REFLECTIONS

REFLECTIONS

Susan Hufford

Seaview Books

NEW YORK

The people and events described or depicted in this novel are fictitious and any resemblance to actual incidents or individuals is unintended and coincidental.

Manufactured in the United States of America.

FIRST EDITION

Seaview Books/A Division of PEI Books, Inc.

Library of Congress Cataloging in Publication Data

Hufford, Susan.
Reflections.

I. Title.
PS3558.U343R4 813'.54 81-50318
ISBN 0-87223-713-3 AACR2

Designed by Tere LoPrete

The author and publisher gratefully acknowledge permission to reprint lyrics from:

For Michael
and for Chester

". . . the past should be altered by the present as much as the present is directed by the past."

T.S. Eliot
"Tradition and the Individual"

PART ONE

"Pursuing an art is not just a matter of finding the time—it is a matter of having a free spirit to bring it on . . ."

Stella Bowen, painter

APRIL 1980
Paris

There seemed to be no line of reason, no logic, nothing to make sense out of the past three days. Or maybe it was the past twelve years that needed clarification. It had been twelve years since she had first met him, eleven since they had become lovers. But her failure—ah yes, failure!—had not dated from their meeting, so maybe it was all thirty-four years of her life that required reexamination. Behind the heavily mascaraed, unfamiliar eyes she had assumed for the occasion, Angelica picked reluctantly at the memories which comprised her life. As she stood in the store window watching the streetlights reflecting in rain puddles, her thoughts were desultory, half-formed, and shimmering like the night outside.

Born Dolores Steinberg, she had first become Anastasia, followed by Serena, then Dahlia, and finally, now, Angelica Stein. All of her names were none of her names. She was a speck, a mote, a mass of impermanent molecules lost in an eternity she could not fathom. He was right about that, too; she did not have the intellectual aptitude or integrity to grapple with universal concepts. In an effort not to cry (she detested tears) she took a deep breath and expelled the air through her mouth so that a loud hissing sound cut through the shadowy silence of the display window.

At night when the crowds were gone, when no one was staring

through the glass at her practically nude body, her mind became a black hole. Terrible images flashed in on her—white arms splattered with blood, her fallen body mangled by a passing car, dead roadside animals, a pelican on the beach with a broken wing, planes which crashed before leaving the ground, and sometimes only dots . . . wavy lines and triangles . . . all of which spelled doom.

Her life, or so she had believed, had been dedicated to preserving the fine distinction between discipline and abandon, between passion and intellect. She walked the high wires, but she walked them consciously, knowing, so she had thought, what it would mean to lose her balance from such a height. And now she had fallen and there seemed to be no promise, no rose garden, no song beneath the yew tree. Only suicide seemed appropriate and though her imagination was rampant with efficient methods and final words she knew the act was out of the question. Life was too sweet to her and she was too ravenous to leave it. But wanting life did nothing to ward off the closing shadows. At the moment her love for life seemed like a slow-growing cancer, an inescapable burden that intensified and prolonged her suffering. Ironically, she felt condemned to live. Dimly, she knew the *black hole* was a familiar place. She had been here before, only not in many years and never so far from the light.

Angelica Stein stood unnecessarily still, feeling death grow inside of her. At three in the morning the crowds which had swarmed around Suzanne's Boudoir were gone and the Rue des Saints Pères was deserted except for a rare figure hurrying along, untouched by the lure of exclusive Rive Gauche shops. A bitter wind from the north sucked the forming leaves from the trees. It was April in Paris but the chestnuts were not yet in blossom.

From the other side of Suzanne's display window, three pale, gaunt mannequins wearing enticing lingerie smiled their carmine, seductive smiles into the rainy night. They were triplets, Modiglianish lookalikes with emaciated bodies, diamond-shaped narrow faces, sunken cheeks, and dark doleful eyes. Two of the thin, curiously sensual dummies lolled against each other at the front of the window, the raven-haired beauty with one arm draped lovingly around her blond sister. Both the blond and the auburn-haired dummy who lounged seductively at the rear of the window were clad in Suzanne's *très très cher* rose silk teddies; while the third sister with the dark punk razor-cut, wore a peachy satin *chemise de nuit* which revealed every nuance of her body—the small breasts, assertive hipbones, and the outline of a soft puff between her slender legs.

Why was she rooted stubbornly to her assigned position, doing exactly what she would have been doing if she had been in a state of grace; if her Lord, Ferris, had given her his benediction and set her on her way with his blessings? She was more dummy than the two mannequins she had created. They had had no choice; she had simply unscrewed their limbs, removed their wigs, and crated them up for the trip to Paris. No one had crated her up, yet she had taken the train, zombielike as planned, from Tours to Paris, compulsively carrying out her little game. Yes, he had called it a game—five nights in a storefront window. Only how had she traveled to the Gare from the farmhouse in Azay? Had Ferris driven her or had she hitched, jabbering like some demented apparition to her crate of dummies? The recent past was a blur.

Five nights in a storefront window? For the past three—yes, it was already three—days from ten in the morning until the shops closed at seven in the evening, Rive Gauche shoppers had been trying to guess which of the three "weird" sisters was the *real* woman.

"You're frighteningly good at this, Angelica. I can't even see you breathing." Her friend Suzanne, who owned the boutique, was ecstatic about the customers flocking into her shop after gaping at the "living" mannequin. She had not yet noticed the bruises, expertly disguised by makeup, on Angelica's inner arms, nor any other indication that Angelica was anything other than her usual unexpected self.

Maybe she wasn't breathing. During the day, Angelica watched the crowd of faces, scarcely blinking her heavily mascaraed dark eyes. Their prying eyes aroused her. Her breasts prickled beneath the clingy peach gown and she soothed herself with erotic fantasies—imagining herself in the cool arms of strangers, occasionally actually feeling their anonymous knowing hands giving her pleasure. She seemed to exist in a state of suspended tumescence, almost as if being constantly on the brink of orgasmic ecstasy was her lifeline, the one thing which could sustain her and give her strength to endure the task she had set for herself.

She was fascinated and repulsed that after all that had happened between her and Ferris, her body could still be kindled by the eyes of strangers. She was, she thought, both exhibitionist and voyeur. She read their faces—their hunger, amusement, fear, and envy while they stared at her body, trying to find some sign of life.

The lighting in the narrow display window, also conceived and executed by Angelica, was dim and sultry. All three dummies seemed to have risen from some primal, disheveled bed. Magdalena's blond, frizzed hair lent her a good-natured wantonness; luxurious-locked Sam, slouched at the rear, seemed to ooze her availability. Ironically it was Mag or Sam that someone spotted moving while the real woman, the most bizarre of the trio, whose close-cropped black hair did nothing to mitigate the severity of her angular features, was passed over. It proved . . . something, Angelica thought with unaccustomed bitterness.

Until only three days before, Angelica Stein had happily thought of herself as a young American artist, living in a mythical tapestry of her own design in France, with her lover:

"Why the hell do you want to spend five days in a goddamned window with those goddamned ugly dummies?" Her lover, Ferris Brown, was not in the habit of suspending his disbelief nor of keeping his opinions to himself. As one of the foremost American artists, with paintings in major museums throughout the world, he had little tolerance for the new avant-garde, the intermedia art forms which Angelica had experimented with from time to time. Lately it had dawned on her that the only time Ferris had anything positive to say about her work was when she emulated his style of abstract expressionism.

Her response to his challenge had been to laugh. She had, after all, asked herself the same question.

"Why are you laughing?" He had grown more irritated.

"I'm no dummy, Ferris!" She had tried for levity in the face of his truculence. She didn't want to fight, not now; not again.

"I'm laughing now so I won't break up when I'm in the window with those two yokels. Weird, aren't they?"

(Would he say they were ugly if he knew I spent the last of my own money—five hundred dollars apiece—for these two stand-up dolls?)

"Why," Ferris had ranted on, "are you wasting your time with crap like this? It couldn't even be considered camp, let alone pop. You tell me you have no patience with Warhol and then you come up with . . ."

"I was curious. I want to know how it will feel to stand in a window with Sam and Mag and . . ."

"Your answer to everything, Angelica, is curiosity. It doesn't pass for art. It's pretentious. I thought you'd given up being an exhibitionist in cruddy windows. Didn't you get enough of that back in New York?"

"Leave me alone."

"Well, maybe you should go back to New York and get a job doing windows at Bloomingdale's."

"Please Ferris, don't be mean . . . you'll just hate yourself for it later." She had reached for him but he had turned away fuming. Why, she had wondered, should this quarrel end differently from the others they had been having recently? Still, she kept hoping.

"Anyway, I'm not calling it art. I'm not calling it anything. I'm just doing it." She had left the room and returned to her studio to crate up Sam and Mag for the trip to Paris. For over six months she had worked on the mannequins, perfecting their bodies, breathing life into them with her spirit as well as with her hands. First she had posed naked in front of the cheval mirror, sketching herself from every conceivable angle before beginning to make the clay model which would serve as the form for both mannequins. Then she had begun the faces, again making a clay model, then dipping strips of celastic, a costly pliable plastic, in acetone. It had been necessary to wear surgical gloves in order not to burn herself as she overlapped the celastic strips in the manner of papier-mâché. Lastly, there had been the final painting, the arduous task of duplicating her own skin tone and texture. There had been costly wigs, artificial fingernails, even a down of body hair on their arms. She didn't know why she loved them but she did. And she didn't know where they would lead her but she was going. *That* was what bothered Ferris.

Since moving to France two years ago she had strayed, not from him, but from his teaching. In her pathetically small studio, which was really the second bathroom in the farmhouse outside the old village of Azay-le-Rideau, she had unhinged herself from all the years of schools, art classes, concepts, and teachers. It was neither folly, ego, nor narcissism, as Ferris had implied, which had driven her to mold Sam and Mag in her own image; it was a necessity which she did not yet understand.

He had also accused her, though always with a laugh, as if it were a joke, of having an artistic relapse. Wasn't she just harkening back to her East Village days when she, as he liked to put it, "did strange things in cruddy store windows for Bowery bums"? But it didn't feel to Angelica like she was repeating herself; though she could not articulate where she was going, she did not really believe she was going backwards.

She was off on too many tangents and it terrified her that she had nothing substantial to cling to except her own appetite. She had tried explaining her fears to Ferris, but at forty-nine he was busy with his own fears and had no desire to reflect on his years as a floundering artist. But then Ferris had been an early, almost immediate success. His floundering, both critical and financial, had lasted a mere three years. At twenty-four the *New York Times* had acclaimed him, and two of the art world's most important collectors, Rockefeller and Hirshhorn, had begun investing in his work. Once the powerful art barons had put their mark of approval on him, the momentum was picked up by museums across the nation and his reputation was solidified. Though he never said so, Ferris assumed that the *Times* and other powerful sources would have acclaimed Angelica, too, had she been worth it.

Everything fascinated Angelica. No selectivity, Ferris said. She was like a child grabbing at everything; except, as he liked to point out, she was no longer a child. Was she an abstract painter, a primitivist, a collagist, a sculptor? In 1969 when she first arrived in New York, even while she was studying more conventional abstract painting with Ferris at the New School, Angelica had experimented with presentational "event" art, or "happenings" as they were often referred to. Angelica had never thought of them as happenings but as true art, however brief and tenuous they might be. Like Eleanor Antin, whose preoccupation with role-defining and character had led her to the creation of *The King of Solana Beach,* Angelica had attempted to physicalize her fears and her fantasies using herself as the main component.

In an East Village store window she had created *Rites of Blood,* a garish, multimedia event using blown-up Vietnam war photographs from the seven o'clock news, a collection of New York street throwaways such as couches oozing stuffing, broken tables, wheelless baby carriages, and herself, sprayed red and garbed in an incarnadine robe also taken from a garbage can. On other occasions she would costume herself as a fantasy—a black man, a baby, a chair. She would blow up black and white photographs of herself in the various disguises, paint them, superimpose other images on them and then appear in dancelike context with the touched-up photos.

Her "art events," while often political in content, were not utterly devoid of humor, though the tone was more macabre than fanciful. In the early days she had pushed herself closer and closer to the edge of her own understanding, acknowledging that as often as not her goal was to terrorize herself, to discover what, if anything, lay beyond her own individual terror. The only time the papers had mentioned her work the *Village Voice* had said she was "a bold exhibitionist." Ferris had laughed at her because she referred to it as "my one good review." Ferris, along with a number of other people, was never altogether sure if she was serious.

She hopped back and forth, immersing herself first in one medium, then in another. Before leaving New York for France she had spent hours studying, meditating on, and copying the paintings of Van Gogh. The Van Goghs could always make her weep, and grief evoked by paintings or images was, she believed, a legitimate cause for tears. Before studying the Van Goghs it was necessary to experience a stab of pain for the man who had created *L'Arlésienne,* using the yellow of an almost jarring intensity, daring to paint Madame Ginoux's face green and somehow making the entirety so moving. Madame Ginoux unfailingly brought tears to her eyes.

Since coming to France she sometimes had four or five totally disparate projects going at one time. She seemed to have no method, no single vision, and it was time, said Ferris, for her to commit herself to something. Something, she now suspected, meant abstract expressionism; something closely allied with his style. Something which critics and gallery owners would recognize—then, perhaps, she might gain entré to that sacred world, as his protégé. It was, after all, his style which had drawn them together in the first place.

She had first seen Ferris's work when the Chicago Institute had purchased two of his paintings, one of which, *The Driver*, a 77-by-89-inch work, perfectly reflected Kandinsky's theory that color and form could exist unto themselves without any recognizable imitation of reality. The gobbets of somber umber and the sweeping romantic strokes were an end in themselves, and as a zealous twelve-year-old Angelica had fallen in love with the passions of Ferris's massive oils. His paintings thundered their cosmic ramifications, and Angelica, the product of political revolutionaries who scorned anything remotely religious or mystical, fell to worshipping his work. She was a contented child, but solitary, with an almost mystical empathy for darkness and suffering. Ferris's desolate, churning cosmos touched her, and she avidly followed his career, imagining somehow that because the critics had had the good sense to recognize his artistic merits they would ultimately do the same for her.

In 1969 she graduated from the University of Chicago and moved to New York City, a self-contained hot wire of sensuality liberated by the sixties and her own intellectual upbringing and proclivities. Identifying totally with the burgeoning women's movement, she knew the seventies were hers. If men had dominated the art world for the past nineteen centuries, the close of the twentieth would herald a new order and she would be among the victors. She felt her logic was infallible; she was a woman who used her head. Her enthusiasm was matched only by her naiveté. She was a new Joan without armor.

Sexual freedom would be the key to her liberation as well as to her ultimate success in the art world. After all, at sixteen she had consciously shed her virginity, for much the same reason that her mother had prophylactically had her brother's and her tonsils removed—to avoid future infection. She was free. There would be no domestic traps.

Angelica, still known then as Dolores Steinberg, was forthright, too—no one had ever accused her of being ambivalent. She was unhampered by traditional romantic notions, although her quietness and gracility made her seem more a cloistered nun than a hot little nymph of the seventies. She was no ordinary vamp. She shunned lipstick, mascara, anything artificial. From her father, an aging underground Marxist radical awaiting the revolution with a faded yellow party card in the secret compartment of his wallet, she had inherited both the heart and the instincts of a revolutionary. She believed that she knew who she was and that she was a product of her own making. Her mind and her body were her own. She would never be dominated.

And so she had sought Ferris out at first as a teacher. As one of ten select students at the New School she had strained to gain his approval, by nothing as simple as mere imitation of his style, but by absorbing herself in the intellectual, metaphysical aspects of his painting. She had an amazing talent: the ability to see with his eyes. There were times during the first year of their acquaintance when her instincts triggered a terror in him. Her concentration was fearless, inexhaustible. She became so sensitive and in tune with him that on one occasion she actually produced a painting he swore he had seen only in his own mind. While she continued to play at her own fantasies in East Village store windows, in class she was his obedient protégé.

Beneath the solitary, cool exterior her mind sizzled. Once she had gained his approval, it was almost inevitable that he would have to possess her.

Even then, ten years ago, when she was still so confident, so sure of her privileges and unconflicted about the artist's right to appropriate whatever was necessary in order to ensure the vision, she was not proud that he had left a wife and daughter so that he could live with her.

They should have remained friends, simply and forever

friends; but there was so much passion between them and love was the only word they could find to name it. At the time they saw no choice. Now, eleven years after becoming lovers, their lovemaking was like a religious ritual and they were two deluded souls afraid to admit their waning faith in the existence of a failing god.

Any normal woman would have cried. Had he said that or had she said it about herself?

Her prearranged schedule for the five-day shop window marathon included three hours of sleep each night. No one had walked down the misty Rue des Saints Pères since four. Angelica dragged herself out of the window and collapsed on the cot Suzanne had set up for her behind the counter. She set the alarm for six-thirty, picked at a baguette and cheese, and closed her eyes. The blackness shuddered inside her head as it had done when Ferris had slammed her against the wall to try to stop her from going to Paris.

If she really loved him she would have cried. He had said something like that before launching another attack which had cost her the bruises on her arms. But of course she loved him. He was a genius. His paintings still had power over her, she was still in awe of his brilliance. He would never have beaten her if he had not been drinking, if he had not finally admitted to himself that she was slipping away from him.

"Don't go," he had begged as he drove her the thirty-four kilometers to catch the train in Tours. "If you go now, you'll never come back."

"I'll come back."

"As who, though? Who will you be?"

"Myself. I'll be myself." She had been too dazed to offer him much reassurance.

"Angelica . . ." It was the first time he had used her new name without a caustic tone. He had taken her hand, kissed it. She had felt his tears on her wrist and said nothing. Her eyes were dry. She detested tears.

"You could stay the night," he had suggested, "and take an early train tomorrow. There's a six-forty."

"Suze is expecting me. She'll be waiting at the shop tonight to let me in."

He had not begun his usual tirade against Suzanne, whom he considered arrogant, ugly, and utterly bereft of any redeeming qualities. Suzanne, in point of fact, was fortyish, blond and dimpled, soft-spoken, and a successful lingerie designer. It was Suzanne's sexual preferences that Ferris could not tolerate. He could not understand how Angelica could be friends with a "dyke" without becoming tainted or, even worse, seduced. Ferris would have rather seen Angelica go off with a battalion of Turks than spend the night alone with Suzanne.

Waiting for the train to come at the Gare he had looked at her as if she were a stranger or a ghost about to dematerialize. In less than an hour he had smoked a pack of Gauloises and seemed on the point of saying something important. It had occurred to Angelica that he was finally going to ask her to marry him. The irony of their situation had turned her breath sour.

When the train appeared he had shoved his knobby hands in the pockets of his faded Levi jacket and walked away, leaving her to lug the mannequin crate and her valise onto the train. He actually had been going to propose but he was suddenly enraged by her apparent composure and dry eyes. He cursed her as he climbed into his battered Renault and headed back to Azay. She had ruined his life and he was glad she was gone, whoever she was.

Who was she? Of course she knew who she was. Even her parents had come to accept her changing names and if anyone had reason to be hurt it was Phil and Myra Steinberg who had given her that first unlikely appellation. Dolores Steinberg? By the time she was five she had known she was not a Dolores, but for eighteen years she had answered to a name that had always pinched like an ill-fitting shoe.

When she had first met Ferris, shortly after moving to New York, she had been heavily involved with her Russian heritage and introduced herself in East Village circles as Anastasia . . . for the fun of it. Still clinging to her family ties, she had not yet dropped the "berg" in Steinberg nor considered making the change legal. The first legal change, to Serena Stein, and the loss of "berg," coincided with a period of intense interest in Eastern philosophies and Cabalistic theosophy. That was ten years ago, just after she and Ferris had started living together. The change to Serena had amused him, as if she had switched for his enjoyment instead of some deeper reasons of her own.

Serena had been less unpredictable than either Dolores or Anastasia and for six years the name had calmed and contained her. She had abandoned the storefront windows for soft sculpture in gaily colored fabrics and this new tact had paid off in the form of a Rockefeller grant. Unfortunately the year's stipend of two thousand dollars scarcely covered the cost of art supplies and was not enough to live on even though she was sharing expenses with Ferris. Consequently Ms. Stein, in addition to devoting herself to her personal work, became a gainfully employed elementary art teacher in Baldwin, Long Island—a reliable commuter for four years. However, finally Ms. Stein was too contained, Serena too earthbound, and the soft sculpture too inconsequential. Prior to moving to France she had changed her name again, this time to the exotic Dahlia. At the same time she had begun a maniacal quest for a new medium, a quest which led to an instant replay of her past endeavors. This time Ferris was not amused.

She was too slippery for him, always out of his grasp in a way he could neither define nor comprehend. Serena Stein had been someone he recognized; he had understood her comings and goings. Dahlia, on the other hand, though she looked exactly like Serena and wore the same somber clothes and no makeup, had escaped him. He had never uttered "Dahlia" without feeling that his universe was doomed to extinction.

Although Ferris Brown was a successful artist with a steady and ever increasing income, Dolores-Anastasia-Serena-Dahlia-Angelica's ability to closet herself off in her studio without any awareness of the passage of time irked him. Living with her in New York he had been unaware of this capacity, since so much of her time had been spent on the Long Island Rail Road. However, since coming to France her patterns had grown unreasonable: he did not like her disappearing like that for so long, especially lately when his own work was a form of Chinese water torture, painfully repetitious, something he felt he had to endure.

Angelica, on the other hand, could spend fourteen hours

without eating or talking to anyone. She would bend and twist wires, fool with old pieces of string, paint, glue, carve, whatever . . . as if possessed. Sometimes he would watch her through the window, observing her serious, almond-shaped eyes, her thin lips poised in a Mona Lisa smile, and her fluid, relaxed movements. She was solitary, the way children who create monsters and flowers out of air are solitary and inviolable.

His own back was so badly knotted with tension that he went to a chiropractor three times a week and could not stand in front of a canvas for longer than two hours at a stretch. He told himself that her easy absorption was her biggest problem, that until she created out of agony and torture her work would be shallow, easy, and derivative in the worst sense. She had made a big mistake abandoning the technique he had given her. If she had only kept working along those old lines, in a year or two when they returned permanently to the States he might have used his influence to get his agent, Aron Loden, to promote her.

However, the mishmash—the dummies, the disjointed bursts of color slopped on glass, the pastel and charcoal portraits of local citizens—wouldn't even make the grade at a crackpot Soho gallery, let alone uptown. He told himself her work was of no consequence but he was not consoled. Several times he even wondered if he was secretly afraid of the competition she posed; but then he reminded himself that she had, in her entire artistic life, sold only three paintings and those to women—sympathetic but unknowledgeable friends. Still, it bothered him that she took so much pleasure in her industry.

"You expect me to call you Angelica . . . just like that?"

He would not stop badgering her. The truth was she did not expect anything. She wanted to change her name. She wanted him to love her and she wanted to love him.

"You could have named yourself Rosa," he had suggested snidely, "after Mademoiselle Bonheur. If you were hell-bent on finding a goddamned role model, she was, for Christ's sake, a hell of a better painter than the Angelica Kauffmann you're naming yourself after."

"You're missing the point!" Angelica had protested.

"There is no point! Angelica Kauffmann was a fuckin' whore,

for Chrissakes. If she hadn't been pretty and screwed everyone nobody woulda paid the least attention to her paintings. She was a lightweight who got herself promoted because she was a whore!"

"I don't care if she was a whore!" This was one of the few times Angelica had raised her voice. "I love Angelica Kauffmann . . . I don't care . . ."

"You're crazy, you know that. You need help!!"

"Ferris!" She had laughed suddenly to let him know that she was above his criticism. "Why are you so upset? Your face is purple. Here, look."

"You're making a fool of yourself, Dah . . . hell, I don't know what to call you. Why can't you see that it's this sort of neurotic irrationality that makes your work so inconsequential?"

"Thank you."

"Why won't you listen to me?" he fumed at a lower decibel.

"I listen to you all the time, Ferris," she had said calmly. "You are my most loyal and loquacious critic."

He wanted to contain her. The name business was like a trigger, something he could feel beneath his finger, something real and specific he could understand. But that night, only one week ago, it had all been solved by slipping into his arms and loving him. How could she be that angry with him when she knew how fragile he was, when she knew all he really wanted was loving? Besides, he really was a genius.

Unlike his massive oils, Ferris Brown was a small man, just Angelica's size when she was in bare feet. He was a shy, uncomfortable man who frowned a lot and appeared to be ill-dressed no matter what he was wearing. He felt his smallness in his soul and compensated by looking at the world with cold eyes. His skin was tinged with gray, his expression always worried; fear and nerves were kept rigidly under control. In his heart he did not understand the paintings he produced; he knew the critics were wrong, that either he was a charlatan or his luck would inevitably change and he would die in poverty. The huge sums of money (fifty thousand dollars for a recent resale of an oil painting done in the sixties) which his paintings now sold for were sent to Barbara, his former wife, now remarried, to be lavished on his only daughter, Sadie, aged nineteen. Years ago Barbara and Sadie had forgiven him for deserting the family to live with a strange young woman artist. Ferris alone pondered the ramifications of his actions in some obscure corner of his mind. He would never marry Angelica. He had made that perfectly clear at the outset and periodically he liked to remind her that the situation had not changed. Only lately her calm acceptance of his terms had begun to chafe.

Without acknowledging it to himself he wanted her tears, her demands, even her resentment. Had she issued him an ultimatum—"Marry me or else!"—he would have understood the situation more clearly.

Until their move to France Ferris had been a wiry, taut one hundred and thirty-five pounds; but the expatriate life had put pounds on his spare frame, all in one place, and his always sparse sandy hair had begun to make its final thinning before baldness. Angelica knew, though only from quiet observation, that he had gone six months without washing his hair, in a futile attempt to preserve his rapidly receding hairline.

How could she not understand and love a man so in need of love, even if he did have a strange way of showing his need?

That night she had been intent on loving him with the voracity she had recently reserved only for her work. As the new, magical Angelica she had covered his body and made him young, molding him with the same fierce dedication she had lavished on Magdalena and Sam. She never spoke. At the start of their relationship he had urged her to speak in bed, thinking her silence was an affliction of her youth, a reserve or even a detachment. But the silence was her core, her most precious gift. When she gave her silence there was nothing more of her to give.

Angelica woke clinging to the edge of the narrow cot and wondered where she was. Glass cases of sherbet-colored femininity, seemingly whispering romance, lace and love-filled nights—she located herself in Suzanne's shop and the alarm was ringing. She was safe. It was all right. He had not followed her.

It occurred to her now that for the past few days she had lived in terror of seeing his face among the faces of strangers staring in the window at her. All of the disaster fantasies had been about him. But Suzanne would have told her if he had called, so he had not come to Paris after her. She was in terror of seeing him and in terror of not seeing him, poised again between passion and discipline.

She sat on the edge of the cot examining the red marks on her upper arm. Now they were tinged with pale blue and there were several mustard-yellow splotches which looked like thumb prints. Odd how they formed almost a rainbow effect now that they had begun to fade. She reached for her purse, removed a small compact and re-covered the bruises with makeup. For the first time the events of four days ago began to take shape in her memory.

"Ferris, you can't stop me from leaving. Be reasonable." When she had lugged the crate of mannequins into the kitchen she had found him, arms resolutely folded, sitting on a chair in front of the door. It was not his usual humor, but she had hoped.

"What do you mean I can't . . ."

"It's only for a week."

"I said . . ." He had staggered to his feet and she was aware then that he had been drinking, and heavily.

"I'm sorry I stayed in my studio so long," she had said and meant it. Lately he complained often about her long disappearances and tonight of all nights she should have been more considerate. She should not have worked so long. His feelings were hurt, that was all.

"Ferris . . ." She had reached for him but he shoved her hand away. "Ferris, I apologize. Let's not fight before I go off. It *is* my fault for losing track of time but . . . listen, I was wrong. Okay? Will you accept my apology?"

He had stared mutely at her, unwilling to read anything in her manner but feminine manipulation.

"Come with me," she had suggested. "We'll stay at the Abbaye St. Germain. We'll have a night in Paris, I'll creep out of your bed before dawn and climb into my window and . . ."

"Stop laughing at me!" He had jerked her arm viciously.

"I'm not!"

"Well, don't ever! You think I'm not serious?"

"I know you are . . ."

"I'll show you!" He had ignored her and thrown her backwards so that she crashed onto the kitchen table.

"What are you doing?" Finally, she had protested, loudly.

"Getting rid of these." He had lunged for the dummy crate, only she beat him to it, kicking instinctively for his most vulnerable spot.

"You cunt!" He had doubled over.

"Ferris, stop it!" They had struggled. A whipping blur of awkward swinging, with dishes crashing to the floor and the sound of their labored breathing and their hatred for each other.

"I'll teach you to kick me," he had threatened, slamming her against the stove. There was a burner on, it singed her arm but she did not feel it. The same arm shot out and connected with his nose, which immediately began to bleed. As far as he was concerned she had initiated the violence and she would pay for it.

"All lies anyway," he had sputtered through the blood. "You're not going into Paris just to stand in some window."

"I am! I am! What did you think I . . . ?"

"Don't I have any rights?"

"What rights? What are you talking about?"

"You know what I'm talking about."

She had circled around the perimeter of the kitchen feeling both frightened and ridiculous for feeling frightened. How could she be frightened of Ferris? How was it possible?

"Slut."

"Ferris, if you want to talk about what you're afraid of let's sit down and . . ."

". . . suppose you wanna see what it feels like to be a whore like your namesake."

"Let's sit . . ."

"Why are you doin' it then?" His speech had become more slurred, almost as if he were making himself more intoxicated in order to say what he could not say sober. "Why you standin' naked in a window if you don't want . . ."

"I'm not going to be naked! And even if I were it's none of your business!"

"Twelve years and it's none of my business. I'm gonna kill you is what I'm . . ."

He threw himself at her, pushing her down, and with both

hands around her throat he began banging her head on the floor. She scratched at his face but could not move him. She wanted to die, gave up completely to his fury and went limp.

"Jesus Christ!" The instant she surrendered he had felt it. "Serena!" He had laid his head on her heart. "Honey . . . I didn't mean . . . My God!" He had sobbed.

Remembering made her sick all over again, just as his sobs had caused her to bite her tongue to keep from vomiting. Angelica folded up the cot and blankets and put them in the closet. That was the way it felt to die, to abandon all resistance, to know that you had been beaten. She had lain on the kitchen floor with Ferris's head on her heart, her eyes wide and dry, staring at the rough white plaster and the old chestnut beams. His body heaved on top of her as he slurred his love for her and prayed that she would forgive him. She hardly heard what he said; she felt distracted, removed. She had had the sense that she was perched above them, on one of the aged beams, viewing the pathetic scene with the revulsion of a passing stranger. Only when he had rolled off her did she make any attempt to move and then she stood up slowly, put on the tea kettle, and sat down and waited for it to boil. She had accepted his apologies without really being there. She had listened to him for nearly an hour from her emotional vantage point on the ceiling and then he had driven her to the train.

By seven Angelica was back in the window with Sam and Mag. From now on, she decided, she would not sleep. Suze had insisted on leaving the cot but she could see now that sleep only made her task more difficult.

Between seven and nine when Suze came to work with fresh coffee and croissants only three people passed the shop. Paris was a late-hours city; mornings were civilized and slow. The sun was out for the first time in over a week and Suze chattered as she dusted and arranged to open the shop. Business was up thirty percent and Suze was insisting she would split the profits with Angelica.

"Absolutely not," Angelica said without moving her lips, but something inside of her released and with a sense of incredulity she wondered if she wasn't finally emerging from the black hole. Money, she needed money!

At the end of the day when Suze left, Angelica closed her eyes, trying not to anticipate the old tower clock which rang off the hours. Tomorrow was the fifth day and then what?

What the hell am I doing in this frigging window? Maybe Ferris is right. Any normal woman would be home crying. Money. Where is the money going to come from? Even if she accepted money from Suze it wouldn't begin to be enough.

Tears, Angelica thought, were vastly overrated. It was one thing to feel them in your heart, another to let them fall without restraint. In your heart they could be channeled into compassion for something or someone, for yourself even. But once you became accustomed to bathing in them they became an end in themselves, a narcotic, a delusion. Angelica's mother, despite her political and intellectual expertise, had cried about everything; about the starving children in Biafra, about the migrant workers and César Chávez, about the Chrysler loan from the government, and about her father's mistresses. Every crisis reduced her to tears, leaving her drained, shaken, enervated, and useless. On the other hand, Angelica had observed at an early age that her father never cried at all; the tears in his heart had dried up. He would hold his breath until his heart exploded rather than shed a tear. In the end his rage left him as ineffectual as tears left his wife. The trick, Angelica thought, was to keep the tears alive in your heart.

She was not the sort of woman that men abuse. She did not hunger after violence, or fall for unpredictable, macho men who must strike out before being overwhelmed by tenderness and tears. She had always chosen her men carefully. Hostility, especially from men, repelled her. She had never, even in the throes of adolescence, wanted to be the girl on the arm of the halfback. She had hankered after the clarinetist, the physics major, or the boy with the stutter, and not in order to dominate but rather to feel safe. When she had first seen Ferris Brown she had attached cosmic significance to his small stature and, despite his bantam rooster bravura, the idea of violence erupting from this sensitive genius had never, not once, crossed her mind.

It had to have been her fault. A man, a genius, who grasped both the magnificence and the torment of infinity could not sink so low unless he had been horribly provoked.

But how? How could it have happened? To her? There was no way she could think lightly about the back of his hand on her face. She felt the imprint of it inside her head.

Now, after nearly five days of holding her pose, the blackness was receding and she was able to look backwards from this fixed, still point. Violence had no place in her life. There had never been violence in her family, she did not travel in violent circles and was not given to drunken orgies where defenses are lowered to the point of unconsciousness. She rarely drank more than one glass of wine, did not smoke tobacco or grass, did not snort coke, take uppers, downers, speed, or even aspirin. At parties she got high on half a beer, and glowed. She appeared to exist in a constant state of intoxication, vague and cheerful, floating and far-off. It was not unusual to find people who were threatened by her purity, labeling her pretentious, superficial, and sometimes even accusing her of lying. Years ago, before Ferris, she had gone to bed with a congenial stockbroker who wore three-piece suits and had wakened to find him looking for needle marks in her arms. A lot of people could not believe it was possible to enjoy life in an unremitting state of sobriety. Recently Ferris had hinted it was proof of her advanced neurosis.

It alternately amused and depressed her that people thought of passion as synonymous with vice and debauchery. "You can't be an artist," someone had accused her, "you have no vices."

It was true. The one hangover she had suffered had convinced her that excessive alcohol was no fun; likewise her experiments with drugs had netted her less of a high than her own unaltered perceptions. Men who wanted to seduce her did not have to ply her with martinis. She was a woman capable of making love in the back seat of a speeding cab in subzero weather, cold sober.

She was clean—inside her mind and in her body—all that she craved was life. If she suffered, from time to time falling into those brief but terrifying depressions, it was not because she sought darkness but because the light which she had envisioned in her mind she had yet to encounter with her eyes.

And yet *it* had happened. With no vices, no storehouse of subtle, self-destructive tendencies to blame the beating on, it had happened. Where, she wondered, was her rage? Her indignation? Her tears?

She wondered if she would leave him. She wondered if the reason she would leave him would be the fight, or if there wasn't another, deeper reason.

On the evening of the final day of her "window art," just before Suzanne locked up for the night, Angelica fainted.

"Hunger!" Suzanne admonished her. "Didn't you eat the cheese I left?"

"I couldn't swallow it . . ."

"*Merde*! If I didn't know you better I'd say you had anorexia and were trying to kill yourself. I'm taking you home with me now. I don't want to find two dummies and a corpse in my window tomorrow."

"It might ruin business!" Angelica started laughing and had difficulty stopping. The laughter brought the blood to her face, her pulse was racing, and she wondered why she felt better after fainting than before.

"I have to finish in the window," she protested. "I'll eat the yogurt. You can watch me."

"And what are these bruises?" Suze touched her arm where the makeup had worn off.

"I fell in the country with the crate." Angelica slid the spoon into the yogurt and was relieved that she did not gag.

"*Tu parles*." Suze was skeptical but she did not pursue the matter.

Angelica finished the yogurt with a sense of triumph. "I feel like celebrating."

"On what?" Suze was aghast.

"Nervous energy . . . let's go to the Closerie for a late supper!"

With difficulty she climbed back into the window and resumed her pose. Her body was one massive knot, every muscle contracted with pain, and the area surrounding her heart felt like a time bomb. Where, she wondered, was the purification from such agony?

It was a bitter victory; meager and elusive like everything else in her life right now. She tried to tell herself it was at least *something*: five days in a shop window, alone with her thoughts, bruises, and passing eyes. At least she had not lost her mind. It was something.

But it was not enough. No more crumbs! When Suze disappeared around the corner Angelica realized she was crying, so softly and unobtrusively crying that had a pedestrian been staring in the window the tears might not have been detected. No sobs cut through the stillness in the shop; her weeping was as steady and unaffected as breathing.

She was dying inside from lack of recognition. And she had no excuses! She was not an artist who never picked up a brush. She had no patience with people who did not try, with artists who *would* paint, writers who *would* write . . . but never did. The world, it seemed, was full of creative souls about to begin. She knew a man who referred to himself as an artist; a man, at least according to himself and his oh-so-supportive wife, of enormous talent, who protected himself from failure by never beginning. He was viciously critical of everyone else's work and smug and certain about his own prodigious gifts . . . were he to decide to bestow them on an undeserving world. Angelica disliked the man more than anyone she knew and in her heart she had not one jot of pity for him.

Of course it was hard to begin, hard to see how inadequate you were at shadows and light and composition. It was agony to see the mystical light in a Rembrandt or the soaring, uncontainable spirit and colossal drawing of a Picasso and then begin. But it wasn't worth talking about. It was hard to begin. It always was, even for her, though Ferris thought it was all so easy for her. At those rare times when it was easy, he resented her. He begrudged her the only pleasure she had, her work, when he had so much more.

She had nothing to hide behind. She might as well have been standing naked. She had no money, not even a glimmer of a reputation. She was surrounded by her work and no one was aware that she was even there—except when she stood with her two dummies in a shop window in Paris. Who the hell could she blame?

She was not some late-hours, sleep-half-the-day, high-on-drugs, laid-back-on-grass expatriate who dabbled and rationalized and dreamed of beginning. She waited on no muse but began every day with or without inspiration. And nothing. She had nothing to show for it!

Good Christ, she was thirty-four years old! Old enough to die like Keats or Janis Joplin or Ruth Silverman who had graduated from high school with her and had died of breast cancer at thirty. No, don't count Janis Joplin—that was self-destructive, to be pitied, yes, but not to be included in her statistics of death from natural causes. Thirty-four. In another year, were she to be in a position to have the child she had always wanted, she would fall into the category of "older mother." Yes, she would be thirty-five and she would have to have amniocentesis to make certain her child was not defective.

And who the hell could she blame?

Now she was hot, sweating in the chilly window, gagging on all her thirty-four years of life. Oh yes, they had meant something, hadn't they? She tried to remember what her years meant but suddenly she felt too flimsy and it seemed that the Rue des Saints Pères was about to dematerialize. What if the world, the street outside, were to vanish? It might. It could. She was convinced it was possible.

She had nothing to show for her life. For the first time since entering the window she broke her pose and turned to look at Sam and Mag. She wanted to clutch them against her burning body and make them live. They were sad and still, watching her, she thought, with pained eyes. Ferris was right. She had sabotaged whatever talent she had by going off on tangents. Maybe she didn't have enough talent? What did it mean to have talent? The thought made her dizzy and she tried to recall a time when Dolores Steinberg was spoken of in superlative terms; but it seemed too far back to count. The past was a lie. Certainly Ferris had never praised her work or challenged her potential. Had he ever once mentioned her potential? Had anyone?

She did not mind growing old. She did not mind that the vertical crease between her eyebrows was getting deeper or that her thinness which at twenty had been dramatic now made her appear haggard. She didn't mind the idea of amniocentesis.

Was it more painful to remember what people had said about her or to pretend they had said nothing? A million years ago people had told her she had great talent. *Great talent.* That pronouncement had seemed then to be the key to her future. A firm hand, unique imagination, explosive sense of color, superb taste, style, intellect, energy . . . that ancient praise was jumbled inside her head. There was always praise when you were young, but now she was thirty-four which was not so very young and in all her years of diligence she had never been able to support herself with her work.

She had no agent, and no gallery (even a third-rate one) was clamoring for more of her work. She had never had a show, though during her years in New York she had beaten paths to every known gallery, carting in canvases and soft sculpture, sending slides of her work, mailing cards and costly brochures, making phone calls to people in power who did not want to receive them. Once she had set up an invitational quasi-show in a friend's apartment but only her friends had come. Apart from the two thousand dollars she had been awarded from the Rockefeller Foundation, in fifteen years she had earned a total of eight hundred and forty dollars for her work. This, and not the back of Ferris's hand, was what was killing her.

APRIL 1980
New York City

Catherine Aimsley came awake with a burst of exhilarated consciousness as if she had been swimming underwater and had suddenly surfaced. It was getting on toward dawn, she could feel it even without opening her eyes. She lay, eyes closed, smiling, smug and excruciatingly excited about the new painting of Tony. She would begin it immediately. She would spend the entire day in her studio and by evening she might have finished —like in the old days. She would take the entire day, giving herself over to this new image which well might be the breakthrough she had been waiting for. She reached for Tony and when she found his side of the bed empty she finally opened her eyes.

Damn him, sneaking off like that in the middle of the night. She hated the emptiness, the pillow still indented from the shape of his head. Ah, but that was the way he was!

She pulled his pillow against her stomach and snuggled into it. He teased her for not wanting to sleep with him in her own bed as long as she was technically married to Lester. But that was the way she was.

Cathy watched the shadows from the streetlights flickering on the pale blue walls of the high-ceilinged guest room. Night light was hushed; even her crimson robe was tinged with something not quite gray. After-dusk light was not the same as before-dawn light; morning light swallowed up daytime colors. If Tony had not bolted from her bed at God only knew what hour, she would have wakened him and sketched his nakedness against the soft gray dawn. The shadows would play soft on his lean, young back, he would be indistinct; perhaps more a part of time and space than of himself.

Now what the hell did that mean? Cathy smiled and stretched and filled the spaces of her mind with muted mysterious colors. She would make it a posterior painting, the darkness would seem to devour his legs, he would be rising into the morning from . . .

She was dying to sketch it! Perhaps even begin it this very minute from some instinctual memory. She watched the light change. Soon there would be no turning back and the night would be gone. After a certain point it happened very quickly. Oh, she should get up and go directly to her studio and make some preliminary scribbles. Yes, soon there would be no turning back.

She squinted at the digital clock. Two more hours until she had to be up to get Vinnie's breakfast.

But she made no move to get up; instead she continued to picture the new painting and watch it materialize in the silent room, watch it rise like the phoenix.

She would abandon her present work in oil and undertake a gouache painting which would give the effect of free, spontaneous, dashing brush strokes. There would be no heavy impasto or thickness of paint, yet it would be more substantial than some of the watercolors she had been doing lately. What she needed to get was a brilliant, light-reflecting quality and that was best achieved with the white pigments of gouache. Perhaps Tony should be turned slightly with one arm limp at his side? Yes, the tight power of his well-rounded buttocks would contrast with the vulnerability of his limp arm.

Forty-six wasn't old. How much sleep did a person need? Cathy threw back the covers and padded down the hall to her studio with the new painting burning inside her. How long had it been since she was really excited like this, since desire to get it down had wakened her in the night and driven her to her studio? Not since Lester had moved out. No, not in a long time, since just after she had begun seeing Tony on a regular basis, juggling her schedule to meet him after he finished teaching and. . . . Don't think about that now, she told herself. Concentrate.

She turned on the light in her studio and frowned because it was too neat. It looked sterile. She picked up a stub of charcoal and drew a few lines, tossed the sheet aside and made another attempt. The light was too harsh, not at all magical like the light in the guest room. It was probably ridiculous to try to draw Tony from memory but maybe she could block out the proportions, the feeling of the way the light would fall—just so she wouldn't forget.

Cathy sat perched on the stool rubbing her cold feet together, staring at the white paper with the inadequate black marks. The excitement wavered. It would really be better to go back to bed. She had slept through the alarm twice during the past few weeks. It wasn't fair to Vinnie.

But back in bed the energy flowed in on her again and she could not close her eyes. She stared at that spot where her mind had fixed Tony and saw the muted life, the swallowing-up of daytime colors, the ingestion of what people called "reality" but which was no more real than the mystical unicorn. And no less real, she thought as her feet hit the floor for the second time in ten minutes.

If only she could fix the vision of Tony on paper, get it down right so that the vision could feed others as it was feeding her now. She felt simultaneously hungry and satisfied and almost dizzy with ecstasy.

Halfway down the hall to her studio she stopped herself. If she began painting now she would be dead by three in the afternoon and that was when a friend of her daughter's was stopping by to garner some advice. Cathy smiled. Imagine! Advice from *her*? According to her older daughter, Laura, the girl wanted to be an artist and her parents were giving her a hard time.

Advice? Well, she could think of a lot of things to tell the girl, Joan-Something was her name, that had nothing much to do with gouaches or galleries. Ha! And then, at four she had to meet with Vinnie's headmaster. Of course Lester would be only too happy to go but that wouldn't be right, would it? And after the meeting at the school she had promised Vinnie . . . something, she couldn't remember what, but Vinnie would remember. She hated breaking promises. And of course now that she and Lester had actually separated, Vinnie was probably under a great deal of strain. Just because he didn't show the strain didn't mean it didn't exist. Poor Vinnie. Hadn't Laura said something about bringing the baby over or was that next week?

For several minutes Cathy stood outside the door to Vinnie's room, then slowly she opened the door, tiptoed inside, and stood over his curled-up little body. Her last child. She adjusted the blanket and he stirred slightly but then resumed his deep, even breathing. Maybe he wasn't her last child! Forty-six was pushing it but it certainly wasn't impossible. Maybe she would have another child—*Tony*'s child!

What would Tony say? Cathy fairly ran back to the kitchen, poured herself a glass of grapefruit juice, and in a daze, feeling herself already pregnant with Tony's child, watched the minutes tick by on the large industrial clock which dominated her immaculate high-tech kitchen.

Her thick light brown hair was long, nearly to her waist, and she pulled a lock around to scrutinize it. The color had not even begun to change. Everyone said it was quite amazing and she had to agree. At forty-six there was not a trace of gray. She kept expecting her age to catch up with her—good God, she'd been anticipating the descent of dowdy middle age since she turned thirty!—but it just wasn't happening. Well, she was a trifle thicker around the middle since Vinnie's birth but actually her body had responded amazingly well considering she had been thirty-seven when her third child was born. She smiled suddenly, recalling that it hadn't been any more difficult regaining her girlish figure at thirty-seven than when she had had Laura at . . .

Twenty-one! Actually the hardest time she'd had losing weight was when Aggie (named after her mama) was born, two years after Laura. Then she had weighed nearly one hundred and twenty pounds. My God, and now she was a grandmother, bless Laura for that, and she weighed one hundred and eight—"lady's weight," as her grandmother used to say. At five foot two and one hundred and eight pounds she weighed only three pounds more than when she graduated from Wayne High School in 1952. Not bad.

There was no doubt in her mind that Tony Casteli was the sort of man who would eventually want children; given the twenty-two year difference in their ages that could prove a problem unless it was solved quickly.

"Jesus!" The sound of her voice cut through the still apartment. What the hell was she thinking? She didn't want the responsibility of another child. She was, maternally speaking, fulfilled, exceptionally lucky with two terrific, independent daughters and a darling eight-year-old son. Oh yes, and Robbie, her new grandson, compliments of Laura. It was lunacy to think of having another child.

She returned to bed for the second time, the ecstasy having escalated into a nervous frenzy. There were streaks of light in the gray sky; only an hour and fifteen minutes until the alarm went off. When she closed her eyes the word *waste* jumped out at her.

After a minute she got up for the third time. The space where the vision of Tony had formed was empty. She took an antihistamine to dilute her feelings and make her drowsy. She was suddenly desperate about getting that additional hour of sleep. When the alarm went off she did not hear it.

"Mama." Vinnie nudged her and turned off the alarm. "You stay asleep," he whispered.

"No!" Cathy protested and pretended she was awake.

"I can make my own toast." Vinnie was already dressed in his navy blue blazer.

"No, I want to!" Cathy heaved her legs over the side of the bed and let out an agonized cry. "Damn!"

The leg pain shot into her heel and she could feel the savage spasm in her lower back.

"Oh no!" She fell back onto the bed and tried not to cry. How many times had she done this to herself? How many times had she squelched that terrible excitement which precedes a creative splurge, turning against herself so that it ended by throwing her entire back into one horrible spasm?

"Your back?" Vinnie asked.

She could not answer, she felt so ridiculous. She was not some unconscious ninny with no understanding of the subtle psychological intricacies of her own personality. She knew perfectly well that whenever she became excited about her work she had to be careful or she would devise some way to stop herself. Always! Always some dark side of herself, some part she believed she had, if not conquered, at least become conscious enough of to control, would overtake her. *You will not be happy in your work. You will not be obsessed, delighted by your own creativity, or free to soar to your own heights.* Like the sole of some giant, clumsy boot, this dark self was always waiting to come down hard on her excited plans, as if to remind her that she was, after all . . . nothing.

"I'm sick of myself," she told Vinnie after she had hobbled into the kitchen to fix him scrambled eggs which he kept insisting he did not want.

"You should spend the day resting," he told her. "You'll be better tonight."

"The point is," she faced him, "I wouldn't be in pain now if I'd stayed up working."

"Why didn't you?" Vinnie was always curious about Cathy's psychological explanations. They interested him greatly; he looked on them as wonderful stories devised for his amusement. Most children's books bored him; compared with his mother's inventions they were too predictable.

"I forced myself to abandon my excitement," Cathy explained, "because I was afraid I'd be too tired to spend the afternoon with you."

"But I'm going to Dad's after school." Vinnie wrinkled his brow. "I'm staying at his apartment tonight, remember?"

Cathy let out a shriek which delighted her son. "You see how I use you, Vinnie? You don't need me to make your toast."

"That's what I told you."

"I wear you like an albatross."

"What's an albatross?"

Cathy dropped a hot English muffin on the floor and was careful to bend down and pick it up with a straight back.

"An albatross is what people hang around their necks when they're afraid they might win the race."

"What's wrong with winning?" Vinnie was fascinated.

"I'm not sure," Cathy said. "Maybe nothing."

By ten o'clock, her jaw clenched like a Marine sergeant, Cathy stood rigidly at attention in front of a 36-by-24-inch piece of roughly textured paper with a partial foundation of watercolor on which she would begin the new gouache. Her back was worse, the Darvon had done little more than dull the pain, and the brace, prescribed by the doctor for "her little setbacks (haha)," made it impossible for her to move like anything but a robot. There were unsightly ridges beneath her jeans; she hated that damned brace. She hated her damned self and her damned stupidity!

On top of everything that girl was coming over to discover the key to her success as a serious artist and to ask her for advice. Some joke. Cathy stared at the blank paper and the minutes passed heavily. Remember the story about *The Little Engine That Could*? All the children loved that story. Laura had loved it, then Aggie, then Vinnie, and now Robbie would love it when he was a little older. *I think I can, I think I can.*

Cathy added a dram of gum solution to an ounce of titanium white, then a touch of black and an infinitesimal amount of Mars violet. After adding more water she grimaced, added more titanium white, then more water. Very rapidly she outlined a torso and watched it dry. She frowned. It was too dark. She added more titanium white, then tried phoning Tony but he wasn't home. He should have been back from the museum by now; he should have been there grading papers. She dialed again and let the phone ring twenty times in case he had fallen asleep. Where the hell was he? She felt a stab of jealousy along with a twinge of pain down her right leg. She tried not to imagine him with one of those tough, young women artists he hung around with—platonically, of course, but even so it made her nervous. He probably lied about going to the museum to do research. He had some other assignation in mind all along, right? That was obviously why he had left her bed in the middle of the night, right? Shit!

She called Lester's new apartment but he was out, too, and

his housekeeper said he wouldn't be back until late afternoon. Of course, he was meeting Vinnie, taking him somewhere after the meeting at school. Cathy hobbled into the kitchen, made herself a cup of tea, and took one more Darvon. I think I can, she chanted, and went back to her easel.

Why was life so hard?

Because you make it hard, Catherine.

Do not!

At eleven o'clock she moved to the window and allowed the rain to mesmerize her as she watched hordes of kids flow out of the yellow school buses lined up outside of the Museum of Natural History. Rain and yellow school buses . . . they seemed to go together. It had been the same in Ohio, only in Ohio there had been mud.

From the cow pastures of southern Ohio to the fifteenth floor of the Beresford and an aerial view of Manhattan—how long had it been since she had seen a cow pie? Those round, crusty disks with diligent flies humming over them? *Long*. And she missed the cows and their musical lowing and their friendly, wet, big pink noses. Cows were the one thing she still missed. But not the mud, she did not miss the mud.

After nine years the view from Lester Aimsley's elegant apartment still enthralled her: to the east, Central Park, dotted with ponds and winding roads, was just turning pale spring green, an indistinct hint still stiff with winter black. Hard turning soft, angles blooming into rounds. Further east she could actually make out a slice of the East River and off to the west a patch of the gray and turbulent Hudson River. But the panorama of mighty skyscrapers to the south was the view which most moved her. Magnificent monuments: from the Empire State Building to the new slanted-top Citicorp, like great pyramids; for her they were proof of immortality. She called them her wildflowers and knew their names by heart. Like a devoted botanist she was intimately involved in their origins. She could quote architects, dates, costs, sources for rare materials such as marble, and other endless anecdotes connected with their construction.

Someday, and it would be soon, when she had to move from the apartment and turn it back over to Lester, when that happened, she would miss the sweeping view of her wildflowers more than the luxurious, rambling living quarters, even more than the impressive studio which Lester had had designed for her.

And regardless of what Lester was suggesting she was going to move. She could not afford the apartment alone and that was that. Even if her next show, which was scheduled for November, netted her millions (which was out of the question) she would never feel secure taking on the monthly nut which Lester paid for the cooperative apartment and its exorbitant maintenance. Besides it was Lester's apartment and the separation (face it, Cathy), the divorce, was her doing. She intended to pay for it. She was not entitled to Lester's money. It didn't matter that he had a lot of it, that he would never miss it, that he would feel better knowing his son was being given the best of everything. Lester knew how she felt about alimony and payoffs for women who didn't deserve it. And she didn't deserve it. Then why was he insisting she stay on? Why did he want to make things easier for her when it was all her fault?

At the window again she surveyed the skyline nostalgically, as if she had already moved to some cramped, dismal studio with a western exposure and an obstructed view. In the rain her wildflowers were like hulking rocks along the foggy Maine coast. She had produced more than fifty paintings of the south skyline, some in ghostly dawn with a dense brume of snow making them less than shadows; some in full, harsh midday light with hard shadows cracking the pavements below; others at night when the buildings were blooming as colorfully and unexpectedly as desert flowers.

She had painted her wildflowers from her first days in the city, long before the Beresford, long before Lester and Vinnie, Laura, Baby Aggie—even before Rosen. She had painted them in borrowed rooms, in apartments of friends, painted them from the streets or from empty offices on weekends. In 1969, five years after Rosen's death and the year of her first show, the critics had seen in her wildflowers "the intense phallic fascination of the liberated woman who has suffered and returned full circle." Full circle to what, she wondered. Of course she recognized that she had gained entré to the select inner coterie of the art establishment by being the widow of the late Robert Rosen. They—the powers, the eyes that pass judgment and make the deals with museums and collectors—had seen her as a hot commodity because of her relationship with Rosen, and every brush stroke, at least in the beginning, had been made to relate to their stormy marriage and Rosen's self-destructive demise.

The critics had always been quick to point out that an artist of the caliber of Robert Rosen would have taken the idea further. Cathy's reviews, though favorable, were niggardly and begrudging. She was forever being compared to her late husband and found wanting. They liked to say she made "brilliant beginnings" and if one powerful critic admitted that her oil paintings were beautifully executed, powerful yet delicate, he felt obliged to observe that Cathy was "irritatingly cautious in her scope."

They found her choice of "wildflowers" whimsical, which in their terms meant insignificant. She admitted it was a trifle precious to dub them such, but that was how she felt about them and she could not see why she should label them with an obscure quote from Ezra Pound or an archaic French word in order to mollify the critics and convince them that she was not merely a lightweight. For her the awesome buildings were not phallic symbols, they were wildflowers. If some people considered New York City, as typified by its concrete and steel skyline, a place of confinement, a jail of sorts, Cathy considered it a place of freedom, as fecund as an Ohio cow pasture and much more exciting.

Damn critics were always dying to read sexual connotations into women's work, and so what . . . maybe they were right. But why was a woman's preoccupation so often labeled "limiting" or "maternal" while a man's sexual explorations were seen in a cosmic light? It took no great mind to figure out that her recent fascination with the male body had *something* to do with sex. What irritated her was the convenient inference that the sexual was lesser, or merely a phase that women passed through before entering the mysterious real of whatever they were supposed to enter. Male critics, thought Cathy, spoke with a forked tongue.

She limped back to her station in front of the vacant paper, aware that she was dangerously close to losing her sense of humor. This was no time to think of Rosen and her gratuitous acceptance into the Mad Ave crowd. At least she had weaseled her way in the door when most other women had been out in the cold. Anyway, things were changing, weren't they? Bad time to think these thoughts. The Darvon had worn off and each throb of pain reminded her that something was running away with her.

Damn. She'd been getting so close to some breakthrough with her work and now it would be impossible to deliver the promised paintings in time for her show in November. She would just have to phone Zed so he could schedule something else. Whenever her back went into spasm her mind obediently followed suit until she was in a total panic and unable to think of anything but the pain.

She was going out of control, slipping into her own custom-made madness, and as always she was shocked that she had not seen it coming on. She left the studio, went back into the bedroom she had shared with Lester, and tried to remove her jeans. It took her fifteen minutes to undress. She could not bend forward and finally she lowered herself gingerly onto the floor, wriggled them off, and inched herself into an upright position. By the time she put on her robe her face was flushed and angry and the tears were falling hard. She dialed Lester again, then Tony, then Lester, then one last time for Tony.

Damn Tony was probably with the Israeli beauty, the one who didn't speak English. Some sucker she had been to believe that he was spending two hours a day teaching her English because he thought she was so special, gifted as an artist. She could just see them together at Tony's Village apartment, smoking dope, learning a few words in the present tense and suddenly falling into each other's arms because it was easier than words.

"Shit!" she screamed, trying to halt the pornographic images of Tony and the other young woman. He had stressed hundreds of times that Lila, that was the Israeli's name, and the other girls who hung around with him were just "buddies." Why couldn't she believe that? Why was she so damned intent on suffering and what difference did it make if he were lying?

But he wasn't lying, right? She dialed his number again and

he answered breathlessly on the second ring. He had just come back with a load of groceries and was looking forward to her coming to his place for dinner.

Cathy hung up, seething. "Asshole!" she hissed at herself, then "asshole! Idiot!"

Too many men in her life, too many. Yes, yes. All her friends told her that. Too many men; "yes," she laughed, smiled, joked, and agreed. They were absolutely right. Too many. There had always been too many men, or at least always from the time of Rosen's death. Before Rosen she had been pure, sweet, compliant . . . the ideal wife, mother, housekeeper, and so on. Smilingly agreeable, she had tiptoed lightly through her life so as not to disturb him.

Before Rosen there had been boyfriends, dozens and dozens of them, and after Rosen there had been lovers in equally staggering numbers. Yes, after Rosen's death there had never been more than a few weeks' respite; actually, now that she thought of it, not from sex but from *love*. Oh, she needed love, thrived on it and ached and longed for it when it ended. Yes, the addiction was definitely to love, not to sex. Not that sex wasn't okay and sometimes she liked to tell herself it was hard-core lust that drove her forward. Wrong, it was love. Actually, if she was in love she could get along perfectly well without sex. She was especially partial to long absences from whoever was her current beloved because then she could have it both ways: she could be in love and still have the time (not to mention the inspiration) to throw herself into her work. She had once quipped that the ideal situation would be to fall in love with a man condemned to a long prison sentence.

Unfortunately she really loved men . . . though not to the exclusion of women, of course. Her closest friends were women but she *loved* men—loved the holding of them and the smell and all the mystery which had nothing to do with her. Men fascinated her in much the same way her wildflowers did. Men's asses had always intrigued her, even in high school when they weren't supposed to and when nobody was mentioning them. Yet she had always studied them, guiltily of course but nonetheless obsessively.

Her friends were right when they said men had dominated her life. She had canceled a show once when things were hot between her and that French marquis. People had been horrified at that. Even in the midst of the man-hating sixties when she was swinging her fists along with her sisters, it had been easy to forgive them. She felt small for that, shallow and apolitical, but it was true.

She called Tony back on the pretext of having forgotten what time she was expected for dinner. He answered promptly and she felt ashamed that she had imagined his cocky kid's grin warming the loins of someone his own age. It was probably true that the sweet young things who swarmed around him were buddies. He was awfully easy to talk to.

Cathy thought of his stocky, firm young body. He was a fierce and passionate lover, vociferous and bawdy yet always he courted her with a hint of humor. He was strong. He could swing Cathy into dozens of undreamed-of positions, laughing at her phony puritan reactions as he thrust himself into her. Hadn't she known the minute she had met those black, black eyes that his gentle, almost docile demeanor camouflaged a raging libido?

She hadn't been particularly looking the night they had first met, at some function, she had forgotten now what, which had been held in the Fountain Restaurant at the Metropolitan Museum. Lester had been out of town, London probably, but she couldn't remember that either. Tony had worn a gray flannel suit and there had been absolutely nothing extraordinary about him, other than his youth and those very persevering black eyes. She had felt him staring at her and, being well over her usual quota of bourbons, had glibly commented that Italian men of his medium (though surely not *short*) stature invariably found her irresistible. She had said it as a joke really, because he was so damned young and except for a weekend relapse in Paris she had been quite strict with herself since her marriage to Lester. Certainly she had not been consciously looking for a lover.

Because his gaze was so dogged she had anticipated an equally glib reply, probably delivered with a Bronx accent. Instead he had engaged her, not in a predictable cocktail party seduction but in a passionately intelligent conversation about her work. His words, coupled with the strain of his gray jacket across his broad shoulders and the apparently involuntary glint in his eyes, had totally captured her imagination.

He was an art teacher and, as he put it, had few pretensions about being a major contributor to the serious art world though he still did some painting on his own. He loved teaching at his private school, loved his Sunday painting, loved the flurry of art activities which the city afforded him. He spoke easily and excitedly about himself, yet his obvious delight in his life was in no way smug. He seemed incapable of restraining his enthusiasm, which had made him seem younger than his then twenty-three years. She had known she was in the presence of a powerful ego yet Tony's egotism had from the start struck her as different from that of most of the men she encountered—all except Lester, who she considered an exception in every way.

Tony Casteli radiated sexuality, not unconsciously, for he seemed acutely aware of his potential, but effortlessly and good-naturedly. Later he confessed to Cathy that he would never have had the nerve even to ask her to have a cup of coffee with him. Instead he had stationed himself outside the museum hoping that she would leave alone and that they would just "happen" to be going in the same direction. He had been even too nervous to plan what he would say. As it turned out, Cathy saw him leave and followed him. Her hasty departure had required no further explanation; it had given him the confidence he needed and they had joined hands, flagged a cab, and driven directly to Tony's Sullivan Street apartment. The thirty-minute cab ride from Fifth Avenue and Seventy-ninth Street to the West Village remained in both of their minds as an unparalleled sensate feast.

"I always wondered how things like this happened," Cathy had mused later, curled contentedly on his lumpy bed, wearing one of his Japanese kimonos. "Do you always go around seducing women old enough to be your mother?"

"You're not!"

"I am!" She had thrown herself on him and they had rolled on the bed laughing hysterically as Tony tried to guess her age.

"You don't seem like a mother," he had said seriously, and then he had proceeded to describe his own mother with such specific and loving details that Cathy wondered if her affair with him was going to be as simple as she might have hoped.

He was a complete person and she had learned during their first long night together that there were no colors of herself that would have to be hidden from him. Soberly she had explored his body with her mouth, finding damp creases, new textures, soft and pungent smells which fed some new desire in herself. His need to please her was like an aphrodisiac, making all things possible for her. Waves of pleasure had vibrated in her body long after he had fallen asleep with his dark head tucked against her breast.

Cathy closed her eyes against the memory which marked the beginning of the now eight-month-long affair. She was a love addict. All right. But how do you knock a habit when it owns not your body, but your heart?

She looked at the clock next to the bed. That girl, Joan-Something, was coming in less than an hour. There was no way to call her and tell her not to come. Some advice she'd give today. She closed her eyes and went over the list of former lovers in her mind. She had a morbid fear of forgetting an old lover, like the woman in the Jacques Brel song who can't remember his name. To forget a lover's name would be immoral. So periodically she reviewed the list, sometimes putting them in alphabetical order, sometimes in chronological order, sometimes, when she was feeling mean, ranking them according to performance. Occasionally, she was even comforted by her memories.

But not today. Today nothing helped, not even the memories of Tony, of the freedom of making love in cabs, on beaches, on deserted country roads . . . nothing helped today. She felt herself growing smaller, like Alice, helpless in a world that was oversized. She began growling at herself in some primitive language in which the only recognizable word was *asshole*.

Forty-six was too old to be doing what she was doing. She was also too smart to be doing what she was doing and yet here she was doing it in the grand style. Well, Rosen had wrapped his car around a telephone pole, was that so smart? She was still ahead of him. She was still alive and she'd never taken heroin. She had been responsible. She had successfully raised two daughters while juggling a sometimes flourishing, sometimes languishing career, hadn't she? Hadn't she always supported herself and the girls until her marriage to Lester? There were worse things, weren't there, than throwing your back out of whack?

But Rosen was a hero. His tragic death at a young age had only confirmed his greatness. She was alive and "irritatingly cautious in her scope." Rosen was dead. Why was she still measuring everything against him? Leave that to the damned critics. Today of all days, why was she thinking of a dead husband?

Resting on her back in bed with a pillow tucked under her knees to ease the pressure on the sciatic nerve, she contemplated the ceiling. She had spent hours mixing the paint, getting just the shade she wanted. "Close-encounter blue," Lester had called it back in the days when they still slept together, before she had grown frightened of his body, half-convinced that she might be contaminated by his sixty-six years. "Close-encounter blue." The tears dribbled into her ears and snatches of an old hillbilly song which had been popular in her youth ran through her mind.

I got tears in my ears
From lying on my back
Cryin' over you.

But crying over who?

How do you think, Jone? No, really, Jone, what is it you think with, since your mind shrinks from words and your brain refuses (or is unable?) to grant words their usual priority. How will you function in a world glutted with words? Like some dumb animal, will you go along sniffing at the pavement, wagging your tail, hoping for a kind touch, a handout? Isn't that what you've always done?

Yes, Jone. Yes. Keep it simple. You do not have to fall in line with the rest of your family, no matter what they say. Is it really a surprise to you, Jone, that your liberal, enlightened family finds the idea of your becoming a sculptor so horrifying?

You're a big girl, Jone, nearly six feet tall. Robust. They've always depended on you, like a rock. They say you never gurgled like most babies. You were serious, an uncompromising infant so large you could not hold your own head up. They always expected a lot from you. But you never gave them words, only actions, strong gestures, your large frame occupying space. They came to rely on you for that. You, the lastborn child of Elizabeth Jones Beele, her final bid for recognition and immortality. Yes, they relied on you like a servant, loyal and dependable. Old black Jone. Only you weren't old, you weren't a servant, and you weren't black. It was all right. They knew what to expect from you. You never minded. No one had to tell you to make your bed. You enjoyed touching the smooth sheets, pressing out the wrinkles with the palm of your large hand, plumping and poofing the pillows, polishing the family silver. You relished the hot dishwater, the waxing of floors, and the shoveling of snow in the winter. They could not punish you with those mundane chores.

You were a silent child, the youngest of four precocious little Beeles. The other little Beeles, like their ancestors, were born elocutionists. They, the Beeles, talked on and on, soothing and scaring each other with words whose meanings were at best ambiguous. They argued cases before the Supreme Court and graduated Phi Beta Kappa . . . in words; they entered law school and left law school with the words spewing out of their mouths. Sister, brothers, mother, father: talking, writing, spelling, reading. The Beele Westchester home seemed to be built of words and books; the maid cooking on a stove heated by rejected novels or first drafts of legal briefs. If you could not put it into words fast enough the Beeles had you trapped.

They were a competitive lot and though they loved you, Jone, and thought you cunning for keeping silent until you were two, they always viewed you as a friendly amoeba, a primitive, indefinite form, possibly parasitic, but certainly nothing to worry about.

They were, however, concerned about your intellect until some great educational authority reassured them. Then they made up words for the reason you were the way you were—so different from them. You were, they agreed, like your grandmother Mary Jones who, while not as reticent as you, had a gift for drawing and making things with her hands. Yes, they declared, you had inherited grandmother Mary's artistic talent, though not, they hoped, her sour, unyielding spirit. Mary Jones. You were named for her. Clever, no, the spelling of your name? Another linguistic trick, something your mother, Elizabeth, author of six rejected novels, thought up as proof of her liberated nature. She never introduces you without spelling your name: J O N E. "You see my maiden name was Jones," she laughs.

You have considered changing your last name to Jones too. Jone Jones. But your family doesn't expect such subtleties from you and you prefer to leave the linguistic sleight-of-hand to the Beeles. And so you will remain a dog sniffing the streets, granddaughter to an impoverished spirit, now confined tidily and at great expense in the luxurious nursing home in Wilton, a woman who died years before your own mother, Elizabeth, was even born.

Poor Elizabeth, who ever since it was discovered that you were living in some filthy place doing your sculpting, keeps sobbing, "I thought I knew you." They are sure you are unhappy because you are growing plump at twenty-two. They can't imagine you don't care to be willowy, pale, and lean like the Beeles. You will need the weight and the muscles to carry tons of steel and marble on your back. They want you thin, Jone, so you can sit in their Bronxville living room and discuss the high unemployment rate with an eligible young lawyer (Catholic hopefully) who will in time join the family legal firm. And talk.

But you want to build monuments and unfix the past. You want to weld metals into undreamed-of shapes and forms. You would like to put your large calloused hands around the white colonial Westchester house and mold it into something new. This, Jone, is something they did not guess about you because they were so busy talking.

Jone Beele shook the rain out of her umbrella as she stepped into the luxurious lobby of the Beresford. She had lied to Catherine Aimsley about being friends with her daughter at Sarah Lawrence. Laura Rosen had been only a face and a name in one of her classes. Laura was part of the elite, comfortable crowd, the crowd Jone's mother would have preferred for her daughter.

Jone mumbled Catherine's name to the elevator man and stood scrunched and dripping in the rear as though the elevator were packed with people. It had taken all her nerve to call Catherine Aimsley, to listen to her gravelly, low voice repeating her name twice, identifying herself as a fellow-artist, a sculptor, who had always admired Catherine's work. Now what the hell was she going to say to a woman old enough to be her mother, a woman who ranked as one of the most important painters on the New York art scene?

My name is Jone Beele. I've been lying to everyone for a year now and I need to talk to someone. I picked you because you are successful and I can mention your name to my parents, who think I am crazy, but they will be impressed because I know someone important like you. Nine months ago I quit my job teaching in a fancy East Side private elementary school. Since then I've been living in a garage in Tribeca sculpting. Now I have a room full of metal, welded pieces which my parents would tell me are junk if they could see them. If they saw these same pieces in a reputable Madison Avenue gallery they might buy them. You see, they claim to love art. I don't know any artists. I don't know what to do with my pieces. I don't know how to begin because all I can do is do. This is hard for me. Coming to see you is hard. I've come to you because you are "someone" and because I can't waste my time drinking coffee with kids I see who are in the same boat I'm in. I want you to help me. I'm not used to asking for help and I'm not much good with words. I want you to see my pieces and tell me if they're junk. If you say they're junk, it won't matter. I'll still keep on working but I'll believe you. I don't believe them. *I've never done anything like this before in my life. My father would have said it was impossible for me to bully my way in here to talk to you. They say I'm not assertive, only now I have to be because in another month I'll need money to buy more metal. I need to sell my work. I don't want to be taken advantage of. I've heard you were a hardheaded business woman, you never gave your work away. You had to be tough. I'm only twenty-two but I know that. I'm here to find out how to survive.*

The elevator door opened slowly onto a small marble foyer with two doors. There was a large "A" on one of the doors. As Jone pressed the buzzer she wondered why Catherine had changed her name to Aimsley instead of keeping the name of the legendary Robert Rosen. For that matter, why had she changed her name at all?

APRIL 1980
Paris

The three final hours in the display window were no less torturous for knowing that soon it would all be over. Angelica felt like the apocryphal drowning man as her life flashed before her eyes not once but many times. She might have quit. At any moment before the end she might have left the window. Who would have known? Her staying was more than endurance, more than will. She stayed because she was curious to see what would happen next, to know where it all would lead.

She knew now why she had come to the window, to frame herself behind glass as part of that ghoulish trio. Now that the images were coming so fast and vividly she knew she had had to make herself this vulnerable in order to regenerate.

> *What we call the beginning is often the end*
> *And to make an end is to make a beginning.*
> *The end is where we start from.*

Random lines and images from Eliot's *Four Quartets* spun themselves around the images of her own life. It was hard to die.

Until now Angelica had not realized that spending two years in France had been a way of finally putting an end to the frustration of trying to find a niche for herself in a world that appeared to have no place for her. In the farmhouse in Azay-le-Rideau there was only Ferris's criticism and rejection; in New York there had been the impenetrable, sophisticated uptown world and the esoteric, equally mysterious and closed downtown Soho world. She had deluded herself into thinking she would be happier living in the bucolic French countryside, within sight of a turreted castle, playing fairy-tale mistress (who also paints) to a genius.

"Don't worry about money," Ferris kept telling her. "I've plenty for both of us. You place too much importance on money! Use the time here to work, to find yourself. Isn't it a relief not to have to take the commuter train to Long Island and teach everyday? Relax. What's mine is yours."

But it wasn't. Ferris doled out money, not grudgingly, but as if she were being rewarded for being a good girl. Anyway, his money was not enough. She was so broke now she could not bear to think of how she might survive alone. How had she allowed herself to drift into such complacency? She was all used up and she couldn't even be philosophical about it and attribute it to a "lean spell."

Forget about earning a lot of money. Her goals were so modest she choked on them sometimes and thought she might die of an overdose of humility. If the gallery in Montmartre sold any of the dozen paintings she had left with them she would feel rich. Imagine feeling rich with two hundred and fifty dollars in her humble lint-filled little pocket—for that was what she would be left with once the gallery took their fifty percent. How revolting! Mentally she could not even grasp the significance of the six-figure sums which Ferris's paintings sold for.

Of course she wouldn't starve, Ferris would feed her. Maybe that was why she had been unable to swallow her food for the past few weeks. At the moment she did not even have enough money to take a plane to New York, let alone set herself up with a studio when she got there. She could wade through the red tape and multitudinous paperwork necessary to apply for either a Rockefeller or a National Endowment grant but that was not an immediate solution. She could try to get her old teaching job back but she knew she wouldn't. Now that she had tasted the satisfaction of having enough time for her work, that avenue was no longer open.

Money for food and a roof, some space, and decent light were all she really required for the moment. She could try peddling her paintings along the Seine or on some street corner and risk being fined or humiliated. There was nothing romantic about an artist selling paintings on street corners. She would almost rather sell her body.

Sell her body? Yes, well, she could make more money with shorter hours than she had made teaching school. And she wouldn't have to ride the Long Island Rail Road. Sell her body? *Really, Angelica, you have been in this window too long!*

At eleven forty-five Suzanne's red Simca pulled up in front of the shop and while Suzanne crated up Mag and Sam, Angelica washed and dressed in the tiny W.C. The black sweater, black raw silk harem pants, and boots which, except when she was working, had been her uniform for the past two years, felt graceless after five days in the peachy *chemise de nuit*. She scrubbed off the exotic mannequin makeup and joined Suze in the car, pale and glowing in her solemn black.

Suze had recently broken off with the woman she had lived with for the past twelve years, so they were alone as they drove up the wide boulevard to the late-hours *brasserie* in Montparnasse. The Closerie des Lilas, reputedly a favorite of both Hemingway and Lenin, was at midnight just coming alive.

"You're sure you don't want to go back to my place and sleep?"

Angelica sniffed the air. "Oysters. Only in months that have an *r* in their name." For the first time since leaving Azay-le-Rideau she felt hungry, *starved* to be precise. Oysters, a glass of white wine, lots of bread, and one of those overwhelming desserts composed of vanilla meringue, vanilla creme, and vanilla ice cream, topped with chantilly *avec* ever so slightly more vanilla would suit.

Suze swept over to a table of rowdy acquaintances, so Angelica gave her name to the *maître d'* and, declining to go to the bar for a drink, waited by his side straight and proper as a schoolchild. So this was what it was like on the outside, moving with laughing strangers on the other side of the glass. She was a mannequin come recently to life, part of a painting she would one day do. The racket in the Closerie was music, the reckless ostentation and far-out fashions of the clientele such a relief after the long winter in the country.

Ferris hated Paris, hated all cities, so that after fleeing from New York he had wanted only to watch the mists play on the soft rolling countryside of the Loire Valley. Even though they were only two and a half hours away from Paris, this was her first trip in over a year.

A man was staring at her. She could feel his eyes on her without looking up. He was young. It seemed to her she could feel his youth in the air between them. She smiled and allowed him to study her without her acknowledgment. When she finally raised her eyes she met his, heavy and dark with intent. She had been right. He was probably no more than twenty. He was callow and expectant, with a strong Gallic face, a face she would love to paint. Men who studied her in bars were special men. She knew she did not draw that response from the hail-fellows-well-met. Her hands were tingling, as if she were about to begin a new work. It was a good feeling. It had been years since she had opened herself to a strange man's eyes in a crowded bar. It had been nine years, to be exact.

"Am I interrupting?" Suze nudged her. Suze would have loved to see her vanish with a stranger, male or female.

Angelica nodded to the man and took Suze's arm. "I was just making sure my powers haven't waned."

"Do you know how erotic people found your little *ménage à trois*?" Suze asked after the waiter had taken their orders.

"So . . . I can make a living as a dummy in store windows. That's always good to know." Angelica laughed ruefully.

"That's not what I meant and you know it. Next time I could get some real publicity . . . photographers. Maybe a Paris gallery would pick up on you."

"As a freak," Angelica suggested, somewhat distracted because the young man at the bar had left. "I know, Suze, that I have all the necessary attributes for being a marvelous freak—I know that's not what you meant. I realize you're complimenting me and God knows it's been a long time since anyone did that.

Standing in your window . . . God, it was like being in a time capsule or the way I've heard people describe their experiences on psychedelic drugs, like a psychomimetic experience. When I first moved to New York after college I did a lot of art as event . . . exhibitionism as Ferris calls it. But this was different! When I started out in the late sixties my events were an end in themselves but this experience with Mag and Sam isn't an end. It's part of a process, see, and I wouldn't want to do it again. The spectrum of possibilities of different types of art is unlimited today and that's good. But me . . . like I said, it would be easy to be a freak. I met a guy at a party before I knew Ferris. He was in with the Warhol crowd and he thought I was really special. What he meant was *freaky* . . . you know, that I could be promoted into a commodity. He kept saying he wanted to 'handle' me . . . what a creepy expression. Anyway, without ever seeing my work he told me he could make me a huge success. You know what? He invited me to dinner at Warhol's and I stood him up."

"Don't you think that was . . . self-defeating, even self-destructive?"

"I never wanted to be a personality . . . I want to be an artist. And what I didn't know when I stood in those East Village windows but I do know now, is that event art isn't *it* for me . . . not ultimately. I know this is going to sound like a judgment for all those people who are involved in this aspect of art but it isn't really. Just for me . . . I'm talking just for me. . . ."

"I've never heard you talk this much," Suze laughed.

"I've been alone with those two yokels. I'm high. I'm just high! And I know that what I want is to do something important, something that people recognize, something that moves them and makes them *see*. Great artists in the past used to make powerful social and political statements . . . not by sacrificing the aesthetic either. Look at David, at Goya. It's not enough just to be unique . . . to try and find some original little space that no one else has occupied. And it's not enough to imitate the past. If I paint like Rembrandt, so what? That doesn't make me a genius, it makes me an imitator.

"But what if I find a way of taking the past, the substance, or all that's valuable, all that I personally respond to in the masters and see it with my own eyes in the world *I* live in? What if I do *that*?" Angelica leaned across the table breathlessly.

"I don't know." Suze was moved. "I don't even know how you continue."

"Of course I continue," Angelica laughed and sat back in her chair. "What else would I do? Only now I'm going to do it, full-time, the way I see it."

"You could do the window again. You could get publicity . . . it might not hurt to . . ."

"No," Angelica shook her head. "I would be imitating something . . . like I've been trying to imitate Ferris, struggling to paint in a way that is totally unnatural to me. Nope. No more windows, much as I love Sam and Mag."

"But Angelica, be honest, you cultivate a bizarre image. Look at you, all in black with your pale skin and almost no hair. Why do you have a burr haircut if you don't want people to respond to you as an eccentric? When I'm with you people always stare."

"That's what I do." Angelica waited until the waiter left, then she turned all the oysters out of their shells and sliced into one of them. "I'm not Bette Midler. I would be a disaster on a talk show. I can only talk to two people at a time."

Suze laughed, enjoying Angelica's delight in her precious oysters.

"Come live with me," Suze said as they were finishing, "and get back into the mainstream. You're not a country girl."

"You mean that I should leave Ferris? Funny, he always said you were trying to lure me away from him."

"But not the way he means." Suze shook her head impatiently. "Ferris is so damned sure that my sexual predilections are the sole basis for our friendship. I'm surprised he didn't show up to make sure I and my perverted band of merry maids weren't ganging up on you."

Angelica finished her oysters in silence, passed on a second glass of wine, and waited the arrival of the vanilla masterpiece.

"I've never been with a woman," she said finally. "I'd be curious . . ."

"I'm warning all my friends," Suze teased, "not to fall in love with you."

"No," Angelica mused, "I'm not an easy person to love."

At one-thirty when they left the Closerie des Lilas she noticed the air had turned sweet and soft. In Azay the lilac bush outside their bedroom window would be in bloom and this time tomorrow she would be sleeping with its heavy scent inside her dreams. It might be the last night she spent with Ferris. Suze had insisted she accept the six hundred dollars which was half of the profit for the week. Six hundred dollars was enough money to fly to New York and last for how long?

As Suze turned onto Boulevard St. Michel, Angelica wondered how much money a prostitute could make if she made her own rules and played it alone without benefit of a madam or, God forbid, a *pimp*. She tried to see herself going up to men in bars, nice men in shirts and ties. She imagined herself explaining her situation to them: "I need to make a fast buck so I can spend the rest of the day painting." Maybe the Plaza or the St. Regis would put her up in a suite in exchange for turning tricks. Maybe. . . . All of her fantasies ended in one-liners. Midwestern, Jewish, quasi-intellectual feminist turns her back on her art to lie on her back.

She smiled in the dark yet she knew that at the root of her absurd scenarios was an important question: How could she live, as an independent artist, and have time to continue her work? It wasn't enough to snatch an hour here and there; she needed time, and time was dollars and cents.

The question, she knew, was an ancient one. If she went to New York, and she was determined that she would, she would have to find a job. Teaching was out even if she could find a job in Manhattan. She would always end up giving too much of herself and having nothing left for her own work. She was not good at pacing herself and that was something she would finally have to face. She had once tried waitressing but had been a dismal failure and was fired afer two days. It seemed ludicrous to her now but waitressing had been beyond her. She had not been able to carry more than one cup of coffee at a time nor to yell out her orders to the chef. Another time she had tried working as a "coder" for a market research firm but that too had ended abruptly when she went to the supervisor to make a deal: since she was twice as efficient as the other coders she had suggested she (a) work half as long or (b) earn twice as much money. The answer to both alternatives was *no,* and for her audacity she was fired on the spot.

The most logical course, one she had avoided primarily because Ferris claimed it was the ruination of any artist worth his salt, was commercial art. According to Ferris, going commercial —magazine layouts, bookcovers, publicity, advertising—was the ultimate prostitution. He insisted *anything* was better than commercial work because it deluded people into believing they were being creative while seducing them with high wages. Well, he could call *that* prostitution but when she weighed sitting behind a drawing board at Benton and Bowles against stroking the corpulent hairy derrière of a stranger, there really was no choice.

Angelica did not return to Azay-le-Rideau the following day nor the day after, nor the day after that. She did not decide not to leave Paris, she only decided to stay on enjoying Suzanne's hospitality, Suzanne's warm and radical friends, and Paris itself. During the day she wandered around St. Germain, the Quartier Latin, along the Seine sometimes as far as the Bois de Boulogne. She climbed to the top of Notre Dame to commune with her beloved gargoyles, mourning over their pockmarked faces, the result of twentieth-century pollution. Once the chestnut blossoms popped she could not be lured inside a museum, except on one rainy morning she spent at the Louvre studying the Dutch masters. She was healing.

Having spent the past two years practically isolated in the country, Angelica craved the chaos and hustle of city streets. From the streets of Paris one could study architecture, people, history; one could listen to music and eat. The streets and the people made her feel strong and full; she drank in the sights and sat in sidewalk cafés reflecting on her solitary encounters. Evenings were social: concerts, avant-garde theater, dinner and dancing in one of several Rive Gauche clubs. Invariably she was surrounded by women, successful, bright, professional women who sought each other's company rather than the company of men. Against Suzanne's protests Angelica paid her own way. Though the six hundred dollars had dwindled, her hopes for the future had escalated. It felt good to pay.

The sexual exchanges between Suze's friends were subtle and unaffected. Even at the Taverne Marie, one of the late-hours gay bars frequented exclusively by women, the signals were inconspicuous. Angelica enjoyed dancing with Suze's band of merry maids, as Suze herself referred to her friends. Dancing with women infused her with memories of preadolescent innocence when girl friends held hands, skipped together, and even kissed without shame. She felt safe with these women. She delighted in the remarkable delicacy of the dancing even when the music turned to torrid disco.

One night, because there was no reason not to, she found herself walking arm in arm along the Seine with Françoise Landes, a young lawyer who, bent on disguising her voluptuous Rubenesque body, wore baggy corduroys, a University of Illinois sweatshirt, and red cowboy boots. Angelica had met Françoise on numerous occasions and been consistently amused by the French woman's sacrilegious humor. Françoise's cruel wit reminded her of the rapier-sharp brilliance of a Wilde or a Gertrude Stein. Consequently, Angelica had spent the entire evening in stitches; the laughter had purged her, leaving her as relaxed and regenerated as if she had undergone a deep, delicious body massage.

When Françoise caressed her head she responded, smiling and moving closer. It felt good, perfectly natural, to be touched by her new friend. And when Françoise took her hand, Angelica reciprocated with a warm squeeze.

But when Françoise opened the door to her apartment in St. Louis-en-l'Ile, Angelica's sense of well-being began to ebb. She wasn't exactly frightened. She thought she knew what was happening and that she wanted it to happen. On the other hand, she knew nothing, had no idea what to expect.

"A cognac?" Françoise tossed her jacket on one of the Louis the Fourteenth chairs. The apartment was unexpectedly elegant, lavishly decorated with beautiful antiques, thick oriental rugs, and crystal chandeliers. There was a view of the Seine off of a tiny balcony at the end of the living room.

"I didn't know you were rich." Angelica felt awkward as Françoise lowered her ample body onto a peacock-blue chaise.

"Papa was a marquis before he was a Communist. You see, *chérie,* we have a lot in common. We're both unscrupulous capitalists sprung from the loins of deluded Marxists."

"I've never thought of myself as . . ."

". . . unscrupulous?" Françoise laughed.

"No, as a capitalist. I don't exactly view life with an economic eye. I am apolitical." In an effort to relax, Angelica stretched out in the middle of the rug.

"But not asexual." Françoise laughed wickedly and poured herself a second cognac.

Angelica's nerves were fused with a wild desire to burst out laughing at the absurdity of the situation; it was more like a Restoration comedy than a lascivious seduction! Here was Françoise casually quipping about her Marxist father, drinking cognac, and here was Angelica deep-breathing on the floor.

"Françoise, I think you should know something. I never . . ."

"So?" Françoise stood over her and smiled archly.

"You knew?" Angelica felt ridiculous, painfully naive. "You knew I'd . . ."

Françoise guffawed and tossed the cognac down as if it were water. "Americans are so naive! Especially you, for all of your no hair, no makeup, no obvious pretensions."

Angelica sat up and chuckled, thinking of the statues Rodin had done of Balzac, of the way the sculptor had captured Balzac's sagacity, his lustiness and gargantuan spirit. Rodin had been obsessed with Balzac not only because of the writer's massive physique but because Balzac's body was the perfect reflection of his inner power. From the moment she had met Françoise, Angelica had sensed her power, an unquenchable appetite, irreverence that somehow managed never to be really evil or mean. What was most astonishing was that Françoise was only twenty-six years old. It was almost impossible to imagine her as a child.

"Did Suze tell you I was a devout heterosexual with this crazy curiosity?"

"I did not need to be told," Françoise laughed as she placed some fruit and a plate of cheese on the low table. "The first time

I met you—was it two years ago at Suzanne's?—I knew you were not a lesbian. However, I'm a terribly open-minded woman . . . as you will see."

"I'm really that transparent?" Angelica rubbed a red apple against her cheek. She did not like to think of herself as transparent but perhaps she was.

"You're beautiful," Françoise said softly. "And no, you are not transparent . . . you are far from that. But then you work at it," she smiled mischievously.

"I don't . . ."

"Of course you do!" Françoise exploded. "We all work at our images . . . those of us with imagination. We create ourselves, don't we?"

Angelica shrugged.

"Listen, I did the same thing you're doing. Once I went off with a man . . . because I was curious."

"And?"

Françoise wrinkled her nose. "It helped me to become a more compassionate attorney. That's all I can say for it. Do you like Debussy . . . Ravel . . . Poulenc?"

"Whatever." Angelica stretched back onto the floor and stared at Françoise's ornately carved ceiling. It was so different from the clean white plaster and rustic beams of the Azay kitchen. She listened to the music Françoise had put on without knowing or caring what it was. Françoise kicked off her red boots and smoked a cigarette. It was eleven-thirty.

At midnight Françoise turned off the music. "My father used to do a lot of business with Chase Manhattan Bank. Chase likes to buy art . . . makes them feel good about themselves. Buying art; funny phrase, isn't it?"

"I always hated that phrase . . . which may be why my pockets are empty. Buying art? Sounds as callous as buying the wind."

"You idiot!" Françoise roared. "You can't afford to think that way—even if there is some truth in it. You must abandon that line of thinking and listen to me. Chase buys art to ease their conscience about screwing the common man out of his daily bread. The truth is they do it mostly for tax write-offs and basically they don't give a flying fuck what sort of shit they buy."

"Where did you learn such colorful English?" Angelica giggled.

"I've been reading *Rolling Stone* since I was ten." Françoise continued, full-voiced, as though she were pleading a case before a blind jury. "Up to a point, making money is who you know—connections. Chase buys mostly crap—paintings of pastel peonies in darling little crystal vases, children with sad eyes who look demented, dogs playing cards . . . that sort of thing."

She shook her honey curls and continued in the same declamatory style with only a trace of a French accent. "Suze says you are very good but you have not had . . . how do you say, a *break*. That is such a strange idiom. I myself know you are brilliant!"

"How?" Angelica asked tentatively.

"Instinct," Françoise declared, "and egomania. I would not have been drawn to you if you weren't brilliant. I have this capacity for sniffing out fellow geniuses. My father finds such immodesty in a woman intolerable but I can see by your smile that you find me enchanting."

"I do find you enchanting. Like something out of Grimm's."

"Naughty." Françoise shook her finger in Angelica's face.

"And I'm flattered you think I'm a genius but how could you know after seeing me in Suze's window?"

"And the two paintings Suze has. *L'Ail et les Framboises.*"

"You remember my *Garlic and Raspberries*?" Angelica was astonished.

Françoise nodded. "And the other, *La Peau de Suzanne,* a very evocative picture of our mutual friend. For the longest time I refused to believe Suze when she said you two were not lovers. Such skin, the way you painted it, the texture so rich, just begging to be caressed. Not a nude in the usual sense but a feeling, like a touch, something to make your hands crave, rather like those smooth pieces of wood one fondles. A touchstone."

"You really remember."

"But of course!"

"I did those a long time ago. I've gone away from painting still lifes, portraits. I've been so damned abstract."

"So perhaps you will try again along those lines . . . whatever. I do not understand a thing about how you would draw a picture or even get an idea to draw a picture. Who would think of garlic and raspberries as . . . partners? But when I see your picture I say these are the perfect couple. They will live happily ever after and the painting makes me smile and feel good."

"Isn't that wonderful!" Angelica clapped her hands gleefully. "And I did that, didn't I? I thought of matching those two. Or maybe I didn't . . . maybe someone else did and I stole it, can't remember who . . ."

"You did! Even if someone before you did, *you* made it specially yours. I'm no critic, but I know that much. Now I want one of your pictures. Any you say and I want to pay."

"I couldn't charge *you,* Françoise . . ."

"Tu es idiote!"

"I guess I am."

"I will not hang it upon my wall unless I pay."

"I have just the . . ." Angelica hopped up excitedly. "It's not realistic like the two Suze has but it's the only decent thing I've done since coming to France. It's a mixed-media, a self-portrait in oil, collage, with photographs. See, I was fooling around with time sequences, trying to capture the Buddhist's Ten Worlds in One . . . only not a composite but an actual singular impact. I think you'd like it!"

"I didn't understand what you said," Françoise roared, "but I know I will like it because you would not sell it to me unless you were sure I would be satisfied. Now . . . Papa, my Papa, has clout with a man at Chase Manhattan, the one who buys the art. I have clout with Papa. I can probably fix it so that Chase Manhattan Bank will buy one of your paintings to start you off in New York. But you must let me help you decide the price. I don't want you giving a painting to Chase Manhattan Bank."

"That would be very nice," Angelica smiled. She did not for a moment believe it would happen.

"You know I'm not lying," said Françoise.

"I know."

"And not exaggerating either."

"I believe you," Angelica said convincingly. She wondered why it was so difficult for her to believe that something would spontaneously fall into her lap, some good fortune out of the blue.

"And I don't care if you've never made love with a woman," Françoise went on. "I don't care if you've never made it with a man but only with roses. I don't care! Even if you eat your apple and go back to Suzanne's I shall still call Papa tomorrow and he will phone the schmuck at Chase Manhattan immediately."

"Where did you learn that English!" Angelica shrieked as she followed Françoise into her large, fragrant boudoir. Again she was flabbergasted by the incongruities in Françoise's taste. Who would expect Fragonard-like cherubs on the headboard of a bed whose owner wore American university sweatshirts and cowboy boots?

Françoise turned off the lights and lit five candles, each in a different silver holder on the bedside table, then disappeared into the bathroom. Angelica slid out of her black harem pants, leaving them in a soft heap on top of her boots next to the bed. Françoise was singing in French as Angelica removed her sweater and sat naked on the edge of the bed waiting for the bathroom door to open.

It was all terribly strange, each moment detached from the one before, each moment and each new sensation provocatively intense. The heavy cypress odor from the candles was dizzying and Angelica gave herself over to the sultry drama, existing only in the moment. Her libido yearned toward some new knowledge—knowledge which like the time spent in Suzanne's window would unleash her potency.

Françoise emerged smiling from the shower and leaped naked onto the bed. Her breasts were like pale bells swaying musically in the dim light. Angelica watched them until they were still and then she raised her eyes to Françoise, who was still smiling.

"Have your shower." Françoise leaned toward Angelica and kissed her gently on the cheek. A child's kiss, thought Angelica, so unexpectedly tentative and shy. Without thinking she reached out and caressed Françoise's head, then allowed her hand to follow the curve of her shoulders into the hollow of her neck. Françoise had the sort of body which was far more beautiful unclothed. Clothes would never do justice to her firm voluptuousness, especially in an era when fashion had glorified bones and found flesh practically an abomination.

When she finished her shower Angelica slipped into bed next to Françoise and they talked, lying on their backs, both watching the same flickering lights on the ceiling. Angelica spoke of her years as a commuting teacher and how impossible it had been to maintain any continuity in her art work during that period. Françoise, ever the defender of social injustice, swore that there was no justice in life unless people made it themselves. That, she insisted, was the meaning of civilization.

They spoke of their childhoods, finding similarities as well as differences. They talked on and on, and the talk seemed to intoxicate them; their shared secrets made their world safe and complete.

Finally there was nothing difficult about it. Words melted easily into touch. Françoise's flesh was warm, she surrounded Angelica's angles with her softness. They whispered in the dark as if someone might overhear, like Brownies at camp or girl friends at a slumber party who should have been asleep hours before. The contrast of their bodies kindled a spark in Angelica and the world of shimmering candle shadows transformed reality into an abstract reflection in the cheval mirror at the foot of the bed. Their actions were simple and prolonged and finally Angelica was able to relinquish the last rational thread which impelled her to compare this experience with others. At length she was caught up in the exquisite sensations Françoise awakened in her and in the blending of familiar fragrances.

At three the next afternoon Angelica boarded a train at the Gare d'Austerlitz. The sun was out, the chestnut blossoms covered the ground, and despite the heaviness she felt whenever she thought of Ferris, she was optimistic about her future. Françoise had called Papa and Papa was calling his contact at Chase Manhattan Bank. In addition, Françoise was calling one of Papa's former lovers, a prominent American artist, Catherine Rosen Aimsley, who had enjoyed financial success as a commercial artist before her acceptance by the critics as a "serious" artist.

"Your father was Catherine Aimsley's lover? When she was married to Rosen!" Angelica had wanted to know.

"A chip off the old block! I'm not sure. I think it was after. I only met her once. She was nice but she wore too much perfume. She has two daughters my age and for a while it looked like the marquis had matrimony on his mind. He's a callous old fart, I think he dropped her."

"I love her work!" Angelica rhapsodized with a little skip.

"I'm so excited, Françoise. I swear Ferris made it a point never to introduce me to anyone who might have been helpful. Sorry, I didn't mean to dish him. I hate Jews who complain. Françoise, I do thank you!"

"No strings attached." Françoise kissed Angelica when she dropped her off at the Gare. "I've no intention of forming a 'pair bond' until I'm forty. I'm content being promiscuous. Call me when you get in tomorrow and good luck with your boyfriend."

Her boyfriend? Angelica frowned as she checked the departures schedule to see which track her train was on. In his entire life Ferris had probably never been the boyfriend type—even at fourteen. Poor Ferris. She wished she didn't feel so damned sorry for him!

She had had no communication with him since he had taken her to the Gare in Tours almost two weeks ago. She told herself she was lucky; since *Le Figaro* had not headlined his suicide he had clearly dealt with the dissolution of their relationship in a temperate manner. She told herself she was relieved and happy for them both. She knew she was on the right course. There was something about Ferris she was no longer willing to accept and two weeks away from him had spelled out precisely what that was. He wanted to keep her for himself. He loved her, yes he did; and in some way he also knew more about her than anyone else in her life. But he also wanted to own her. Without meaning to he had tried to imprison her.

Angelica was in no way prepared for what greeted her when she returned to Azay. Later when she recalled her last week there she chided herself for thinking that it would be easy.

MAY 1980
New York City

The girl, Jone Beele, was talented, there was no doubt about that. Catherine Aimsley limped self-consciously from the derelict garage where the young sculptor lived to her sleek black chauffered limousine. The driver, a dignified black man who had been with Lester Aimsley long before Catherine, leaped out when he saw her approach.

"Please Morris, don't jump when you see me. It makes me feel so old."

Morris laughed and opened the door for Cathy. "You're moving easier today, Mrs. Aimsley."

"Nice of you to say so." Cathy inched her way into the powdery blue interior of Lester Aimsley's car. The minute Lester had learned that her back was in spasm he had ordered his car to be put at her disposal. I suppose, she thought, glancing out the tinted windows at the unfamiliar downtown streets, that I should be grateful to be somewhat protected against the potholes during my infirmity.

"Actually"—Cathy slid open the glass shield which separated her from the driver—"I do feel a tad better. You know, Morris, I think it's the yoga. Before I did yoga an attack could put me out of commission for months . . . not to mention what it did to my mind. Really, I'd never have believed yoga would work, but take it from one who has suffered since the age of sixteen with this damned degenerated disc. . . . Isn't that a disgusting ailment, Morris? Anyway, I do believe exercise is the one thing which enables a person to spring back. Believe me, Morris, I've been to the best damned surgeons in the city . . . hell, in the world . . . and when it comes to backs they don't know their asses from a hole in the ground."

"I won't argue about that," Morris laughed.

"That's right," Cathy nodded, "we're both fifth-lumbar people."

"We are indeed," said Morris.

"Only . . ." Cathy started to lean forward, thought better of it, and took a deep, relaxing breath before continuing. "When your back goes out on you, do you—even in the midst of your most excruciating pain—do you feel guilty?"

"I don't understand," said Morris, glancing up into the rear-view mirror at his passenger's pert face peering out from her beige slouch hat.

"Do you feel you did it to yourself?"

"Shoot no," said Morris. "Why would I?"

"I don't know." Cathy shook her head. "Sometimes I think I do it to myself and sometimes I don't. It makes my head swim trying to figure out what I'm doing when I'm doing it."

"I guess I know what you mean." Morris stopped for a red light at Hudson Street. "I had my back go out on me once before a vacation . . . like maybe I was nervous about leavin'."

"Yes," said Cathy, leaning back into the seat.

"Radio?" asked Morris.

"Please." Cathy closed her eyes, thinking of the young Jone Beele and her garage full of metal sculpture. God, that girl was a different breed, so self-assured, single-minded, unencumbered by romantic illusions. She envied the girls who were her daughters' age. They could see so much clearer and further than she had been able to see. Next to Jone Beele, Cathy had felt like a chipmunk again, scurrying around exclaiming over Jone's work, making high squeaking noises, limping, talking too much about herself and Tony and Vinnie and Laura. Thinking of it made her feel ridiculous. And through it all Jone Beele had been so unaffected and direct. Shit, thought Cathy, Jone Beele's back would never go out on her. Jone Beele would always know what her motivations were. Funny how many of the kids, contemporaries of Laura or Aggie, gave her a shaky, insecure feeling . . . even Tony sometimes. She had come to New York City almost twenty-seven years ago but from her present perspective she felt as if centuries had passed. It seemed to her that the new generations had aged while she had grown younger and more inconsequential.

Good God, she had moved to New York in the summer of 1953. Cathy smiled wanly, remembering.

In Wayne, Ohio, during the summer of '53 there was nothing to do after watching the rerun of *Mighty Joe Young* but sit inside the Snack Shack and listen to the boys drive by in their cars and nurse a chocolate coke and a breaking heart. A breaking heart, painful as it was, made the time go faster. In Wayne, Ohio, in 1953 there was nothing else to do but fall in love if you didn't have a car and couldn't get out of there.

She was Cathy Harder then and her folks were country people eeking out a living from twenty acres of corn, a sty full of muddy Chester White hogs, and innumerable chickens which pecked away at her mother's purple petunias in the summer. Cathy's one year at Ohio University in nearby Athens had not impressed her family. Her three older brothers viewed her suspiciously, her parents said she had changed. "Changed" was one of the worst things a person could say about another person living in a town of 2,037 steady citizens. It was important to remain the person you had always been—whoever that was.

The Kiwanis Club scholarship which had made possible the year at Ohio U. was no longer in effect and even if Cathy had been able to save enough money to cover the tuition she was not positive that Athens was far enough away from Wayne. Athens, though not as muddy as Wayne, was still too muddy and she was tired of seeing her shoes caked with dirt. Her father accused her of being a snob and she thought maybe he was right.

So the summer of '53 was even more tedious, more demanding, than previous summers. Just as she had done every summer since she was fourteen she waited tables breakfast and lunch at the only café in town. The café was closed at night so that left a lot of time in which to try not to lose her virginity or her mind. The only way to avoid either consequence was to fall in love, to dream, moon, and suffer. Once her soul was on fire she was able to vent her emotions by painting. Whether in a state of euphoria or in the throes of agonizing unrequited love, Cathy Harder painted.

He would swing the car into the dusty lane which led to the peeling white farmhouse, one arm pulling her to *Him*, the other draped casually out the open car window. *He* would be strong and brown from working in the hayfields, sweet-smelling of Old Spice, and there would be dozens of colored plastic spoons from the local Dairy Queen fastened on the car's sun visor. The Four Aces would be singing, or Nat King Cole, and the lightning bugs would part as the Chevy moved slowly toward the house. *He* would park near the barn, off to one side, so that the car was in the shadows—so her parents could not see inside, could not see that *He* had eased her down onto the front seat. Maybe *He* would be from a neighboring town, maybe *He* was a boy from Wayne who had joined the Marines and was home on furlough, maybe *He* was an old flame from high school. *He* was always unbearably sweet, dying from love and passion, moist and longing to tear off her shirtwaist dress but, out of respect, never daring. *He* was always decent, even in his persistence. *His* tongue probing inside her mouth seemed almost a sort of proxy for the other—the thing they could not do. In the front seats of cars.

Love! Cathy would stuff a pillow under the bathroom door and stay up all night making pictures and at seven o'clock she would arrive at work invigorated, her eyes shining with love.

Or: *He* would not notice her. *He* would be in love with Marilyn Hagers, a cheerleader from Seaton, and she would see the two of them in *His* red Ford convertible and *His* arm would be around Marilyn Hagers. Then Cathy would lie sleepless with the tears in her ears until she finally dragged out of bed, stuffed a pillow under the bathroom door, and stayed up all night making pictures. Either way.

The pictures kept her going and they piled up under her bed in the room she shared with her two younger sisters. Nellie and Brenda were the only members of the family who did not think that Cathy had "changed." They thought Cathy's pictures were beautiful and regarded Cathy, who let them use her tangerine lipstick, as some magical goddess whose strange ways made their lives like something out of a book.

But what to do with the pictures? There were so many and the hours spent painting them eventually made the rest of her life seem pallid, even the palpitating moments in the front seats of cars. As the summer wore on, Cathy left *Him* in the car before her mother flicked the porch light.

She showed the pictures to her mother. "Nice," said her mother and patted her hand. The Harders had always liked to draw pictures and her mother's people, the Tuttles, had run an upholstery shop. Her mother showed Cathy a needlepoint picture of Wayne, Ohio, circa 1890 which Cathy's great-grandmother had designed and executed.

"Why do you keep it in the chest?" Cathy had asked.

"To keep it clean." Her mother had wrapped the needlepoint in tissue paper and replaced it in the cedar chest.

"But it's beautiful! It should be out where people can see it." Cathy had felt inexplicably sad.

"Good Lord, Gramma did plenty more of them. Quilts, afghans . . . Lord knows where they are. Mama used to tease her she couldn't sit still without stitching at something. Here."

She had handed Cathy a patchwork quilt done predominantly in vibrant reds, oranges, and yellows. It was not a conventional period quilt; it had a distinctive look all its own. In some ways Cathy thought, it resembled a mosaic more than a quilt because Gramma had used very small slivers of fabric instead of the customary patches. The needlework was also minute. Cathy had to squint to see the tiny stitches. She couldn't even begin to conceive of the patience, the years of painstaking labor that had gone into the creation of the quilt's exquisitely embroidered bucolic scenes—the red barn in snow, a sparrow on a sunflower, a field of mud surrounded by a broken fence, a row of crimson hollyhocks.

"Why didn't you ever show me this before?" Cathy had asked her mother.

"I don't know," Aggie Harder had answered. "It makes me sad. Never liked looking at it. Maybe cause Gramma fussed so with it, always tryin' to get it just so. She started years ago, when I was a girl . . . younger'n you are now. See, there's a square here she didn't finish. I bet she worked on this thing more'n half her life. Now I guess I oughta finish it up, only . . ."

Cathy nodded understandingly at her mother. "It has an almost abstract quality."

"What?"

"Abstract. See how she didn't feel obliged to make everything the color it is in reality . . . like the little orange dog and the purple spruce over here."

"It's so strange." Her mother had grabbed back the quilt as though afraid someone would arrest her for having it in the house. "You never saw nothing like that before, did you?"

"No." Cathy tried to remember her great-grandmother Tuttle, tried to imagine the blank-eyed old lady who had rocked away on the back porch for the last ten years of her life ever creating something so original. Her mother was right. The quilt was strange; it was different, the way dreams were different from waking.

She had gone to her room and cried. Everyone in Wayne had supposed she would be an art teacher—a nice, steady lady urging first-graders to cut out even, orange circles for Halloween, turkeys for Thanksgiving, and snowflakes for Christmas. They saw her teaching in Wayne or in a neighboring town just like Wayne; she saw herself dying.

She had told her little sisters she was crying about *Him* because that, she knew, was something they would understand. The two younger girls looked at Cathy sympathetically and turned the lights off without being asked. When she had heard their even breathing Cathy had slipped out of bed and gone out into the starry August night in her ruffled shortie nightgown and her bare feet. She had sat on the fence watching the cows graze in the asparagus patch her grandfather had planted thirty years before. Beneath the flimsy fabric of her nightie she had felt the peeling paint and splinters from the old fence. If she left Wayne her father would see it as a rejection. No one had ever left before—no brother, cousin, or uncle had ever struck out on his own.

She had felt guilty about wanting to leave. For so long she had wished that something would miraculously make her life exciting so she would not have to leave. Oh, she might complain about all the mud and that the only movie theater in town which showed only third-rate pictures was open just on weekends, but the truth was she loved the faces, the familiarity of the people in Wayne.

The only thing was, if she stayed in Wayne she was bound to slip up—and pretty soon, too. She would slip up, panic, like so many of the girls she knew, and end up having to get married to some guy she didn't love. She'd teach school until the baby came and that would be that. Eventually she would stitch quilts for her own grandchildren.

Well, what was wrong with that, she thought, hopping down from the fence into the field with the friendly cows. The ground was spongy from yesterday's rain and she dug her toes into the damp earth. Her mother, Aggie Harder, had spent her life ministering to the needs of others and it had been enough for her. Shouldn't it be enough for Cathy? Wasn't there something wrong with her, being so restless, wanting to spend all of her time painting pictures? "Wasting time" was what her father called it, even though he had sometimes complimented her on her ability to "make things look real." She had noticed that her father didn't mind one picture a week but twenty frightened him. If she painted one picture that was nice, but if she painted many she was nuts.

But she was obsessed with making pictures and that night in August of 1953 she had been too restless to go back inside the Harder farmhouse. She had felt like one of those Gothic-romance victims shivering half-naked in the moonlight, menaced by the shadow of the haunted mansion which signaled the poor thing's inevitable doom. Then, with pellucid clarity, Cathy had realized that if she thought for very long about leaving Wayne, she would never go. She would be caught in a trap of her own desire; tongues would wag and people would count backwards on their fingers and she would turn in her watercolors for a cheap diamond ring.

"Mama!" She had gone into her parents' room in the dark, stiff with childish terror at invading their privacy. Her father was snoring. She had never seen him asleep—it was like seeing him naked—and she had turned away, looking only at her mother. "Mama, wake up!"

Mama had struggled out of a deep sleep and followed her oldest daughter into the kitchen.

"Mama, I gotta go away. I'm too afraid to do what I got to do here . . . too afraid I won't have a chance to try. I wanta go now."

"Your father won't like it." Aggie Harder had not seemed surprised, only concerned. She rubbed her neck thoughtfully as she looked steadily at Cathy.

"What about you, Mama? What'll you think if I go off?"

"I'll be afraid for you." Aggie glanced down at Cathy's muddy feet. "You're wild with the boys. You think I don't know you're boy-crazy?"

Cathy had started to protest. Though it was true that was one of the reasons she wanted to leave home, it was not the main reason, nor did she want to leave just to run wild and do as she pleased.

"But that's not why I'm goin', Mama. Not because of the boys."

"Because of the pictures." Aggie had smiled vaguely.

"I guess so," Cathy had stammered uncertainly.

"Well, is it?" Aggie had asked her sharply.

"Yes, Mama."

"You can paint them here . . . you can go back to college, I'll find a way . . ."

"No! There's not enough for me to *see* at the university. I need more things to see . . . more paintings by famous people and just . . . *more*."

Aggie had nodded reluctantly. "Paris?"

"Oh God, no!" Cathy had exploded, laughing to cover her fear. Paris? She had never even thought of it. "New York, Mama. I could at least find out . . ."

"I want you to be happy," Mrs. Harder had said, pulling out a chair and sitting down at the red Formica kitchen table. Cathy had stood with her back against the laboring Frigidaire and it seemed to her she saw Aggie Harder for the first time, saw the hardy lean female body beneath her worn summer nightgown, the face still with a youthful sweetness at forty-seven. Odd that she had come to her mother when Aggie was the strong disciplinarian in the family, the moral barometer, assigner of tasks, nay-sayer.

"You're a special girl," Aggie offered after a moment of sitting with both elbows on the table and her chin centered in her folded hands. "But girls don't go off alone. It's not right."

Cathy's heart had constricted.

"I want you to be happy." Aggie had looked at her with the unnatural sternness she had perfected over her years as a mother. "And I know you won't be happy here . . . same as Gramma never was. I got a hunderd and thirty dollars on the third shelf of the cupboard above the Frigidaire. You can add that to whatever you've managed to put away over the summer."

It was the same thing as a blessing. Mama wanted her happiness even if she didn't understand. On August 18, 1953, Catherine Harder left behind the drawings and paintings under her bed and caught the seven o'clock bus for Cincinnati where she changed for a Greyhound to New York City. She had never heard of marijuana or artichokes, and the idea of becoming an artist—someone like Picasso or Renoir—was outside the realm of possibility. She simply wanted to be able to earn a living with her artistic talent and her goal was modest: a job decorating windows in some big department store such as Macy's (she had never head of Bloomingdale's), a wardrobe of sophisticated clothes in chic colors such as plum and cranberry, and enough money to support herself so that she would never be beholden to anyone else for her existence. Also, it would be nice to have some free time and enough space to experiment with her pictures. It would be a relief not to have to hide them under her bed.

MAY 1980
Azay-le-Rideau

When Angelica appeared at the back door around sundown, a full week later than Ferris might have expected her, if indeed he was expecting her, she was armed for four possibilities: another woman, a cold shoulder, another brawl, or an empty house. Instead she found Ferris sitting quietly at the kitchen table sipping a cup of thick black coffee and reading the newspaper. The kitchen was spotless, there was one of her ceramic cups bursting with violets, and the delectable aroma of one of Ferris's *daubes* was in the air.

"Hello," he greeted her as if she had returned from a quick drive to the village to pick up some *crème fraiche* for the strawberries.

"You're expecting someone?" Angelica stood just inside the door with her arms dangling. She had left Mag and Sam and her valise in Paris. Her intention was to spend no more than one night in Azay.

"I was hoping," he replied, neither repentant nor hostile. Actually he seemed happier than she had seen him in two years.

He moved to the stove, poured a cup of coffee, and handed it to her. "I thought you might come Monday, then Tuesday . . . then when you didn't I thought you might come today. And you did."

"Yes." Angelica sat down warily and sipped the coffee.

"How was Paris?"

"Fine. Smoggy but. . . . You've been cooking the *daube* since last week?" She wondered why he didn't reproach her for not phoning to tell him she had changed her plans.

"I added sausage today. Last night's was all right. Tonight's will be even better."

"It smells wonderful," she sniffed, "lots of garlic." How absurd this conversation was. She glanced quickly at him but there was not the usual tension between his brows and she was confused. "Is something the matter?"

"Never better." He moved back to the stove to adjust the flame under the *daube*. "I'm glad you're back, Angelica."

She felt her stomach tighten as he came toward her. "I have something to show you."

Now, she thought, the shit is going to hit the fan. This is some perverse trick of his, some maniacal new tack he's taking. But there was no odor of liquor, he was drinking coffee without cognac, his shoulders were not hunched to his ears and . . .

"Come." He took her hand and led her back outside toward his studio which was at one end of the former stables. His hand was cool and confident, he squeezed her fingers, and as they approached the studio door he kissed her wrist. He read the amazement in her face and, cupping his hands loosely around her boyishly short hair, he kissed her. He kissed her so tenderly that she gasped. She had never imagined she would ever again be moved by his kiss.

"I have something to show you." He unlatched the door and stood aside. She stared at him, still uncertain, doubting, and cautious. "Go on in, Angelica. Go on."

Angelica's being was geared to meet the unexpected; her imagination thrived on what was impossible but Ferris had done something she had not counted on. The depth of her silence as she stood staring in the open door was proof that Ferris had guessed right.

"I can't say anything," she uttered after several moments. "Ferris! My God, you did these in two weeks?" She moved closer to the triptych, a composite of three large paintings which could be viewed either as a whole or separately. They were a combination of acrylic and oil on canvas, executed over layers and layers of luminous washes of color so that the images appeared to grow out of the paintings. The brush strokes were light (another change from the more aggressive heaviness of his former work), lending a fragile oriental quality to the triptych. The whitish yellows and pale cerulean blues were almost translucent; Angelica had never seen him use such colors, had rarely seen such delicate hues put to such a commanding end.

"They're beautiful!" she cried. "My God . . . I . . .!" She was galvanized, her astonishment almost existed on some other plane of reality, for Ferris's new works reflected something she had never guessed. The shock would not have been greater had he, the man, assumed some new physical countenance.

"Look what you've done here!" she exclaimed, pointing to the canvas on the right. "Look how you've textured it so I can detect the form underneath! I mean . . . I really see forms, right? Like there is the castle, huh? Am I right? Yes? That's the castle, isn't it?"

She was sobbing with relief when she threw her arms around his neck. He felt so small, so fragile. Good God, after Françoise he felt absolutely delicate.

"You've lost weight." She covered his face with kisses and began to worry about his health. It seemed she had never really seen him, never known him before. For nearly ten years she had looked without seeing; until this moment she had missed him entirely. These new paintings were so much more than the abstract expressionism which had gained him his reputation. Why he was off on a whole new tangent, an original vision of his own making. And she was part of that vision. She knew that she was inside those paintings, that something in their last violent encounter had released a new vision in him as well as in her. In a sense, she had inspired him. But she was not flattered at having been his inspiration, she was in awe.

He was all new to her. She felt like the little girl at the great Chicago Art Institute seeing his work for the first time. He was alive in three canvases in a way she had dreamed he could be. And he was kissing her, for the first time in months, maybe even in years, he was kissing her not perfunctorily as an accepted prelude to something more. And her body was not detached as it had been with Françoise. Her body was her mind and everything in her was straining toward him, wanting to take in so much of him that she became him. His hands moved slowly down her body. They were new hands with new ways; the hands of a genius, of a man who could shock her, not the way Françoise had shocked her with her acerbic wit, but profoundly shock her out of life into death and back again. It was a relief to love him, to feel passion flare in a way it had not done in years. This, she thought, is the purification!

She continued staring at the paintings as he unfastened her black pants and kneeled at her feet. She dropped to her knees and loosened his belt; her movements, like something from a Japanese Noh drama, were slow, sustained with the concentration of a ritual. The sunset made magical light on the canvases, the smell of turpentine blended with spring green and pale lavender lilacs. So much more erotic, she thought, than the scent of Françoise's cypress candles. And his hardness was better, it was all so much better. Angelica ground her body into his, bone to bone, touching, it seemed, in new places, places always hidden until now.

"That's why you didn't call me," she breathed as her arms went around him, coming to rest on his buttocks, pressing them tighter into her. She cried out as she exploded but Ferris continued to move on top of her and when she had her breath back she wrapped her legs around him, arching her body so forcefully into his that he shouted exultantly. When he paused to prolong his pleasure she felt compelled to move, driving him further into ecstasy until he cried out for her to stop.

"Stop!" She liked him near the brink but wanted the moment to last. She smiled at him. His face was crimson, he was concentrating on his endurance, but she liked it better when he was more nearly out of control. She rolled on top of him, straddling him with her head tucked under his chin, moving mercilessly, stopping only when she felt he was too near the edge and then only for an instant.

Half laughing, she gulped for air, then she rose above him until they were nearly separated and he pulled her back down to him. His eyes were shut, his mouth set in an exquisitely tortured smile.

He groaned as she initiated some maddeningly slow rhythm

only to change abruptly, digging her fingers into his back as he rolled over her to the original position.

"Forgive me." His tears fed his desire and he was finally unable to control himself.

Still, Angelica was far from finished and as he faded she revived him and to his amazement it was all beginning over again.

"I can't stop," she cried, laughing, but her body seemed to become savage in its need for him. This, she thought, was the purification, the "in the beginning" of that first, violent Creation.

"Ferris, those paintings . . . are . . ."

He silenced her with a kiss, then gave a wild shudder. Angelica's hair was damp, she smiled languidly and ran her fingers lightly over his back, feeling pleasantly drained and healed. It had never been like this. In all of their years together they had never been so close or so free with one another.

"I love this farm!" Angelica announced later as he gave her another portion of the *daube*.

"And I love you." He watched her eat with a satisfied smile.

"Ferris, I swear to God your hair has grown back . . ." She broke off and laughed because she was not supposed to have noticed nor to have known the extreme care he had taken to preserve and maintain the patch which remained.

But now all the strictures were off. She tossed her napkin into the air and ran to hug him. When she told him she knew he had gone for six months without washing his hair, he actually laughed. Now it was all right for her to know that. Now, she told herself, he was no longer threatened by her candor nor by intimacy. They were close. It was all new. Repeatedly she told herself how he had changed over the past two weeks, how they had both changed. They had broken through the suffering of their karmic relationship and from this point on their lives and their individual work would flourish. They would feed each other, support each other, and cherish each other. He had finally seen her true value.

"Paris was *extraordinaire*!" She was confident enough even to talk about her experiences in the store window. "I did some sketches after the marathon was over . . . some of the faces looking in at me and Sam and Mag. It was very weird, Ferris, and I know you thought it was pretentious and risqué but I learned something. Wouldn't trade it for . . . I've zillions of new ideas . . . faces! Can't wait to get back to my studio and see what happens."

"But not tonight." He took her hand and kissed it.

"Of course, not tonight."

For five days they lived in each other's arms, went on picnics with bread and cheese and Ferris's special *pâtés*. They drove to Chenonceaux and toured the magnificent castle, wandering hand in hand in the spring gardens planted by Catherine de' Medici. In five days they did all the things Angelica had hungered to do since their arrival in France nearly two years before.

Ferris was ecstatic about his work. His agent was flying over to see the paintings and personally accompany them back to New York. He was confident that these first three paintings were only the beginning. As they went about their sightseeing he pulled a ravaged notebook out of his Levi jacket and scribbled notes for another new painting.

"We'll go to New York this fall." When Angelica indicated she had been thinking of returning to the States sooner, he became not defensive as he would have previously, but firm. "Fall is best . . . just in time for my retrospective at the Whitney . . . in high style. It ought to be fun."

"But . . ."

"And it's best for you, too," he told her. "You'll have the whole summer to put something together."

"I suppose . . ."

"Absolutely!"

"And we'll stay in New York?" Angelica wondered vaguely why she was asking him what they would do, but when he replied they would do whatever she wanted to do, she dismissed the matter.

"I've got to go to Paris and get my things," she told him, "and Mag and Sam."

"We'll drive up for the weekend," he suggested. "We'll stop at Blois . . . it's on the way and you've been wanting to see the cathedral at Orléans."

"You mean it?" she cried.

Yes, he meant it. Yes, he would try to forget how much he loathed cities, he would try to see Paris with her eyes, and he would even climb to the bell tower at Notre Dame. It seemed there was nothing he would not do for her, and Angelica thought she had never been happier. It did not seem to matter that she had not set foot in her studio since returning to Azay.

Actually she was tired. It was unusual for her to sleep past eight o'clock but since returning to the farm she had slept past ten. She told herself she had spring fever, that she had exhausted herself in Paris, and that she was storing up for a great burst of creativity. She generally worked in spurts, so this was probably just a low ebb. And Ferris indulged her, encouraging her to sleep late, to relax, take it easy. After a week in a store window, didn't she deserve a vacation?

He, on the other hand, was up every morning at five. He seemed possessed of superhuman energies, making love to her in the morning, waking her in the middle of the night, and still rising before the sun. By the time Angelica was out of bed he had done a day's work and was ready to picnic on the grass.

The day they were to leave for Paris she sat quietly in the corner of his studio and watched him begin a new painting. She was ambivalent about the trip; she would have preferred to take the plunge and spend the weekend in her studio but Ferris had made reservations, he was excited about the trip, and God knows how often she had nagged him about going to Paris. So she said nothing. Her work could wait till Monday.

After an exhaustive tour of the castle at Blois they drove further north and stopped for the night at a little *auberge* outside of Orléans. Their tiny room had a fireplace and it looked out over a meadow where four black-and-white cows grazed happily in the moonlight.

"I didn't know cows ate at night." Angelica curled against Ferris in the narrow fourposter bed. "Do you suppose they'll eat all night?"

"Why don't you stay up and see?" he laughed.

"Ferris, what really made you change?" Angelica sat up abruptly and studied him. "We haven't talked about what happened before but . . ."

"I don't think there's any reason to talk about it."

"I'm just curious," she persisted. "I always loved you and I thought, in spite of our differences, that you loved me. But there was always something, some little snag that made me feel, not exactly inhibited around you, but that I had to be careful."

"I never noticed you being careful." He pulled her back against him and for a moment she said nothing but allowed some idyllic dream of the future to overtake her. In the dream she and Ferris had moved into a spacious, sun-filled loft in Soho and Ferris was helping her select the paintings which would be hung in her first, one-person show. There was a child crawling on the floor between the stacks of paintings and there was a big dog and a profusion of large, prickly but flowering cacti in primitive terra-cotta pots.

She opened her eyes and smiled lazily. The past few days had been something of a miracle—a flowering of both their sensual and spiritual bond. Marriage *per se* had never been terribly important to Angelica yet she knew Ferris, knew that in the recesses of his Victorian, moral mind, he revered marriage as the ultimate statement of a relationship between a man and woman. At times she had even considered that the only reason he had not suggested marriage was as a way of keeping her in line—as if an acknowledgment on his part that he desired her to be his wife would dissipate the power he wielded over her. Or perhaps he was simply afraid she would say no. That was possible too. In any case, she felt that marriage was the key which would allow them both to forge ahead, to continue to explore all the potential they possessed as two creative equals who valued and loved each other. It was time for him to relinquish the guilt from his first, failed marriage and see that their union was different—born not of worn-out conventions but of hope.

"What are you thinking?" he asked.

"So, so much," she said, savoring her excitement. "I feel we're on the brink of something, Ferris. That we truly understand each other. You know, I did something in Paris that I was always curious about but was never quite sure I could go through with. I took a plunge. Sometimes I think it's necessary to take a plunge . . . even when you're frightened, not sure. Life shouldn't be too safe."

"I shouldn't think you need worry about that," Ferris smiled.

"You're talking about posing in the window for five days, I suppose?"

"No, I always knew I could force myself to endure the physical agony. That sort of physical agony—with me being conscious and in control as opposed to, say, going under the knife while under anesthesia, is no problem for me. I've always been confident of my physical stamina; it was my *mental* strength I needed to test. Like Eliot says: 'We shall not cease from exploration.' That horrible brawl we had before I left for Paris pushed me over an uncertain edge. Without that I might not have gained as much as I did."

Ferris nodded. "It pushed us both over an uncertain edge. I resented you for flaunting yourself in some cheap erotic sideshow."

"Yes!" Angelica bobbed her head. "You were afraid and you thought you could make your life safe by keeping me here. And nobody can keep their life safe, especially artists. Eliot was saying those lines to everyone but I've always felt they apply especially to us. We're the seekers. I know a lot of people think I'm weird, that I do ditzy things, am purposefully obscure—but it's because I'm looking."

"Don't you think there's a limit?" Ferris asked stonily.

"There can't be," Angelica said. "Exploration is the only thing we have control over . . . I don't mean the outcome, only the effort. Even in that window with my poor body like a steel rod I was able to explore, and then later, when I was staying with Suze and wondering what the hell was going to happen to my life and what I would say to you when and if I ever saw you again, I was able to keep myself open to possibilities, to exploration."

Ferris seemed uneasy but Angelica continued intensely. "See, you knew the window was going to be erotic. I didn't. I didn't, I swear. It was a shock to me when . . . but Ferris, the main thing is, *I* was the voyeur. I read so much in those faces staring in at me. You know how a person looks at himself in the mirror? You only look at yourself that way, right? So unless you are a mirror you never see other people looking at themselves like that, right? Those faces looking in at my dummies and me were unguarded, as if they were alone. Even those who laughed gave the distinct impression of being isolated. It was as if I became a camera, registering their secrets, and in turn their secrets triggered off memories in me. God, my mind is so full of things I want to get down on canvas or in my book . . . mostly faces."

She broke off and looked hopefully at Ferris, who seemed almost depressed by her enthusiasm.

"You've done portraits before, Angelica. Why do you think this is different?"

"This *is* different!" Angelica struggled not to fall into his mood. She smiled buoyantly. "I just want you to understand that I'm really serious about my seemingly daffy schemes."

"I never said you were daffy." Ferris was defensive.

"I know." Angelica's smile stiffened. Could a trap be forming now?

"Anyway, you don't need my permission to carry out your explorations."

"The night I left for Paris you didn't feel that way."

"Are you going to keep reminding me?" Ferris shut his eyes against the memory and Angelica placed her hand over them.

"No," she soothed. "I'm sorry. I'm sorry for going on about it, Ferris, only it was important to me. It feels like maybe a turning point for me. Don't you understand?"

"I do." He removed her hand and smiled. It wasn't enough, she wanted something more from him and her pulse accelerated as she continued.

"I guess because Suze is gay I started thinking about what it would be like to be with a woman. Then I noticed the way the women who came to Suze's boutique looked at me and I began to have an inkling of the difference between the way a man experiences desire and the way women do. Then I was hit with a barrage of memories of myself as a preadolescent, around nine or ten, and the joy and comfort I took from being physically close to my girl friends. It seemed to me if I could feel that again—in all its innocence—I could understand something . . . about myself, about other women in order to paint them. Then I ran into a friend of Suze's . . . a woman I'd met several times before and had always enjoyed."

"A friend of Suzanne's?"

"Only a lot younger. I guess you'd say she was a radical but that would hardly do her justice. It's the contradictions in people which really fascinate me. Françoise is a gay Marxist lawyer who wears red cowboy boots and comes from a very rich, royal old family."

"So . . ." Angelica heard a familiar tone come into his voice, but she did not want to acknowledge it. She dismissed it as impossible.

"What the hell are you telling me?" Ferris sat up abruptly.

Angelica knew she should stop, that she should lie or omit a crucial detail in her narrative. "It's something I don't imagine I'll do again but I don't regret it. I mean, frankly I prefer . . ."

Ferris took her arm roughly. "You're telling me you went to bed with a woman?"

"I did but . . ." Angelica continued optimistically, "but we're friends and . . ."

"You actually . . .?"

"You make it sound as if it was something sordid. It wasn't! Haven't you been listening to me? I'm telling you it confirmed my heterosexual inclinations but beyond that it opened me to a part of myself that was locked and . . ."

"I don't believe you." Ferris jumped off the bed and moved to the window with his hands clenched at his sides.

"There's no reason for you to be threatened by this," Angelica said softly. "I love *you*. I don't plan on leading a double life, if that's what you're worried about."

"What the hell are you trying to do to me?" Ferris turned on her furiously.

"Nothing," she stammered and unnecessarily added, "You don't want to hear, do you?"

"But you had to tell me!" He leered at her. "What is it you want? Forgiveness? For Christ's sake, am I your confessor?"

"I wanted to share . . ." She reached for her robe, feeling violated and ashamed, not of what she had done but of her own stupidity for thinking she could make him understand. And she felt she had betrayed Françoise as well as herself.

"There is nothing to forgive." She stood up and faced him defiantly.

"Why the hell did you have to ruin everything?" he blazed.

"I didn't think it would . . . ruin . . ." Or had she? She met his eyes and saw how quickly love had been transformed into hate. She saw the same hate she had seen the night she had left for Paris. How was that possible?

"I shouldn't have," she apologized. "Can't we just forget it?"

His arm shot out like a reflex in answer to her question and his other arm followed, knocking her off balance. She blinked, felt her soul start to abandon her as it had done in the Azay kitchen. She forced her concentration back to earth, planted her feet on the floor, and started for the bathroom. "I think I'll get dressed."

Her voice was cold, her will was inviolate. She could not believe it was happening again. How dare he shame her over sex, over anything she might do. He had slept with three other women in the past year and he had made certain she knew about it. Each time he had done it to hurt her, to keep her in line and bolster his own fragile ego. Each time she had seen his motives and forgiven him. The knowledge of what he had done had not threatened her, she had mostly felt bad for him because it had cost him a great deal of guilt and self-loathing. He had tried, always, to use sex as a weapon against her and all he could see now was that she was doing the same thing.

His rage was out of control and this time he did not have the excuse of being drunk. He lunged for her and she dodged him.

"Stop it!" she demanded. "You and your goddamned fragile male ego!"

Suddenly he *did* stop and Angelica understood why his rage was cut short. They stared at each other and she knew by his expression that he was reading in her face something he had never seen there before—the same hatred she had read in his. There was no more understanding.

After a moment she picked up her clothes, went into the bathroom, turned on the water so that he could not hear, and threw up. Their brief period of remission was over.

MAY 1980
New York City

Cathy looked away from her estranged husband, painfully conscious that the mortified expression she wore was incompatible with the restrained, classical elegance of one of New York's most acclaimed restaurants.

"But it's not even a *ménage à trois*! I could understand a drunken, debauched orgy, for Christ's sake . . . I mean . . . I mean, I *might* understand something one just falls into blindly with the senses, but that is not what you're suggesting!" If only he had chosen someplace else to say what he had said. In the car, on the street, on the phone even, but in a place of perfection with everything so nice . . . it was too jarring.

She had anticipated nothing like this. She had foreseen her evening with Lester as an academic soirée, a critical feast, an intellectual inspiration, for God's sake. She had missed his opinions and was eager to hear what he thought about various new exhibits in town. Lately she had been restudying Manet's work and she had even compiled a list of questions to ask Lester about Manet's reduction of images to essential planes, the reduction of shadows, for example in *Le Déjeuner sur l'Herbe* . . . five or six points, all of which now made her feel even more absurd.

"Catherine, I only suggested that we all might make a go of it."

"A go . . . a go? I never heard you use slang before." Cathy flushed. Here she had spent the day looking forward to an informative conversation about Manet while he had been waiting to spring this on her. How could Tony move in with them? Was he out of his mind?

"Lester, could we please talk about Manet?"

Lester Aimsley laughed helplessly at the only woman he had ever wanted to marry, the only woman he had been lucky enough to marry, and the only woman he ever would be married to. He reached for Cathy's hand and held it a moment across the table.

"If that is what you would like, we can talk about Manet."

"Good." Cathy wished she did not have the unfortunate talent for observing every situation in her life from the outside and commenting on it. She was so intent on watching herself and Lester that it was very difficult to go on with the Manet questions.

"It wasn't that he was precisely a naturalist, Cath, but then your latest work, the canvases I've seen in any case, could not be termed naturalistic . . . purely. The nomenclature is misleading. I really find those classifications intolerable, not to mention inaccurate, because anytime a great artist comes along, no definition can contain the work. I don't think Manet ever succeeded in integrating the separate parts in *Déjeuner*. The picture was comprised of separate studies—the nude figure, the tumbling fruit, discarded clothing. I feel I'm rambling."

"No," Cathy shook her head. She treasured Lester's ability to articulate entire art movements so that she, who had practically no formal knowledge of art criticism, could make real use of his understanding. Often a single phrase of his would elucidate a problem and enable her to approach her own work from a fresh point of view. And there was nothing stuffy or self-important in his attitude as there had been in Rosen's. Lester only *looked* like a brittle academician.

But she could not fully concentrate on what he was saying about Manet.

"You should fly to Paris and see for yourself. Spend a few afternoons at the Jeu de Paume. You're due for a trip to Paris."

"Perhaps we should *all* go," Cathy suggested and was horrified at the petulance in her voice and the pettiness of the remark. Why was he being so nice to her?

Damn him for shocking her. She needed no more shocks in

her life. She wanted everything to run smoothly now. She did not want to become emotional. But there he sat in his classic navy linen jacket and his immaculate white yachting shoes, making a positively seedy suggestion.

Cathy felt foolish. Lately the old chipmunk syndrome had been reoccurring. Good God, she'd thought she was done with that phase of her development. Didn't anything ever change? She still felt embarrassed recalling the time the DAR had given her a special award for one of her paintings. They, the DAR ladies and their progeny, were the well-dressed, educated denizens of Wayne and she, at sixteen, had been extremely nervous about eating dinner in their presence and later mounting the platform to receive her award. She had been mortified, too, when after receiving her award she had seen the cakes of mud on her shoes like some old cluck, some old hillbilly. To compensate she had rattled on, her voice accelerated and high . . . like a chipmunk.

Cathy shuddered at the memory and tried to meditate on the peachy-pink walls of Dodin-Bouffant . . . like the color of a muted Tuscany sunset. Lester had said the decor was an aesthetic triumph and as usual he was right. He had known she would love the daring of the uncluttered walls—not even one painting to mar the perfection of that slightly jaded peachiness which was a bold contrast to the powdery-blue-gray upholstered chairs. The *nouvelle cuisine* had arrived on oversized white china plates, the food arranged to create a visual balance of color, texture, and form. She had laughingly suggested that she felt as though she were taking part in a Japanese tea ceremony and should consequently commit *seppuku*—such perfection could surely not be surpassed. Yes, she thought now, she should have definitely committed *seppuku*.

She hated feeling stupid and provincial. She looked back at Lester, who was studying the dessert card with a beatific smile. His thin, heavily lined face was beginning to acquire the tender rosiness of affluent old age, an almost boyish softness. She wished she could find one malicious line in that face, but he was aging like a goddamned angel. Rosen had looked like a debauched Beelzebub at forty but Lester, the last of the nineteenth-century "gentlemen," had managed to retain the countenance of a child at sixty-seven. Cathy reminded herself that his blue eyes were always watery, that he was not weeping. Damn, he was a good man. If only he were intolerant, petty, or demanding . . . but he was so good!

Considerate, humorous, respectful, loving without being cloying—she could enumerate Lester's virtues *ad infinitum*, but it was just another form of torture, for she always came back to her desire to be free of him.

"What you are suggesting is a home-sweet-home threesome!" Cathy whispered, needlessly, since there was only one other couple in the room and they were at the far end.

"I am not!" Lester fought back a smile.

"You are! No, it's worse than that, Lester. A foursome. What about our son? What about Vinnie?"

"Vinnie knows you sleep with Tony."

"My God!" Cathy gasped. Of course it was true. She knew it was true. Why was she playing the hypocrite?

"I'm sorry, Catherine, that you find the topic so disquieting, but there's a lot at stake here . . . not the least of which is your work. Vinnie tells me you haven't been working at all since . . ."

"Oh, Vinnie, Vinnie, Vinnie!"

"Catherine, I'm not suggesting a *ménage à trois*, you know that. Not that I wouldn't like us to resume. . . . But then I know you don't think of me in *that* way anymore."

"Why are you so damned articulate?" Cathy felt a hot flash. My God, he'd frightened her into menopause.

"I'm a critic," Lester smiled. "Have you forgotten?"

Cathy smiled begrudgingly. "I feel so foolish."

"I just see no reason for us to dissolve a perfectly amiable relationship just because you have a lover."

Cathy squirmed in her gray silk dress, touched the pearls at her neck, and crossed and uncrossed her feet under the table. It was pleasantly cool yet she was perspiring . . . between her thighs. It was ludicrous. Was it realism, she wondered, or naturalism? If she painted a picture of an elegant, middle-aged woman, how would she—artistically of course—suggest the sweat in her crotch?

"Clothes definitely do not make the person." She observed herself wryly and Lester chuckled, knowing how she adored clothes, was a slave to fashion, yet flogged herself after every shopping spree.

"Listen, Cathy, I'm not bringing this up to make you feel uncomfortable."

"I know."

"Or guilty."

"Me? Guilty? Ha!" Cathy tossed down her cognac the way she remembered Rita Hayworth doing in some movie about monsoons.

"I'm sixty-seven years old, Cathy. My self-image is not dependent on the mightiness of my . . . do you prefer cock or penis?"

I might as well go back to the cow pastures, thought Cathy as her face turned scarlet. "That's very blunt," she said. "And not like you. Are you insulting me?"

Lester shook his head solemnly. "I just wanted to startle you, I guess."

"Well, you did. Is this what it means to be civilized, Lester? Lovers and husbands and sons all under one roof? I'm not French and I'm not trying to be funny. I've led a very . . . unconventional, some might even say promiscuous life. I am not a prude."

"No one could ever accuse you of that," Lester twinkled.

"Right! But I . . . I can't accept this. . . . Vinnie could turn out to be a homosexual. It would be my fault!"

"Cath . . ." Lester reached for her hand.

"Lester, I am going to get blamed. I'm a mother and I am going to get blamed!"

"Don't you think my attitude will have something to do with whether Vinnie blames you or not? Vinnie is my only child . . . thanks to you and, yes, you must allow me to be grateful to you for that. As a pedantic old bachelor thought by many to be 'gay,' these past ten years with you have brought me unexpected joy. And it's not as though you don't like me."

"Like you? Of course I . . ."

"There will, as I've told you before, never be any question of a custody fight over Vinnie, so you must not let that enter your mind. However, I want to be a presence in Vinnie's life . . . more than a visiting dignitary."

"I understand that . . ."

"And I love you, too. I want you to be happy, Catherine . . . as happy as you've made me. Your affair with Tony Casteli is not . . ."

"Don't call it an affair," Cathy protested, then burst out laughing. "Lester, I'm still married . . . to you!"

"And I'm suggesting you stay married to me, that you continue with your life and your work. We're extremely compatible, Cath, why should we get divorced? Unless you plan on marrying Casteli?"

"No!" Cathy was emphatic. Actually she had never even thought of marrying Tony, which was odd because she had thought of having his child, had projected herself into a melancholy future when he would leave her for a younger woman.

She looked at Lester as though seeing him for the first time. How could she have anticipated that Lester Aimsley, former Metropolitan Museum curator, stalwart art historian, the epitome of the conservative Establishment, could come up with such a solution?

"You and I were friends and colleagues before we became lovers," Lester continued evenly. "Our marriage works in very concrete terms and I would like to maintain its continuity if not its sanctity, which I swear to you I don't give a damn about."

Cathy felt claustrophobic, on the point of screaming or throwing over the table and running hysterically out of the place. She had a well-honed instinct for histrionics and Lester knew it. He was watching her closely. It was not beyond the realm of possibility that she would bolt. He was literally suggesting that she might have her cake and eat it too. But the idea made her queasy and what did *that* mean? Life with Lester had been full, productive, everything except . . . wildly erotic. But, as she thought of it now, she had not become involved with Tony for that reason. She had thrown herself into the affair, accidentally, of course, but during a lull in her work, as a shot in the arm, a stimulus to revitalize her vision. She had not been looking to have an affair, of that she was positive.

"Why do you find my proposal so outrageous?" Lester persisted. "Remember Harold Wiseberg?"

Cathy nodded glumly. During the early days of her relationship with Lester, when she had still been juggling money and jobs, raising two children, and trying to free her mind and soul for concentration on her serious work, she had joked about how she wished she were Harold Wiseberg. Harold was the only member of Rosen's old group whom Cathy had continued to see after her husband's death. He was a moderately successful sculptor, married to the same woman for thirty years, the father of five apparently happy children. Harold was amiable and obese and for as long as Cathy had known him, in good times and in lean, Harold had spent all day at his work while his wife Sophia worked to support the family. In theory Cathy hated Harold Wiseberg, only in reality and having been a close friend of Sophia's as well, she knew it worked. Sophia created a beautiful, carefree ambiance for Harold; that was her job and one she carried out with love and dignity.

"But Harold Wiseberg doesn't have a mistress!" Cathy replied triumphantly.

"And that's not the point." Lester was ready for her.

It wasn't the point. Cathy moped. Lester wanted to make life easy for her, he had been her biggest fan, just as Sophia was Harold's biggest fan. He had introduced her to her present gallery, the prestigious Porter Gallery, he had negotiated contracts, made connections with collectors . . . all without trying to control her. Most of the male artists she knew had amazingly serene domestic situations, the logistics of their lives taken care of for them by smiling, worshipful women, some of whom were admittedly miserable but some of whom were content. She tried to recall if she had ever heard a man lamenting his sense of guilt. Slaves and masters? Sometimes, sometimes not. Lester wasn't even going to be standing over a hot stove all day.

"What will Vinnie tell his friends?" she asked cautiously.

Lester smiled. "Cath, we needn't put a neon sign outside the building. Anyhow, I never knew you to be concerned about what other people think."

But it wasn't her concern about other people that was the stumbling block. Cathy rubbed her calves together, wrinkling her stockings so that she felt slightly tawdry. "You have really shocked me with all this. Do you mean Tony should move in with us and we should all eat breakfast together?"

"I mean you should feel free to make whatever arrangement feels best . . . and Tony, too. I rather like him. Is that perverse?"

Cathy shrugged and looked away.

Lester cogitated briefly, then leaning toward his wife, with a hint of sadness in his pale eyes, asked, "Would you prefer a duel?"

JUNE 1980
Paris

"I'm pregnant!" Angelica announced. Her dark eyes narrowed with amusement when Suze and Françoise blanched as if she had just told them she had contracted a fatal disease.

Suze shook her head and did not try to hide her irritation. Angelica had returned to Paris bruised and morose and now she was blithely telling them she was going to have the child of the man who had abused her. She was about to return to New York penniless and pregnant and she was actually joking about it.

"If this isn't proof that biology is destiny, I don't know what is!" Angelica giggled irrepressibly.

"Merde!" Françoise lit a cigarette and blew the smoke in Angelica's face. "You are full of shit."

Angelica stuck her tongue out, playing the child. "Maybe the baby is yours, Françoise."

"Angelica," pleaded Suze.

"I know what I'm doing," Angelica said sanguinely. "The worst is over."

"That is what you think." Françoise stomped angrily to the bar and poured herself a brandy. "How the hell are you going to paint with a baby crying? How the hell are you going to work to support your artistic addiction? Angelique, listen . . . the only women who can afford to have children and not trade in their professional lives for snotty noses and diarrhea are *rich* women. And no matter what conclusions you might have drawn in your deluded state, surely you know that you are not rich."

"But I might be." Angelica refused to be brought down.

"Am I talking to a serious person?" Françoise shouted again.

"Yes, you are," Angelica remarked quietly. The two women stared at her as if she were a creature from Mars but she could not stop smiling. A high note reverberated in her right temple and she had the image of herself as a wire—a fine golden wire which could sound a pure note, a high C on a magnificent gleaming concert grand piano. The sound she made created fertile hues, colors she had seen once in a dream but had never been able to recapture until this moment. It was difficult to listen to Suze and Françoise because she wanted to be somewhere mixing colors, trying to duplicate the numinous, spiritual shades which had been prompted by her note. Some Force that was herself and yet was beyond herself had struck the note. She believed in that Force and in the purity of her note.

"Babies are always shitting," Françoise said grossly. "Do you know how their shit smells?"

Angelica nodded and listened to her note.

"Does Ferris know about the baby?"

Angelica shook her head.

"Christ, you are stupid, you know that? If you insist on having his child, at least get some financial support from him."

"That wouldn't be fair." Angelica had already gone over it all in her mind and rejected asking Ferris for anything.

"Why?" Suze felt her friendship with Angelica strained to the breaking point. "Why do you want to jeopardize your chances for success now, just when you've pulled yourself out of a terrible relationship, just when you've decided to put all of your energy into your work? Angelica, did anyone ever tell you how tired pregnant women get? Sometimes they even throw up. They often sleep whole days away. They do not stand in front of an easel painting for eighteen hours a day, which is what you claim you want to do."

"I know it won't be easy."

"But why do you want to make it hard for yourself?" Suze persisted.

"I think," Françoise said, "that unconsciously you are using this to get back at Ferris. You can hurt him with this child."

"Wrong, Françoise! I don't consider it is his child. It will be *my* child because I will take the responsibility for it."

"You haven't even been able to take responsibility for yourself," Suze said gently.

"I'm thirty-four," Angelica said solemnly. "I want this child. Whatever my feeling for Ferris is at this moment, there was a time when I did love him. I don't now, but I did. I'm not looking for love from a man but I know that my spirit needs to love. I will love my child. It is a necessity. There is no choice."

"But you have plenty of time." Suze recognized how futile it was to plead with Angelica but a sense of outrage forced her to keep trying.

"Maybe I don't have time," Angelica reflected as her note became pianissimo and was gone. "I've *had* my abortion. I'm not afraid of that. I know what my options are, but I want this child."

"And you want your work! Damn it, Angelica! Why can't you see that you are making things impossible for yourself!"

"If I want it, why can't I have it?"

"You can, if that's all you want."

"I want both!" Angelica stopped smiling.

"I think you want this child for the same reasons you wanted to go home with Françoise. As an experiment."

Angelica met Suze's eyes. From the outside she realized her life must look like a lesson in anarchy but now there was blooming in her a conviction that her Dream World *should* exist, that she could under no circumstances bow down to the old order. The only relevant choice was life or death. She chose life; all other choices were unholy.

"You're probably right," she answered Suze after a moment.

"Babies are not experiments." Françoise massaged Angelica's shoulder lightly.

"I know." Angelica smiled sadly and squeezed Françoise's hand. She didn't like them being angry with her but she understood how they could be. Everything they said was true but that did not alter her conviction that the life growing inside her would feed her creative spirit. Maybe that was selfish. But if she was too tired to stand at the easel eighteen hours a day, then she would work for only six hours or four even, but they would be potent, productive hours. She had already made too many compromises in her life and could not afford even one more. She wanted her work and she wanted her child. She was sure only of those two desires.

For the past week she had had difficulty communicating with people because of the plethora of images and ideas flooding in on her. She craved solitude to explore these new patterns. At night her dreams were peopled with uncommon figures, powerful, robed figures on fire from within. Perhaps they were the Eumenides existing in Eliot's "time past and time future." These dream figures had wills of their own and they moved forcefully as if to impart, or so it seemed to her upon waking, a promise. Sometimes they were beneficent, sometimes like hounds of hell pursuing her down unfamiliar alleys. But regardless, whether angelic or demonic, they fed her vision.

Even her waking vision was tinged with sparks of electricity and there were moments, both dreaming and awake, when she believed she glimpsed those strange, undefinable colors. She wondered if it weren't a prelude to some madness, the kind of madness which drove Van Gogh to mutilate himself.

The momentum toward her new life as *une femme seule* had begun: yesterday Catherine Aimsley had phoned to tell Françoise that she had arranged for Angelica to share a studio with a twenty-two-year-old sculptor named Jone Beele and that two publicity firms that hired free-lance artists were expecting to hear from her on Monday. What Suze and Françoise could not know was that the drain of a job, pregnancy, and a baby could not compare with the emotional exhaustion of living with a man like Ferris for nine years.

PART TWO

". . . women come into opposition to civilization and display their retarding and restraining influence—"

Sigmund Freud

Civilization and Its Discontents

JUNE 1980
New York City

When Angelica came out of the Customs area at Kennedy International Airport and saw a hefty disheveled blond in baggy khaki army trousers scanning the crowd with the earnestness of a large-pawed puppy awaiting the reappearance of its mistress, she knew instantly the young woman had to be Jone Beele. Jone's ash-blond hair escaped from its barrette in a natural frizz. At first glance she appeared to be heavily rouged but upon closer examination Angelica saw that Jone's cheeks were naturally ruddy, her lashes and eyebrows nearly black in contrast to her light hair.

"I just *knew* you," she said to Jone on the way into the city. "You looked like who you should be. You looked like the person I wanted you to be."

"You must be psychic," Jone laughed, responding immediately to the thin woman's ascetic black attire, her searching gray eyes, and fluttering, graceful movements.

"Nope," Angelica confessed. "I'm wrong a lot of the time . . . it just never stops me from going up to strangers. Once in Heathrow Airport I saw a man from the rear and thought he was my father . . . ran right up to him and said, 'Hi, Daddy.' It made no sense at all to think I'd see my father in England."

"Was it your father?"

"No."

Jone laughed again.

"How do you know Mrs. Aimsley?" Angelica wanted to know.

"She'd die if she heard you call her Mrs. Aimsley. She's like a little girl. I went to school with her daughter, Laura. Even her daughter seems older than her."

"Really?" Angelica was intrigued. "Now, you see, I imagined her all wrong. I imagined her svelte and terribly sophisticated, willowy and grand . . . certainly taller than me and I'm only five five."

"She's tiny."

Angelica rubbed her nose with her forefinger. "I guess I imagined her as a *grande dame* because a friend of mine in Paris said she wears too much perfume. God, am I glad to be home! What a nice surprise that you met me."

Angelica pressed her nose against the window of the pickup truck Jone had borrowed to meet her at the airport. They were passing a large cemetery in Queens and Angelica shook her head, remembering. "You know, I used to turn my head the other way every time Ferris . . . my 'ex' . . . and I drove to or from the airport. I never wanted to face that sprawling urban cemetery. Ferris used to tease me, said it was sign of how unrealistic I was. You know, I don't mind looking at it now. I think that's a good omen."

Jone smiled. "I think you're right."

"And I can't wait to see my new home!"

"Well," Jone twinkled, "you should find that amusing."

JULY 1980
New York City

Angelica and Jone laughingly referred to their place on Charlton Street as a "basement studio," which had a certain pithy, bohemian ring to it. Their friends gasped that it was "terrific space" and "unbelievable" for two hundred dollars a month. It was actually a derelict Mobil garage with no windows facing the street and the customary pull-up garage door opening onto a thirty-by-fifty-foot slab of cement stained with oil and gas. Her first night there in June, Angelica christened the floor with a bottle of Joy perfume which Ferris had given her for Christmas, but by July the stale gas and grime odor had triumphed over the Joy.

In ludicrous contrast to the automotive austerity of the place, the former tenant, a quasi-architect/artist/short-order chef, had installed three pairs of elegant, glass-paned French doors through which the sunlight poured from early morning till midafternoon. For curtains Angelica stitched together the sexy lingerie Ferris had awarded her over their years together, an ingenious patchwork of pants, gowns, and nighties. Catherine Aimsley, their matchmaker and sometime benefactress, had suggested Angelica might go into business marketing the "undie drapes"—they were just the sort of trendy item that Bendel's would adore. But no, Angelica was not interested.

"But," Cathy reasoned, "it would be better than working at

Far Out Inc.!" The older woman could not understand why Angelica would not prefer going into business for herself and possibly making a bundle if she got in in time for the Christmas buying, to doing layouts for movie posters at Far Out Inc. for seven dollars an hour.

"You have such wonderful, funky ideas," Cathy told Angelica.

"I know," Angelica had smiled, and that had been the end of the discussion.

At the rear of the long cement room which Jone and Angelica used as a work area was the former Mobil office, now divided into two sleeping alcoves and a sitting area. A miniature refrigerator, hot plate, and toaster-oven passed for a kitchen. The bathroom was a Stygian cubbyhole next to an old laundry tub which was the kitchen sink. There was no wiring in the bathroom so Angelica had transformed it into a religious shrine with candles lining the walls and a constantly smoldering cup of jasmine incense on the toilet. There was a *mezuzah* on one side of the door and holy water for Jone on the other side. On the ceiling Angelica had rendered a smiling, chubby, androgynous Buddha riding blissfully on puffy white clouds. The bathroom, she declared, was the only room that was really finished, they would decorate the rest of the Mobil in good time. It was, she insisted, a place of infinite potential.

The two women divided their work areas with strips of metal, welding rods and assorted booty from Jone's trips to the metal junkyard in Brooklyn. Steel sheets, stampings, angle irons, rods and pipes in varying sizes and shapes; aluminum, brass, bronze, copper, and stainless steel stacked between two oil drums. There were old bedsprings, broken grocery carts, sections of pressed-tin ceilings and rusted car fenders. Angelica had tied bright ribbons —reds, purples, zippy yellows, and oranges—at strategic points so that vivid colors leaped out from Jone's metal work.

Jone relished her trips to the scrap yards where she would chat with the men who worked there and wander around in her hard hat, using her magnet to unearth something precious to be employed in her sculptures. She found she had just the right words for the men at the scrap yard and she was not even shy about doing a bit of bickering when it came time to negotiate prices for the materials. She liked the junkyard men, liked how they responded directly to what she was doing in their territory. They had metal in common; it was more than enough. It was simple; she liked that. She liked the overhead cranes, the functional weighing scale where they tallied up her bill, and mostly she liked driving the borrowed pickup truck jammed high with her metals back across the Brooklyn Bridge to Manhattan.

"Like a scavenger," her mother had winced when Jone had explained her trips to the junkyard.

"Louise Nevelson probably did it." Jone had hoped the mention of the famous woman sculptor would mollify her.

"Jone," her mother had used her best Bridge Club voice to explain, "I've met Louise Nevelson, well, not actually met her but she was a speaker at the Junior League . . ."

"The Junior League!?"

"Well, maybe it was the League of Women Voters. It's not important. What I'm getting at is you're nothing like her. She was a born maverick, an iconoclast, and all along her teachers, everyone, said she had extraordinary talent. No one could stop her, no one ever could. She wears very long eyelashes, and I've seen pictures of her wearing them at the junkyard."

"What does that mean?"

"Jone, dear, it means that trying to hide behind Louise Nevelson's skirts was a foolish idea. Now listen, Jone, you're nothing like her. That is my point in all this. Forget about the Junior League. I know you think it's foolish for me to go to the meetings. I know what you think about that. However . . . my point is that you're not nuts like she is. No, I didn't mean that. I meant that you . . . you're far too quiet to be successful. That woman talks a lot. Wait . . . don't interrupt. My point in all this is that with my own ears I heard Louise Nevelson say that she experienced almost no recognition at all until she was in her fifties. That's thirty years from now, Jonie."

"I can count."

". . . and not only recognition. What about money? Oh, I know you expect to inherit money from your Grandmother Mary, but isn't that a sad way to live? You'll be waiting for her to die just so you can live decently."

"Did you ever think I might sell my sculpture, make money without wearing false eyelashes?"

"You don't understand a word I say."

Jone had wanted to say, "True," but she had kept silent because she believed in the commandment: honor thy father and thy mother. It had always disturbed her when her mother and Grandmother Mary picked, sniped, and fought with each other; she had determined never to duplicate their behavior. Sometimes she chewed the insides of her mouth raw listening to Elizabeth prattle on and on, but she was going to honor her if it was the last thing she did!

Driving her skeleton metals back to the Mobil Garage she invariably thought of her grandmother, Mean Mary Jones, locked away at the Wilton Retirement Manor, snarling at the staff, worrying Elizabeth and almost getting herself expelled. Every week Jone thought: this week I'll go visit grandmother, but there were always reasons why she couldn't. She had not seen Mary Jones for six months, had not written or even phoned.

"Why can't you call? What is so difficult about making a phone call? You were always her favorite . . . the only one she cares about." Her mother badgered Jone constantly about her insensitivity and lack of responsibility.

Of course she had chosen the Brooklyn junkyard because of Mary. The Bronx was more convenient, even the scrap yard in Queens was easier to get to, but she had chosen Brooklyn in order to be with her grandmother. Crossing the Brooklyn Bridge (surely the most beautiful bridge in the world) with its plaintive, innocent Gothic arches, Jone moved through the same space Mary had traveled through on her trips back and forth from Brooklyn to the Dream City, which was how Mary had always referred to New York. The Dream City. Jone wondered if she didn't absorb actual electrical vibrations from the past, picking up fragments of Grandmother Mary's passion along the way. Whatever her grandmother had lacked, she had not lacked passion. However much it pained her to think of Mary's wasted life, Jone thought, she needed the old woman's passion.

She would make up for the past. Each trip strengthened her resolve to become a successful sculptor; not in theory but in fact, not in words but in her body as it moved through space above the East River. She saw Bartholdi's Statue of Liberty, knowing that her grandmother, then Mary Gregory, had looked out across the waters at the same colossal figure made out of hammered plates of copper. The sparkling waters were the same, the shoreline could not have changed significantly since the trolley had run along the bridge at the turn of the century.

"When I was a girl . . ."

Every conversation Jone could remember having with her grandmother had begun with those same words. "When I was a girl it was all wide open and we knew we lived on the most beautiful spot on earth and we knew, you see, how very smart we were because we had made so much out of it. Technology, we had it and it was efficient. You can't imagine how efficient it was when I was a girl. Horse-drawn trolleys were out by the time I went to study at the Art Students League. That was 1906 and oh my, we thought it was amazing to be without the aroma of the horses; my dear child, it was a miracle! We thought ourselves quite civilized and we were. The pinnacle. Yes, and we had the first subway, finished in 1904 and not patronized by rude, ignorant, antisocial types who only want to deface the walls with their initials. People of quality rode the subways. Papa, your great-grandfather, rode them and of course I did, too. I wore gloves because mother insisted and it was the least I could do to please her. The fare was five cents. We would buy our tickets and throw them into the gateman's glass box—a 'chopper box' they called it and there was one at the entrance to each platform. It was an event. Every day, during the time of my studies at the Art Students League, was an event of going and coming, of movement and seeing. I think I should have been content only to make journeys. It seemed so rare to me."

. . . only to make journeys . . . it seemed so rare to me. Stories from her grandmother's past, stories of *when I was a girl* ran through Jone's mind as she moved across her grandmother's bridge and the tears which were part of the ritual only strengthened her determination to make it up to Mary Jones.

The garage studio, the dank, junked-up environment her parents saw, was to Jone as sacred as a chapel, a place outside of time in which all things might be possible. The oxyacetylene fuel gas tanks, vise, C-clamps, anvil, metal sheers, sledge hammer were all things which could be relied upon. As her welding became more proficient they were becoming absolutes in her hands.

There were no illusions here and she wanted none. Painting was an illusionary art and that was why she had not flourished there. Let them call her average, mediocre, but only as a painter. Now that there was substance beneath her, she was safe. Her work, open, sensuous metal figures neither male nor female, consumed space. It *was.*

Some of the welding rods she used were bronze, some flux-coated bronze, some nickel silver—though that was very expensive and she had nearly depleted her savings buying basic equipment and supplies. The rods were a quarter-inch in diameter, three-thirty-seconds, one-sixteenth, three-sixteenths, one-eighth. There were a different number of rods per pound: twenty-nine one-sixteenth bronze rods per pound and one three-eighths. She could tell by touching; it was all clear, distinct. One lifted, one knew.

Until she had enough money to install a ventilation fan system (hopefully by winter or they would freeze) it was necessary to work with the French doors open so they would not be overcome by the fumes.

Wearing a flameproof welding jacket, gloves, and goggles, Jone heaved a large sheet of metal onto the fireproof worktable and secured it in the vise-grip before turning on the valves of the torch to release the gas mixture. *Playing with fire—danger—DON'T!* All terribly familiar words. She smiled as the sparks danced out of the nozzle. *My God, you'll kill yourself! Burn yourself up. That thing could explode, Jone, what in God's name are you thinking of?*

And she wasn't even a dainty little thing like her sister Sarah. Imagine the outcry if Sarah had donned goggles and picked up a welding torch. Thank God I'm an oaf, thought Jone as she began a string-bead effect as part of the process of fusion welding.

The metal had already turned cherry red, becoming soft and wet as she made small circular motions which produced a series of welded puddles as the metal melted, then holes, and finally the welding bead itself: a straight line down the edge of the large sheet. There were hours and hours of precision work, mistakes which led to innovations and insight; mistakes which hurt, infuriated her, and made it impossible to do anything but start again. She knew she had only begun to learn the skill of welding but she was also convinced she would become an expert at it because the method suited her so perfectly.

When she began with the cutting torch (and much later when she would be grinding and polishing the completed form) it was necessary to wear soundproof earmuffs. It was this particular aspect of the technique which had sent her spinning off into uncharted euphoria when she had first learned the skill in an adult education class at a vocational school in her former neighborhood. The combination of muted sound which obliterated everything—street noise, phones, memories, plans—together with the passion of the heat which could cut, join, and transform ordinary metal into mythical forms was indescribably exhilarating to Jone. She was strengthened by the violence—the transformation of metal into form through fire. She thrived on the physical demands the work made on her body, the dexterity of balancing pieces to get a perfect corner joint, the surgeonlike control necessary to make a perfect braze weld. Vision was not enough. She was still not certain she had the vision, the raw, uncontrollable originality of someone like Angelica, but she knew she had the tenacity, the stamina, and—how was it Cathy had put it?—the girth!

"Stop!" Angelica, pale and wraithlike in what looked like, and was in fact, a nun's habit, appeared on Jone's side of the barrier waving a red rose. The robe was her recently adopted "painting habit" and she slipped into it every morning and worked in it until three in the afternoon, when she replaced it with black overalls which she wore to work with one of her handpainted T-shirts. The "habit" and the overalls, together with black harem pants, a black velvet bias-cut thirties gown, and a black faille fifties Dior suit, were her entire wardrobe. Shoes were black pumps, black ballet slippers, or black boots. It amazed Jone that with these limited items and a few scarves and shawls Angelica managed to create an infinite number of outfits and always came off looking as though she were in the process of inventing a new trend in fashion.

Jone turned off her equipment, smiling at Angelica's talent for materializing out of thin air.

"Your mother's Mercedes. I saw it go by the window. She's circling like some rare silver bird on the verge of distinction. Sorry, I meant extinction." Angelica moved her hand across the midsection of a female torso. "I like this piece, Jone. The openness is something new. It's good."

Jone checked the valves on the tanks to make sure they were closed. "She'll want me to come out to the car to talk to her. She's afraid of leaving her stereo unguarded."

"I could tell her you're not here," Angelica volunteered.

"She can smell the acetylene . . . so she says."

"I could tell her I'm Sister Angelica now, that we've just been accepted by the Polish pope as a new experiment in sisterhood. Does she know I'm pregnant?"

Jone shook her head, took off her mask and gloves and hung both the oxygen and the acetylene cylinders on the wall.

"Do you think she thinks I'm gay? That you and I are . . ."

"I don't think she thinks I have that much imagination," Jone commented dryly.

"She'd feel better if you wore false eyelashes," Angelica chuckled. "Listen, I'm going to the Whitney after work. I'm taking off early. Tonight's free and I want to see the Nevelson retro again. Can you meet me?"

"You should get more rest." Jone frowned as Angelica waved the red rose and floated into the Mobil office living quarters. "I mean it. You're pushing too damned hard."

"You're a good mama." Angelica reappeared in the doorway. "But I feel fab now that I've stopped throwing up every morning."

"I still think you should come home after work and let me make you dinner."

"I wish we were gay," Angelica sighed and ducked out of sight.

Elizabeth Beele parked her silver Mercedes across the street and stared at the garage where her youngest child was living with a freaky girl who wore her hair in a punk cut and dressed only in black. OBIL, the sign said . . . the "M" had flaked off years before. Elizabeth shook her head and looked in the rearview mirror, smoothing her perfectly coiffed blond hair with a sudden jerky movement. She had thought the cool green Monets at the Metropolitan would soothe her but they had only made her feel worse. There was too much to do. There was nothing to be done.

She lit a cigarette and hoped Jone would come out so she would not have to go inside. OBIL. Last week Jone had mentioned that her roommate thought the sign might be an omen and was considering changing her name to Obil. Jone thought that was funny. In fact she had never seen Jone laugh as frequently as she was doing since the punk girl had joined her. There was nothing to be done.

Boccherini was playing on the stereo, the car smelled of an expensive clovey potpourri from Bendel's. Elizabeth pressed her forehead against the leather-bound steering wheel and tried not to cry. Everyone in the Beele family had always said Jone and her grandmother were alike but maybe they weren't. Elizabeth herself had said it. Only, Elizabeth rationalized, she had made the comparison between her daughter and her mother to make the old woman feel as though she belonged, as some means of communication that wasn't completely hypocritical. Actually they weren't alike. No, only insofar as they were both artistically inclined. Not even talented, just inclined. Dear God, thought Elizabeth, please don't let it be true.

There were schools of psychiatric thought which held that mental illness, like certain physical diseases, was transmitted from generation to generation, sometimes skipping one generation. Elizabeth was thankful to have been skipped but she was filled with dread for the agonies in store for her daughter if it turned out Jone had inherited Mary Jones's flawed psyche.

Smiling, Jone loped across the street and slid into the car. She kissed her mother gingerly, careful not to smudge her cheek or brush against Elizabeth's crisp linen dress. Elizabeth felt Jone's dry lips and did truly try not to cry.

She turned away. "I tried to call. You never answer your phone. You might as well be living in Rhodesia."

"It's the racket from the grinder. I don't always hear the phone. Mother, I'm not trying to avoid you. I was going to phone . . ."

"Your grandmother tried to kill herself."

Elizabeth saw Jone's face reflected in the side mirror and wondered at the absolute coldness in her daughter's eyes.

Cathy let herself into Tony's tiny apartment on Sullivan Street with the key he had presented to her as proof of his monogamous intentions. She had not mentioned Lester's proposal to him so far but told herself that very soon she was going to broach the subject. Having her own key made her more secure about all the lithe young girls flitting in and out of his apartment; some were modeling for him, some were students, and some, he continued to insist, were just buddies. She was suspicious of that word *buddies* but she had to believe him, didn't she, since he had given her a key?

She whistled to herself as she emptied a few ashtrays and washed out the cups he had left in his sink. She enjoyed sprucing up his meager quarters though he teased her mercilessly about her domestic predilections and had threatened to cut her off for a week should she dare to wax his floors. She, who wouldn't dream of scouring anything in her own home, simply adored working up a sweat over the brown stains in his bathroom sink.

Silly, silly silly, Cathy told herself. You are a silly! She leafed through a stack of charcoal drawings done by beginning students at the Fashion Institute where Tony was teaching a summer course. For no apparent reason the image of her first husband, Robert Rosen, flashed in her memory. Well, probably, she thought, looking around Tony's threadbare surroundings, it was because she had imagined, prior to moving to New York, that she would lose her virginity in just such a bohemian setting. Romance! But then Rosen had had other plans and, besides, he had already been making a comfortable living by the time they met. There had been no leisurely love-filled afternoon with Rosen.

And so, Catherine, have you come to remedy that gap in your experience? Is that why you are here? Cathy glanced critically at her reflection in the mirror which hung above Tony's only decent piece of furniture, the Victorian oak chest she had given him for Valentine's Day.

Ever since she had thrown her back out of whack she had had the damndest sensation that Rosen's ghost was stomping around after her. What would he think of her now, she wondered?

She took off her crisp green linen dress and sat on the edge of Tony's lumpy bed wearing her white silk slip. She loved being in his apartment alone, waiting for him . . . in her slip. She stretched languidly as the late afternoon sun filtered in through the rickety shutters. Really, there was nothing sexier than a plain white slip. Eva Marie Saint had worn a white slip in *On the Waterfront* and somehow Cathy always thought of Eva and Marlon when she visited Tony's seedy brownstone with its dark, narrow halls and the old claw-foot tub which was in the kitchen. Life was so different than it had been back in Wayne. She loved the ritual of making love in Tony's place—loved arriving alone, loved leaving afterwards (sometimes with her stockings and her panties stuffed recklessly into her purse) to cab back uptown along the deserted Avenue of the Americas at three in the morning.

Maybe she hadn't mentioned Lester's suggestion because she was reluctant to give up her illicit, bohemian afternoons, afternoons where she could feel like Eva Marie Saint . . . young. Yes, she felt young and free and unencumbered when she was at Tony's.

The phone rang and Cathy answered it, thinking it was Tony. Whoever it was hung up and in spite of the symbolic key, she immediately fantasized a willowy twenty-two-year-old beauty with legs like Cyd Charisse.

Nonsense, she told herself, pouring a glass of Soave and lighting the remains of a joint Tony had left for her in the black lacquered box next to the bed. She had always been a person who examined the past—some would say she thrived on, even wallowed in nostalgia—but nowhere was the past as sweet to reflect upon as in Tony's little "pad."

"Hello, Rosen." She blew a puff of smoke at the imagined apparition. "I'm in love with two men who have never made me weep. Now what do you think of that?"

Cathy giggled, already high from one drag of the marijuana. "Dope fiend," she exclaimed and laughed again.

If Rosen had not wrapped the car around a telephone pole

in 1964, how would he have continued? Cathy tried to imagine him living in 1980, having gone through sixteen years of therapy, EST, yoga, Rolfing, Transcendental Meditation, primal marathons . . . all the mind-expanding adventures which had marked her own eclectic struggle for survival. Unlike Tony and Lester, Rosen would have seen all of her pursuits as a sign of weakness. Rosen would have preferred a Bowery gutter.

"Yes, you would have!" Cathy shook an accusing finger at the haze of Rosen's aura. "I know you think my back spasms are laughable and inconsequential compared with your broken neck and charred remains. You and your cosmic demise. And you were right, they still love you for your self-destructive egomania. Ah well . . ."

Cathy sank back onto the pillows, pleasantly drifting into the past where it had all begun.

From the moment Cathy Harder stepped off the bus in August of 1953 she knew she had made the right decision. She sniffed the gas fumes in New York's Port Authority Bus terminal as a mustached man jabbed her in the ribs and then grimaced as if she had jabbed him. It was all right. She had arrived and it was all right! Her pulse quickened as it had done when *He* would appear silhouetted in the door of the Snack Shack back in Wayne. There would be no more mud to wade through, she had eluded her fate: the odor of sour milk which permeated school cafeterias.

When she applied for a job decorating windows at Macy's they had told her she was not qualified; but she was hired to sell costume jewelry and with her beautiful new wardrobe (bought at employee's discount) in autumnal plums and chocolaty browns, she was a success, with more dates than she could handle. She continued to *make pictures,* watercolors mostly and a few pastels which she, for some reason, continued to store neatly under her bed in the furnished room she rented from an Irish family on East Eighty-second Street. After a week at Macy's she volunteered to stay late and assist whoever was doing the windows. By September she was working four days in jewelry and two days as a junior window designer. She flirted and talked constantly, took orders easily, and won the hearts of the men at Macy's.

Back in Wayne family and friends had scoffed at museums as outmoded relics which could have no possible significance or value in their lives. People who frequented museums, so they thought, were themselves relics—old people with nothing else to do, Jews, or captive schoolchildren on a day's outing. Museums were too much like graveyards, reminding one of the past. Unlike cars they could not get you anywhere, unlike food they did not nourish you, unlike television they did not amuse you and make you forget who you were and what your life did or did not mean. And in fact, the people of Wayne, according to their own experiences, were correct. The Wayne Museum, the only museum most of them knew, was a smelly, olive-drab room in the old wing of the town hall where the fire chief, an amateur taxidermist, displayed his foxes, chipmunks, muskrats, etc., in glass cases. Cathy actually mounted the steps of the New York's Metropolitan Museum half expecting to be greeted by Chief Folborn's mangy stuffed animals. Instead she entered a magic world where lines in time were not drawn, where one could exist in the seventh or the seventeenth century, in Greece, Rome, or the gardens of Monet. She later remarked that the Metropolitan Museum was the first real miracle in her life; having discovered such visual ecstasy she began spending most of her free moments inside its palatial walls. Gradually the men receded and the mighty Met took over the number one spot in her life.

Then the second miracle: someone told her about an art school called the Art Students League. She enrolled immediately and by Christmas her life in New York had surpassed anything she had been able to imagine back in Wayne. The only thing she lacked to make it perfect was a Great Love. *Him.*

On December 31, at a party given by one of the students at the ASL, a tall man with piercing black eyes and a bushy black beard stared at her from across a crowded room. Finally she giggled because it reminded her of the song "Some Enchanted Evening," where the stranger stared across the crowded room and "the sound of his laughter will ring in your dreams."

Who can explain it, who can tell you why?
Fools give you reasons, wise men never try. . . .

What was so hilarious was that the song made it all sound so romantic and civilized—beautiful people in gowns and tuxedoes—whereas in her case the stranger was a Heathcliffian beatnik. He was not only wearing jeans but sandals with bright red socks . . . in winter! Like a remote figure in a Gothic mystery he took two giant steps across the crowded room, and without smiling asked her to dance. Locked in his tense embrace Cathy felt even tinier than her petite five feet two. When she tried to look up at him he pressed her head into his chest. He had dirty fingernails and smelled of turpentine and cigarettes. When she introduced herself he seemed not to be listening and at the conclusion of the dance he returned to his station across the crowded room and fixed her with his melancholy eyes.

One of the other girls pulled Cathy into the Ladies Room to warn her that her admirer was Robert Rosen, renegade king of the inner art circles. He had been on the cover of *Time* and five pages had been devoted to his controversial mammoth paintings, his questionable technique of hurling buckets of paint at the canvas to create his masterpieces. He and his cronies were the Rough Riders of the art world, the one-hundred-percent, all-male, new-wave artists who eschewed any trace of nineteenth century gentility.

Although he had been accused of being a fraud, of hoodwinking the public into thinking his new spatter-and-hurl technique could be considered "art," Rosen was nevertheless the dominant figure on the American art scene. If people rejected his work, they were still drawn to his audacity, the vitality of his male ego which had dared to hurl instead of paint, which had broken from centuries of the tradition which many believed had gone stale.

Later that night, after Rosen was drunk enough, he suggested Cathy leave the party with him. He seemed shocked when she turned him down, explaining that she was only nineteen and that he was too old for her. He was at least thirty, wasn't he? Rosen thought about it for a moment, then turned and left. Cathy was positive she had seen the last of him.

Who can explain it, who can tell you why?
Fools give you reasons, wise men never try. . . .

The sound of his laughter did not ring in her dreams. Even had there been laughter, which there hadn't—not even a smile—it is doubtful whether it would have rung in her dreams. She had found Rosen foreboding, too quiet, cold, and rather "scary," as she described the incident to one of the girls at work. She was, however, flattered that anyone as important as Robert Rosen would find her interesting enough to ask out. For the next few days she used the memory of their brief dance together to bolster her ego. In retrospect her pulse began to quicken whereas at the time she had been quite uncomfortable.

As the days wore on she thought of the Great Man more and more, focusing on him as a renegade genius, a misunderstood maverick. In her imagination she had always seen herself married to a Great Man—a senator, a movie star, a president even—a man who wielded power. Yes, power had always been more important than money, though it was true that they generally went together. None of the boys she had dated in Wayne had had any real potential for power, though several of them had had modest fortunes behind them.

A Great Man! She could be the wife of a Great Painter, the inspiration behind his work. The idea appealed to her. Some people were saying that Rosen was as important an innovator as Picasso. Only how, she wondered, having rebuffed him, was she to contrive to meet him again?

She did not, as it happened, have to contrive anything. Rosen had been unable to put her out of his mind. Perhaps he was initially intrigued by her gentle rejection, something he was not accustomed to receiving from women. Her petite yet sturdy body, her light brown curls, ingenuous smile, and bright clothes played on his mind, enchanting him. He thought of her as a tiny princess; unlike the older, "used" women he and his crowd associated with, Cathy exuded purity and that, he was sure, was a rarity in 1953. A week after their first meeting he was waiting for her outside her house on Eighty-second Street. His unexpected but prayed-for appearance seemed like a sign from God. He took her to his studio and showed her his work.

"My God." She had been flabbergasted by his huge loft with its north-windowed walls, twenty-foot ceilings, the huge tubs where he mixed his paints, the cans of exotic oils such as oiticica oil from Brazil, lumbang oil and stillingia oil from China. Everything about Rosen's studio affirmed his greatness, his larger-than-life heroic nature.

"I always just buy my oil in tubes," she had admitted when he demonstrated his various methods of grinding the pigment and under which conditions he would elect to use certain oils.

"God, this is neat! Wow . . . it must be incredible to have a studio like this." Cathy cringed at the sound of the chipmunk voice, her humiliating chipmunk behavior.

All of Rosen's paintings were enormous abstract improvisations of form and color. Sometimes he painted with brooms; often the colors were splashed or shoved onto the canvas; occasionally, he explained, he might even feel the need to paint with his body.

"But never a brush?" Cathy blushed at her stupidity and was gratified that Rosen gave no sign of being put off by her naiveté.

She did not know what to think of the paintings. They were certainly overpowering, and his use of color was often moving in some mysterious way.

They had coffee and before she had finished the first cup she was shot with Great Love for the Great Man. Rosen was HIM. She understood the way he looked at her—men had looked at her that way all her life—only now her desire was inflamed by her mind, by Rosen's power and all the mysteries he symbolized.

Outside his studio Rosen was again reticent; their conversation came in spurts, awkwardly. Cathy's nervousness and inability to think coherently convinced her that this was Great Love. She had never in her life been speechless; usually she chattered away nonstop. With Rosen she had dried up—struck dumb by the power of love. She was miserable, lovesick; and when she looked into his dark eyes she was terrified of the anger and power she saw. Her paralysis and terror convinced her that this was finally the real thing.

She forced herself to speak; felt the words come haltingly and heard her voice like that of a stranger. She told him about Wayne, Ohio, and for the first time he smiled in recognition, saying that he had known all along she was a farm girl. Yes, that was what had attracted him. He had lived in Iowa until he was eighteen. He didn't much like city women because they were hard. They talked of farms and country life; it was their one true bond and it might have been an important one.

He offered to teach her how to paint after his manner and of course she responded with enthusiasm, though by then she would have been receptive to another offer. The idea of having Rosen as her first lover consumed her thinking for the three days following, and on the evening of their second official date she was determined. But already they were, unconsciously, at odds with each other: Cathy was in love with the illicit idea of herself as (at least for some time) mistress to a great artist, and Rosen wanted to maintain her purity forever. He wanted her as a wife.

Two weeks later they were married and immediately, at Rosen's insistence, Cathy quit her job at Macy's in order, as Rosen explained, to begin to take her art seriously. She set up her easel in their bedroom. It was out of the question, he said, to have her working in his studio with him. Understandably he could only fully free himself when he was alone. But the bedroom was tiny, the light was mediocre, and having to drag paints and canvases in and out and to clean up after every session was not conducive to working. Then, of course, there were Rosen's friends, always stopping by, drinking and talking until dawn. The men treated her kindly. She cooked, made coffee, refilled drinks, emptied ashtrays, and grew dizzy listening to their marathons about the meaning of art from an existential point of view. Almost nightly they argued in loud angry voices, downing quarts of brandy; like Baudelaire, they seemed to have a "horror of being easily understood." She felt obliged to be the perfect wife and hostess even when her presence went ignored. She could not grasp what they were saying and felt stupid because most of the time she was not even able to concentrate on their words. Their art was their religion. She knew by their tone and manner how important they were. They detested anything easy, anything literal or fraught with human feelings. They perceived themselves as artists to be the only truly moral men living and agreed wholeheartedly with Richard Pousette-Dart that only the artist "has the courage to create his own soul and live by the means of the light of it." Like Duchamps they forced themselves into self-contradictions in order to avoid following their own tastes.

They were a secret society unto themselves and they tolerated

Cathy's work, which was crammed into a corner of the small bedroom, with quick smiles. By "truly moral men" they meant exactly that: men. There was a brief period during which they admitted one lone woman artist to their ranks but she soon fell into disrepute and quickly became the butt of some of their less-inspired comments.

Cathy's appetite was for things she saw: the tall buildings, Robert's naked body. She had wanted to paint Robert nude standing beside one of his huge canvases, but she was afraid to ask. She knew her ideas were inconsequential because they could be understood. She was not original. She painted pictures, they created art. Finally she began hurling her own paint onto the canvas, but even their compliments did not assuage the loss she had felt. When she became pregnant she was relieved. The baby, their Laura, gave her an excuse to absent herself from their nightly evangelical tirades and she could sit quietly sketching. She drew pictures of the baby and hid them so Rosen would not tease her about being shallow and wasting her time on such sentimental subjects. She guessed he was right but she continued doing the drawings anyway.

She knew the marriage was a failure but the combination of her midwestern morality and the belief that love was painful made the idea of leaving Rosen impossible. By the time their second daughter, Aggie, was born in 1957, Rosen's handsome face was as puffy and pink as one of her father's Chester White hogs. His constant drinking and eventual reliance on pills and drugs to help temper the extreme vacillation of his moods had made her life with him miserable. His own daughters withdrew from him, for though he never struck out against anyone, there was always the sense of violence about him. Whereas initially he had been furtive and often withdrawn with Cathy, now he was pointedly nasty in his refusal to communicate. He ignored her with a vengeance and when the money came in he spent it lavishly on himself as if he had forgotten that anyone else existed. In 1964 he killed himself by wrapping his new MG around a telephone pole in Southampton. His body burned to ashes, there were only his paintings.

Cathy felt she had lived with a ghost for ten years and at thirty-one she cried herself to sleep listening to sad music, just as she had done back in Wayne the summer Billy Thomas ran off and married Patty Elsworth because he had got her pregnant. She wondered why she was crying if she hadn't loved him. But then perhaps she had loved him. She had cried harder, certain that she would never know the answer.

AUGUST 1980
New York City

Just like that the work stopped. Dried up. Dead. The strange metal objects, some of them seven feet tall, stared at Jone and she stared back as though seeing them for the first time, as though they were no relations of hers. Angelica told her not to worry, to pick up the torch regardless.

"It will well up again, stronger," Angelica reassured Jone. "My God, you've produced so much and now you're going to be showing your work. You need time to fill up. Don't be afraid."

"Right." Jone smiled and continued fixing dinners, adding thyme to casseroles. Dependable Jone. She continued to see that Angelica took her vitamins and lately had even found herself giving advice to Cathy Aimsley on whether or not to proceed with her divorce. Dealing with Cathy as a contemporary and confidante had at first been flattering. Now it was depressing. As much as she liked Cathy, and no one it seemed could dislike her for long, it was maddening to see how she wasted her hours in trivial worriment: one minute she was divorcing Lester, moving in with Tony, and the next minute she was moving to Montana to live by herself.

Angelica's increasingly protruding belly frightened her. Somehow she had thought Angelica, of all people, would come to her senses before it was too late. But Angelica showed no signs of vacillating and it was already the fourth month.

Ever since her grandmother's "accident," as Jone's mother referred to it, Jone had moved through her days without feeling space, as if she were bound and gagged. She had almost depleted her savings by stocking up on bronze and buying into a somewhat shoddy, recently organized cooperative gallery on Mercer Street. Actually, she told herself, she was only going through the motions of placing her pieces in the large, columned Mercer Street loft. She did not foresee that anything good would come from her effort since the show was tacky and the work of most of the other artists was quirky, punk, really almost embarrassingly bad. But it was August and there was no one around anyway. Cathy and Angelica had both encouraged her to buy into the show; maybe that was why she felt slightly irritated with both of them lately. Well, she didn't let on and she wouldn't blame them when nothing sold and she had to find part-time work like Angelica. Even before the show opened she wanted to quit. Angelica said that wasn't unusual but Angelica didn't know.

No, she had not gone to see her grandmother. Seeing the wasted old woman would only depress her further. So much waste. Instead she diligently sent four get-well cards a week, bright, optimistic wishes for Grandmother to Get Well with pictures of smiling blond grandchildren jumping rope or little black dogs on crutches with bandages on their heads. All smiling.

She spent hours browsing through card shops selecting safe, noncontroversial messages and praying that none of her cards would be responsible for sending Mary into another suicidal state. She signed the cards "Love, Jone" and told herself she would visit Mary when she wasn't quite so down, when she had some good news of her own.

The more Jone perceived the growth in her work, her newly acquired expertise with her materials and the torch, the more frightened she became that something might intervene. She was beset with childhood memories of her grandmother, incidents half heard, perhaps only dreamed, which led her to believe that Mary's entire life had been one insidious attempt to destroy herself.

No one had ever admitted it but Jone was certain that Mary

had attempted suicide before. There had been whispers in the hall and it had been a cold Christmas night. Jone had been twelve and the whispers, uncommon in a home where people either read themselves to sleep or listened to Bach, had hissed outside her bedroom door like a blizzard. Her father had tiptoed in to see if she had heard. "It's all right," he had said.

Of course it had not been all right. The next morning they told her Grandmother Mary had twisted her ankle and could not be disturbed. They were lying. A twisted ankle was no reason to call an ambulance in the middle of the night and sedate the patient for a week after.

How she wished she were making it up, wished she could obliterate the whispers in her memory. Was it possible that her grandmother's existence had been so miserable that she had been driven to try to take her own life, not just once but several times?

A week before the quasi-show which Jone's parents knew nothing about, her mother took her to lunch at the Sign of the Dove.

". . . and . . . ? The men in your life?" Elizabeth tried in vain for subtlety.

"There was one," Jone lied to make her mother feel easier. "It's over."

"Oh, darling," Elizabeth sounded both pained and relieved. "Then, darling, please, please take time off from your metal and pay a visit to Grandmother Mary. I can't understand . . ."

"Was Grandmother this unhappy when you were a girl?" Jone asked.

"Of course not! Mother was perfectly fine until the past few years. She's old, that's all."

"Once I heard sirens."

Elizabeth laughed convincingly. "You never did."

"Mother, please admit it. Grandmother did not simply twist her ankle that Christmas!"

Elizabeth's mouth twitched imperceptibly and her eyes became dreamy, moist, and utterly beneficent. "Your grandmother, Jone, was a highly respected woman. She gave birth to eight children, six of whom survived and are happy and prosperous. Look at me? Do I mope? Never! For three years, in case you have forgotten, Grandmother Mary was the chairman of the Catholic Fund and in one of those years she raised more money than any of her predecessors. She absolutely worshiped your grandfather and when his gout forced him to retire at eighty she literally carried him up and down the stairs so that he would not have to . . . Jone, in case you have forgotten! . . . would not have to spend his last months in a hospital. Your grandmother is someone you should be proud of. My God, she's a saint and you can't even find an afternoon to pay her a visit."

Jone nodded and picked listlessly at the salmon mousse her mother had insisted she order. A saint? How could her mother have said that?

"Why are you putting me through this?" Elizabeth asked with a tortured smile.

"I just asked," Jone said. "I have these memories . . . I need you to tell me what really happened. Remember the stretched canvas she used to keep in her . . ."

"This isn't like you." Elizabeth tried to chuckle. "I'm worried about you. You're strange."

Like Louise Nevelson, Jone wanted to say but instead she nodded her acquiescence.

"I'll go to see her."

"We could drive up after lunch," Elizabeth suggested.

"You and Grandmother always fight."

Elizabeth moaned through her martyred smile. "My God, Jone, I'm hardly going to pick a fight with a woman who just tried to slit her wrists!"

"I'm sorry." Jone reached for her mother's pale, smooth hand. "It's just that there are questions. Things that have been bothering me for . . ."

"You're not like her!" Elizabeth snapped. "If that's what you're thinking, forget it, because you are not like her. Jone, forget about the past and just go to see her."

"She was an alcoholic," Jone tried again.

"She is Irish," Elizabeth answered and Jone nodded. She directed her attention to the salmon mousse, knowing there could be no answers from Elizabeth, only smooth sailing.

Old people should be above suicide. Old people might be arthritic, lonely, afraid of being mugged, but they should not get angry enough or be perverse enough to jab at themselves with a broken glass. Old people might be enlightened and wise enough to elect euthanasia. In their right minds, old people might instruct their families to unplug their life-support systems but they should not curse like thugs and flail about and dirty their beds with their own blood. Old age should be dignified. The wisdom gained over the years should make them calm, serene, accepting. Should. As the body shrivels the spirit becomes enlightened. *Them*, make *them* peaceful, make *them* more angel than mortal, yes? Aren't cataracts just another step toward enlightenment? As they form over old eyes, dimming and distorting, don't the old people begin to see a deeper reality? Yes? Mightn't they actually see into infinity? Oh, no, nothing hideous in death. Nothing. At death the body secretes peaceful toxins which, if not subverted by drugs and medical abuse, precipitate the "passing on" process. Right? Isn't that the way it should be for *them*?

"Endotoxins," Jone told the man sitting across the table from her at McSorley's Bar. "You ever hear of them?"

He shook his head and poured them another glass of beer from the large pitcher. It was ten o'clock and they had been drinking since late in the afternoon. He wondered if he would be able to stand up and steer her back to his loft if it came to that. He hoped it would.

"Endotoxins," she repeated, enunciating emphatically. "They're substances that're released naturally upon the destruction of cells. The cells produce them, see? It's all natural. See?"

He did not see. Mostly they had been drinking in silence. She did not have much to say and he had rather liked that about her, especially since when she did speak he understood practically nothing of what she said.

"You said you were an artist?" He tried vaguely to draw her out.

"A welder," she replied without looking at him.

"I thought you said . . ."

"I know."

He looked down at his beer and felt stupid for hanging around a girl like her. He was shy—a short, unsuccessful actor, balding at twenty-four. He assumed he would be a failure and the assumption kept hurting him. She was statuesque and didn't seem to mind that he was so short and such a poor conversationalist. He hoped he could get her home with him but he just couldn't imagine how, couldn't picture it somehow.

"You said your grandmother was sick?"

"Insane."

"I see."

"My mother says she's insane."

"Who? Your grandmother or your mother?"

"My mother says my grandmother's insane." Jone lit the last cigarette, puffed hard, and began to unseam the package until it was one flat surface. Then, very carefully, she began folding it back and forth like an accordion.

He watched the process with a fascinated expression and when she had finished he complimented her, hoping to make a joke, but either it fell flat or she didn't hear. It was hard to tell.

"If a person is unhappy enough, does that make them insane?" Jone looked at him hard. "Does it, do you think? Do you think . . . there's a . . . corollary"—she broke off with a laugh.

"I don't know." His palms were sweaty. He guessed he was boring her. "I guess I'd better go." He stood up, threw down too much money, and moved rapidly like a wind-up toy toward the door.

Jone's vision blurred. For an instant she thought she felt cataracts forming on her eyes but then she realized that he was moving through space too fast. He was leaving and she was alone. When he stumbled she felt herself starting to cry.

All the while he was making love to her she was trying to remember his name and how she had moved from the bar to his bed. She thought she had cried for a long time but she wasn't sure. He was nice, though, and gentle, and she enjoyed touching his abdomen which was soft, like foam rubber. She guessed he was more than generously endowed though she was probably not a good judge. But even in the dim light he had seemed almost awesome, which was odd because his manner was so impotent. Obviously there was no correlation between form and content. He was not at all firm and had a light red fuzz over his chest and back, rather like a bear. She hadn't slept with many men, never one with fuzz.

How was it possible they were making love when she was still so dizzy, when the room was still spinning and everything still so blurred? He ran his hand between her breasts and down to her pale mound of hair. She heard herself moan and opened her legs. Angelica would be proud of her for taking care of her biological needs, something Angelica found easy to do. She called them her "sensible one-night stands with clean men." Jone found it impossible to create the circumstances which would lead to sex. The games which preceded the actual event involved words, even when the men were not interested in the words. This man, Bear, had been content to sit in silence and drink without any words.

Bear moaned on top of her and she clasped her legs around him in gratitude as the room spun faster and faster.

❀

"My God, don't move, Tony! Don't move!" Cathy's studio smelled of dying flowers, kerosene, and the usual turpentine. Her back pain, much improved, was obliterated by inspiration and a gram of cocaine which Tony had provided. "Oh, this is wild, Tony!" Her hair was tangled, she was nude, and Tony, bathed in light from a dozen kerosene lamps, was posing naked for her, surrounded by a sea of daisies.

Cathy felt exhilarated. Her brushstrokes were bold and heavy. No one would accuse her of being cautious in this painting.

"Hey Babe, I'm happy you're havin' such a good old time in your Garden of Eden but I got only another fifteen minutes before these legs give out."

"Right!" As she painted Cathy dragged a stool across the floor with one foot then climbed on the stool to flesh out the detail at the top of the large canvas. She had been working since five in the afternoon, blocking out areas even before Tony arrived at eight. Now it was after midnight and the nude was almost finished.

"See how much work you get done when Vinnie's not here?"

"I know." Cathy puzzled over a shadow and added a dot of cobalt violet. "Poor Vin. It's not his fault though. Anyway . . . I miss him. When he's with Lester I wish he were here and when he's here. . . . Don't move!"

"I should be painting you at the same time," Tony laughed. "You look like a sexy demented witch. I love the slash of vermilion on your left boob."

"That's one of the liabilities of painting in the raw . . . now, don't move!"

"I'm going to ravish you under your easel."

"Good." Cathy clenched a brush between her teeth and reached for a larger rounded brush to smooth out the cobalt violet. "I love painting in this light," she said with the brush still in her teeth.

"Are you going to make me famous?" Tony teased, "like the Mona Lisa?"

Cathy laughed. "You don't need me to . . . now, don't move, Tony." How curious, she thought, that the total effect of his body was so moving when detail by detail there was nothing extraordinary about the separate parts. Actually his legs were too short to be in perfect proportion with his torso, yet even in repose his body seemed on the point of springing forth, action being implicit without any effort on his part. He was a child really, and sometimes his youth, the energy which he simply took for granted, stunned her, humbled her the way the Grand Canyon had done the first time she had seen it in the purple shadows, just seconds before the darkness swallowed it up. Because he was twenty-five he was unlike any other man she had ever encountered. Comparing him to Rosen was like juxtaposing apples and oranges, though they had the same male body, the same well-defined yet smooth musculature. She had seen young men like Tony escorting her two daughters. Escorting, hell: sleeping with. The ease with which they mingled with women had intrigued her, though as long as Laura and Aggie were under her roof she had not even engaged the young men in conversation for fear of indulging in the slightest flirtations, like a Mrs. Robinson. God forbid! She had a horror of being a Mrs. Robinson, of seducing some poor innocent young man.

But Tony wasn't innocent and most of the time, God bless him, she actually felt he was older than she was. She had come to depend on his opinions about her work in much the same way she depended on Lester's criticism, though of course Tony was not as well versed in art history and lacked Lester's experience. Still, he was astute and had a nice, constructive way of stating his criticism, like Lester. Tony called it being supportive, a word he used frequently together with words like "relationship," "space," and lately "karma." He believed his "relationship" with Cathy was "karma" and was (at least he insisted he was) completely satisfied with their situation because unlike most younger women, he said, Cathy had learned how important "space" was. He had no suspicion that on several occasions she had rather mechanically entertained the notion of having his child in order to cement the "karma." Of course she would never do it.

"I haven't ever seen you this fired up about a painting." Tony bent forward from the waist allowing his body to go limp before he resumed the pose. His lean face was all bones and impeccably serious except for his liquid dark eyes which seemed to send erotic messages even when he was doing nothing more than asking for milk in his coffee.

"It's that girl," Cathy said, "the big blond, Jone Beele—you met her—the one that went to school with Laura. She and her roommate, Angelica, my *enceinte* friend, they make me feel so guilty. God, they're so productive, those two . . . and not just turning out junk either. They work hard. Jesus, I felt so guilty whining around here in my eight-room mansion with a cleaning woman twice a week and . . ."

"So what's new? Stop feeling guilty, damn it!"

"Guilt can serve a positive purpose." Cathy crouched in front of her painting and considered a thigh tendon with a frown. The painting was far less abstract than her previous work and she was concerned about her technique. She needed to work harder and she knew it.

"What possible purpose can guilt serve? You'd better make it good," said Tony.

". . . can propel you into action. Isn't that what happened to me? The nun and the blond were a goddamned inspiration and here you see the results. Therefore, I am finished with guilt—except for positive guilt."

Tony dropped to the floor and assumed an exaggerated fetal position, rolling with laughter in front of Cathy's sea of daisies. "I love you." He staggered to his feet, still chortling. "What a morass of contradictions you are: a Calvinist, hedonistic, midwestern farm girl skipping through life in her Gucci shoes."

"Is it good?" Cathy stood back from the painting suddenly uncertain. She shivered and reached for her silk kimono.

"Such delicate feet." Tony walked over to her and ran his hands along her slender flanks, down her smooth muscular legs, and finally rested them lightly on the tops of her feet.

She should feel elated. It was possible now to rally her forces and be ready for the November show. She should call Zed Porter tomorrow and have him take a look; his praise would fortify her. Or Lester . . . she could call Lester and get his opinion.

Tony kissed her on the cheek and resumed his position. "I'm good for another hour."

Cathy was exhausted. Small chores—a get-well card for a fading uncle, a checkbook to be balanced, tennis shoes for Vinnie—filled her mind, preempting her professional concerns. Her mother's birthday was next week and she hadn't even sent a card. Well, she could wire some flowers, couldn't she? She felt annoyed with herself for holding on to the petty details of life. Why wasn't she like O'Keeffe, capable of leading a solitary life in her own Abiquiu? Alone? Alone in New Mexico with the coyotes? My God, she hated even to stay alone in the apartment and there were two doormen, neighbors, and a burglar alarm system. When Vinnie wasn't here and Tony didn't stay over she slept with the lights on.

"You're not quitting?" Tony's voice sounded far off. She answered "yes" and began cleaning her brushes. She was doomed to fail.

"Cathy?" Tony broke his pose and cuddled her for a moment

then held her at arm's length, studying her intently. "Baby? What is it?"

"It's me. I'm afraid of the dark." She felt stupid telling him and looked away. "I bet those girls downtown aren't afraid of the dark."

"Cathy, I don't understand what you're talking about."

"Fear. I'm talking about fear. I still sleep with the lights . . ."

"You're too hard on yourself." Tony hugged her.

"Or not hard enough. I feel old . . . like there's no way for me to break out of . . . I don't know. Sometimes I feel trapped but I can't see what's trapping me. Too often I feel I'm not living as myself."

"Well, you don't feel old to me." Tony caressed her head gently. "I think you can do anything you put your mind to. I really do."

Cathy bit her lip as the tears formed in her eyes. There was Tony being so "supportive"; God, she was going to miss him when. . . . Now, why was she thinking about his leaving when he was stroking her? Why couldn't she relax and give in to the sensations as she had done before that damned conversation with Lester?

Tony's chest was smooth, hardly any hair. She knew that someday he would leave. Someday she would not be enough for him and he would move on and there would be an empty space in her life and she would cry. Then the space would be filled and on and on and more tears and more and more. She would continue to feel weak and her work would continue to reflect her diffidence. Tomorrow Lester was bringing Vinnie home, they would exchange a few words, mostly about Vinnie, and then he would leave gracefully, without pressuring. He would never inquire whether or not she had discussed his solution with Tony; he would continue to leave the entire decision up to her.

These two men were so different from Rosen, who had been harsh, arrogant, taking everything for himself, leaving her and the girls practically for dead. She *did* love them both. Cathy closed her eyes, suddenly nauseated by the odors in the studio. How had she fallen so swiftly into despair?

"I'll take you out for pizza," Tony suggested.

"Let's make love first." Cathy swept around behind him, lowered her head and butted him out of the studio, down the hall to the guest room. Maybe it would be better tonight and if it was, then she would know what to do tomorrow when Lester came. If her body came alive as it had in the early days of their affair, she would have the answer.

Only it wasn't better and she resorted to fakery as she had been doing since that night at Dodin-Bouffant when Lester had made his absurd proposal. She wondered if Tony hadn't noticed her pretense and just wasn't saying anything—giving her "space." She nuzzled under his chin, praying to be miraculously aroused.

Jone was horrified at what she had done; not that she had slept with Bear, but that she had fallen into his bed blindly, witlessly, taking no precautions whatsoever. She woke up queasy and staggered into his bathroom the way she had watched Angelica do for the past two months. Trapped.

Hadn't her grandmother been trapped by six live children and two dead ones? Hadn't the children, a husband, the obligations of supervising, organizing, buying, and selling devoured her time and sapped her energy until there was nothing left? The answer was obvious. And hadn't she stopped painting, finally, after the fourth live child, and hadn't she, until they moved her off to a rest home some forty years later, lived with a stretched canvas next to her bed?

"Why, Grandmother?"

"Just in case . . ."

For forty years, *just in case*? What else was there to do but tease her about it? It was one of the few times she actually smiled, as Jone recalled. Why don't you paint, now that you have the time, her children urged her, Elizabeth's being the most poignant voice of the lot; but no, no, the time had gone by and nobody really knew why. Living with that canvas, Jone thought, was like keeping the corpse of a dead child around as a reminder.

And was Angelica any different? Wasn't she, despite her yoga, meditation, Carl Jung, quotes from T.S. Eliot, trips to psychics, and astro dance classes, trapped? How could Angelica, of all the women Jone knew, so determined, and so talented, not see that the risk she was taking was too great?

My God, at this very moment, she, Jone Beele, for all her historical platitudes might be a candidate for the biologically defeated! Jone pressed a cool cloth against her eyes. She reminded herself that this was 1980, but it did not seem so. Wasn't this the age of OPEC, abortions, solar energy, sexual freedom, human liberation, and nuclear power? She wanted comfort; she knew she would feel more at ease living in a cave on the side of a mountain. On her sixteenth birthday her mother, ever the liberal even if she was Catholic, had given Jone the liberated woman's manual: *Our Bodies, Ourselves.* It explained everything, Elizabeth had announced: how to, how not to; it gave information, anatomical names for parts of the body, facts to eliminate mystery. The thrust of its message—Responsibility!—was admirable, of course, and most of the women Jone's age claimed the book as their biological Bible. Who would argue against Responsibility?

But it was a slippery word; hard to hold on to. There were too many dark variables; in the end she too might be trapped. She did not believe in the curse of the Furies, but looking in Bear's toothpaste-splattered mirror she could feel them breathing down her neck.

She felt like a jerk leaving him a note so she simply left him cuddling a pillow against his soft stomach like a child. She knew he would feel rotten and rejected but how could she explain something to him which she did not understand herself?

When Jone arrived around dawn at the Obil studio she was shocked to find Angelica standing in front of her easel, one hand massaging the small of her back. The painting, executed in a controlled, linear style with a Botticelli-like elegance, was a still life in which the translucent pomegranates, lemons, onions, and walnuts gave off an aloof purity. The work, like others in the recent series of gouaches, had a definite, austere, religious quality which remained intact despite Angelica's use of highly saturated brilliant colors. The painting was fragile, filled with mystery, numinous, like Angelica herself.

"You haven't worked all night?" Jone felt her facial muscles arrange themselves in a statement of horror as her mother's had done yesterday. Her face was not her own, nor her mind, and certainly not her body.

"Nope." Angelica continued painting. "I went to bed early, got up at three, drank my quart of milk, did my yoga, said a coupla Hail Marys, and went to work. I love getting up in the middle of the night. I never could with Ferris. He'd come wandering in . . . was I all right, was I all right, was I all right? You know, whenever he wantd me to stop doing something he'd become frantic, suddenly, about my health, and you just can't tell someone who's *soooo* worried about you to go fuck himself." Angelica put her brush down and turned to Jone. "My God! Are *you* all right?"

"Sure," Jone smiled with her mother's face, and patted Angelica on the shoulder as she headed for the other room. "Met a guy. You know. I'm fine." I'm still breathing, she thought. I am alive. There's still time. I can make it up to her.

"You don't look fine." Angelica followed her.

"My grandmother's ill. After I had lunch with my mother I went to see her. It was a shock . . . that's all."

"Oh, no," cried Angelica. "The artist grandma you told me about, the one that went to the Art Students League and hung out with O'Keeffe at Stieglitz's 291?"

"Did I say that?" Jone snapped testily.

"You said . . ."

"She didn't know O'Keeffe. She was there around the same time . . . had some of the same . . . teachers, that's all." Jone stripped off her clothes and flung them in a heap.

"I'm really sorry. You were so close to her. Will she . . . ?"

Jone shrugged. "She's ninety. Who knows."

"If there's anything I can do . . . ?"

Jone went into the shower to wash off the dried semen. Had she actually told Angelica she was close to her grandmother? Was that true? Once she and Grandmother Mary had picked berries in the woods outside her grandmother's summer place. Silently avoiding the blackberry thorns, they had smiled at each other, and when Jone had found the partially decayed corpse of a red fox her grandmother had waited under a tree while Jone examined it, poking at the fur with a stick. Jone's mother would have screamed or thrown up at the sight but Grandmother Mary had waited in silence under a tree without saying no.

And later they had taken off their shoes and sat on a rock with their feet in the stream, popping berries into their mouths and listening to the rush of water. They had played canasta and watched sunsets together without sound; and once, when there was just the two of them, Mary had put on one of the boys' baseball caps backwards and sung some old ditty, clowning and kicking her legs for the amusement of her eight-year-old granddaughter. And that was all. Only those few memories but they were sharp and real like the metal she transformed into shapes.

The sacrificial child. How much easier, Jone thought resentfully, to have been the granddaughter of Georgia O'Keeffe, an image of strength, an iconoclast, not even bucking tradition but simply following the vision. Instead she was stuck with Mean Mary whom she loved, hated, and feared.

Ah, thought Jone, but you can't be the granddaughter of a woman who didn't have children—a woman who traded a family for work and was rumored to have referred to her paintings as children. Was there no middle ground between Georgia and Mary?

Jone attacked her body with a loofah sponge. What would happen to her if she ever did really love a man? How much of herself would she be willing to give, unwittingly, until it was perhaps too late to gain back not only her physical strength but her emotional and spiritual strength? Well, she probably never would fall in love like that, but what if?

Jone did not like the thoughts she was having and she scrubbed even harder as if to erase them. Children had trapped her grandmother, wasn't that right? Wasn't that what had finally depleted her Grandmother Mary's energies and stolen her spirit? Well, it wasn't necessary to give birth to eight children. But maybe even one was too many? One sick child or a child that needed and needed and needed . . . or a child one ended loving too much. The reality was, it wasn't possible to know how you would react until you were faced with the total responsibility for the well-being of another human being. Before the fact it was all conjecture, after the fact it was too late. Her older sister had a friend who had been adamant about not wanting children but she loved her husband and he had convinced his wife that his life would be incomplete without children. Now her sister's friend had two children under six and no husband. Of course she had child support and even a generous alimony settlement but the children were hers. There were, to be sure, the Kramer-vs.-Kramers, but mostly there were mothers and children and more children and mothers. Jone knew no one would ever suspect her of having such dark unnatural thoughts. Angelica was always telling her she had a finely honed maternal instinct, Cathy had lately taken to calling her for advice until she felt like *her* mother, her brother's kids flocked to her side at family gatherings, and even strange children in the park seemed to zero in on her. Or was she imagining it?

She was angry in a way she had never been angry in her life. She had no temper, they all said so. She was docile, *too* docile, her father said. "Healthy," said her mother Elizabeth, "well-adjusted, easygoing, she rolls with the punches." Passive.

She had snapped at Angelica before getting into the shower and now almost in a rage she wanted to run dripping into the studio and scream that Angelica was playing some crazy game, deceiving herself into thinking that in this world she could bring up a child and continue her work. And she wanted to call up Cathy and tell her she was a middle-aged neurotic, just like her own mother, worrying and fretting over children who didn't need it, meddling, playing the goddamned martyr!

Jesus, she should have never gone to visit her grandmother! That was what all of this was about. She was like a sponge where her grandmother was concerned, sopping up all of Mary's anger, misery, and resentment. Even as a child she had taken on her grandmother's moods as if her own suffering would in some way alleviate the terrible pain she sensed in the older woman. It almost seemed that Mary was capable of possessing her with her demonic spirit.

The rest of the family hated Mary Jones, she was sure of it. Even Elizabeth, though of course it was complicated and she would never admit to anything less than the appropriate filial feelings. Two of Mary's children had written her off entirely, not even corresponding with her for the past ten years! (Was that the reward for being a mother?) Drastic actions, thought Jone, from well-brought-up Westchester children. The rest of the grandchildren smirked and joked—every family had its cross to bear.

The shower dribbled and finally stopped altogether. Jone did not notice and toweled herself dry without bothering to rinse off the soap. Why had Mary Jones, with fifteen other grandchildren to choose from, decided to reveal herself to Jone—for that, Jone was convinced, was what had happened. Mary Jones had claimed her while she was still too young to resist, had left fragments of herself and of her past for the child, Jone, to glimpse. And why? It couldn't have been merely the innocuous spelling of Jone's name, which was nothing more than Elizabeth's poetic peace offering to a mother who had done everything to thwart her.

Even as a child Mary's frequent lapses into melancholy had chilled Jone. Without really thinking about it, Jone suited up in her flameproof apron, gauntlet gloves, and soundproof earmuffs and went to work on a new piece: *Lilith.* She had made preparatory notes and sketches for several weeks and now she worked, almost automatically it seemed, her mind dwelling in some muted, nonverbal past. When she was too exhausted to manipulate the torch she went into the other room and slept. After five days of concentrated work the torso was finished except for the final polishing. Only it did not resemble the preliminary sketches, did not resemble a human torso at all. It was gnarled, an almost primitive form, and something in its tight curves reminded her of her grandmother. When Angelica studied the huge amorphous sculpture, she said it looked like it could not have been made from metal, for it seemed to have no edges, seemed rather formed of clay or cut from marble.

"What will you call it?" Angelica wanted to know; one of her great joys was naming her paintings.

"Not Lilith anymore . . . I don't know." Jone threw on a raincoat on over her work clothes. "You're out of milk."

"You don't have to go out in the . . ." Angelica protested but Jone waved her off.

"I need air."

The thing she had created frightened her. Angelica was right, it was good; but it still frightened her. She bought two quarts of milk and a package of Fig Newtons for Angelica but she felt feverish and the rain had slacked, so she walked until she found herself in front of McSorley's Bar. She ducked her head inside to make sure Bear wasn't around, then went in and ordered a beer.

She did not lack passion. She knew that now. The piece was telling her that. She wasn't like her mother or her sister or most of their friends, but she did not lack passion. She had thought she did.

Very calmly she finished her beer. There was one sure way to stop the panic and avoid the motherhood trap and she finally understood what it was. As soon as her show was over she would make the arrangements. Yes, with the Right-to-Lifers breathing down the neck of the Supreme Court, there was only one sure way of preparing for the future. Jone smiled at the bartender and went out into the drizzle and back home to Angelica with the milk and the Fig Newtons.

SEPTEMBER 1980

New York City

"They're not bad . . . are they, Zed?" Cathy sat perched on a counter littered with tubes of paint and Yuban coffee cans filled with brushes as Zed Porter, her gallery owner, perused her new work.

"They're fine." Zed, who was known more for his business acumen and his laconic prowess with women than for his effusiveness, gave a charming but typically oblique smile.

"You shit!" Cathy screamed. "They're not just fine, they're better than any goddamned thing I've done."

"Well, they're very different."

"So?"

". . . such a departure from . . . and I mean, this one, with the young buck and your son. How does Lester feel about that?"

Cathy struck her hand against her head, too hard. "Did you just say that? Am I hearing things? My God, I thought you guys loved the sensational and now all of a sudden you . . ."

"I've been a friend of Lester's for . . ."

"Jesus!" Cathy leaped off the counter, turning over several cans which clattered to the floor. "Get out of here."

"Let's talk." Zed started toward Cathy with a conciliatory outstretched arm.

"No!"

"You've misunderstood . . ."

"No, I haven't. Either the paintings are good or bad. Lester doesn't enter into it. Just get out of here!" Cathy lunged at the suave man whose Madison Avenue gallery, one of the most prestigious in the world, had shown her work for nine years.

"Catherine . . . calmly, calmly . . . let's . . ."

"No, I'm not calm." Cathy clenched her fists to keep from slugging him. She wanted to fight. She actually wanted to take him on.

"You forget Lester introduced me to your work." Zed, who was several years younger than Cathy, adopted a patient, paternal tone. "If it hadn't been for Lester . . ."

"You're telling me if it hadn't been for Lester my work wouldn't have received the attention, the critical notices . . . wouldn't have brought bucks into your establishment? Listen. I was well on my way before I started showing at Porter Gallery. Just because Lester introduced us doesn't give you . . ."

"I think you should lower your voice and the two of us should go for a nice martini, have some lunch, and talk this thing out."

"No! You think, the same as most of Lester's friends, that the only reason I married him ten years ago was to *use* him. 'Poor Lester,' is what you think, and now 'poor, poor Lester,' because the slut is sleeping with . . ."

"Catherine, nobody called you . . ."

"We would not be having this discussion if I were a man and you know it. You would not dare criticize my . . . my content! The paintings are either good or bad and that is the end of it!"

Cathy opened the front door and before she could shove him out he had the good grace to leave. She slammed the door, then leaned against the jamb trying to preserve her anger against Porter. Christ, people had been expecting her to double-cross Lester since they were married in 1970!

She wandered stoically into the living room, flinging herself onto the couch into an attitude of classic despair. The shits! When Lester had singled her out at that first show in '69, the tongues had shifted into automatic, wagging about how conniving she was to latch herself onto one of the most influential men in the business, gossiping about her past, making lurid predictions about her future. Even her own friends, loyal feminists picketing the Museum of Modern Art, had sensed her supposed, underlying motivation and (1) accused her of selling out or (2) cynically congratulated her for her cunning.

And it seemed they had all been right. Cathy tried to remember the early days with Lester: their initial encounter at the Ludlow Gallery where her first major show had been held replete with celebrities, collectors, champagne, and an impressive glossy color catalog of her work. She had rarely experienced the glittering first night of art shows because Rosen had not believed in either champagne or civility and had always made it a point to be absent from his openings.

The night of her show, Cathy had relished the crowd of fashionable spectators, finding humor in the abundance of phoniness and pedantry. Lester Aimsley had been a quiet, distinguished, white-haired gentleman at the far end of the gallery. He had stood so long in front of one of her paintings, *The Fuller Flower,* a 40-by-60-inch oil of the Fuller Building, that eventually his silence had drawn her to him out of curiosity to know what exactly he was finding in the painting to engage his attention for such a long time. As far as she knew, he was simply another guest, rich no doubt, a potential buyer. As far as he was concerned, she was a pretty child, for, at thirty-five she looked little more than twenty with her long hair tied back with a red ribbon and the lacy collar of her frilly Victorian blouse rising to the pointy chin of her valentine-shaped face.

He had called *The Fuller Flower* a vital, energetic abstraction in which one could see (she remembered his exact words!) "the progression through realism beyond a conventional interpretation of expressionism." Too embarrassed then to allow him to continue praising the piece, she had owned up to being the artist and he had been as delighted as a child that "such unprecedented power could come from such a delicate form." In the midst of so much loud, effusive commendation Lester Aimsley's quiet, decorous response had had a real and soothing effect on her, beyond flattery. She had liked what he had seen in her painting and although she would never have phrased it as he had, his interpretation and skill in pinpointing what for her had been mostly hard work with a modicum of "inspiration" somehow opened her eyes to her own potential for growth. As a former critic he could tell her things about her work she might never have seen. From the start she had trusted both his instincts and his intentions so that she had *heard* what he was saying without feeling threatened.

After that first evening which still, when she recalled it, gave her the feeling of having met someone one has always known, there followed weeks of concerts, lingering lunches, her first white truffles, long loquacious walks and no, not even a trace of tension. She had been unable to imagine a quarrel with such a man and remarkably, for she was not known for her control, there had never been one. It had never occurred to her that they would marry even though from the start she had found she preferred Lester's company to anyone else's. But was that love? Love minus sex, was that love? Love plus sex, was that love?

But Lester had wanted them to make a home together and her daughters had adored him. There had been warmth and a home, her work and her family for the first time in her life. She had been happy. Only then she had become afraid that she was using him, and to console herself, and prove to herself and to the world that theirs was more than a marriage of convenience, she had decided to have his child. A simple solution, one he had not asked for, but once it became a fact, something of a miracle to him.

The irony was that for years before she met Lester people had urged her to stop turning out floral paintings for DAR ladies and get on with her serious work. Forget that she had two small daughters whose lives, both economic and emotional, were entirely dependent on her since Rosen in his self-absorption had not calculated the possibility of a future for anyone other than himself. His friends had scoffed at the money she made on the floral paintings and later on at the sheets she had designed. They had teased her for succumbing to the midwestern Puritan work ethic, accused her of self-deception for equating money with fulfillment. And when she had married a man who could provide her with emotional, physical, and financial *space* they had accused her of . . .

There was no way to win.

"Go to another gallery." Angelica sat with her legs curled under her on the red-cushioned banquette at the Russian Tea Room. She was on her third glass of milk, Cathy was on her third vodka.

"Cathy, it's simple. You don't need Zed Porter. He needs you."

"Why is that simple?" Cathy frowned and lit another cigarette. The cigarettes tasted horrible but that was what she did when she felt like killing herself.

"Cathy," Angelica began for the third time to explain, "there is some gallery who will take your work. It may not be as flashy as *Porter* but someone out there would *die* to give you a show. If you believe in the paintings . . ."

"I do," Cathy said automatically, without conviction.

"You're Catherine Aimsely. People pay attention to you. You have a gallery in Paris . . . show your new stuff there and shove the brilliant reviews down his . . ."

"But maybe he's right. Maybe the paintings are . . . I don't want to hurt Lester. What the hell am I going to do?"

"Oh, listen, I'm getting pissed off."

Cathy looked up, sobered.

"The paintings *are* good. Anyway, what's good? We could sit here and talk about that for the next millennium. Do I know what's good? Does Hilton Kramer? Who knows? We do the work, let people have a look, and hope we can buy our apples and oranges as a result. Anyway, what do I know?"

"I think you know a lot more than I do." Cathy allowed the tears to stream down her face.

"Don't cry." Angelica, reminded of her mother, reached for Cathy's hand.

"Well, I am a shit," Cathy sniffed, "and a baby, and I can't stop crying. Porter wants to see more stuff so he can put the catalog together for the show . . . Jesus. He sends messages to me through Vinnie because I won't talk to him on the phone. Poor Vinnie. Lester's in England . . . I don't know." Cathy sank deeper into the red cushions.

"Call Porter. Give him an ultimatum."

Cathy shook her head miserably.

"So," Angelica shrugged impatiently, "wait for Lester to come home or Tony . . . or call your grandson to take care of it. Listen . . . I envy your dilemma so maybe I'm not the best . . ."

"You're right!" Cathy sat up straight and looked reluctantly at Angelica. "I bet you wonder how I raised two daughters."

Angelica shook her head, again thinking of her own mother who had fretted so long and hard about her own inadequacies that eventually she had become inadequate.

"Well, it's good Jone sold those pieces." Cathy's smile was sincere. "Is she ecstatic?"

Angelica smiled. "Jone is too composed to be ecstatic. She is perhaps the only enlightened twenty-two-year-old extant."

"I know I'm a bore, Angelica, but I do appreciate your listening to me. I've already bored all my old friends so I'm branching out to the new ones."

Angelica laughed. "You're not boring. Look, I'm meeting someone at the Whitney for the Hopper show . . . you're welcome to come along but . . ."

"Go!" Cathy waved her off. "Don't worry, I'll sport you to the milk."

Cathy stared after Angelica's expanding black figure. Was it her imagination or did the sophisticated crowd actually part as she moved to the door? Danced to the door. *The Girls Downtown*—that was how she thought of Jone and Angelica, and "downtown" was a remote world, as remote as Wayne, Ohio. "Downtown" the music was different and the smells, the clothes, and the mingling of the sexes were different, too. Tony was at home downtown, even Lester was more at home downtown than she was. How was it that Georgia O'Keeffe, as much of a midwesterner as she was, was not afraid of the dark? Maybe Rosen and his crowd had been right. Maybe women were intellectually and morally inferior and maybe O'Keeffe was nothing more than the exception to the rule.

Cathy ordered another vodka and settled in, almost comfortably, having forgotten that she was alone. Maybe she should paint them, that unlikely couple: the oafish blond covering her Rubenesque body in baggy army pants; Angelica a swift dark line made perfectly in one movement. Yes, paint them in their strange clothes with their uncompromising eyes. Her mother would call them "unfeminine" but Cathy knew better. What they were was UFOs. Yes, they were proof and she would paint them and in their midst she would put the body of a naked man, as Manet had done in *Le Déjeuner sur l'Herbe,* where he planted the glowing, milk-white body of a woman between two well-attired nineteenth-century gentlemen. The woman's body was as ripe and lush as the fruit which remained from their picnic. The implication was aesthetic, not social, but very erotic. The woman's body was incandescent in the midst of the male umbers and Tony's body would be the same in her painting—supine and rich. But would the girls be seated like the men in Manet's painting or perhaps standing in a contemporary pose? And where would they be?

The goldenrod grew as mighty and tall as oaks in Ohio and the fields were dotted with thistles, prickly and purple. A rose could not compare with a thistle, and how long had it been since she had walked in the fallow fields where her father had once grown corn to feed the Chester Whites? Maybe twenty years? And there was no mud in September, no reason not to go.

But how could the girls survive in a field of goldenrod? They could, of course, because they were *The Girls Downtown.*

Cathy made a rapid, bungling exit from the Russian Tea Room, digging desperately in her purse for her wallet, dropping her change. She chuckled, recalling Angelica's graceful floating departure.

Face it, kid, you will never be a *grande dame* despite your Guccis and your pearls. Resign yourself to being small and slightly silly.

"Vinnie!" she shouted as she let herself in the dark apartment. "Vinnie, how would you like to fly with me to Ohio and stay at Gram's for a few days?"

"Can I take my skates?"

"Where will you skate in Wayne . . . there's only fields. We'll be lucky if we don't drown in mud. Pray to God it doesn't rain . . ."

"Then I don't want . . ."

"There's nobody to look after . . . your Dad is . . . oh, damn, there goes that idea."

Vinnie grinned. "Go without me. Where's Tony?"

"Away."

"I'll stay at Steve's."

Cathy shook her head.

"I'll stay with Mrs. Morgenstein."

Cathy shook her head.

"Laura . . . I can help her with . . ."

"I can't impose on Laura. She's got enough to do with the baby and the book she's writing." Cathy felt the knots retying themselves. She couldn't go. She couldn't leave poor Vinnie. She would just have to stay. She slumped down on the sofa and leafed through a magazine, trying to look interested.

"Oh, all right," said Vinnie. "But I really don't think you want me along."

It was true, she didn't. "Of course I do," she smiled at her son and hugged him.

"Just don't blame me if I'm in the way and you worry about me. You coulda left me here."

"Vinnie, you're starting to talk like a goddamned analyst. Oh, what the hell! Call Laura and see if it's okay."

"Yea!" Vinnie gave her a hug and raced off to call his half-sister.

"So you're a friend of Catherine Aimsley?" Dr. Fuseli smiled like a man who wanted to be nice and pumped Jone's hand. He gestured for Jone to sit, then took a seat behind his very large, immaculate desk. There were no papers on the desk, only one solitary pink rose. On the wall behind him were pictures of various mammals and their offspring, a photograph of a poodle catching a ball, and a photograph of Dr. Fuseli with his brother, a former United States Senator.

"Well, well." Dr. Fuseli withdrew Jone's folder from his drawer, glanced at it briefly and returned it hastily to the drawer so as not to litter up his desk. "I understand you're thinking of having your Fallopian tubes blocked off?"

"Not thinking," said Jone. "Going to."

"I see." Fuseli smiled understandingly. "And what does Mrs. Aimsely think of your idea?"

"I didn't tell her."

"But you said you were friends."

Jone looked at him steadily, waiting for him to continue.

"You're very young to contemplate this sort of . . ."

"I'm not contemplating it, Doctor. I don't want children. Ever. According to New York City law I have to be over twenty-one to undergo sterilization. I'm twenty-two."

Dr. Fuseli chuckled lightly as if she had made an amusing point. "Well well. Miss Belle, I'm not being presumptuous in asking you these few questions, I don't think. You know that for all intents and purposes the tubal ligation is irreversible. This is a decision you will have to live with for the rest of your life."

"I know that."

"It's important for me to understand . . . to know that *you* understand."

"I do. I do understand."

Fuseli cleared his throat uncomfortably. "Most of my patients are women in their forties who have several children."

"I've given this a lot of thought."

"It's just . . . a young woman like you . . . there are so many reliable means of contraception. Look, Miss Belle, if you came in with your husband and said the two of you had arrived at a decision to remain childless I would feel confident that you had . . ."

"I've no intention of getting married, Doctor."

"I see." Doctor Fuseli stared at Jone a moment, then shook his head. "I know it's become a rather trendy . . ."

Jone laughed unexpectedly. "Do I look like a trendy person?"

"I'm just doing my job." Fuseli smiled to hide his irritation.

"I know you are."

"Sometimes I suggest a woman have a psychiatric consultation before . . ."

"I'm not going to do that. My decision is moral. I was brought up a Catholic. I believe in abortion, on principle, but I don't think I . . . I can't afford to squander my energy worrying about . . ."

"All right, there are several techniques. The one I would recommend for you is a minilaparotomy. It requires a small incision above the pubic bone, the tube is cut and secured with a band. The procedure usually takes about thirty minutes using a local anesthetic. You can leave the hospital the same day, barring complications which I do not foresee."

"How soon?"

"I don't see why we can't schedule you for next week. My secretary will phone you. Oh, yes, the fee is five hundred dollars. If money is a problem I'm sure you can get it for less at Planned Parenthood."

Jone shook her head. "I have the money."

"Well." Fuseli stood up and gripped Jone's hand again. "I think you know what you're doing. You've thought it all out. I'm confident of that."

"Thank you, Doctor."

It was hot and muggy on Fifth Avenue; a bluish vapor hung over St. Patrick's Cathedral. Jone stood outside Fuseli's office building and studied St. Patty's, which had been restored to its original resplendence with steam cleaning for the Pope's visit in '79. She didn't like Fuseli and toyed with the idea of checking out another doctor except it would take too much time. Besides, Fuseli was one of the best and, judging from the sterility of his office decor, he should have no problem rendering her equally sterile.

She crossed the street and waded through the Japanese tourists and their fancy cameras to enter St. Patrick's. Inside it was cool and fragrant with the heavy odors of her childhood. She had not been inside a church in four years, not since her sister's marriage. She found a statue of the Virgin and knelt down.

Dear Mary, Mother of God. The Pope will not understand but I think you will.

For the first time in her life the act of crossing herself did not feel like a superficial gesture.

PART THREE

"How much courage it took to go beyond the image one has lived with, to move on to the next concept."
Beverly Pepper, sculptor

SEPTEMBER 1980

New York City

Angelica's desk, one of a dozen identical white laminated boards laid across chrome sawhorses, faced a wall covered with gaudy posters advertising the latest grade-B films. Far Out Inc. specialized in designing graphics for inferior films and uninspired rock albums. Everyone who worked there was young and groovy and into a lot of other things. Like Angelica, their jobs with FOI supported their outside artistic habits. No one that Angelica had spoken with, and she spoke very little when she put in her six hours from four to ten, worked at Far Out Inc. with the idea of moving to the top of the corporate ladder. Everyone at Far Out was looking for a way out.

However, the money was good and Angelica blessed Catherine Aimsley every time she picked up her pencil. By the time the baby arrived in January she would have saved enough to live, albeit frugally, for the next six months without taking an outside job. Ideally she would like to find a gallery, at least one which would take her work on consignment, before the baby was born; but she was making every effort to be realistic and that just might not happen. She was trying not to project goals in terms of time; she was simply studying and working.

It seemed to her that the weight of the child inside her was grounding her, connecting her to what was real in herself. Freed from Ferris's critical eye, her own vision was coming into focus. The world had new colors and these she transmitted to her work in a new, highly controlled style. Although she was still focused on still lifes in her work, it was color, now, which absorbed her when she went to museums and galleries—color and light. One entire afternoon was spent gazing at the Vermeers in the Metropolitan, another evaluating Van Gogh's yellow, the earth tones of Cézanne, Matisse's pink. At night her dreams were unprecedented rainbows and whereas in the past she might have been content to be dominated by the suffusion, she now insisted on a more analytical, less abstract approach. She knew at least that her concern and fascination with color would have to be connected to some meaningful content. For her, form alone would never suffice.

It was odd, at thirty-four, to be one of the two oldest employees working in an establishment, but on the other hand she considered it a benefit. With Ferris she had always felt flimsy; at Far Out Inc. she felt positively monolithic. She knew her coworkers thought she was unfashionably weird, as opposed to fashionably eccentric like themselves. Occasionally she was tempted to boost her ego by revealing her most fetching absurdist traits. All she would have needed to do was show them the satirical drawings she had made for *Lavender Bog*, an ostensibly erotic movie about two half-naked, idiotic-looking adolescents trapped in a bog in south Jersey. The film was the blockbuster of the summer and whenever things became unbearably dull or she felt herself on the verge of depression, Angelica would entertain herself drawing grotesque genitals coming out of the loony-eyed boy's ears. However, she resisted the impulse to become the darling of Far Out Inc. and took the drawings home to Jone instead.

"This is better than the stuff we saw last Saturday," Jone commented over the Thursday night tuna fish casserole she had prepared for them.

"Don't remind me." Angelica felt a twinge of hopelessness. There was a dearth of good art at most of the Soho galleries.

"Seeing that crap inspired me," said Jone. "I can't help but succeed."

"It was so ugly." Angelica winced as she recalled entering one prestigious gallery where the show consisted of free-standing papier-mâché walls on which the artist had scratched out obscenities and graffiti. Entering the gallery was like getting on the West Side IRT subway.

"Who needs that?" Angelica was on her feet in a rage. "There's no illuminating social comment in *Fuck You*: no technique—no . . ."

"Finish your dinner," Jone soothed. "You haven't started trying to find a gallery. You will. Your work is . . ."

"I know it's better, I know, I know, I know." Angelica sat back down at the table and struggled with black despair. "But my work was better, more interesting, more intelligent than that crap five years ago and I couldn't . . . oh, you don't want to hear this again."

"I don't mind." Jone helped herself to more casserole. "I added thyme, do you like it?"

Angelica sighed and put her head down on the table and cried. A moment later she looked up, smiling. "You're such a good influence on me. Let's get married!"

Jone guffawed as Angelica continued.

"I forgot to tell you, I had an appointment with Dr. Nigel today. He asked about you."

"Me?" Jone stopped laughing suddenly. She had confided in no one about her recent surgery but had checked into New York University Medical Center early one morning and left the same evening, arriving home before Angelica was back from work.

"What's the matter?" Angelica asked.

"Why did your doctor . . ."

"Silly!" Angelica exclaimed. "You . . . Mr. Stein. He asked about Mr. Stein. You're the only Mr. Stein in my life, you goose."

"Oooooh," Jone sighed. Angelica's doctor always referred to her as Mrs. Stein so Angelica had obligingly created a Mr. Stein, a dependable and affluent Wall Street broker, eager to participate in the birth of his child, determined to share in the later nurturing.

"I told him that Mr. Stein—I think I referred to him as Arnie—was as excited as I was about taking the Lamaze classes. You're still willing to do it, aren't you?"

"Of course." Jone smiled, relieved. Several times she had been at the point of telling Angelica what she had done, only the words would not form themselves. It was her secret, hers alone, and she told herself there was nothing wrong in that. They had cut chunks out of her tubes, she had felt nothing. Certainly she had not felt remorse, not really. Dr. Fuseli had stared at her prior to the procedure, scrutinizing her for signs of hysteria, a flicker, even, of trepidation. She had taken responsibility, yes? She had removed, for all time, one obstacle from her course, thus fortifying her commitment to her work. It was all right to keep that a secret, wasn't it? All this talk of openness, Jone thought, could be carried to extremes. There was still some value in privacy, wasn't there? And this was like a sacred covenant with herself. It concerned no one else. The only reason it was on her mind so much now was that she was still adjusting to the idea that she would never have to be concerned about that biological aspect of her life again. In a few weeks she probably wouldn't even be thinking of it any more.

"I still think," Angelica prattled on, "that you should reconsider going through the whole ordeal in drag."

"Won't they let me in the delivery room unless I'm a man?"

"Sure they will but it wouldn't be as much fun. Laughter is healing. Imagine laughing the baby out . . . a new method. Ha! I wonder if anyone's thought of it? I could write a book: *Laugh Your Child into Life*. Actually I'd like to have the baby here in our own home but Dr. Nigel is balking. Anyway, it's too expensive, you know, to hire . . . I thought of asking my parents for a loan."

"You should ask Ferris."

"Never!"

"Then what about your parents?"

"I don't know," Angelica mused. "They'll worry. It's a drain to have people worry about you . . . you know, it makes you feel so weak. It's one thing if I'm worried about me; I can handle that. No, I don't think I'll tell them. I'll wait till I can present them with their healthy grandchild. It will be a real test of their liberal principles to see how they take to little Zoe."

"Angelica, aren't you a little nervous about naming the kid before . . ."

"It's either Zoe or Zeus, and yes, I am nervous but I'd be nervous if I didn't do it. If it bothers you I'll keep quiet about it when you're around."

"That's all right," Jone smiled.

"You seem sad," Angelica observed. "Ever since your show and selling those three pieces you seem melancholy. Are you worried about having the baby underfoot around here?"

"I swear I never thought about it."

"Me neither." Angelica frowned. "It could be a problem."

Jone shook her head. "I don't think so. I've got my earmuffs."

"That's right!" Angelica cried. "Jesus, if I believed in fate and all that, I'd say you and I were destined for each other."

Jone stood up from the table and stacked the dishes. "I think I'm going for a beer. Want to join me?"

"Fat chance you have of having fun with a pregnant nun at your table." Angelica took the plates from Jone and moved toward the sink. "I want to get in three hours of work tonight. Tomorrow's my holiday . . . all day with Picasso. I may even add some padding to my stomach. I can't imagine the guards asking a docile pregnant woman to leave the museum, can you? Of course I won't be wearing my habit."

"I think you should do a self-portrait," Jone said on her way to the door. "I've always thought so."

"Maybe." Angelica stared at the stack of dirty dishes. A roach scuttled across the counter but she did not scream at it as she usually did. Screaming took energy and she needed all the energy she could summon up.

Angelica stood outside the Museum of Modern Art savoring the last of a large Baskin-Robbins vanilla cone. This was the first full day off she had had in over three months and she couldn't have asked for more perfect weather, the temperature a cool, dry sixty-eight, the sky cloudless like a brilliant opaque blue canvas. Fifty-third Street was like a carnival. It had been that way for the duration of the Picasso exhibition and several times Angelica had stopped on her way home from Far Out Inc. just to watch the crowd, the eclectic group of Picassophiles. Today, the long-haired students with backpacks and hiking boots were sitting on the sidewalk, their faces turned toward the sun. There were the usual sleek limousines, the chatting white-haired matrons on their way to lunch after their allotted time inside the museum. The city was mad for Picasso. There were Picasso pennants, Picasso T-shirts—everything was Picasso. Even Hoving, head of Tiffany's, was hiring Picasso's daughter, Paloma, to design jewelry, for the name itself was pure gold, the mere signature familiar.

Angelica had secured her ticket months ago and now, on the point of finally getting inside, eager as she was, she felt reluctant to leave the crowd. She studied the faces, moved by the diversity of form, line, and plane. It was as if the man, the great God Picasso, so diverse himself, had conjured up the crowd as a reflection of the many faces of reality which he had portrayed. The outside of the museum, thought Angelica, was perhaps the true measure of the man.

Inside Angelica spent much of her time studying the progression of the great man's work, the unnatural evolution from *Corina Pere Romeu* in 1902 to the 1905 portrait of *Woman with a Fan* to *Woman-Flower* in 1946, and finally, Angelica's favorite, *Jacqueline with Black Scarf,* painted in 1954. Having taken a fairly cursory look at the rest of the exhibit, she moved back and forth between these four paintings hoping to shed some new light on her own artistic development. Without question she was most enthralled by the portraits.

She was having a cup of chowder in the cafeteria overlooking the sculpture garden when she saw Ferris standing next to one of the Rodins, looking up, perhaps at a plane or the top of some building, his hand shading his eyes. He was wearing his familiarly ill-fitting Levi pants and jacket but the pants, she noted, were baggier than usual. He looked like a gnome receding into a giant's clothes. He shoved his hands in his pants pockets, hitching them up slightly as she had seen him do hundreds of times before, and swayed back and forth, still gazing steadily upwards at the now fading light.

How odd to see him here, she thought, for time after time he had disdained the works of Picasso as if it were possible to neutralize such a vast and threatening talent through criticism.

She had argued that he might disagree with various works, with various styles and periods even, but that it was blind and stupid to disregard Picasso entirely. But there had never been room for her opinion and he had scorned her for idolizing Picasso, whom he accused of being a "media man," a "master of gimmicks." Now Matisse was another matter. Matisse was a true innovator with taste, so were Kandinsky and Cézanne and, it went without saying, Rembrandt and David, but other than those five artists, for Ferris there were only inferior doodlers. In the past it had irked Angelica that he could condense and telescope art history so efficiently without any doubts whatsoever; now, however, watching him craning his neck still searching out some mysterious sight in the sky, she found herself laughing out loud at him. Viewed from this perspective, the balding awkward man who had abused and insulted her was a sad, clownlike figure dwarfed both by the city and the greatness of the Moores, the Rodins, and the Nadelmans.

Would it be malicious to creep up behind him, to simply be sitting there when he stopped searching the skyline? She knew the look that would come to his face, how he would immediately twist his surprised, initial reaction into a controlled, stern expression. Ferris was never one to enjoy surprises, viewing them as an invasion, an insult to his mastery of life.

Odd how her reaction to him was still the same as it had always been. She had always wanted to tease him out of his agony, to startle and shock him.

She concluded that she was not being malicious, that any other form of greeting him would be inappropriate. The truth was she was even happy to see him.

"Hi," she said softly.

He was lighting a cigarette next to a fecund reclining Henry Moore figure and he did not look up when she spoke.

"Hi," she repeated but he only exhaled the smoke and closed his eyes as if her voice had been in his mind. Then—and it must have been the sense of her presence, for she said nothing else but simply stood next to him—his eyes snapped open.

"I might have known," he exclaimed, starting to smile, stopping himself, then smiling in spite of himself. "I might have known you'd catch me here."

"But I know you're not here to see the Picassos . . . you just came for a smoke."

"Right," he laughed and through his laughter she saw him take in the well-rounded protrusion beneath the loose black dress. "I heard you were in New York."

"I suspected I'd see you, too." She sat down next to him on the low wall. "Your retrospective opens at the beginning of October, right?"

"How are you?"

"I'm pregnant." She smiled, looking down at her mound of tummy.

"I wondered." He bit his lip, nodded, then looked back up at the sky. "Most expensive air in the world."

"Oh, you mean where they're going to add on to the museum? Very weird, don't you think . . . air rights? Something spooky about air rights." She shivered.

"I was going to call you." He scratched his head miserably.

"I'm sure. We would have met . . . I mean . . . look, Ferris, I don't want to spend time regretting . . ."

"I've sure as hell spent time doing that."

"I am glad to see you." She touched his elbow firmly until he turned and looked at her. "I'm doing all right . . . have a job, a great place to live with a sculptor . . . a woman who likes to cook with thyme the way you loved the rosemary. And I'm working hard and . . . getting somewhere. I'm enjoying the city, the craziness . . ."

"You teaching again?"

"No." She didn't want to tell him about Far Out Inc. She might be able to make everyone else laugh about the goings-on there but Ferris would find it too insignificant and that would sting, even now.

"Could we have dinner?"

"I want to go back inside," she said. "I'd planned on sneaking in for another look at *Jacqueline with Black Scarf*."

"I'm staying at Rex's . . ."

"I figured you'd stay there." Suddenly it was too painful to talk to him and not to answer his question, the one question he wanted her to answer and the one question he would never ask. In spite of not wanting to, she felt angry—not at anything in their past together, not at the bruises or the ugly words, but at his inability, in the present, to ask a simple question about the paternity of her child. She even wondered if he would have mentioned her all-too-apparent pregnancy if she had not.

The palms of her hands were wet, she was angrier with him now than she had ever been during their years together. She was not given to bursts of blinding anger but she wanted to scream until the shock of her voice shattered his damned anti-social composure, until he begged her to stop. *Whose child is it?*

As usual, he was sidestepping any communication with his silence, waiting for her to place the power back in his hands.

"If you want to phone me . . ." She scribbled her phone number on a piece of paper and handed it to him. The child inside her kicked hard for the first time as she hurried back inside the museum to study the best portrait Picasso had done of his last wife.

"I'm not going to talk about it." Catherine Aimsley was perched incongruously on Jone's steel-and-bronze-littered work table. Today Cathy looked very '40s with her light brown hair in a sophisticated upsweep, slim skirt, dangerously high heels, and a creamy crepe blouse with padded shoulders.

"For once in my life I am not going to dissipate my work, the impetus for breaking new ground, by blabbing about what I'm doing. I didn't even tell Tony! Can you imagine? Lester had an inkling of where I might be headed but not because I've shown him anything or talked about what I've been painting out in Wayne. He just always *knows*. I'm afraid Vinnie has inherited his father's frightening critical clairvoyance. I hate mothers who rattle on about how extraordinary their kids are, but Vinnie really is!"

Jone laughed as she shoved a heavy cast-iron torso out of the center of her work space.

"God, you're strong," Cathy said in an awed voice. "Did you pose for that yourself?" She jumped off the table and examined the voluptuous seven-foot piece. "Sexy," she whistled. "Is this the one the Whitney is having another look at?"

Jone shrugged. "Angelica shouldn't have told anyone. The Whitney does a lot of looking. They have a very large permanent collection that nobody ever sees. It doesn't . . ."

"Very sanguine, my dear," Cathy observed.

"Angelica gets excited enough for both of us."

"Don't talk about me," Angelica cried from the other room. "I'm depressed and I only want praise. I'm coming in now with the spinach painting I told you about and I want you to . . ."

"Jesus." Jone dropped the bronze rods she was clearing from her work table and ran into the other room to help Angelica lug in the huge canvas for Cathy to have a look.

"You idiot! I told you not to lift that. Damn it!"

Looking very disgruntled, Jone returned with the 48-by-54-inch canvas. "You tell her," she nodded at Cathy. "Tell her it's one thing to be relaxed and to consider birth a normal, natural procedure and it's another thing to . . . shit!" Jone turned on Angelica. "Don't you ever do that again! What do you do when I'm not around?"

"I'm glad to see you two aren't perfect." Cathy chuckled as Angelica fought back a smile and tried to look repentant.

"She works too hard." Jone glared at Angelica, then laughed.

"She's the best mother I ever had," Angelica teased the big blond. "Okay, Jonie, heave that canvas up onto your table so Cathy can have a better perspective. That's right, prop it against that empty regulator there." Angelica watched Cathy's face with a half-smile.

"That's incredible!" Cathy exclaimed. "Fabulous. Jone was right. Yeah . . . shit. Zed will thank me for sending you to him. Really . . . Angelica. Jone was right . . . never seen anything quite . . ."

Cathy laughed as she moved closer to *Spinacia oleracea*. She kept shaking her head in wonderment and saying "shit, man" under her breath.

There was a savage, vehement, erotic quality to the leafy viridian-green spinach plants which Angelica had set up on an old table. The surface was heavily textured oil. The background was a solid, brilliant yellow—resembling the hue which had obsessed Van Gogh in *L'Arlésienne*.

The simplicity and forcefulness of Angelica's lines, a suggestion of crimson where the paint had peeled off on the old table, put the composition into perfect balance. Yet beyond that was more and this was what fascinated Cathy and caused the laughter to continue to bubble forth. In addition to the sensual impact Angelica had achieved a lighthearted, robust absurdity in the sexuality of the two spinach plants.

"They really do exhibit sexual dimorphism," Angelica explained. "I read it in the *New York Times*. Fascinated me. I mean spinach! I realized I'd always felt strongly about spinach . . . not just liked it with bacon crumbled on top, creamed, souffléed, or whatever but identified with its . . . power. Nothing pedantic about spinach though. See those little prongs on Butch Spinach? It was curious to me that the male spinach as well as the female spinach flowered. I mean we generally think of the female as flowering, right? Interesting."

"You really did a lot of research?" Cathy was still smiling, glancing from the painting to Angelica and back to the painting again.

Angelica laughed. "I'm not exactly a spinach *aficionado*. I surveyed the field in my intuitively haphazard way."

"Can I phone Zed from here?" Cathy asked.

"How does he feel about recommendations from friends?" Angelica wanted to know.

"Jesus!" breathed Jone, "would you let somebody put in a plug for you?"

"I don't like rejection . . ."

"So who does?" Jone shouted and then to Cathy, "My co-op gallery rejected her series of gouache still lifes."

"It was the first time I'd shown my stuff since coming back to New York. I'm still recovering," Angelica admitted.

"But you didn't show them this," Jone offered. "The other series is too cerebral for them, too spiritual. What do they know from spiritual?"

"They're your gallery!" Angelica pointed out. "You're spiritual. Don't pamper me, Fritz. They just didn't like it."

"What about the phone?" Cathy looked at her watch. "I gotta meet Vinnie after school, then he and Les are driving me to the airport."

"You're going back to Ohio?" Angelica asked, and Cathy nodded.

"So do I make the call or what?"

"Porter Gallery . . ." Angelica felt queasy. Porter was one of the four or five most prestigious galleries in the city, in the world actually. Somehow she had, with all of her boring humility, she thought now, imagined she would start with a lesser gallery. If Porter took her on, the powers in London, Paris, Florence—everyone—would know about her. She wanted it too much and she knew it. With all of the important people Ferris had known, she had never come so close to actually making contact with the Powers.

"Sure, call," she said briskly. "Time for my milk." She escaped to the kitchen so she would not have to hear what Cathy said to Zed Porter, so she would not have to have the bubble burst quite so soon. Why would he want to see one painting? What could he do with one painting even if she did explain her ideas for a series, even if she told him that she knew . . . God, God, knew what? She had been thinking that she knew, finally knew, that no one and nothing could stop her from being a major artist. But the moment she had felt the rush of confidence, the dizzying surge of ego, her mind had backed off.

Angelica poured herself the milk and strained to hear what Cathy was saying in the other room. The baby kicked her as if to tell her to please start breathing again.

"You're all set." Cathy came into the kitchen and shook Angelica's hand. "He's expecting to hear from you. He'll come down here to have a look whenever you say. I left my Ohio phone number with Jone. Call me and let me know."

"Oh, my God!" Angelica covered her mouth to keep from crying but her voice was shaky when she spoke. "Thank you."

OCTOBER 1980

New York City

Jone's co-op gallery on Mercer Street was bust. The very nice man who had passed himself off as an artist and out of the goodness of his heart acted as business manager for the group of fifty unknown artists, had skipped town.

"How much of your money?" drawled the striking young cowboy who was having some difficulty keeping stride with Jone as she sloshed through the Soho streets late on a wet and windy Saturday afternoon.

"It's not the money," she said. "I hated that place from the start. The guy had rotten taste . . . I mean not so far as we're concerned but . . . I shoulda pulled out as soon as I got those favorable notices two months ago . . . gone looking. I shoulda found another gallery but what did I do? Stayed home and worked . . . put out more money for more materials and . . . I think I knew all along the guy was a crook. I feel dumb."

"But how much money?" Whittemore Russell, his friends called him Whit, was a twenty-three-year-old sculptor from Houston, Texas. At something over six feet tall with broad shoulders, a lean waist, and a stiff-legged walk, he would have resembled a cowboy even if he had been wearing a three-piece pinstripe suit. However, Whit, not being one for understatement, was dressed like the lead in a 1950s television Western with hand-tooled leather boots, spurs, tight jeans, a fringed leather jacket, and a cowboy hat. He had started out sculpting realistic, medium-sized bronze horses but now he said his work was "turnin' serious" and he was working on more abstract western forms.

"He just sold two of my large pieces," said Jone. "The last two pieces he had. One for five hundred, the other for eight."

"Jee-zus Kee-*riiist*!" Whit screwed his almost too handsome face into a scowl and held it there.

Jone glanced sideways at him with his face all screwed up. She stared, waiting for his expression to go back to normal, but he held his facial muscles in an agonized scowl. She wondered how long he would hold it and finally, after they had walked nearly a block, she laughed.

"Why are you laughin'?" He finally relaxed his face to pose the question.

"I've seen you do that before," said Jone, still laughing. "The expressions on your face . . . get stuck. Like at the gallery, I've seen you laugh and when you stop your face keeps on laughing. You're like a silent film actor." Jone doubled over laughing.

"I think you care more about losin' that money'n you think," smiled Whit. "Look at you . . . you're hysterical. Jee-zus, after throwin' your fifty percent back into the co-op you coulda had seven hundred bucks in your pocket right now. How much rent you pay?"

"My share is a hundred and a quarter. I have a roommate."

"Shit, that's good rent. I pay two but then I live by myself."

"Yeah?" Jone turned the corner and headed toward Dean and DeLuca for something dreadfully fattening like a whole loaf of raisin pumpernickel with cream cheese or even a six-pack of Beck's with Italian salami and a loaf of seeded Italian bread.

Whittemore Russell, whom she had known for several months, but with whom she had never carried on a conversation, turned the corner with her.

"I'd like to string that buzzard up is what I'd like."

Jone smiled and continued walking. Everyone teased Whit about his western identity which also included a plethora of good-ole-boy saloon talk. People were always asking him where his horse was tied and informing him of rustlers on the IRT.

Jone had observed that he tolerated the teasing with an easy Texas grin. She had also observed that he was never without the equivalent of a sexy young Belle Starr on his arm. The city was full of cowboys these days but she had never seen one to rival the authenticity of Whittemore Russell.

"You could form a posse," she suggested.

"Not a bad idea." He narrowed his brown eyes and walked that way for a while without saying anything.

"What about you?" Jone asked. "Did he owe you money?"

Whit shook his head. "I had shitty luck at that place, not like you . . . for all the good it did ya. But you got those notices. You shouldn't have no trouble findin' you another gallery. I got some stuff in a gallery up in Woodstock. Cheap stuff though. I'm not proud of it. If I didn't need the dough I'd, you know, pull it all back in and work in this new vein I'm into. Jee-zus Kee-rist, it costs a helluva lot of money to be an artist . . . just puttin' out for the bronze. Writers are lucky, you know, they can always write on the other side of the paper."

"The piece you brought in last week was nice," Jone said. "I liked it. It was different."

"Yeah. It wasn't a horse is what you mean."

"No, not just that it wasn't a horse. I liked some of your horses, too."

Whit laughed. "Is that a compliment?"

"Yes." Jone stopped in front of the famous gourmet shop. She was already salivating thinking of the endless possibilities inside. Angelica had been depressed lately, working herself into a state of exhaustion, trying to accumulate more paintings which satisfied her before phoning Zed Porter. A gourmet picnic from Dean and DeLuca would cheer her up. Maybe, Jone thought, I will even buy caviar to celebrate having to learn a lesson the hard way. Only I don't like caviar.

"Wanna come over to the O.R. Corral for dinner? I been cookin' beans for three days. They should be 'bout ready."

"What did you say?" Jone felt her own face twist into an incredulous expression and she held it there to see how it would feel. It felt like sculpture and she began thinking that it would be interesting to create a piece not by duplicating the form visually but kinetically . . . to work blind.

"Well?" Whit was waiting. "I been cookin' beans for three days. It's a special dish. I didn't just forget to turn them off."

"Oh," Jone laughed. "I don't know . . . I have a pregnant roommate who's been depressed and . . ."

"So bring her along. When I cook beans I cook a lot of 'em, otherwise it's just not worth it."

Jone laughed again. Whit's line of reasoning was not unlike Angelica's; in fact they would probably hit it off quite nicely. Jone had always thought the tall Texan, though vaguely humorous and certainly handsome, a real macho type. It would never have occurred to her that he was the kind of man who would cook beans for three days. The idea of spending an evening with two off-the-wall characters like Whit and Angelica made her feel giddy . . . or maybe it was Whit who was making her feel giddy. But she was no Belle Starr like his other girls so she might as well forget it.

"Okay," she nodded and beneath her baggy canvas clothes her body turned soft and warm and she was aware that he had taken her arm. His forearm felt like sculpture, all hard and cool beneath his shirt.

"They're pinto beans," he grinned at her.

"I'll call my roommate." Jone pulled her arm away and ran to a phone booth up ahead. She put in the dime and was just dialing when she heard the door to the phone booth open and felt him press in against her back, felt that he was feeling about her the same way she had been feeling about him. She hung up the receiver as he moved his mouth slowly along the back of her neck, nuzzling her like one of his young colt creations. The streets were crowded with Saturday shoppers but in Soho the most bizarre behavior was granted only a cursory stare or a smile. Jone closed her eyes to the crowd as he kissed her neck, gradually moving his hands down the sides of her body.

He let out a sigh. "Jee-zus!"

Most unlike me, most unlike, she thought as he slid his hand inside her shirt placket, caressing her bare skin.

"I wasn't lying about the beans," he whispered into her ear. "I really have been cooking for three days. I betcha they'll be the best damn beans you ever ate."

OCTOBER 1980
Wayne, Ohio

"Mama, did I ever tell you how much I love you?"

Mrs. Harder looked shocked, as if someone had walked in on her as she was stepping out of the bathtub.

"Well, never mind." Cathy laughed at her mother's expression and continued working on the large canvas. *Mother in the Fields* was a naturalistic rendering of seventy-four-year-old Aggie Harder, tall and slender as a girl, her silver hair cut short in a stylish cap and wearing her Sunday best, a sophisticated, nubby Italian knit which Cathy had sent her for Christmas last year. Cathy had wanted to paint her mother in the loose-fitting cotton dress she usually wore and her raveled, dog-chewed pink cardigan but Aggie would not hear of it. If she was going to have her picture painted (and if it had to be in the cornfield for land sakes!) she was at least going to wear what she wanted to wear. It had taken all of Cathy's cunning to keep her mother from making a special trip to the beauty parlor to have a blue rinse put on her hair so it wouldn't look so "awful silver."

So here was Aggie Harder, a mature, midwestern Vogue model, with a gold scarab pin from Tiffany's on her lapel and gold hoops in her ears, also gifts from Cathy over the years. The result of Aggie's insistence on "dressing up for my picture" was a painting of far greater complexity and depth than Cathy had originally conceived. Between the artist and the subject there existed a state of perfect balance and equality as if they both had a stake in the outcome.

Cathy marveled at and was humbled by the presence of the many-faceted country woman whose mystery, even to her, remained intact and limitless after so many years. For two days now they had stood under a clear blue sky, mostly silent except for when they took a break and sipped from the thermos filled with cold lemonade. It was real Indian summer, hot as July and humid as only Ohio could be. Most of the corn had been gathered into shocks for drying and in the composition they stood like sentinels ready to march at the word of their stately commandress.

Cathy worked quickly so as not to tire her mother, who she knew would never admit to being tired, continuing to hold the pose for as long as Cathy needed her.

How incredible, thought Cathy, that she had been prompted to come back to Wayne in order to solidify the idea she had had for a nude of Tony and *The Girls Downtown,* Jone and Angelica, only to find herself swept into a vortex of personal memories and to end by painting her mother in the cornfields. She had stifled virtually none of her impulses, and she had created ten oil canvases in the past three weeks since returning home. Home?

It amazed her that after more than twenty-five years of cultivating urban perceptions and sensibilities her imagination was struck by the eloquence of her roots, the dowdy little burg of Wayne, Ohio. God, it wasn't even picturesque like those little New England towns with their pristine church spires and rolling hills dotted with sheep. Wayne wasn't even a village, it was a burg with three filling stations (for all the four-car families), a bar, a hardware store, a drugstore-diner, and a drygoods store which featured Orlon sweaters.

But there was nothing sentimental in Cathy's new approach to her work; rather she employed an almost classical, purist technique in various compositions: the weather-worn, sliding barn door in which her father (probably more than fifty years ago!) had cut a round hole so the cats could go in and out; the lane which led to the main road, dry now but washed out and rutted from years of neglect; the meadow, rampant with autumnal colors: wildflowers, purple thistles the size of a fist, goldenrod, not dainty and low as it was in the East but waist-high, with cumbersome clusters which turned her hands buttery when she touched them.

She had even done a picture of the remembered once-detested mud, a swampy, fecund stretch out behind the barn where no matter how dry it was elsewhere one could always ooze about in the rank, rich muck. Wonderful! The mud she had complained about and had been humiliated by when it had clung to her shoes in proper company was a source of inspiration, a symbol of regeneration.

No matter how insignificant the subject may once have seemed, if she saw something which piqued her interest she painted it. From the perspective of her old room on the second story she painted the window with a faded blue curtain billowing out and in the yard below, just at the outer righthand frame of the window, seated in an aluminum chair on the browning grass, the back of her mother's left shoulder. The composition was heavy on the right and it created the illusion that Aggie might at any moment slip out of sight. Cathy tried to paint it the way she saw it, without comment, demanding from herself more technical virtuosity than she had required in years. The only comment she allowed for was in her choice of compositions, the scenes she elected to frame for her canvas. No doubt there would be those who would find flaws in her technical skill but Cathy herself, while not satisfied with every detail, was encouraged that after years of painting in a more abstract manner she could, because of her desire to represent these simple rural scenes, demand and receive a high degree of exactitude from herself.

She had been in Ohio for almost a month, up everyday at dawn lugging a tool box full of paints and a makeshift easel to various locations on the Harder farm or into the town itself. She had made three brief trips back to New York to see Vinnie, who was staying with his father, and to spend time with Tony, who was "one hundred percent supportive" and hinting that he would be willing to spend the next year in Wayne should she decide to stay on. On her last trip east she gave Zed Porter an ultimatum: "Hang what I want in the November show or I'll hang it somewhere else." He had been sanctimonious and aloof with her in the confines of his office but when she had phoned him, just before leaving New York the last time, he had been his old charming self, saying he would be delighted to make a special trip downtown to have a look at Angelica's work. If he had still been feeling antagonistic he would have invented some petty, perfectly obvious excuse to make her feel unimportant. Anyway, she told herself, she did not care if she parted company with Porter Gallery. Zed had been playing too safe lately, insidiously censoring the spirit of adventure in his artists by urging them to repeat old patterns. Now that Zed was big business there was too much at stake for him; more and more he was leaning toward past masters instead of risking criticism with new artists. She really should call Angelica and tell her that so she wouldn't get her hopes up.

That damn Zed had so bloody much power. Better not to tell Angelica anything which might inhibit her, better just to let her go on working out of her own optimistic spirit. If Zed didn't come through for her, Cathy was convinced some other gallery would.

She was giving him one more week; then if he continued to play his waiting game she would spring a little surprise on him. She knew he had not scheduled another show, knew that he had a partial catalog set for the printer and that the invitations were also set except for choosing which painting would be reproduced on the catalog's cover. All of those details were costly and Zed was nothing if not frugal with his millions. It was likely he would hold out until the last possible minute, waiting for her to phone him in the middle of the night and submit to his word. Only she had contacted her old friend M. Landes in Paris and if Zed persisted in playing God with her she would show her new work there, at her former gallery's Paris affiliate!

It was remarkable to her that she viewed these business machinations with such detachment. Maybe it was being in Wayne, so far from the cocaine existence of the city, but the whole system of intrigue with collectors and galleries and critics seemed irrelevant. She wondered if, for her, the answer to life didn't lie in being a long-distance commuter. The flight from Dayton, the nearest airport city to Wayne, took about an hour; including transportation to the airport at both ends she could make the trip in under three hours. Some people took that long to drive to work every day. Her trips back to New York were not problem-plagued, even the meeting with Zed had not been the usual ordeal. She had laughed more with Les than she had in years, her conversations with Laura had been stimulating and unmarred by the painful soul-searching criticism they often leveled at each other. Most amazing, Vinnie's missing her had not wrenched her heart, because it had been clear to her that as long as he had his roller skates, earphones, and Ernie Tomelli as best friend, his world was the best of all possible worlds.

Her nights with Tony had almost recaptured the old feeling of romance and she had even managed to squeeze out a few pleasant tears when she said good-bye to him at the airport. In the past she had always hated leaving people. There was a time when leaving Vinnie to go out to dinner had thrown her into paroxysms of terror despite the security system. She was always sure a mysterious intruder would gain access to her apartment and rape the babysitter, then kill Vinnie, or Vinnie would fall in the bathroom and die of a concussion or bleed to death silently on the floor while the babysitter ate popcorn in front of the TV.

Sometimes during a two-hour dinner she would make three or four phone calls home to make sure everything was all right. She had been humiliated and embarrassed by her fears but they had been overwhelming. Now when she waved good-bye to Vinnie she no longer saw his body crushed and bleeding; she saw a happy kid with a missing front tooth who felt secure in the love of both his parents. No tears. Vinnie was lucky to have a father, not just in name but in deed. She was lucky to have a husband . . . now that was curious, too, because she did think of Lester as her husband, in the deepest sense, and what did that mean?

Stop thinking, she told herself as she wiped off her brush and began to gather her equipment. It was good leaving people, she thought, when you were the person doing the leaving and you knew you were coming back. A small smile crossed her face. She was having her cake and eating it too and it wasn't half bad. It was something she might even get used to.

"All finished, Mama. No, I'll carry this, you go on."

The dried corn husks crackled under her sneakers as she followed her mother back to the house. In moments such as these time had no meaning. Walking a few paces behind Aggie she felt like a little girl trailing Mama into the house where she would sit at the familiar red Formica table and watch Mama fix something nice . . . macaroni and cheese or corn fritters. Just the two of them inside the large run-down house, eating alone at the red table with memories between them. They really had very little to say to each other after they'd discussed Vinnie, Cathy's siblings, various grandchildren, and ailing relatives. It had been over twenty-five years since she had spent more than an occasional night in her former home with her mother, and when Aggie visited New York it was different. In the city their continuity was interrupted, but here in Wayne past, present, and future existed in one moment.

Occasionally Aggie would reminisce about her late husband, referring to him as "a good man." Only once had she asked Cathy what she planned to do about her marriage to Lester Aimsley. She had welcomed her daughter home in 1980 as easily as she had let her go early that morning in August 1953.

Sometimes when they lingered at the supper table Cathy wanted to reach out and take Aggie's hand, to explain at great length, as was her habit, about all that she had discovered in her forty-six years and that, had it not been for Aggie's easy letting go, she might have been either too afraid to leave home or lost her sense of power in an effort to forget what she was leaving. But she didn't. Some of Aggie's wisdom was beginning to tell. She was her mother's daughter and it had taken forty-six years to know and understand what that meant. Perhaps as much as all the therapies—the EST, primal, meditation, yoga, the self-help books, and the prayers—being the daughter of this particular woman had insured her survival. Cathy had always thought of herself as having a completely different temperament than her mother. She was flighty, Aggie was solid; she was loquacious to the point of absurdity; Aggie was reticent to the point of annoyance; she was short, Aggie was tall . . . on and on. For so long she had seen only the dissimilarities which had served to make them strangers, remotely exchanging yearly Christmas gifts across the miles. Now Cathy saw that she had in her life done no less than her mother and maybe even in some respects more. She had that same raw corporeal tenacity which her mama possessed. She had never thought of her mama as weak, though perhaps Aggie's tight-lipped manner was merely her armor against her own doubts and feelings of inferiority. But her mama wasn't weak and neither, Cathy knew, was Cathy.

Upstairs in the room she had formerly shared with her two sisters, Cathy scrutinized the nearly completed canvas as if it were the work of someone else, as if the woman in the field was not her mother. The woman in the cornfield was eternal, she looked in her contradictory clothes as if she would live forever.

With the concentration of a priestess Cathy kneeled down and placed the canvas under her old bed. As she slid under the cool sheet she understood that the new silence growing inside of her was finally giving her freedom.

OCTOBER 1980

New York City

Angelica, her nun's habit now almost filled out by her swollen body, was perched on the edge of a high stool to which Jone had secured a metal back lined with foam rubber so that she would have support for her spine during the long hours she spent in front of the easel. Only she could not paint without leaning forward and throwing her entire body into the process; most of the time, except when Jone was around to nag her, she could not accomplish a thing sitting down. Well at least, she thought, the vomiting and fatigue had let up; now there were just swollen ankles and frequent trips to the bathroom to interrupt her.

Today, thank God, Jone was gone—off with her cowboy lover, off to the Hopper exhibit at the Whitney, off to a luncheon meeting with her new uptown gallery, then to dinner to celebrate her good fortune, then to a Halloween party with her new red cowgirl hat, compliments of Whit, then . . .

Angelica heaved her brush at the floor, red paint splattering in all directions. It was no good trying to imitate the past. The painting she was working on, *L'Ail et les Framboises II*, was a variation of an earlier version which Suzanne had in Paris. As far as Angelica was concerned it was a disaster no matter what Whit and Jone said. What did Whit and Jone know anyway? They were in love. Jone's pieces seemed to sell as fast as she could turn them out and now the Whitney was considering a piece and several large collectors were interested.

Angelica picked up the brush and cleaned it off with a paint-stained rag. There was an advantage to living in a garage, for the place was indestructible and today she felt like destroying everything in sight. She kicked the stool over for good measure and stood glaring at the painting.

Ever since Cathy had telephoned Zed Porter, Angelica had been in a panic. She had cut back on her working hours at Far Out Inc. in order to complete more paintings along the lines of *Spinacia*. Only now she hated still lifes and wondered how she had fallen into doing them in the first place.

Nothing felt right to her and she wanted to scream, only she thought it would be bad for the baby. It seemed that everything she might want would be bad for the baby. She picked up the stool slowly, trying to relax. All of the weight was in her torso, her face was gaunt, her arms beneath the sleeves of the nun's habit were like reeds. It seemed to her that she ate all the time, yet in her sixth month of pregnancy she had gained only a total of ten pounds. Despite Dr. Nigel's reassurance that hers was a normal pregnancy, Angelica had become obsessed with eating only the most nutritious foods, spending more and more money on costly organic products.

Ferris had called four times and she had told Jone to tell him she wasn't home. Today, however, the loneliness was intolerable. The idea of going to a bar even to engage in a conversation let alone to pick up someone was odious to her. It had been weeks since she had felt in the least bit sensual; instead she continually felt lethargic and sad. For the past two weeks the sight of the enamored couple, the looks which passed between them, and their inability to keep their hands off of each other had been a torment to her. She felt like a turtle inside a shell and the delight she had always found in solitude was gone. She wanted to be held. Sometimes she thought of her mother, of how it would feel to fly to Chicago and curl up in her mother's arms. Only that was impossible. Her mother had long ceased to exist in that way for her. Her mother touched no one and her father had never touched her in that way. Recently someone at Far Out

Inc. had just slightly patted the top of her head in passing and she had nearly cried out. The casual gesture had brought tears to her eyes; she had actually had to retreat to the women's room and allow herself a brief cry. It had never happened before; she had never been so long without some physical connection. She had written Françoise: "If it is any comfort to you, though I'm sure it isn't, you may have been right about me and my Joan of Arc plan. I am as lonely as if I were living in exile on some far-off barren island."

Good fortune seemed to fall on Jone as naturally as a spring shower; there was a logical progression, an order to Jone's life, which was missing from hers. Of course she was glad for her. Jone deserved the recognition. Yet Jone's success made her even more ravenous and more uncertain about her own future.

The tension between the objects in *L'Ail et les Framboises II* was weak and she did not seem able to get it right. The painting lacked spontaneity and she was tempted to open the front door and hurl it out into the street for one of the clangorous mail trucks to run over. She needed time away, time to gather her resources in order to return with a fresh eye. She thought nostalgically of Paris and Suzanne and Françoise and sidewalk cafés, of *café au lait* and of just sitting and watching the people pass. Françoise had kept her word about putting Angelica in touch with the man who bought art for Chase Manhattan Bank, but Angelica was putting him off until after Zed Porter came down.

The baroque music which had been playing on WNCN changed to strident Stravinsky and she lumbered awkwardly, or so it seemed to her, into the living area to switch off the radio. One had to be very stable to listen to Stravinsky indoors. The only time the *Rite of Spring* had not acted as amphetamine on her system was one summer at Tangelwood when she and Ferris had listened to the piece outside on the grass.

Without the music or the hum of Jone's equipment the Obil was ominously silent. Angelica changed into the black jumpsuit, one of the few things which still fit. The buttons were beginning to strain so she put on one of Jone's white men's shirts over the top. She was almost out the door to take a walk when the phone rang.

"I don't believe I finally reached you. I was sure you were avoiding me."

"I was," Angelica admitted ruefully. The moment the phone had rung she had been sure it would be Ferris. Oddly, she felt relieved, almost happy that he had called again.

"Can I take you to dinner?"

"All right."

"Tonight?" he asked quickly. "I know it's short notice but . . ."

"No, I'm not busy. I mean, I am busy but not that way busy."

"Well, I didn't know," Ferris said. "I didn't know what your situation . . ."

"Where shall we go? No place fancy."

"Do you have an address . . . can I pick you up or what?"

Angelica paused, glancing over her shoulder at the unfinished painting. She did not want him here, did not want to hear his comments.

"Maxine Sobel said she ran into you at a show at Paul Cooper's, said you were living in some garage over by the river."

"It's not as bad as it sounds." Angelica laughed, imagining what he was thinking.

"Maxine was hurt you never called her back. You didn't call any of our old . . ."

"Ferris! I know you don't mean to criticize me. No, I didn't call our old friends because they were *your* friends and at the time I did not want to have anything to do with your anything."

"They really were your friends, too, especially Maxine."

"Maybe," Angelica replied stonily. "Is the dinner invitation contingent upon my calling Maxine?"

There was an uneasy silence, then Ferris said, "Does the Trattoria at eight sound all right?"

"Fine. I'll meet you there."

"You know where it . . ."

"On Hudson. See you at eight."

She hung up feeling more ambivalent than before and wondering at the perversity of Providence in arranging for Ferris to call when she was at her most vulnerable and in need of spending the evening with anyone.

She stared at the painting. She had been going for a walk but maybe she would stay and work. Maybe it could be salvaged if she strengthened the contours of the berries and improved the texture of the garlic, perhaps pulled back one of the bulbs to expose the reddish hue of the papery skin.

She worked for two hours in a self-induced trance, an act of will set in motion not today when she was on the brink of the black hole, but months before when she was stronger. Still in a fog and without really deciding to, she called Zed Porter's office and through his secretary made an appointment for him to come down to the Obil on the following Wednesday. Dimly she heard the secretary say Mr. Porter had been expecting her call and when she hung up she felt nothing—not fear, not anticipation, and certainly not a sense of accomplishment. It was as if she had not made the call and nothing whatever was at stake.

Ferris and Angelica had finished a politely talkative dinner and were walking down Bank Street toward the Hudson River when he finally broached the subject of her pregnancy.

"Look," he tapped her arm as if it were a hot stove. "I did try to call you after I ran into you at the Modern . . . a number of times. I just think you should have told me about . . . ," he trailed off uneasily.

Angelica nodded and looked at the charming red brick town houses which lined the block.

"You had a good dinner, didn't you?"

She nodded again and smiled at him. "Food's great there. Still. Always is."

"Good tortellini."

"And cream sauce."

"Angelica, why don't you admit . . ."

"Look, Ferris, we had an enjoyable dinner. Maybe we should leave it at that. Let's just talk about shows and friends. Isn't it odd how city leaves stay green well into winter? Look, only a few have turned brown so far."

He stopped her and put his hands on her shoulders, gazing plaintively at her under a streetlight. "Why won't you let me help you in all this?"

The bitterness she had worked so hard to overcome tempted her to reply that a man who hits a woman for a second time deserves nothing. Nothing ever.

"I could help you. It isn't right that you should have to take all the responsibility for the . . ."

"The *baby*," she finished his sentence crisply. "Why? That's what I want."

"But. . . ." He looked away miserably as she remembered him doing. It was an easy gesture for him, she thought. One he had perfected above all others. It was too easy. She liked him better when he was defensive and mean; at least she could be sure he meant that.

"Well, at least you're not accusing me of being crazy for getting myself into this."

"It's a little late for that." He looked regretful.

"You're right. It is too late for that. But it always was. I never considered not having this baby."

They walked in silence and she could feel the one question he wanted to ask. It was ludicrous, almost funny, that he could not come right out and ask if the child were his. The pleasure she took in his diffidence was perverse but she didn't care. The longer he waited the more confident she felt about her own decision. Finally, when they turned onto West Street she heard herself saying, "No, it's not yours."

She was not sure if he looked relieved or disappointed.

"Wouldn't I have told you if it was? Really, Ferris, did you think . . . ? God, no! It all happened after I left you for the second time. You have absolutely no reason to feel responsible for . . ."—she patted her well-rounded belly with an intentionally ambiguous smile—". . . this."

"When is it due?" he asked evenly, watching his shoes as they walked.

"Ferris, let's just be friends. Just that. If we could do that we will have accomplished a lot."

"But even a friend would know when a baby was going to be born to another friend."

"Late February," she hedged by a month to make the lie seem plausible.

"And the father . . . ?"

"You don't know him." Angelica tried to sound genial and contained, but she was a novice at lying to friends, and she knew she had failed. The lie existed between them as a convention, as something too dangerous for either of them to comment on or examine further at the moment.

Compared with the Obil Garage, Whittemore Russell's apartment was palatial. It was a loft on the top floor of a prewar factory off Houston Street, with two immense windows facing the Hudson River. Although the light was not as good as the Obil's eastern and northern exposures, Whit had transformed it into a rustic showplace with hand-hewn beams and functional wood furniture reminiscent of the Shakers in its simplicity. Every detail had been designed and executed by Whit himself including the gaudy sleeploft which was every cowboy's fantasy of a house of ill-repute with its mirrors, crystal sconces equipped with dimmers, crimson drapes, old Playboy calendars (prepubic classics, Whit called them, dating back to the fifties), and a big bear rug for a spread.

Except perhaps for the satiny Bunnies which looked seductively down on Jone as she lay next to Whit, everything about the O.R. Corral suited her perfectly. Certainly everything about Whit suited her, even his boastful confessions that there were more than a few brokenhearted, sad-eyed Belles still phoning and pleading to see him. He joyously claimed to have gone "cold turkey on chicks since I first had beans with you." He was amazed that "it" had happened to him and Jone was equally amazed that "it" had happened to her. When they weren't making love or staring blissfully at each other with their mouths full of one of Whit's Texas gourmet treats, they were elaborating on how incredible it was they were so in tune with each other and how everything else in life had receded and how it was really true what the poets said about love.

"Rare," Whit repeated again and again. "Real rare. Real, *real* rare is what this is . . . like the first time I got thrown from a horse."

"What!" As she was with Angelica, Jone was the perfect foil for his nonsequiturs.

"It's like you can git it explained to you how it will feel fallin' off a horse and you can think about it and wonder 'will it hurt?'

and be afraid or brave or whatever, but till it finally happens there is no way you kin know."

This sort of exaggerated explanation, performed with an equally exaggerated Texas drawl, inevitably elicited laughter and kisses from Jone. Knowing this, Whit played his role to the hilt, reveling in his own charms, enjoying his own artistic cleverness, wit, smarts, looks, sensitivity, liberation, and good cooking.

Jone felt wanted. Whit's flagrant, insatiable desire for her was the most surprising thing that had ever happened to her, more surprising even than her latest sales, her newly acquired Madison Avenue gallery representation, and the Whitney's purchase of one of her pieces (still stored and unseen by the public). She felt as if the skies had opened and showered blessings on her, felt that with Whit she had finally surmounted the past, shedding the last of her fears that her own life might be as wasted and miserable as her grandmother's.

She also shed her baggy khakis and wore tailored pants and pastel hand-knit sweaters which revealed her generous, strong curves. Her body, which had always seemed large and unwieldy, suddenly began to fit and she became absorbed in her own anatomy and how it might relate to her work as well as how it so obviously related to Whit.

Whit proclaimed the absolute inferiority of any woman under five ten and one hundred and fifty pounds. He said Jone's heft reminded him of Gaston Lachaise's *Standing Woman* and insisted on taking two rolls of film with Jone posing beside the sculpture at the Museum of Modern Art.

"Only thing is you got to wear your clothes," he complained over his Pentax as Jone, following his orders, mimicked the woman's stance with her hands on her hips and her left leg thrust to the side. "Jeee-zus, I'd like to see you . . . I know! I can shoot her, shoot you at home, then superimpose the nude you on her negative."

And put me up next to the Playboy Bunnies, thought Jone with an amused smile.

"Now let me shoot you from the rear. Right, hold it just like that. Jeee-zus!"

Whit, who had been working on horses for the past two years

except for an occasional departure into Brancusi-like simplified forms, elongations of brass and wood carvings, was obsessed with the female body—Jone's body to be precise. Her every gesture intrigued him and he was continually asking her to hold some mundane pose so that he could sketch it for later reference.

"I never thought of myself as a model," Jone confessed to Angelica on one of her rare evenings at home in the days after her initial encounter with Whit.

"You wouldn't listen to me," Angelica joked. "Didn't I tell you you had a splendid ass? But no, you wouldn't believe *me*. It's a good thing I'm a perfectly secure person without a single self-doubt or I would wonder if perhaps my opinions were meaningless."

"When am I going to get to meet Ferris?" Jone asked.

Angelica rolled her eyes.

"No, really. I think the four of us should . . ."

"A double date." Angelica waltzed around in a little circle, flapping her thin arms like a loony adolescent. "You've got to stop worrying about me." She stopped mid-gesture, feeling fat and ridiculous. "I may be jealous of what you and Whit have going, but I am happy for you. I like Whit."

"He likes you." Jone chewed at a nonexistent nail.

"Ferris is a part of another life. He doesn't belong in the Obil Garage . . ."

"Angelica, what are you trying to prove?" Jone backed up as she asked the question. "You're working yourself into a state over this meeting with Zed Porter. You should be taking it easy now and not . . ."

"No," Angelica interrupted quietly. "No, I don't want to take it easy. But yes, you're right, it would be nice if I could . . . not put everything on the line like I'm doing with Porter. That would be nice. But it's not me. I don't know how not to put it all on the line. Anyway, I am finally getting organized. I bought some secondhand baby blankets, little shirts, a stuffed rabbit, and I have dibs on an antique cradle through a woman at work. I know it's probably more expensive, but I've arranged for a diaper service. Can you imagine the guy's face the first time he drops off a load of diapers down here? It seems to me I am as prepared as a good Brownie should be."

"But let Ferris help. Christ, you lived with the man for ten years; he must have some good points!"

"He has many," Angelica smiled softly, "but he doesn't know what they are . . . or whence they come. Please stop worrying about me."

"I can't, damn it!" Jone raised her voice.

"And go live with Whit if that's what you're worried about."

"I have no intention—" Jone broke off.

"I don't believe you."

"I couldn't leave you here," Jone said.

"Oh, fine. Make me feel like your poor decrepit mother, the albatross around your young neck. Would you stop!" Angelica swatted at Jone with a smelly turpentine rag. "You'll be glad you've gone when *l'enfant terrible* arrives."

"Anyway, it's too soon to think of moving in with him," Jone insisted. "So far the only person who's mentioned it, the only person who is dying to have me move in with Whit, is my mother."

"The Lady Elizabeth." Angelica smiled. "I'd like to do a portrait of her sometime. You think she'd pose for me alone here?"

"I don't think so," Jone guffawed. "She's afraid of you. She's never said so but I think you scare her. Like Louise Nevelson scares her . . . like . . . like you and Louise remind her of something in herself that's gone."

"Heavy." Angelica shivered tragically. "I like your mother. She's very funny. Maybe when I'm no longer pregnant, when I'm a mother, she'll feel safer with me, you know?"

Jone nodded ruefully. "As soon as my sister became pregnant and not just a lawyer with a Phi Beta Kappa key, my mother's attitude toward her changed. She stopped nagging her and accepted her as a responsible adult. Anyhow, there's no hope for me there, though with Whit in the picture Mother already hears wedding bells and the pitter-patter of tiny feet. As far as they're concerned my future is finally shaping up. Like they really love Whit. Even my father, who wouldn't be caught dead in anything but a white shirt and a striped tie. I swear it's because Whit is a cowboy. My father feels safe with him because Whit reminds him of *Gunsmoke* and Wyatt Earp. For real! And they love it that he's taller than me and that he's from Texas. Being Catholic and from Texas seems to cancel out the negative aspect of his being an artist. And he's clean! One of Mother's first comments when we were alone after she and Dad came to Whit's for dinner was how clean he was . . . how clean he kept his bathroom, his kitchen, etcetera. He *is* one of the cleanest artists I've ever met."

"I've noticed," Angelica laughed. "Even his fingernails."

"Yes," Jone reflected with a fond smile. "Isn't that funny? He's cleaner than I am . . . cleaner than you. I don't mean we're dirty . . ."

Angelica giggled. "I noticed that he had one of those things in his toilet that turns the water blue. I loved that about him!"

"Me, too!" Jone grew animated thinking of Whit's constantly surprising complexities. "You should see his closet, it's all compartments."

"He's not German, is he?" Angelica asked.

"Irish. All the way Irish. Comes from a big family, well-off . . . a lot like me. Catholic. Jesus, it's a good thing . . ."

"What?" Angelica looked quizzically at Jone.

"I wasn't going to tell anyone." Jone grabbed her raincoat off the shabby couch and fished for her cigarettes. "Will the smoke bother you?"

"Not if I don't breathe," Angelica said and Jone stuffed the cigarettes back in her pocket.

"Whit doesn't smoke."

"I know." Angelica studied Jone curiously. "What were you going to say that you weren't going to tell anybody? Those are usually the best things to talk about."

"I know that's your theory." Jone frowned. "And maybe you're right. It makes it too big a deal if you keep it in. Right?"

"It could," Angelica said. "But if it nourishes you to keep it for yourself you should."

Jone shrugged. "Remember just after Labor Day when I said I was laid up, couldn't work 'cause I'd pulled something here?" Jone put her hand on her lower abdomen.

"You said you were afraid it was appendicitis," Angelica recalled.

Jone nodded. "I was lying."

"You were pregnant? You had an . . ."

"I had my tubes . . . I had myself sterilized."

Angelica gasped and stared at her.

"Why did you do that? Why didn't you . . . ? What happened . . . I mean why didn't you say something? I can't believe it."

"You would only have tried to talk me out of it," Jone began.

"You're twenty-two. My God . . . how could you decide a thing like that?"

"You sound angry." Jone forgot and pulled out a cigarette.

"Go on, smoke. One. You can have one. Jesus, you really shocked me. And now . . . ? Now you've met Whit and . . ."

"And now I'm damned glad I did it when I did it. With my luck and Whit and my inherited Irish fertility I wouldn't stand a chance no matter what I did."

"It's irreversible, isn't it?" Angelica was trying to understand how she could have overlooked the desperation which must have driven Jone to such an extreme act. Jone Beele was the last person she would expect to take such a drastic step. Jone was a rock, she was solid, reliable, quiet but not furtive, not given to impulses. Angelica had always thought of the younger woman as an earth symbol, rooted in reality, basic in the best sense, primitive even.

"And you didn't tell anyone?" Angelica asked finally and Jone shook her head. "Then I guess it's a good thing you finally mentioned it."

"Yes." Jone exhaled and stubbed out the cigarette before it was half finished. "I was aware of the ultimate dangers in not telling anyone, especially you. And I'm really glad, especially now, that I followed my instincts and had the operation. The point is, I never want to think about the possibility and the only way to do that is to do what I did. Listen, if later on I become overwhelmed by the desire to nurture I will buy myself a golden retriever, or an ocelot maybe. I mean it. Or . . . or I'll adopt a child. There are plenty of children who could use a good home."

Angelica sighed and ran her thin hands through her short dark hair.

"Children ruined my grandmother's artistic life." Jone met Angelica's eyes.

"Are you sure?" Angelica queried. "Did you ever ask her?"

"How could I ask her? No one is supposed to know that it even mattered to her that she never . . ."

"Well, then, how do you know?" Angelica persisted.

"It was six children," Jone went on urgently. "It was the burden of being the teacher, the organizer, the cook, the disciplinarian . . . it was all the things we now know get in the way. The things that drain you, that take away your spirit and your freedom. Of course I know. Anyway, why am I telling you this? You're the socialist with the political conscience."

Angelica pondered for a moment, then asked: "Are you going to tell Whit?"

"Of course! But it's a little early, isn't it? We've only been seeing each other for three weeks. We haven't reached the point where the future is an issue."

Angelica laced her pale thin fingers around Jone's calloused hand and walked her to the door, the two artists swinging their arms together like schoolgirls.

"You sure you don't want to have dinner with us tonight?"

"I'm sure." Angelica gave Jone's arm a final swing.

"But we'll all have dinner at Whit's after your meeting with Porter tomorrow, okay?"

"Stop worrying about me." Angelica kissed Jone on the cheek. "My God, you're even wearing perfume!"

❁

Zed Porter was coming down after work, around six the secretary had said. Angelica, taking yet another full day off from Far Out Inc., had spent the morning meditating and the afternoon making a final selection of work to present to Mr. Porter.

At one o'clock her selection consisted of four oil paintings in the recent series of still lifes, including *Spinacia oleracea,* and two earlier, more cerebral still lifes in pastel, a large abstract oil done prior to moving to France, and a dozen charcoal portraits chosen from the hundreds she had executed by studying the faces of tourists who had come to visit the nearby château at Azay-le-Rideau. At two o'clock the selection looked paltry and at three she added several early multimedia collages and a mammoth political piece from the East Village store window days.

She showered and dressed and tried to keep her imagination from creating new compositions, but the prospects of having her existing work judged by someone as important as Zed Porter had released a torrent of new ideas. At four she did a sketch of Jone's mother from memory, threw it away, and removed five of the charcoal portraits. She read out loud from T.S. Eliot's *Ash Wednesday* and made a litany of the lines:

> *Teach us to care and not to care*
> *Teach us to sit still.*

She danced slowly about the Obil Garage, hoping to calm the fetus inside who was as restless and nervous as she, and finally she put on her jacket and stood outside on the street to keep from tampering with her selections.

With her hands shoved into the pockets of a World War I army coat she watched the hulking U.S. Mail trucks sputter diesel fumes into the late afternoon shadows as they pulled in and out of their terminal across the street. It was better outside, away from her work. Leaning against the building, she closed her eyes and listened to the grinding of the gears, the aggressive male voices shouting directions for the truck drivers to "cut the wheels hard" as they backed the clumsy giants into the narrow loading area.

The comings and goings of the groaning trucks gave her a sense of continuity and as always when she stood outside watching them she was calmed by the noisy energy of the automotive sounds, the lumbering movements. The baby relaxed inside her and for an instant she felt in perfect harmony with the universe and absolutely confident of her ultimate success. *She had to succeed.* With her eyes shut she smiled at herself for meditating on trucks. This was her urban version of a rushing country stream.

"Pardon me, you wouldn't be Angelica Stein?"

"Yes, yes, I am. I am." Angelica's eyes flew open though she continued to lean lazily against the building. "You're Mr. Porter."

"Zed." He smiled and extended a hand still tanned from the summer, or more likely, she thought, perpetually tanned.

"I like mail trucks"—she nodded across the street—"no pun intended. Did you ever see a new mail truck, one that didn't rattle and belch and seem on the point of exploding or breaking down?"

"I don't recall." Zed took in Angelica's pale face, her high cheekbones and the too-dark circles ringing her steady gray eyes. Giacometti elegance, he thought, except for the punk haircut which he found offensive and her body, which, he was surprised to see, was well advanced into pregnancy. Odd that Catherine had given him the impression of a gorgeous young nymphette.

"I've been trying to figure out what there is about these trucks that makes me feel so peaceful."

"Perhaps a sort of Zen contemplation."

"Fabulous!" Angelica applauded as a truck finally jockeyed into position. "It's the simple things." She turned to Zed laughing. "Did you enjoy the show?"

"It was a first," he admitted, settling against the building.

"I come out here when I need soothing and it makes absolutely no sense because I despise cars. I wouldn't own one! I'm a fanatic about them, in fact. I believe there is something evil in the automobile; if not basically evil, then at least some element which has tempted humankind into the basest behavior by giving everyone who can stumble behind the wheel of a car—genius, psychotic, killer, and moron alike—a sense of power as unrealistic as it is lethal. Of course the automobile industry has not only robbed our resources but deluded people into thinking that the car is the symbol, mind you, of the independent American spirit and that public transportation is somehow suspect because it involves *masses* of people in *common* circumstance and is therefore in league against the capitalist system . . . and smacks of communism! So you see why it is so difficult for me to understand my fondness for . . ." Angelica broke off breathlessly. "I rarely talk this much."

Zed laughed. "You sound like a politician."

"I have a few political pretensions." Angelica flinched as his shoulder grazed hers. Cathy had warned her she would find his classical blond elegance attractive. "But my politics are dreadfully inconsistent and I am only fierce on several subjects, one of which you have just been lucky enough to hear about."

"I have a BMW," he baited her with a smile, and she looked directly into his eyes trying to read her future. She reminded herself that he had come down here on business.

"It's very nice down here." He folded his arms and looked around appreciatively as if he might buy the place. No doubt he had a place in the Hamptons, Angelica thought, imagining him clad in tennis whites, his lithe form hurdling across the net to congratulate his opponent. He would always be a winner, even in defeat—unlike Ferris, who would always be a loser no matter how often he won. Cathy, who was, to say the least, not overly fond of Zed, liked to say he had perfected the art of appearing chic and shallow as a form of snobbery in a world that valued depth and openness. Apparently very few people had seen anything beyond his surface charm. His reputation with women was one of generosity, if emotional vapidity; he had two ex-wives and three children who received charitable settlements. There was, Cathy had told Angelica with heavy cynicism, "no bitterness whatever on his part." Curiously he was renowned in the art world as a man with infinite sensitivity, eclectic tastes, and, until recently, a great experimental sense.

She could feel him studying her profile and turned to him. "I came out here because I kept looking at my work through your eyes, trying to imagine all of the possible outcomes of our meeting. I shouldn't be saying this."

"It's all right." He put his arm on her shoulder in an amicable gesture. "I'm very used to nervous people."

Angelica wondered if she would have noticed the empty ring in his voice had Cathy not critiqued him so harshly. He started speaking of Cathy now, of his recent trip to Ohio to see her work—which he hailed as quite a departure from her previous *oeuvre*. Had Angelica seen samples of the new Aimsley naturalism? No? Well, she would, because amazingly, against his better judgment, he had allowed Catherine to talk him into including six of the new paintings in her November show.

He seemed in no hurry to go inside to attend to business and chatted easily, inquiring into Angelica's past training and commenting dryly upon the dearth of substantial art on the contemporary scene. The sound of his voice aroused an acute loneliness in Angelica. She felt lonelier even than she had felt in the presence of the two lovebirds. She listened to the timbre of his voice more than his words, feeling almost compelled to nestle against him and take some brief comfort in the sense of intimacy.

As he smoked a cigarette she found herself imagining that once they were inside she would perform some primitive ritual seduction for his enjoyment, perhaps even expose herself unexpectedly or make some out-of-context erotic gesture like a soul-devouring vampire. Crude and improper images flashed in her mind. She saw him tied to a chair while she circled him, shedding her clothes and dipping in a low primeval dance like one of the figures in the Matisse painting. She saw his shocked face and then his back as he retreated, leaving her alone with her work.

After he finished the cigarette she suggested they go inside. She wanted the erotic images to stop but they continued and she could not look at him when she handed him the glass of Jack Daniels which Cathy had advised her to have on hand. She was possessed by the spirit of the evil Lilith and felt herself about to break some sacred principle. Was it his authority, she wondered, his inviolable power that had aroused her? Or was there something more? Her imagination was making extreme demands—or was it her body only?

"Cheers!" She toasted him with her own glass which was filled with water and savored the movement in his throat as he swallowed the bourbon.

"I do thank you for coming down." She moved to the screen she had placed in front of her work. "Would you mind if I waited in our back room? Through that door . . . we euphemistically refer to it as our living quarters."

"Relax," he grinned at her, "I'm not God."

"You could have fooled me." Angelica bowed her head and hurried into the other room.

Oddly inappropriate as her thoughts were, they did not weaken her, rather they made her feel powerful. It was as if he was not here to judge her work at all, but rather as an emissary, the missing link from her ancient past. Angelica stretched out on the broken-down sofa and pictured the way his blue, Harvard eyes narrowed when he smiled, making tiny creases on his well-lubricated skin. Probably he used a moisturizer, probably he jogged or played squash twice a week, without fail. He would do everything regularly.

Her supine body grew light and luscious as she entered his body in her mind, possessing him on every level until she was able to perceive the world as he did. Imagine! Cathy had warned her and here *she* was in danger of making a blatant pass at him. What would happen if she took the scenario out of her head and played it through for him? It wasn't done. This was business. She was a professional: a professional doesn't mix business with pleasure!

When she opened her eyes he was standing in the doorway watching her. She sat up, confused. Twenty minutes had gone by. She wondered how long he had been watching her and what he had read behind her closed eyes.

"The news is good." He sat down next to her, not businesslike at all. "The technique in the portraits is impressive, the lines alive and forceful. At the risk of offending you, I'd have thought the portraits in particular had been done by a man. That's a compliment. It's also obvious you have a fascination as well as a feeling for color; you are clearly inventive, your compositions are unique without being forced. You have taste . . . which you don't always use . . . and in the *Spinacia* you show the sort of restraint that in my opinion creates exciting tension in art."

Angelica was concentrating so hard on his words that the sounds seemed distorted, unfamiliar. Her body was lead, no erotic energy coursing through her now, no sense of power, only her own hunger. She wished he were speaking on the telephone or that she was reading his words so that she might understand his meaning.

". . . no way I could give you a show."

"What?"

He put his hand on her shoulder. "I'm not certain Porter Gallery is for you and to tell you the truth, I'm not certain it's not. I'm very impressed with your work . . ."

Angelica stared at her hands and thought dispassionately that they looked like the claws on a skeleton. After a moment she was aware that he had handed her a Jack Daniels which she accepted though she could not recall the last time she had tasted hard liquor.

"Now listen." His voice was soft, more intimate and less congenial than it had been earlier. "What I saw out there was very impressive. That should mean something to you. I don't believe in being polite or in flattering an artist even when they were sent by a client or friend of mine. But your talent is oozing out in all directions. It's as if you start something ferociously, then either become bored or back off from it before you're really there. Frankly, I wouldn't know how to assemble a cohesive show with what you've shown me."

Angelica gulped down the rest of the bourbon. "Son of a bitch!" she screamed and her face was scarlet and she was blinking back the tears so fast the room resembled a flashing-strobe-lighted disco.

"It's not an uncommon dilemma."

"But I never seem to go beyond that point," she snapped at him as if it were his fault; anything to keep from crying. Her earlier sense of power was totally dissipated and she was ashamed for having revealed so much of herself.

"I'm very sorry for the outburst and I do thank you for coming down. Forgive me—I don't want to seem ungrateful—but I feel like killing myself . . . don't worry, I won't, but you'd better go."

Zed considered for a moment, then nodded his head as he stood up. "I'll make you an offer, Angelica. Choose any of your bents, don't worry about making the *right* choice, don't even think about it, just make a choice . . . go in one direction."

"I'm not going to do anything desperate," she interrupted. "I live on the ground floor and we don't even have an oven. Believe me!" She tried to laugh.

Zed put his arms around her unexpectedly. "Make a choice.

I guarantee at this point it doesn't matter what choice you make as long as you commit yourself to it. Call me in a month—say the first week in December. If I like what I see I will include you in a large and what promises to be a very exciting group show in March of '81. Does that interest you?"

NOVEMBER 1980

New York City

"She's not doing well." Jone shrugged off her down parka and sat hunched over a stool adjacent to where Whit was hacking away at a large piece of smooth, close-grained sandy limestone. "She hasn't been going to work, which means she's living off the savings she was supposed to live on after the baby was born."

"What do you think?" Whit removed the protective mask he was wearing and gestured to the piece of limestone.

"Yeah, it's coming along." Jone gnawed at her little fingernail until she tasted blood. "I agree with Cathy that there was something perverse in Porter's telling her to turn out four or five cohesive pieces and call him in a month. For Christ's sake, she's going into her seventh month and anyway who the hell knows what's *cohesive*!"

"Why is that perverse?" Whit wiped up the film of limestone dust which had settled around the large tarpaulin he had used to cover the floor of his work area. "I should be so lucky. Angelica has a shot at the best damned gallery in town."

"But look at her! Anyone with eyes can see. . . . How could he put her under that kind of pressure now? Why not tell her to call him when she's ready, that he believes in her and will consider her work when *she*'s ready. Why a month? Why is he in a hurry, huh? I mean, why rush for this particular show of his?"

"Just is." Whit moved to the other side of the limestone. "The guy runs a business, Jonie."

"I thought you liked Angelica."

"I do." Whit picked up the chisel and gouged out a loose particle.

"You don't think Porter's playing God?"

"Oh, come on, Jone!"

"She burned the collages, threw out . . . Shit, I couldn't have done that. You know those fragile, translucent still lifes—the one the Mercer Co-op turned down? She dumped those too. She's calm now but I can just imagine the state she was in to do a . . ."

"You worry too much about her."

"Well, if I don't, who will?" Jone hopped down off the stool. She was close to tears and Whit was so involved with his new limestone piece he didn't even notice.

"I just don't understand why she has such rotten luck!" Jone muttered and went to the worktable Whit had set up for her. Having sold several more pieces, she had reinvested in more expensive materials and was trying her hand on a block of Alabama Cream marble and on a smaller block of Rockingham Royal Black, an inky Virginia stone with white veins.

Jone stared at the Rockingham Royal, trying to penetrate its density and visualize its potential form. Except for her metals and welding equipment she had moved in with Whit three weeks ago and now used the Obil Garage rarely and only as a studio. Even though her present work space was smaller and the light less favorable than it had been at the Charlton Street studio, initially the move had inspired her. She and Whit had engaged in friendly competitions to see who could conquer the Georgia White or who could best deal with the unforseeable flaws and defects which occurred in the various blocks of marble. Since they were both learning a new technique, both studying with the noted sculptor Hans Laeger, there was a great deal of give and take, of excitement and shared experiences. Usually Jone felt invigorated working alongside him. But today his absorption irritated her and she found herself silently criticizing the way he was demolishing the huge chunk of limestone.

Maybe she was getting even with him for being so hard on her work with the Alabama Cream. So what if she had failed to create a sense of spatial movement? It had, after all, been her first attempt at a large piece of marble and she was only beginning to familiarize herself with the various grains and textures. She had observed that Whit was far more meticulous in his approach than she was and while she admired the detailed drawings which served as his models, she was presently intent on exploring her own kinetic responses to the various stones. She did not want to hold herself to a prearranged plan, no matter what he said.

There was also the question of money. Since her pieces were selling and since her new gallery had scheduled a New York show for May and a London show for April she was in a position to speculate and invest money in most costly grades of marble. Whit, on the other hand, was showing his work at yet another unreliable Soho cooperative gallery, and although he joked about the discrepancy in the quality of their materials, Jone sensed his resentment. They were neither one of them accomplished enough to attack the most desirable Carrara marble, that snow white or creamy white stone known as Italian Statuary, but Jone had already decided that as soon as Hans gave the word she would come up with enough money to buy a large block for Whit to work on.

"You're nuts if you do that," Cathy had counseled her. "You start buying him Carrara Blanco and you have just become an addict. A guilt addict, kiddo, because there's no way around it . . . *you* want the marble! If you start giving away what you want, what you need, you're in big trouble. *I* know. It'll kill you to watch him chipping away at a block that you want to sink your chisel into. And I guarantee you won't like anything he does with it . . . then you'll either lie through your teeth or tell him what you really think. You're gonna lose, kiddo, if you buy the Carrara Blanco for the kid!"

She's right, thought Jone, as Whit hammered away at his limestone. There could be no Italian Statuary in her future until she had enough money to buy two pieces. She would feel just too guilty working on it as long as Whit was working on the damned limestone.

"I'm going out." Jone grabbed her parka and started for the door.

"Whoa there, lady! Hey, you just came home." Whit tossed aside his hammer and stopped her. "I thought we were going to get ourselves all dolled up and go to Aimsley's show at Porter—free champagne, maybe some Ohio chitlins!"

"Let's go another time when we can really see the show instead of being shoved and jammed and . . ."

"You're in a swell mood."

"Porter Gallery will be like the BMT at rush hour only the people will smell sweeter."

"Jeee-zus kee-rist!"

"I'm sorry." Jone frowned miserably. "I don't feel like a gay gallery opening tonight."

"I could fix that." Whit nibbled at her neck but she twisted away from him.

"I just feel like being alone."

Whit dropped his arms and looked stung.

"It's not you . . . it's Angelica," she said by way of a halfhearted explanation.

"You're not her goddamned mother!" Whit shouted and kicked the hammer across the floor.

"Maybe I am," Jone snapped.

"What the hell does that mean?" Whit's face froze in one of his most disgusted grimaces.

"It means that she's hurting, that she's afraid, that she's had rotten luck which she doesn't deserve. You know how that bastard at Chase Manhattan Bank led her on about buying a painting and now Zed Porter is leading her on."

"Leading her on," Whit mimicked. "You're out of your mind. Is that what Angelica said?"

"Of course not." Jone fought not to cry. "She takes everything she can get as something positive. She always expects the best. She pretends to accept the possibility that things won't work out favorably; but I've watched her . . . I know her hope is as stubborn as this goddamned Rockingham Black!"

"Well, that's good," Whit continued to shout, "so she's a goddamned optimist. So why are you so fucking worried about her?"

"Because," Jone marched over to him and thrust her chin in his face, "she is killing herself!" She held her hands clasped tightly behind her back because she wanted to put them around his neck and throttle him for not understanding. No one had ever made her this violently angry.

"So screw Angelica's rotten luck." Whit met her eyes defiantly. "People make their own luck."

"Is that so?" flared Jone. "I'll remind you of that the next time you feel like jumping out the window because . . ."

"I don't get depressed and suicidal because of a little setback."

"Neither does Angelica!" For the first time in her life Jone's voice reflected the dynamic power of her body.

"Then why do you worry so much more about Angelica than you do about me?"

Jone wished he had simply asked the question instead of loading his voice with an angry accusative tone. She moved a few feet away from him, trying to understand what was really happening between them, but then the thought of Angelica and her resentment against a system which could not seem to accommodate someone so vastly and richly talented exploded back against him.

"I worry more about her because she's a woman."

"Oh, shit!"

"I worry because Porter Gallery's roster of artists includes only five women. I worry because there is not room in this system for . . ."

"I did not know you were a fanatic." Whit's cooly superior reply fed her anger and she looked around for something to throw.

"Stop your bellyachin'," he told her. "You're doin' all right."

"So far," she snapped.

"Oh, shit," Whit glared at her, "don't talk to me about discrimination."

"The Royal Academy in London in planning an international contemporary painting exhibition for thirty-eight artists, all living except two. There is not a single woman in the show."

"An echo from the seventies. Besides, all that's changed." Whit turned away. "I am so tired of feminist rhetoric. Please spare me."

"But it's true."

"I don't want to hear it." Whit smiled, picked up his hammer, and returned to his limestone. "Anyway, you know I believe in equal rights, so fuck off!"

Jone ground her teeth. She wanted to tell him his piece was ugly, that she could do better, that her present moderate success was only the beginning and that she was going to surpass him in every possible arena.

Only the thought of her success made her sick. It was all a fluke. She would be punished with it or without it.

As she ran from his apartment she was surprised at the odd sound she was making. She was sobbing as she had never in her life sobbed. It was their first fight and already it was a blur. She had no idea what it had been about, only that she was feeling a new agony, more bitter and consuming than anything she had experienced in her twenty-two years.

Angelica sat propped up in Cathy's king-sized bed and smiled wistfully at the ceiling, which was painted the deep blue of a starry night, at once mysterious and soothing. Cathy called it "close-encounter blue" and that, Angelica thought, was accurate.

"Hey, Vinnie!" Angelica's face lit up as Cathy's eight-year-old streaked by the door wearing only his underpants. Vinnie trotted backwards and stuck his face into the room.

"Come here so I can kiss you," Angelica teased and Vinnie smiled shyly and shook his elfin head. Since Angelica's arrival five days ago he had become totally smitten, peeking in on her, sitting on the edge of her bed listening to stories about her Dream People.

"Would you like some milk?"

"When you have time." Angelica resisted the impulse to jump out of bed and chase Vinnie, hug and wrestle his little body. Although the spotting and the pains had stopped three days ago, the doctor had ordered complete bed rest for a week.

"I have time right now." Vinnie winked, then disappeared. She heard his bare feet slapping against the parquet floors and laughed. God, he was a great kid, sensitive, funny, and independent. She really thought that Vinnie's presence, as much as anything, had contributed to her rapid recovery.

After the horror of the near miscarriage, calling Jone at two in the morning to rush uptown to Lenox Hill Hospital, Cathy, ever the fairy godmother, had insisted she leave the often frigid Obil Garage and recuperate in uptown luxury. Angelica had not objected. She was just grateful that she had not paid for her fervor to Zed Porter's deadline with the life of her baby. Now, stretching beneath the pale blue irises which were sprinkled liberally on Cathy's lavender-scented sheets, she felt blessed. It seemed to her, having so narrowly escaped disaster, that her life was about to blossom. The child was safe. She had never meant to come so close, had not realized the lengths to which her mind could drive her body without its knowledge. So she had learned something and that in itself was a miracle. She had learned that, unlike many people, she could not trust what her body told her because her body would always be ruled by her mind and her mind lived in many mansions. She felt stronger and more focused than she had felt since that first burst of exhilaration after leaving Ferris in France.

All of her friends, including Ferris, had rallied around her; even acquaintances from Far Out Inc. had sent flowers or stopped by to see her so that in the course of a few days her perceptions about her effect on others had altered. She had never asked for an acknowledgment of her power over other people, but seeing the deep concern and loyalties which her trouble had evoked in so many people gave her a renewed sense of hope. Because of her solitary nature and the constancy of her own imagination she had always thought of herself as a loner, as someone passing unnoticed through society, except of course when she donned some theatrical apparel and appeared as a presentational art object. But that was different. Now she felt the power of her own presence and that was giving her the courage to look at the world with her own eyes. She wondered if the baby was making her feel more a part of things—this new life inside who was such an important part of her.

Ferris had been to see her every day and yesterday he had, not unkindly she thought, asked her which was of greater importance to her—the child or her work. He might as well have asked if she preferred life or art. The question had no answer, for it was an ultimately absurd question. Like theological questions about the existence of God, the answer could be read only in individual lives, in the expression of faith which, as she had tried to explain to Ferris, on the part of the conscious person meant simply the dedication to act *as if* something were so. Sometimes, she was convinced, the act of faith, the very gesture of a belief, could alter reality.

Now she understood that Jone had perceived one reality correctly and that Jone's decision to have a tubal ligation had been a rational one, given her hunger for work and society's assumptions about childrearing. For the first time Angelica saw how right Jone's decision was for Jone; while on the other hand her own decision to have a child alone was an act of faith—her *own* act of faith. Jone's decision was pragmatic, solid, like Jone's work, and as lucid and logical as her Beele legal heritage had ordained. Angelica's decision, however, while not without thought, was, in society's terms, illogical; it was based on hope, not fact. How was she going to care for the baby, bring in money, and continue her painting?

She *hoped* to find a communal play group, she *hoped* to organize a collective of working mothers, she *hoped* to rally her considerable creative energies and provide a warm and loving environment for her child while continuing her own pursuits. She was brimming with idealistic theories of how she would function in her new mother-woman-artist role. As soon as she left Cathy's she would post notices in the Tribeca area, inviting other women to pool their resources to begin to provide some day care, a support system. There was no getting around it, she thought, she was a pain-in-the-ass crusader just like her socialist father, and the only thing she could hope for was that she, at least, had a better sense of humor about it . . . sometimes.

Cathy burst unannounced into Zed Porter's dimly lit office, a small room adorned with a Gucci leather sofa, an antique Persian rug, Giacometti sculpture and dominated by one large de Kooning oil.

"Who the hell do you think you are?"

"Hello, Cathy." Zed looked mildly amused as he always did with her. "You're not upset by the review in the *Times,* I take it."

"No, I'm not. I didn't come here for consolation."

"I understand that *Time* and *Newsweek* are giving you accolades if that's any . . ."

"You're not listening. I'm not here about my paintings. I'm here about the way you treat my friends."

"I have no idea what you're talking about." Zed looked bewildered and reached for a cigarette.

"Angelica Stein." Cathy advanced until she was standing directly across the desk from him.

"A very strange lady." Zed laughed ambiguously. "I don't understand."

"You *do* understand!" Cathy slapped his desk with the palm of her hand. "Why did you bait her with a promise of a group show in four months?"

"Why shouldn't I?" Zed looked surprised as if his opponent had lobbed a good one just inside the line.

"Because I know how far in advance you plan shows and I also know who will be represented. . . ."

"You're assuming a lot," Zed interjected as if she were joking. "Everything is subject to change, especially in a group show."

"But why tantalize her? Why tell her to call you in a month when she's seven months . . ."

"Oh, I see." Zed shook his head but continued to smile. "I was insensitive, is that what you're getting at? What should I have done . . . offered her maternity pay? I can't plan my shows around someone's . . ."

"You could have, if you were really interested in her work."

"Of course I'm interested."

"Then you could have *asked* her, in her condition, *when* she thought she *might* be able to pull together a cohesive collection for you. See? You could have created a *positive* situation for her instead of putting her under such goddamned pressure."

"No." Zed stopped smiling and put out his cigarette. "No, you're wrong. The girl needs this sort of pressure in order to get over her artistic schizophrenia. I did her a favor."

"You bastard! You think you are God. You only just met her . . . how do you know so much about what she needs?"

He laughed again. "She needs some outside force like me . . . I'll wager that the pressure I've put her under will be just the impetus she needs to . . ."

"Zed, she nearly had a miscarriage trying to meet your deadline."

"Well, I'm very sorry to hear that," Zed replied smoothly, "I truly am."

"Then call her," Cathy urged. "She's staying at my place. Call her and tell her how sorry you are and that you will look forward to seeing her new work *whenever* she's ready."

"I can't do that." Zed fingered a small bronze female figure on his desk. "Of course I'll send her flowers . . . wish her a speedy recovery. I'm not an ogre, Catherine, but I told you I cannot schedule my exhibitions around someone's baby."

"Hell! I've seen you change your shows just because one of your artists was on a bender or . . . or last year when Roberto Diez was strung out on amphetamines."

"That's different."

"Why? Why is it easier to take someone off the hook when they've behaved irresponsibly than when . . . that is if you're really interested in her work."

"I don't want to debate this issue, whatever this issue is, with you. In the first place Angelica Stein is not a client of mine. She is your friend. I did you a favor by going all the way down to some godforsaken deserted trucking zone and I was intrigued by what I saw. She is talented but . . ."

"Don't you understand," Cathy asked softly, "the power you have? If you don't give her more time she's going to take herself right back downtown and work six hours a day again on top of the six she works in an office to support herself."

"That's her choice, then, isn't it? You make her sound like a poor little match girl which is, most definitely, not the impression she gave me. She didn't strike me as a weak, neurotic woman, which is the way you make her sound."

Cathy stood for a moment studying the elegant bronze figure on his desk. Nothing she could say to Zed would shatter his well-bred composure. She picked up her clutch purse and headed for the door.

"Say hello to Lester," he called after her. "I'll send a messenger over with the *Time* review as soon as I receive it."

❁

One more day in bed. Angelica, still propped up in Cathy's bed, drifted peacefully between waking and sleeping in the late autumnal afternoon. She had the sense that she was sleeping with her eyes open, for she could see the quivering, liquid orange light reflected in the large beveled mirror above Cathy's Art Deco vanity. The intoxicating pleasure of sleep was combined with an unusual awareness, like a double image in a mirror—the immediate sensual knowledge of one's existence plus the visual reflection. Angelica heard Cathy come home, saw her sleek chignon reflected in the mirror as she removed something from a drawer. But Angelica lay silently dreaming. It was extremely pleasurable to linger on the plateau between sleeping and waking. Even the contagious laughter of Vinnie and his two pals racing down the hall signaled only a deeper state of relaxation, as did the traffic noises and the faint strains of a Bach prelude which Cathy must have put on in the living room. Something mattered and yet did not matter. She was a person who would never be able to avoid excessive expectation and it was all, all right. For the moment now she truly existed in a state of harmony, somewhere between what might be and what is—yet accepting everything. In this dreamy floating state she recalled snatches from Eliot's *Four Quartets:*

A condition of complete simplicity
(*Costing not less than everything*)

This was that condition—costly and rare but worth the price. She dreamed, or thought of, or saw, or *was* the ghostlike portrait Edouard Vuillard had painted of himself and his friend Varoqui. It was actually a double portrait, a shrouded asymmetrical composition of soft greens and beiges. The glass bottle in the lower right corner was the only indication that the portrait was a mirror image, a reflection revealing a mysterious dialogue between two realities. In this suspended crepuscular state Angelica summoned up memories of wet Chicago springs along the shore of Lake Michigan. She saw her own adolescent face looking out at her. Hadn't she always been intrigued by the many ways reality presented itself? Even her experiments with mannequins in Suzanne's window had primarily stemmed from a fascination with what was happening on the other side of the glass—the reality which is against the reality which is. The layers of life: the face of Angelica inside the lake as opposed to the face of Angelica. Or the face of Angelica in Ferris's eyes?

Beneath the flannel gown Cathy had insisted she wear Angelica's body was damp and clammy. She was even fortified by this awareness as she drifted between past and future, in a place that was not quite the present. The perspiration which poured from her felt more like cosmic energy flowing, freely generated by her body. When the room was finally dark and the remaining reflections were only gray shadows, she switched on the light, reached for her sketchbook and colored pencils, and began drawing the faces of memories which had appeared to her during the day.

❋

Jone brushed all the connections of her torch with a solution of Ivory soap and water to make certain there were no leaks. She had already tested the hoses by immersing them in water and once she had ascertained that the connections were lead-free she was ready to begin. The fire shot out of the nozzle and she began welding two jagged pieces of aluminum. It was the first time since Angelica's near miscarriage that she had been to the Obil Garage to work. It was a relief, too, not to be chipping away at the block of marble to locate the form inside. The process of welding was almost the reverse—here she would watch a piece grow almost as if by some strange process of osmosis between herself and the materials.

It was also a relief to be away from Whit since his new gallery had sold two of his sculptures for an amazing sum and the *Village Voice* had given him a glowing review for one of his abstract bronze pieces. His first success, Jone thought, had given him a messianic complex.

You're just jealous.

Am not, she answered herself. Why would I be jealous? Things have been easier for me than for him. I'm happy for him. I'm happy for him. I'm happy for him.

But he made more money selling one small piece than you made selling three larger ones.

That's petty.

Maybe, but it still irritates you. What are you going to do about it?

I'm happy for him.

She concentrated on maintaining an even, circular motion on the bronze section she would be adding to the multimetal piece. Whit said she was copping out with the marble, that it was too early to tell whether or not she had a feel for it. He kept urging her to abandon the metal work and concentrate on the marble. She didn't care if she *was* copping out, it was a relief to be encased in her apron and gloves building something instead of tearing something down. Whit said that was a simplistic evaluation of sculpting with marble. Lately she had been able to make few observations which did not elicit some disagreement or clarification from him. It was as if he was a judicial committee of one in charge of making amendments to her character.

Jone tried to remember how many arguments or minor disagreements they had had in the past week and came up with four. That wasn't many. Probably most couples had more, and there was still a lot of laughter and of course when Whit lit his incense and candles and they touched without words it was all just as it had been that first day in the phone booth. Cathy said she was being unrealistic, expecting that two people could live together and work together without some kind of friction. Angelica had also urged her to keep her studio separate, to continue working at the Obil. Only Whit wanted her working there with him, crammed into the space he had alloted her. Well now, what was she to expect; he had been there first. It was his loft. Then why did he feel rejected when she spent a day at the Obil Garage?

The reason, Jone had decided, in one of her angry, irrational moments, was that he was an exhibitionist. He sang when he worked. At first it had been funny, his singing bawdy cowboy ditties, or country and western love songs, each one more ridiculously heartrending than the one before. But he was never quiet, unless he was licking his wounds because Jone had not responded appropriately. She was learning that he required constant care, like a baby. True, he did most of the cooking and he was a good cook, but he wanted her there watching, admiring his proficiency as he deglazed.

He did not mind intrusions, seemed almost to thrive on them. In the same spirit, he was always interrupting Jone and if she timidly and delicately hinted that he might postpone his question, his joke, or his song, he accused her of being self-absorbed. The fact was, most of their mild disagreements were rooted in Jone's selfishness, according to Whit.

The bead she was drawing with the torch became wavy as she started to laugh. When she wasn't embroiled in one of their mild disagreements, their life together took on comic-strip proportions. Their tiffs were absurd and trivial, especially when she thought about how much they had in common and how much they loved each other. When she thought of these confrontations in retrospect she was actually amused by the very facet of his ego which had the power to disrupt her concentration and throw her into an emotional tailspin. She could not decide, however, if his ego was immense or painfully small and fragile; either way it was clear that he expected life to revolve around him. He just assumed that it would and was stunned when it didn't.

The large multimetal scultpure Jone was working on looked like a fecund, tenacled plant, a giant bromeliad with natural voids and a seductive vortex. She was preoccupied with shaping the voids as well as the mass. It was not a new concept, Moore was a master of giving form to space, but Jone was, for the first time, specifically addressing herself to this one particular challenge. The piece, which Angelica had named *Peloria*, was growing. Jone was concerned that its ideal proportions might exceed even the wide door to the Obil Garage. Angelica had suggested with her own inimitable candor that Jone's daring piece was a warning to Whit.

"What do you mean?" Jone had hooted.

"Oh." Angelica had gazed off into space with one hand, palm down, moving back and forth above her prickly new haircut. "You never went in for monstrously large pieces before."

"So?"

"You really want to hear?" Angelica grinned. "I love Jung. I should have been an analyst."

"Why is this a warning to Whit?"

"Maybe I'm wrong," Angelica mused.

"You don't believe that," Jone laughed. "You're never wrong!"

"I'm thinking," Angelica went on, staring at *Peloria,* her title —a gift to Jone—which the dictionary defined as unusual regularity in the form of a flower that is normally irregular. Jone, who, if left to her own devices, would have numbered her sculptures, was as usual astonished that Angelica even knew such a word and that she had instinctively grasped what Jone herself could not begin to articulate.

"I've got it." Angelica beamed at Jone. "You're in a double . . . is it blind or bind? I can never remember. Anyway, you're terrified of really competing with him; that's why you've fudged with the marble. Jone, you know I like Whit, but I've seen his work and it doesn't compare with the natural eccentricity of your designs. In your heart you know that—don't you?"

"No," Jone shook her head adamantly. "I think Whit is just finding himself. You and Whit are a lot alike. You both have one foot in the ninth dimension . . . you both have difficulty focusing in on . . ."

"Maybe," Angelica interrupted, "but you're not afraid of competing with me."

"You and I do different things," Jone protested.

"Nope, we're in the same racket, only you're more successful and I'm sure sometimes you feel bad about that. I know you'd enjoy your success more if I was able to get my act together, but you don't suffer because of me . . ."

"Because I believe in you," Jone interrupted. "I know someone, even if it isn't Zed Porter, is going to recognize how brilliant you are."

Angelica waved her hand in front of Jone's nose. "The point is, you didn't suffer on my account when the *New York Times* singled you out as someone to watch. You didn't worry that I was going to fall into a decline because . . ."

"So you say I'm afraid I might be more successful than Whit? Then I should be relieved by the good things that are happening to him now. That should take the pressure off me, right?"

Angelica shook her head, perplexed. "It's hard to keep it straight. Love mucks up your mind . . . women's minds. Mine at least and I think yours, too. So . . . we have to be very precise. Precision is essential. Okay?"

Jone laughed at Angelica's fierce staccato intensity. She was speaking in a stentorian voice Jone had never heard, pacing around *Peloria* like a mad logician with her hands clasped behind her back.

"Now! You would like to be happy with Whit's good news. Right? But you can't! Because: you are pissed at him in other areas . . . for all those interruptions you told me about."

"I used to be quiet inside myself," Jone volunteered. "I would accumulate quietness, in the midst of my very talkative family, by going off alone. Now, even when I'm not with him, my head is noisy. I think about him constantly. It's like going over the last argument we had or . . . figuring out what I'll say to him about something. And . . . and it's not all negative. I'll see something on the street and the words will form as part of my intention to tell him. I can't just register the experience for myself any more. Shit!"

"Very good, Jone. Your forty-five minutes are up and that will be sixty dollars."

"Yeah." Jone gave a wan smile. "I've never been in therapy."

"Me neither"—Angelica paused impishly—"because I am so *awfully* normal. Actually I've never had the money, though Ferris once offered to send me. Imagine! That was rather a classic example of the pot calling the kettle black." Angelica reflected a moment, then continued. "Cathy's been in therapy for eighteen years. She loves it . . . compares it to exercise class. I guess what she means is she exercises or stretches her feelings or her knowledge of her feelings."

Jone closed her eyes and shook her head. "I'm in love and I'm miserable. What the hell am I going to do?"

"Do your work here. I'm not being selfish. I like having you here, but that's not the only reason. If you don't keep that for yourself you'll start turning into Whit. Jesus, I sound like I know something, don't I?"

"Turning into Whit?"

"Possession." Angelica made her hands into claws as she started for the other room.

"Shit!" Jone picked up the torch and put it down again. "I feel like an ungrateful fool for being miserable!"

She followed Angelica into the living area and watched her change out of her nun's habit into a roomy new jumper. "I've got everything," she lamented. "Sex, a guy who loves me and who I love. I got, not a lot, but *some* money coming in and I got a big show scheduled at a really great gallery. You've got no sex, no guy who loves you or at least not one you can trust, no money coming in, and . . . let's face it, Angelica, you must be more realistic, an *iffy* possibility with Porter. Now, why do I have the impression that you are happier than I am?"

Tears came to Angelica's eyes as she pulled one of Jone's big bulky sweaters over her jumper. "I'm just lucky, I guess. Anyway, don't get hung up on happiness. People who are happy all the time are missing out on something . . . and I don't mean suffering."

Angelica gave Jone a big hug. "Go on back to work, kid!"

PART FOUR

"If the past year or two or three has taught me anything it is that my plot of earth must be tended with absurd care. . . ."

Georgia O'Keeffe, painter

DECEMBER 1980

New York City

Angelica ordered a tea with lemon and two brownies, one for herself and one for the baby inside. It was after two so the dining area at the Whitney was almost deserted. She and Ferris would be able to talk at leisure, without being rushed. As the waitress came with her order she noticed a smart-looking, forty-ish, Westchester matron sit down at the table in front of her. The woman's back was to Angelica but she could see her reflection in the window which looked out onto the vacant sculpture garden.

Angelica studied the reflection of the strange woman and heard her order a lemonade. The woman stared at her own reflected image for a moment, then reached in her Gucci handbag and, in one practiced movement, extracted a compact. Angelica watched, fascinated, as the woman powdered her nose with a fluffy pink powder puff, a perfect 1940s movie-pink powder puff. The gesture was enthralling; somehow it seemed to imply so much more. Angelica had the uncanny sensation that because so much was implicit in the gesture the woman was bound to do it again.

A moment later the woman took the pink powder puff out again and Angelica felt a shiver of recognition. She told herself she was creating a fiction out of something as ordinary as a well-dressed lady sitting alone at a table; but then the woman took the powder puff out for a third time. Angelica wondered if she wasn't conjuring up this woman as a psychic projection, a figment of her own imaginative fears. Or perhaps the woman was a walking avant-garde sculpture, a creation of the Whitney Museum's unorthodox inventions? At the Whitney one could never be too sure where the boundaries between art and reality were located. Segal sculptures more real than the people they were cast from seemed to exchange looks with Marisol swimsuit-clad flappers: things were seldom what they seemed.

Still, Angelica was mesmerized by the blond woman and her pristine pink powder puff. She hadn't even known that women still used pink powder puffs. Each time the woman took out the powder puff and gazed at her own reflection, Angelica was seized with a peculiar, ominous sensation. Outside the window the sky had turned steely gray, a few reluctant snowflakes fell. Angelica saw the woman's eyes acknowledge the hesitant flakes but mostly she seemed to be staring blankly at her own reflection. The woman's eyes were blue; faded eyes, eyes which had looked too long at the sun.

What had brought her here, Angelica wondered. A trip to the museum to distract her from what? A clandestine meeting, a tryst, a sudden loss? As surely as she had known the woman would repeat the gesture with the pink powder puff, Angelica knew that some deep sorrow had driven her to perform the compulsive primping. And why had she ordered a lemonade when a glass of wine or a Manhattan with a red cherry would have been so appropriate?

After ten minutes the woman slipped on a pair of enormous dark glasses. She continued to sip her lemonade, confronting her own image and the slate gray of the deserted Whitney sculpture garden. She was so alone, her dead eyes now obscured by the very dark glasses.

There was another powdering; then she removed the dark glasses to scrutinize her solemn face reflected against the gray and the snow. Angelica considered touching the woman on the shoulder, to tell her how beautiful she looked, to interrupt the eerie ritual and give her assurance. But assurance of what?

It was a quarter past two and knowing Ferris's habitual tardiness as she did, Angelica realized it might be another hour before he showed up. She just couldn't wait, not today. She pulled on her ratty olive-drab Army coat, stuffed the uneaten brownies in her pocket, and took one last look at the woman with the pink powder puff. The woman was adding a lip gloss to her already moist lips. Angelica felt like crying; instead she tossed some money on the table and on the way out left a scribbled note with the waitress explaining to Ferris that she had gone back to the Obil Garage.

The Woman with the Pink Powder Puff was alive inside of her, breathing alongside her unborn child. She was so excited, so eager to begin, that she blew seven dollars on a cab.

Jone's unfinished *Peloria* had not been touched in two weeks and though Jone had phoned that morning to say she would be over to work, she was not there. Angelica thought the garage seemed warmer than usual but perhaps it was her own desire which heated her. By five-thirty she had sketched the woman in charcoal. It was a good drawing, and strong. She knew it was. The vision was so deep inside her and she was so connected to it that it never occurred to her that it would not come out. Oh, it would need touching up, adjustments, but it was alive and it was all hers.

The phone rang three times, but she ignored it. Reflections. Ever since that strangely healing experience in Cathy's bedroom she had improvised on the concept, turning out numerous drawings in charcoal as well as some pastels and watercolors. But not until today at the Whitney had she solidified her intellectual and emotional concepts into something *naturally* visual, something not contrived, forced, or simplistic. And she knew that what had happened to her at the Whitney, her own unique perception of the woman, could never have happened without all that had gone before: Angelica inside the mud puddle as opposed to the face of Angelica. Or the face of Angelica in Ferris's eyes.

Ferris! She thought of him first at nine o'clock and, having forgotten that the phone had rung, wondered why he hadn't called. She ate a can of tuna fish and two hard-boiled eggs and sipped at a lukewarm beer. Cathy would say she was being self-destructive for working so hard when she had nearly suffered a miscarriage. But it didn't feel self-destructive and looking at the work-in-progress, she was convinced, for the first time in her life, that she was on the right track. Illusions had always fascinated her but the fascination had been so much a part of her that she had never considered drawing on them for her work.

She thought of all the weird tangents she had gone off on, hoping to come up with something original. Now, viewing the painting, she was struck by how original it was; yet it was the reality she had perceived all her life. She could hardly wait to get on to the next project. Her mind was bursting with ideas. The surrealists had experimented with the illusory nature of reality, but Angelica's vision was more realistic. She was painting more simply than she had painted in her life, yet the result was infinitely more complex and arresting than any of her previous work.

At eleven she called Ferris.

"What the hell?" he exploded.

"Didn't you get my message?" His irritation escaped her. She was still too excited.

"Of course I got your message . . . something about a pink powder puff and to call you. I've been calling you all evening. I was worried."

"Can you come over?"

"Is something the matter?"

Angelica bit her lip to keep from laughing. He was worried; she had better go slow. She wanted him to be the first to see the painting but she couldn't tell him or he'd never come.

"I'll explain when I see you. Please!" She hung up before he could protest. She gulped down a glass of milk and ate a peanut butter sandwich, not because she was hungry but because the baby needed the protein. She was high, high, high. She showered, perfumed, put on a clean sweat shirt over which she pulled a bright caftan Cathy had given her. She dialed his number to make sure he was on his way, then she made a gigantic bowl of popcorn and took out the bottle of champagne she always kept on hand "in case of celebration." She really didn't like champagne but gloried in the ritual it afforded. Ferris would drink the champagne, she would eat the popcorn. She stood back from the painting and cried. If he hated it she would not believe him. She had finally created something she would stand by.

❁

It was two-thirty in the afternoon and Jone, still in her robe, sat brooding and smoking in Whit's bordello bed. Below her, Whit worked happily, whistling and singing along with his favorite yodeling record. Jone had never heard a yodeling record before Whit, though she had, of course, heard of yodeling. Someone had yodeled briefly in the movie *The Sound of Music* and it had added an authentic Austrian touch; but it was best, she thought, when it was brief.

"It's such a happy sound!" Whit had exclaimed when after two months she had confessed that yodeling at breakfast made her gag on her grapefruit.

"It sounds like a very uptight person gargling."

"Does not! It's pure, country, primitive sound. It takes gettin' used to is all. I betcha you didn't like Bach the first time you . . ."

"You can't compare yodeling to Bach!" Jone had identified her mother's cultured Westchester twang in her response.

"Why sure." Whit had been nonplussed. "Bach wrote pieces where the same notes are stressed again and again . . . repetitions, fast pulsations. I see a great similarity . . . except a good yodeler has the spontaneity of a great jazz musician."

"You're joking!" Jone cried apprehensively.

"You gotta listen, Jonie. I've noticed how you always make quick judgments."

Jone considered this for a moment. It was true that she was inclined to know where she stood so far as her tastes in art and music were concerned; but her decisiveness, which had come up for criticism before, was not really the issue, was it?

"I don't like it," she had said bluntly. "I know you do and that's fine. You should be able to listen to it since it's your apartment."

"It's *our* place, Jonie."

"Okay, it's *our* place and you should still be able to listen to your favorite music, only . . ."

"That's what I say!" Whit had interrupted her with a broad grin.

Jone watched him spread a thick glob of honey on his English muffin.

"Only I can't work with the yodeling," she had said after a moment. "I've tried and . . ."

"But you sure can you-know-what to it. Man, you get going real good when Flaxton Teadmeyer starts in with that husky voice of his. Rare to hear someone with a low voice like that get the flexibility in yodeling. But ole Flax sure gets your hips swiv'lin'. Yahhhhhhhhooooo!"

"Be serious." Jone smiled as Whit did a strenuous bump.

"Oh God, I love you!" Whit wiped the honey off his chin and kissed her. "Honey, did you see the way your ass came out of that piece of Vermont stone I was working on? Like it had been livin' right inside for the past million years . . . ever since the Ice Age maybe, just waitin' for me to come on and free it. Did I tell you Larry came by yesterday . . . thinks it's pretty wild. Jeezus, Jone, if he comes through with a spring show in Paris I am . . . *we* are gonna spend April in Paree! Me and my honey strollin' down the Champs, wouldn't you like that? Maybe we'll ride horses, huh? Wouldn't that be somethin' . . . right around the Place de la Concorde . . . in our western finery. Hey, great idea! Two beautiful all-American kids like us, we could knock 'em dead, get tons of publicity. Shit, what an idea. I'm gonna tell Larry he should mention our potential for publicity when he talks to the guy in Paris. Jeezus-shit, wouldn't that be great, Jonie . . . good for us both, huh? Europeans love cowboys!"

Had he totally forgotten she was having her first European show in London in April? "What about the yodeling?" Jone had felt like a bitch for pressing the issue but Whit didn't hear her. He was galloping to the phone to call Larry, slapping his thighs in excitement, and making what Jone had come to think of as rodeo hoopla.

Still sprawled on the bordello bed, she lit another cigarette and rolled over on her back, staring at her reflection in the mirror above. She hated the red drapes Whit had added to accentuate the already tawdry ambiance which he found so erotic. Of course she hadn't mentioned that.

As she could have predicted, Whit had made a huge splash at the family Thanksgiving two weeks before. She wondered if her irritation with him didn't date from that day as much as from anything else. And it wasn't his fault, that was the confusing part. It wasn't Whit's fault at all that her entire family, with the exception of Grandmother Mary, had gushed over him and his loquacious ideas about art and freedom. That one day had convinced Jone that even in the eyes of her own family, Whit's talents and ideas were superior to hers. Her father had hung on every word of Whit's (they called him Whittemore) analysis of Moore's *Internal and External Forms*; both her mother and sister appeared to have memorized the portion of the *Voice* review which called Whittemore Russell's recent bronze abstracts "a fierce and powerful example of the new wave of spatial freedom in sculpture."

Whit fitted right in with the Beeles, topping them with his loquaciousness, mesmerizing them with his western drawl and his size 13-D clunking cowboy boots. She had actually observed her father staring wistfully at Whit's boots, as if he were wishing to be in them. Her family was so relieved that she had found someone—and Whit was surely a more impressive someone than they had ever expected from her—that they had in Jone's opinion behaved like fools. Only her grandmother, sitting quietly in front of the fireplace, had seemed dubious. But what did that mean? Jone frowned at her own sloppy image. Shouldn't she be happy that her family had fallen in love with Whit?

On the train back into the city, she had picked a niggardly fight with him, accusing him of interrupting her every time she opened her mouth to make a comment. When he had been unable to remember the incidents, Jone had said that was because he had never shut up. In rebuttal Whit had raved about her family, about how warm and hospitable they were and how peculiarly Jone had behaved with them. There had been no way for her to tell him how hurt she had been by their interest in his work when all along, even with her recent success, they had never encouraged her or expressed their pleasure, let alone their *awe*, at her success, as they had with their (so they thought) potential son-in-law.

She felt like an outsider, caught between her family and her lover, and since Thanksgiving she had spent a total of seven hours working. Whit said that was fine, that she needed a vacation. He seemed happier since she spent her days sleeping. He said her prodigious output during the past year had sapped her strength and she needed time to accumulate her own power again.

When Jone arrived at Cathy's apartment later that afternoon Bing Crosby and the Andrew Sisters were cranked up full in a perky rendition of *"Mele Kalikimaka,"* which Vinnie, who answered the doorbell after the third ring, translated as "Merry Christmas" in Hawaiian.

"Come on in, I'm getting into the spirit!" Cathy, in jeans and an Ohio State sweat shirt, was surrounded by boxes of all shapes and sizes and rolls of colorful Christmas paper and ribbons. "I promised myself I'd get these in the mail by December first and I'm only three days late so I'm ahead of schedule."

"That can't be a new song. He's dead, isn't he?" Jone thought irritably that Cathy's music was almost as offensive as Whit's yodeling.

"*Mele Kalikimaka,*" sang Cathy along with Bing and the Sisters. "You're so damned young. I keep forgetting that about you. This music is my vintage. For once I am going not only to be ready for the holidays, I am going to *love* them! Did you know we were going to France for . . ."

Cathy broke off and yelled at Vinnie to turn the record over so that Jone could get into the spirit.

"You sounded bad on the phone, honey. Is something the matter between you and Whit?"

Jone shrugged and began making a large red bow for Cathy to use on one of her packages. "I have a sense of *déjà vu* coming here like this. I think I've come for professional advice again, only I'm not sure."

Cathy nodded.

"I'm not sure what's personal and what's professional. I'm not sure of much right now."

Cathy waited for Jone to continue as the strains of Bing's sonorous voice began "Silent Night."

"I'm in a slump. Can't work."

Cathy put the wrapping aside and perched herself on the corner of the long mahogany banquet table with her legs folded into a tight lotus position. "Shall I say I told you so? Honey, you gotta move your work back to the garage. It's no big deal."

"It's a big deal to him. He wants us to be equals . . . no, 'an egalitarian relationship' is what he calls it. He read about it in *Ms.* magazine."

Cathy chuckled. "I'm sorry, Jone. I know you're upset but just the image of him . . . sorry, go on."

"Well, you're right. He's cute. He means well. That's what's so . . ." Jone broke off, exasperated.

"I know. He told me all about how he worked for the ERA and we both think that's just great. But honey, with all his good intentions, he's still operating with batteries that were manufactured in the fifties. He told me his Mama was FFV and DAR, didn't believe in contraception, let alone the other, and never worked a day in her life. He may be struggling against it, but his little heart is still beating to the rhythm of horse's hooves on the open range. I betcha if you kiss him good-bye every morning and go off to work, when you come home things'll be a lot better."

"I don't think that will solve it." Jone shook her head. "I'm jealous of him. I shouldn't be but . . ."

"Shouldn't," interrupted Cathy, "is a word we could all use a little less frequently. Why are you jealous?"

"It's so petty."

"We're the petty sex," laughed Cathy. "Why the jealousy?"

"Because when he finally started selling . . ." Jone tossed her blond head and felt nothing but the futility of her situation.

"It brought more money than yours, right?"

"A lot more." Jone gave a self-deprecating smile. "Before that happened I felt guilty for making more money than him."

"Damned if you do and damned if you don't," Cathy said. "So you're thinking of bagging out?"

Jone nodded. "I guess. It's too exhausting having an egalitarian relationship."

"Only you love him."

"It doesn't seem to be a problem for him." Jone looked perplexed. "And he does all the things my sister used to gripe about her husband not doing when she got married . . . he cooks, he cleans, picks up his socks . . ."

"You're always worried about him, right?" Cathy asked. "He's like a constant voice inside your head and you want to make absolutely certain that what you do will be good for him, won't harm, hurt, or anger him?"

Jone nodded.

Cathy clicked her tongue against the roof of her mouth. "Honey, it's a tough one but you put him inside your head and you can take him out. Jesus, when I think of my first husband . . . the poor bugger was plagued his whole life with an overabundance of testosterone! Honey, Whit is a find. Don't bag out completely. You're just learning to enjoy men and, take it from me, it won't be easy to find a replacement for Whittemore Russell. He's a good kid."

"My parents think he's Michelangelo. The only woman sculptor my mother's heard of is Louise Nevelson and she's got a vendetta against her because of her eyelashes."

Cathy's smile faded as she hopped down from the table and placed an F.A.O. Schwartz mechanical spaceman in a box.

"God, I'd like to do something as spectacular as Nevelson's *Frozen Lace*!"

"You will." Cathy smiled gently.

"No," Jone shook her head. "I feel like everything in me is drying up. Who the hell ever started the rumor that love inspires people? But if I'm this unhappy maybe I don't love him."

"Jesus, I hate to see you like this, Jone. Maybe you should talk to my doctor, honey. Might do you good just to let it all out to a professional. It doesn't have to be a long-term thing, you know . . . just a few visits might help."

Oh, terrific, thought Jone, just what I need—a goddamned shrink! She was furious at herself for coming to Cathy for advice. After all, Cathy was still floating in limbo between a husband and a lover half her age. What the hell did Cathy know? Jone felt like pointing out that to begin with she did not have twenty years of her life to spend in therapy as Cathy had, and that even if she did she wouldn't choose Cathy's psychiatrist because he clearly had not cured Cathy.

Jone disguised her flash of anger with one of her mother's cheerful smiles and followed Cathy into the kitchen for a polite cup of tea.

". . . and we're all going to France," Cathy announced gleefully. "I can't wait. We'll have a week in Paris to do business—I'm gallery shopping since I've decided to dump dear old Zed."

"Really?"

"Can't believe it myself." Cathy stood with her hands on her hips waiting for the kettle to boil. "I mean he's Lester's friend, for Christ's sake, and he virtually put me on the map in Europe and nice little old me can't stand to offend anyone. Only I did it! I am out in the cold, honey . . . same as Angelica."

"Hardly," Jone said tightly.

"You're right," Cathy admitted. "Anyway, after Paris we go to a darling little French village on the Swiss border. Lester's hired a chef and everything!"

"You and Lester are reconciled?"

"Hmmm." Cathy smiled ambiguously. "Well, we are spending the holidays together . . . Tony, too. It's an experiment. You might say we're taking our show on the road—then maybe we'll get our act together back here! Well . . . it should be fun."

"And Vinnie?" Jone could not hide her shock.

"Of course Vinnie's going." Cathy took the whistling kettle off the stove.

Bing was crooning "I'll Be Home for Christmas" and Cathy's eyes were moist as she dropped a thin slice of lemon into Jone's tea.

A husband, a lover, and a son? The logistics made Jone squeamish and she could hardly bring herself to look at the older woman, the woman she had admired, the woman she had come to for advice. Jone felt set adrift on an unfamiliar sea.

Cathy wiped the tears from her eyes as Bing sang that he would only be home for Christmas in his dreams.

She's so bloody sentimental, thought Jone, hating Cathy, hating herself for being there.

"I'm such a sentimental slob!" declared Cathy, unabashedly crying and smiling as she sloshed the tea all over the counter.

❀

Next to *The Woman with the Pink Powder Puff* were three large completed canvases done in the same simple, realistic style. The second oil painting was an agonizing interpretation of an Atlanta black mother gazing at a picture of her missing child; the third was a variation of the same woman and child from a different perspective, and the fourth and largest painting was a circle of black children staring at their reflections in an idyllic lily pond.

For months the horror of the missing black children had weighed on Angelica, yet she had never considered translating her responses into art. Then immediately upon completion of the painting conceived at the Whitney, she had visualized these three paintings in their entirety. The reflections of the children's faces in the lily pond were haunting not cloying, and in the other paintings there was a bitter, cutting quality to the black mother's resignation as she gazed at the picture of her missing son. They were good. Even Ferris, who was not inclined toward this particular style, was impressed.

Not that it would have mattered if he had not liked them, Angelica told herself. But he did and there was, she grudgingly admitted to herself, a great pleasure in having his approval.

She had not gone back to work at Far Out Inc. since Thanksgiving, but her dwindling funds did not concern her. In any case there was enough money in reserve to cover the maternity costs and to live for a month after the birth. The woman in charge of hiring at Far Out Inc. had promised that she would give Angelica whatever outside free-lance work she could. Ferris had tactfully proposed a no-strings-attached loan to tide her over until the new paintings sold. The promised cradle was installed next to her bed, and a shower instigated by one of her co-workers at Far Out Inc. had netted her an appealing array of pastel baby apparel. Angelica had never felt more prepared in her life.

On December 8, having completed four paintings (the largest was 36 by 28 inches, the smallest 18 by 20 inches) she phoned Zed Porter's office.

"The paint's not even dry," she said breathlessly. "And not only that, I have some rough sketches for three more ideas. I feel like I can't stop."

"Sounds good," Zed responded. "I have an opening at eight, and I'll stop by afterward."

"Yes," Angelica replied confidently, "they *are* good!"

Angelica and Jone spent the afternoon setting up the show. Jone had moved Angelica's easels and her own sculptures (all except for the still growing *Peloria*) into the living area. Angelica had spent over a hundred dollars on track lighting which Jone had installed above the paintings, so that Zed would have ideal conditions in which to view the new paintings. That evening he knocked at the door. Angelica, who was stationed doorside, like a butler, opened it immediately.

"I see you're smiling." Zed kissed her warmly on the lips as if they were old friends and he stopped in like this every week. "Not going to hide in the other room this time?"

Angelica blushed and took his coat. She stayed at his side as he approached the paintings and watched his face as he studied them. He was very serious, moving closer to *The Woman with the Pink Powder Puff*, then away, twisting his head to one side, then to the other. After less than five minutes he turned to her and opened his arms. Angelica looked at him blankly.

He smiled slowly. "Come here."

She obeyed him in a daze and he hugged her.

"I was right," he said. "I knew you had this in you. My dear, the Porter Gallery would be proud to represent your work."

Angelica went limp against him and he held her. She couldn't say anything and made no effort to pull away. He looked as though his body would smell of sea water and the Caribbean sun and she was surprised at the stale odor of tobacco which permeated his clothes. But tonight that usually offensive smell was alluring in its masculinity and she relished it for a moment before pulling away.

"The show is in March." There was a familiar challenge in the way he was smiling at her and she smiled back as a sense of absolute power surged through her. Tonight there would be such a celebration with Whit and Jone!

"Will you need money to live on until then?"

Angelica exaggerated a blink and moved her shoulders up and down and up and down still smiling at him. She needed nothing to live on; he had already given her all that she required.

"When is the baby due?" He appraised her with a succinct smile.

Angelica was flustered, there were too many conflicting signals emanating from him. She could still feel the lean hardness of his chest on her breasts, it was the first time in her life she had ever had large breasts and the sensation of a man's body against her was a totally new experience. Of course she was reading his signals correctly, she affirmed to herself.

"Late January . . ."

He nodded without taking his eyes off of her. They stood facing each other. Angelica felt at the edge of a new precipice.

"What's going on?" She bit her lower lip as she asked the question.

"You must know." Zed held his ground, still gazing at her.

"I do know," she said haltingly. "Yes, I do."

"I've made you an offer." Zed broke his meaningful stare with a little laugh and a boyish smile. "It's one you can't refuse. The show, I mean." He laughed infectiously and moved toward her.

"You'll want more paintings." She glanced at *The Woman with the Pink Powder Puff*.

"If you can manage. We can talk about that later. I don't usually make an offer like this but . . . but in this instance, because of your situation, I'd like to forward you an advance on the sale of these four."

"I could use it." Angelica was aware that he had moved closer, that he had encircled her neck with his hand.

"Giacometti," he said.

"Very thin," laughed Angelica. "Too thin. Like a giraffe almost."

"A swan." He moved his fingers lightly just above the surface of her skin.

Angelica laughed a false, unfamiliar laugh, one that she hated. She caught herself and turned to him.

"How about taking a rain check," she blurted out and knew instantly that it had been a clumsy, stupid remark. His seductive smile went cold and Angelica blundered ahead with her usual candor, except that she was stammering and her face was pinched and tense. "I was very attracted to you but . . . it would be difficult being in my . . ." She laughed self-consciously. ". . . condition . . . but . . . I mean, you must understand we're not just two people meeting under normal circumstances."

"Of course we're not two normal people." He laughed a contained, country-club laugh. "We knew that about each other instantly, didn't we? I'd say we both knew that the last time I was here. I suppose you'd like to go to dinner?"

The question was a savage challenge couched in a charming insinuation, a form he had perfected. Angelica paused, uncertain about how to continue but wanting to salvage something. She decided to answer him literally. "I would like to have dinner with you. We could celebrate. I would treat."

He moved off the stool to get his coat, chuckling good-naturedly as if she had uttered some witticism.

"Actually I have a dinner engagement . . . somehow it slipped my mind . . . some pain-in-the-ass meeting at that new hotel, the Palace. Have you seen it?"

"No," Angelica shook her head mechanically. What had happened, what was going on?

"It's over the old Villard Mansion on Madison and Fifty-second; you know, the one modeled after the Palazzo della Cancelleria in Rome. Perhaps the most famous room is the Gold Room with the La Farge mural . . ."

"Mr. Porter . . ." Angelica interrupted incredulously.

"Are you all right, Angelica?" He extended a gloved hand and she grasped it.

"I haven't offended you?" she asked, knowing that anything she said would be wrong.

"Of course you haven't offended me." He tilted her chin up and smiled warmly at her.

"Your attitude toward me changed so suddenly and I . . . I only wanted to explain. I didn't mean to be glib when I said . . . You see I've gone through my life hopping on one leg—you know, with the other foot in my mouth."

"You mustn't worry," he ordered her with paternal firmness. "I'll send someone down for those paintings this coming Thursday . . . I believe it's the eleventh."

"But do you understand," she persisted, "what I was saying to you?"

"You're too sensitive," he said at the door. "I wonder that you've survived so long." He kissed her lightly on the cheek and left her standing in the open door watching as he climbed into the back seat of his waiting limousine. She stood in the door for a long time after he had driven off and when she finally went back inside she studied her paintings, weighing their merits against whatever resentment Zed Porter might be feeling against her.

She had wanted him, that was true. Had he seen that? Had she been so obvious in their first interview that he had returned expecting . . . ? How could he have expected that? She was almost positive she had contained her fantasies, that nothing had spilled over. And anyway, she told herself, that sort of behavior from a man, the continual sexual bartering, had been eliminated by the sexual revolution, hadn't it? No, she had to be deluding herself. My God, of all the women he must come in contact with, why would he be interested in her with her unwieldy swollen body? No, it couldn't be. She had to be imagining . . . Only his reaction, once she had addressed herself to the situation, to what was unmistakably a pass, had been to pretend as if nothing had happened.

Angelica switched on the small black and white Zenith television which Jone's sister had dedicated to their cause. Maybe nothing had happened. Maybe her vulnerability and desperation had made her imagine, or project, what she really desired. Maybe being so close to her heart's desire was making her hallucinate, making her nearly mad . . .

Angelica gaped at the television. The Beatles—Paul, Ringo, John, and the one whose name she could never remember—were singing "Hey, Jude." They were young, the way she remembered them when she marched in antiwar demonstrations. They looked like children with their hair in bangs, long but not too long. They were innocent and fresh, and their music, the music of the ever-hopeful . . . and John Lennon was dead. He was, he was dead.

For the next hour Angelica sat transfixed in front of the television watching the network's instant replay of John Lennon's life. How had they accumulated an entire life on such short notice? It was if they had been preparing for the memorial service for months.

It was bad for the baby. She turned off the television but her sense of horror, the overwhelming futility she felt, was too acute to face the night alone. She thought of going uptown to stand in the rain outside the Dakota with the throngs of Lennon's mourners but that was out of the question. She sat rubbing her bulging stomach and reminded herself that she was carrying life. Poor Yoko.

It was all too much to bear alone. She phoned Ferris, relieved that he was home, that he had no plans for the evening and was eager to meet her for dinner.

"It's terrible," he said later over coffee, referring to Lennon's murder. "I wasn't a fan but it's still . . ."

"I know," Angelica interjected and then abruptly she said, "Porter liked my paintings."

"I'm not surprised." Ferris smiled. "Is this a celebration then?"

"I don't know," Angelica shrugged, unable to sustain any hope. "He said he was sending someone to pick up the paintings."

"My God!" Ferris jumped up from the table and hugged her with unprecedented spontaneity and enthusiasm. "So smile . . . I mean, I know this other has complicated your feelings but my God, Angelica, this is some helluva piece of good news!"

"I'm afraid to believe him," Angelica said soberly.

"But if he said . . . Come on now, of course it's hard for you to believe your good fortune. Angelica?" Ferris made a funny smile, the way adults do to children when they want to cheer them up. He had never done that before, had always either wilted in the face of her unhappiness or become impatient.

She smiled to please him. "I am glad that you were home when I called. I didn't want to be alone tonight."

❁

"Where have you been!" Whit yelled as Jone came in the front door at ten o'clock at night.

"Would you believe sitting in the Temple of Dendur thinking?" Jone asked sheepishly.

"Jeeeee-zus Keeeee-ow!" Whit hollered.

"I guess I should have called."

"You guess?"

"I just lost track of time." Jone tried to hug him. "I'm sorry."

"The Met closes at eight or something."

"Don't cross-examine me, Whit. That's where I was."

"Shit!"

"Whit, it's no big deal. It may not be the last time I lose track of time. You might even lose . . ."

"No way, lady. No way I'd . . . 'sides it's different for me. I s'pose you took the subway home?"

"Of course I took the subway."

"JEEE-ZUS!"

"Oh, stop." Jone glanced at his limestone piece which was coming along and back to her Rockingham Black which looked like a wad of Black Jack gum which had been chewed too long. "Shit!" Suddenly she was angry, too.

"Jesus!" Whit shook his fist at her. "Why are *you* mad? I'm the one who's mad. I'm the one who has a right to be mad."

"So only one of us can be mad at a time? Are those the rules?" Jone yelled.

"I'm the one who's mad because I'm the one who's been sittin' here imaginin' you been raped or mugged or somethin'."

"Why would that happen to me?" Jone looked surprised.

"Jesus, you're naive. Don't you read the papers?"

"No, I'm tired of reading about the hostages and the kids in Atlanta. No, I don't read the . . ."

"You live in a dream world, lady, and that's what has me worried. You shouldn't be out alone this late."

"Ten? Ten is late? I don't believe you said that!"

"I sure as hell did say it."

"How did I get around before I met you?" Jone shoved her hands in the pockets of her parka as if she were outside in the middle of a blizzard.

"I wonder that myself," Whit fumed. "Jee-zus, I was worried!" He hunched his shoulders forward and began to cry. Jone blinked. She had never seen him cry before.

"Oh God." She burst into tears and threw her arms around his neck and they stood there sobbing in each other's arms.

After two all-night marathons of tears, talk, and lovemaking Jone and Whit decided that for the time being they could not technically live together. By the end of the week Jone was back at the Obil Garage trying to funnel her energy back into her work but mostly she was wondering what Whit was doing and when he would phone. Her agent, David Epstein, was pressuring her because he had expected to see two pieces before Christmas and so far he had seen none. The Whitney Museum had made a last-minute alteration in its February group show of new American sculptors and was considering Jone Beele along with four other candidates to fill the vacant position. It had been this news which had impelled Jone to return home to the Obil; however, she had been afraid to tell Whit her news and therefore had told no one of the Whitney's interest.

She was wearing her soundproof earmuffs for the final grinding and polishing of *Peloria* and did not hear Angelica come home in the midafternoon. Around five she stopped for a break and found Angelica lying on her bed with a pillow under her legs.

"I thought you were working till seven."

"I thought so, too," Angelica said. "I had a little pain."

"How little?" Jone forgot completely about Whit for the first time in four days.

"Minuscule," Angelica assured her. "Honest, I'm not being brave. I called Dr. Nigel, he didn't seem worried . . . said to rest when I got home. He didn't even tell me to leave work early. I just thought it'd be a good idea."

Jone stooped down and examined Angelica's face closely.

"I'm not lying." Angelica tried to smile. "But I'm tense. Too tense, I know I'm too damned tense and I can't seem to . . ."—she broke off and took a deep breath— ". . . relax. Did anybody call me today?" Jone shook her head. "And nobody stopped by to pick up the paintings?"

"I didn't know it was today. Damn!" Jone slapped her thigh. "I had my goddamned earmuffs on!"

Angelica brightened. "Maybe they came and you didn't hear!"

"Shit, what an oaf. Let me call, okay? Jeez, I'm sorry. If you'd told me . . ."

"I didn't want to think about it," Angelica said, "not out loud anyway. Zed said he'd send someone on Thursday and that's . . ."

"Let me call and find out. You lie still. Shit, they could have come this morning and I could have phoned you at work and you wouldn't have had the fuckin' pains!"

"Stop already," Angelica told her, feeling another sharp twinge as Jone dialed Zed Porter's office. She closed her eyes and tried not to listen to the conversation.

"There must be a mix-up," Jone said sharply. "No, it was *today* . . . Angelica Stein, Charlton Street, for a March show . . . the group show, right." Jone shook her head impatiently as she waited for the secretary to come back on the line. "You're sure? You checked?"

There was another long pause. Jone's own stomach knotted up as the secretary responded. "Then give me his number in London because there's been a mistake!"

"Don't tell me." Angelica smiled feebly as Jone hung up the receiver.

"She could be wrong," Jone said. "Maybe Cathy knows where he stays in London."

"The Connaught," Angelica said automatically.

"How do you know?"

"Where else would a man like Zed Porter stay?" Angelica adjusted her position on the sofa. "Jone, don't bother Cathy . . . forget about calling London. Nobody is coming for the paintings today or any day."

"But . . ."

"No," Angelica interrupted firmly. "I just want to concentrate on staying calm. Jesus, what timing! But you know what? I keep thinking of John Lennon. It's all very brief, Jonie, and very relative. I just want to concentrate on staying calm. I'd even eat one of your tuna casseroles if you could be persuaded to fix one."

Jone frowned miserably as she began dinner preparations. "The son of a bitch. Why would he . . . ?"

"Some people just can't stand to say no to someone's face. Maybe he didn't have the heart to disappoint me."

"Oh, shit, Angelica. It's one thing to be philosophical and another to be a goddamned Pollyanna. Stop being so understanding!"

"You're right," Angelica admitted after a moment.

"Let me call Cathy." Jone started for the phone.

"No! She's done enough. Anyway, there could have been a mix-up. Let's wait till tomorrow, okay?"

Jone gouged the can opener into the can of tuna and twisted it vehemently.

"I'm glad you're here," smiled Angelica.

"Yeah, me too," Jone smiled back. "And I guarantee all that work you did for Porter is going to pay off. I just bet that by the time the baby's here you'll have gallery representation for those paintings. You know, I should call David."

Angelica took a deep breath. "Tell me again what his secretary said."

Jone added a can of anchovies to the casserole. "She said Porter had left detailed instructions, as he always did, to be carried out in his absence. There was no mention of your name in either the instructions or in his date book. He didn't even have you scribbled in on the day he came down here to see the paintings. The eighth, wasn't it?"

"The day John Lennon was shot."

"She also said Porter had okayed the galleys for the March show catalog a week ago."

"Why do I feel I've escaped with my life?" Angelica asked thoughtfully, watching Jone chop some scallions. "I mean John and Yoko were coming home from recording an album and then it just happened."

The next morning when Angelica went to work at Far Out Inc. she was surprisingly relaxed and contained. She trusted Jone's belief in her new work and although she was deeply disappointed she was at the same time relieved to be rid of the ambiguity surrounding her relationship with Zed Porter. Oddly the whole ordeal had not been so much a blow to her ego as it had been a lesson in the art of self-preservation. After work she did not rush back to the Obil to paint. With the Porter pressure off she shopped for a few Christmas gifts and went to see a Japanese film. She arrived at the Obil around nine, experiencing a very slight abdominal pain, which she interpreted as the last stab of hope that the four paintings would have been miraculously called for.

But no, the paintings were just where she had left them and

Jone, in goggles and earmuffs, was engrossed in a preliminary polishing of one portion of *Peloria*.

Briefly Angelica returned a call to Ferris. She had poured herself a glass of milk when an abrupt pain seized her uterus with such force that she fell to the floor. The glass flew from her hand and she screamed.

By the time Jone reached her the unremitting pain was unbearable. She struggled to remain confident, to remember the Lamaze breathing instructions.

"Labor," Jone kept saying. "That's all. Just breathe. One, two . . . hold. So what if the baby's early . . . better than late, huh? Just breathe!"

While Jone ran outside to find a cab Angelica tried to do the impossible. It was all happening too fast. She felt as though she were falling from some great height and there was no way to break the fall. She put her hand between her legs—the blood was warm and dark; the knifelike pains seared her body like flames. By the time Jone carried her to the cab, Angelica had stopped screaming and had gone into shock.

At three in the morning Whit and Jone left Cabrini Hospital and took a cab back downtown to Whit's loft. The baby girl had had perfect, wrinkled hands, shiny pink fingernails, and Angelica's narrow face and coal-black hair. It would not have been quite so devastating, thought Jone, had she not resembled Angelica so much.

They rode all the way downtown without talking; Whit smoothed the top of her head rhythmically. The night, which had begun before ten, seemed much longer than it had actually been. In reality it had been only four hours of agony, then hope, then panic, and then hope again. Angelica had suffered from traumatic internal bleeding. The separation of two thirds of the placenta from the uterus, known clinically as *abruptio placentae*, had occurred with characteristic speed and almost no premonitory signs.

The cab stopped in front of Whit's building and Jone, still

clinging to his hand, waited numbly while he paid the driver. Still in silence he led her inside, undressed her, and helped her into bed. All night she had been on the verge of nausea and now she curled her body into a tight fetal knot and squeezed her eyes shut to keep from vomiting. Although Angelica had lost over three liters of blood she was going to be fine. Ferris was with her now. The baby had lived for two hours and twenty minutes, something of a feat in these cases, according to the doctors. The loss of blood had, of course, affected the baby; she had been born fatally anemic and Angelica had never even had a chance to hold her.

❁

On Christmas Day the temperature plummeted to a frigid eleven degrees with gusting northwesterly winds, but Angelica, who was staying uptown at the Beresford while Cathy was vacationing in France, had asked if the four of them might take a Yuletide walk. Since this was the first request she had articulated since the baby's death, Ferris and Jone had whipped up a frenzy of enthusiasm for the midafternoon trek through snowy Central Park.

"This is not fun!" Whit pulled Jone aside so that Ferris and Angelica who were walking up ahead could not hear. "I am not having fun with you, Jone!" A dense cloud formed in front of his face as his warm breath hit the frigid air.

"Well, I'm not having fun with you either." Jone's eyes blazed behind her red ski mask. "So go back inside and sulk. I don't care."

"Jee-zus, it's not the cold I'm talkin' about. I can deal with environmental frigidity."

"Oh God," Jone interjected sarcastically.

"I mean this walk could be the highlight of the goddamned day!"

"Don't talk in circles," Jone told him. "What do you mean?"

"We coulda had a relaxing, good old time with your folks. Who needs to be depressed on Christmas?"

"Apparently you do," said Jone, and tucking her head down

she trotted ahead. Whit had been miserable all day, for that matter he had been edgy for the past week, and she was no longer able or in the mood to rationalize his moodiness as the Christmas blahs.

She had gone back to living with him at the O.R. Corral the night Angelica had gone into premature labor. Their first week together had been perfect. He had seemed either to understand or to be reconciled to her preference for solitary work and on the days when she did not go over to the Obil to work on her welding there had been very few interruptions and no yodeling until four in the afternoon. Angelica's loss seemed to have intensified and strengthened their love, or so Jone had thought until the past week.

"Why don't you just come out with it?" Jone asked as he caught up with her. They paused at the bridle path as two horseback riders approached. The snow was so dry and the air so frigid that the horses' hoofs stirred up a white wake as they galloped past.

"Would you talk to me!" Jone tugged at his arm. "Angelica and Ferris are going to think all we do is fight. We had that argument last week when we went to dinner with . . ."

"Don't remind me!" Whit interrupted, kicking the snow with his big boot. "Look, the snow doesn't even stick, it's so cold. I never seen snow this cold, did you?"

Jone glared at him and ran off again; this time she caught up with Angelica and Ferris. "We'll meet you back at Cathy's, Whit wants to baste the turkey once more before it's done."

Angelica, swathed in one of Cathy's bright scarfs, nodded to Jone.

"You're sure you don't want to go back?" Ferris asked her, but she shook her head solemnly and looked off toward the Delacorte Theater and the frozen pond beyond it.

Ferris and Jone exchanged worried shrugs. "Tell Whit to open the Lafite so it can breathe," Ferris called after Jone.

Whit was still kicking the snow, his face drawn into a petulant scowl.

"Please," Jone begged," can we go back and talk?"

The smell of roasting turkey permeated the Aimsley apartment as Whit and Jone let themselves in. Whit folded up his gloves and scarf with his face frozen in a look of fierce concentration, then he slid them neatly into his pocket. Jone watched him, finding it more and more difficult to stay angry. His face was red and blotchy from the cold and Jone kept seeing him as a scared little boy.

"A brandy to warm up?" he asked.

"We shouldn't drink Cathy's . . ."

"Jesus, Jone, she said help ourselves."

"Okay." Jone took off her boots and padded across Cathy's deep crimson Oriental rug to accept the brandy. They clinked glasses grimly and sat side by side on the velvet sofa staring at each other.

"I feel like a shit," Whit began finally. "But I can't help it." He looked hard at Jone as if no more explanation was necessary, then he took another swallow and studied his feet as he wrinkled his toes inside his heavy gray thermal socks and continued.

"You know when this started, don't you?" he asked.

Jone made no sign. She knew when his attitude toward her had changed but she could never have articulated it except in anger and now she was no longer angry at him. She was frightened.

"You're right," Whit nodded as if she had answered. "When your agent called and said the Whitney had chosen you as a replacement. That's right, babe, that's when it all started to go sour."

Jone remained silent. They sat motionless for some time, poised like stiff, ill-conceived statues on the edge of the sofa.

After a while Jone, still staring off, said, "We should be able to deal with this."

"It's not *we*," Whit said hotly, as if she had insulted him. "It's me. You didn't do anything. I'm the pig."

"You're not a pig." Jone began crying and reached for his hand.

"No, I am," he shoved her off. "Here you get this great break and all I can think is it didn't happen to me. I wasn't even in the running, for Christ's sake. I mean, let's face it, I'm not that much of a contender."

"Not yet!" Jone shook his shoulders. "But you will be. I know you will. I just got lucky. That's all it is, believe me! It's so much luck. I don't deserve it anymore than . . . Look at Angelica . . ."

"I know that's the example you always use," Whit said dubiously.

"But you agree," Jone persisted. "You agreed how incredible her last work has been. You said yourself Porter was an idiot for not taking her on."

"I just don't think . . ." Whit stood up suddenly, smoothing the wrinkles out of the thighs of his jeans. "I'd better baste that turkey."

Jone put her arms around him and laid her cheek against his fanny, hugging him to her. She began to kiss his buttocks, making little smoochy sounds in an effort to lighten his mood.

"Jone! Stop!"

She followed him into the kitchen, agonized by his feeling of insecurity and his sense of worthlessness.

"Whit, we just can't let this get us."

"You keep saying *we*!" He turned on her furiously. "It's *me*. Stop taking everything for yourself!"

"I didn't . . . I just mean, when two people are competing in the same area there are bound to be times when one of them seem to be doing . . ." Jone broke off, unable to think logically. She watched Whit meticulously basting the turkey, tucking the aluminum foil neatly around the breast to keep it from drying out. In her memory Christmas had always been a lonely, miserable gathering characterized by excessive gift-giving, forced bonhomie, and too few unadorned gestures of real closeness. Her mother, inevitably frazzled and tense by the time the big day arrived, usually broke down crying in the early evening when faced with considering her day—now dissolved into a stack of greasy dishes. Her father, irritated because his wife could not control her emotions for just one day out of the year, would often end up spending the night in one of the guest rooms. Then, of course, there was the one Christmas when the ambulance had come to tend, so Elizabeth would have had her believe, to Grandmother Mary's twisted ankle.

"I thought this Christmas would be different," she said softly, almost to herself.

"Go ahead, blame me." Whit flopped down on one of the high stools across from her. "Make me feel worse."

"Can't I say anything?" Jone asked morosely.

"You can't blame me for having a miserable Christmas. That's one thing you can't blame me for because I didn't want to spend it here with a woman who's practically catatonic because her baby died and a man I hardly know but who seems pretty strange on first look, and about as cheerful as Scrooge . . . and who, on top of everything, doesn't even know that the kid who died was his. It's all too weird for me. I would have preferred a nice quiet . . ."

Jone interrupted him with a loud cynical laugh. "How do you know Christmas in Westchester would have been so jolly?"

"It would have been jollier than this."

"Well, this could be jolly," Jone raised her voice, "if you and I could get this straight. That's the only thing stopping us from being jolly."

"I see." Whit smiled falsely. "You mean the way Angelica rushes out of the room from time to time, speaks in whispers, doesn't complete her sentences . . . all that would have contributed to the merriment? Ho ho ho!"

Jone struggled not to respond in kind and after a moment she said, "I only meant that if you and I felt good about each other nothing else would matter. Please, let's try?" She reached out for him and after a moment he took her hand.

They sat in silence again. "I wish you wouldn't feel bad about yourself for being in conflict about the good things that are happening to me."

"Yeah, well I wish so too."

"But at least you've admitted it, Whit. That's a start. As long as we can talk about it, don't you think we'll be able to fix it?"

Whit squirmed down off the stool and fixed his eyes on Cathy's large clock. "Shit, I believe in equal rights . . . only the thing is . . . inside me. I feel all achey and nervous about how I'll behave when everybody comes up to you at that opening party at the Whitney. I mean, it's really dumb but I keep thinking they'll wonder who I am and I'll be just nobody. Some stud . . ."

"Stop!" Jone pleaded taking his hand again. "I don't want

you to feel bad." She leaned her head on his shoulder. "I do understand, because when you sold those two pieces in November for so much money, I couldn't stop myself from thinking 'why should he make so much more than . . .' "

"Jee-zus!" Whit exploded. "You mean you begrudge me that? Shit, man, we got problems!"

JANUARY 1981

New York City

Of course she was glad to be staying in Cathy's beautiful apartment, which smelled of lemon wax and was filled with sunlight and the sense of lives well lived, of accomplishment, intellect, and love. Cathy's apartment was a reflection, thought Angelica, of all the positive values in Cathy's life and, of course, she was glad to be here because how could she be at the place where *it* had happened? The idea of returning to the Obil Garage did not exist, even as an involuntary flash in her mind. Her future did not include the past.

Angelica cried now as often as she liked, and she liked to cry. It was one thing she did well and it passed the time. Jone said that was good, that her former attitude about tears was inappropriate under the circumstances, that her tears would eventually heal her. And so Angelica cried, though never in front of others. Even Jone had not witnessed one tear. Angelica would leave the dinner table, the movies, her desk at Far Out Inc., she would disappear while standing next to Ferris at the Guggenheim or while walking down the street. She would vanish quickly without warning, without apology, and later she would reappear and quietly resume her place in the lives of others.

Everyone guessed she was crying for her baby girl, but she was not. Angelica refused to weep for a soul which she knew would exist again. No, the child, she thought, was free. She believed she was crying because of the reflections, the mirrored images which, when she had first seen them, seemed to be harbingers of a new and fruitful life; a perspective on the past. Now she seemed to have no choice but to see everything as a reflection, and what had begun as a method for the clarification of reality was now an agonizing reminder of the way patterns merely repeated themselves in the lives of women. There were *only* reflections. Angelica discovered the world was filled with a myriad of surfaces which could facilitate this magical act of duplicating reality. Wherever she went—in the supermarkets, on the bus or the street—she studied the faces of women as reflected in a car fender, a highly polished counter top, or a shop window.

She framed the isolated little dramas she saw in her mind, allowing herself to be swallowed up in their contours. She would go beyond her stop on the subway because she had become so engrossed in the graphics of two hysterical, gum-chewing adolescent girls wearing lavender lipstick and she would lose all touch with time, studying their faces in the grimy windows of the decrepit train. She would forget engagements and return to Cathy's luxurious studio and paint the reflections. She told Jone she had no appetite for painting, yet when she wasn't working at Far Out Inc., that was all she did. She painted without thinking. Her pastel of the subway girls had a ghoulish quality, their lavender lips had come out a sickly, unintentional yellow.

Most of the paintings were not only shocking but ill-conceived and carelessly executed. However, that was of no relevance, for Angelica never looked at them once they were finished. Painting had become an inconclusive, ephemeral way to endure time—like long hours spent in idle talking on the telephone, she merely engaged in the conversation of art. Jone spotted stacks of complete canvases after Angelica had only been at Cathy's a week.

When Ferris had finally contacted Zed Porter in London, Porter had claimed to be deeply distressed that Angelica had misinterpreted his words of encouragement. He told Ferris he had never mentioned sending someone down to the Obil to pick up Angelica's paintings for a March show. That was not, he had said, the way he did business.

Aloud Angelica insisted that Porter was lying but when she

woke in the middle of the night, as she usually did, to spend hours replaying the events of the past two months, she was convinced that she had fabricated the praise Porter had lavished on her work as well as his promise to include her in a show. She had imagined all the compliments, fantasized him saying what she had wanted to hear. Even with Jone and Cathy to support her side of the story (Cathy insisted Zed was capable of *anything*) Angelica found it easier to accept the notion that she had deluded herself rather than to examine how and why Porter had treated her as he had.

The extended cold spell had created frosty etchings on the outside of the windows in Cathy's studio and Angelica set to painting the window with the streetlight reflecting below.

"Very beautiful," Ferris praised the painting the next day when he came to take her out to dinner.

"It's been a month," Angelica replied absently as if no compliment had been paid.

"I know." Ferris put his arm around her waist, still considering the gelid painting.

"How can it have been a month since the baby died?" she asked earnestly, as if Ferris might give her a satisfactory answer.

"Cathy's due back in two weeks," Ferris changed the subject. "Angelica, you and I could try again. We could look for a large place with a studio for you. We could find something that would match this . . ."

"I know," she smiled briefly, then moved to the door of the studio and turned out the lights.

"I've been thinking," Ferris said over dinner. "I want to show those four paintings to Aron."

Angelica shook her head.

"Why?" Ferris's hands contracted into tight fists. "Aron hasn't seen your work in years. The Loden Gallery is as prestigious as . . ."

"Ferris, I know you're worried about me. You and Jone. I know you're both trying so hard, but don't. I can't go any faster than I'm going."

"I don't understand," Ferris said nervously.

"Neither do I." Angelica considered her half-eaten portion of fettucini.

"Those paintings are good. I think Aron would like them. Please, let me do something!"

"You've done a lot," Angelica replied. "You've been my friend through all of this."

"But I want to be more. Angelica, I see now what you're doing . . . I never did before. No, let me talk. I understand what's inside your pictures now—the you I first fell in love with and still love. I see that. Maybe I see it because you never put it there before or maybe . . . maybe because I was so damned screwed up I couldn't see it before. Whatever. Anyway, things could be different now. We've come a long way together. I can't lose you now."

"You'll make me leave the table," Angelica joked faintly.

"Was that a laugh?" Ferris smiled unexpectedly like a child caught from behind. "I made you laugh!"

"But only almost." Angelica was struggling not to cry. She clenched her fists beneath the table. "Ferris, don't talk about us picking up where we . . ."

"All right." He held his hand up in the most amazing gesture of self-control she had ever seen from him. "We won't talk about it tonight. Now," he frowned at her uneaten fettucini, "would you like an arugala and mushroom salad? You have to eat something. Really, we're not leaving until you eat a little arugala like a good Italian rabbit."

Angelica did laugh this time and the tears spilled out of her eyes. "Okay, I'll eat it, Signore Mangia!"

❀

The frost-etched window had thawed slightly, so that now in addition to the delicate icy tracery there were rivulets of water and some areas where the window was once again transparent. It was another vivid, blue, sunny day and as Angelica stood looking out at the Museum of Natural History across the street she saw fragments of her face reflected in the midst of the cold lacy designs.

It was Sunday and by noon, when Jone stopped by, Angelica was well into the new painting: a ghostly, reflected self-portrait.

"Hi!" Jone looked sheepishly down at her friend when Angelica answered the door.

"Is it you?" Angelica stood back flabbergasted as Jone entered wearing a fashionable fuchsia down coat with a hemline that dipped longer in the back, mauve stockings, and chic, raspberry suede shoes, strappy and with very high heels.

"Whit's parents are here from Texas. I'm meeting them at the Plaza for tea and Whit bought this for me. How do I look? I feel dumb." She tottered on the unfamiliar spike heels as she took off her coat.

Still incredulous, Angelica backed up and regarded her. "You look like Ginger Rogers with your hair up like that. Did Whit do your hair, too?"

Jone hugged Angelica impulsively, relieved that the tense, lean woman before her was beginning to act more like her old self after a month of near inanimateness and listlessness.

"As a matter of fact, he did." Jone's smile was excited. "Whit can do everything. He's really amazing."

"So I've heard." Angelica smiled softly.

"I'm getting married," said Jone as Angelica was about to sit down.

"Today?"

"No, not today but . . . I wanted you to be the first . . ." Jone pressed her lips together and a moment later she was crying.

"Did I say something wrong?" Angelica was bewildered.

"No, you didn't . . . I . . . I don't know. I think I'm doing the right thing. Whit wants to. We've found this enormous loft on King Street. I'll have terrific space for my work . . . it's all going to be equal and I guess it's silly not to . . . I wouldn't need to but his parents . . . his mother especially wants it. Funny, mine doesn't care. As far as my folks are concerned, wherever I am with Whit by my side, it's all swell. I could be in El Salvador and as long as Whit was . . ."

"What's the matter?" Angelica interrupted. "Why aren't you happy?"

"Because," Jone hesitated, "because what the hell are you going to do when Cathy comes back?"

"You and Ferris." Angelica frowned. "Anyhow, I don't have

to be out of here as soon as I'd thought. Cathy phoned yesterday and said everything's up in the air, whatever that means, and somebody—I didn't catch who—is bringing Vinnie back so he can start the semester and she asks—would I look after him?"

"Fabulous . . ."

"But I'm not going to." Angelica seemed suddenly remote. "I think I'm going . . . someplace. South. Maybe Savannah. I want to be warm and overwhelmed by history and magnolias."

"That's the dumbest thing I ever heard," said Jone.

"When's the wedding?" Angelica ignored the criticism.

"You can't go to Savannah." Jone was worried again.

"Let me guess." Angelica manufactured some enthusiasm. "February third, the day of the opening at the Whitney."

"How do you always do that?" Jone asked, unsmiling. On second thought Angelica seemed worse, not better. At least when she had been staring vacantly and vanishing in mid-sentence Jone had recognized her behavior as an expression of grief. But now she seemed to be neither in mourning nor at all like her old self.

"Well, you're right, we are planning the wedding for the third, only Whit doesn't want to call it a wedding. It's a *celebration* and it'll be at our new loft. We both want you to be Best Person."

"Good," Angelica nodded distantly.

"How's Ferris?" Jone knew perfectly well how Ferris was because she spoke with him about Angelica on the average of three times a day.

"Would you mind if we didn't talk about me?" Angelica was wearing jeans and she curled her legs under her body in one fluid movement. Her body had resumed its former proportions but she felt strange in it. She avoided looking at herself naked in the mirror because of the unsightly, loose flab where the baby had been.

"Sure." Jone smiled artificially, then stopped herself. "We're all so worried . . ."

"My God, you think I don't know that?" Angelica jumped up agitated. "Stop it, damn it! All of you leave me the fuck alone. My goddamned child died and . . . and you're all like vultures, hovering, watching. I'm not a machine. I don't snap back when I'm oiled and have my parts replaced. I may never snap back."

"You will!"

"Maybe not the way everyone thinks I should," Angelica said harshly. "I mean it, Jone, I want you and Ferris off my back!"

Jone nodded, stunned by the outburst. In her mind she was already dialing Ferris.

"I hate people worrying about me," Angelica continued angrily. "I thought you knew that about me. I know you think I'm having a breakdown. Well, so what if I am?"

"I didn't say that."

"Don't lie!" Angelica snapped.

"You're still painting," Jone offered submissively.

"Babies die all the time," Angelica continued. "There are worse things than the death of a newborn child."

"I suppose there are," Jone said helplessly.

"Oh, there are!" Angelica replied resentfully.

"Whit and I thought you might want to take over his old loft after we move."

Angelica shook her head stonily and sat at the far end of the living room watching the sunlight reflecting off the plastic top of Cathy's sleek turntable.

Countless times she had tried to remember the pain of the birth in her body, but she could not. They had given her Demerol, she had refused anything else. Jone's hand had been in hers almost the entire time, that big palm, calloused but thick and spongy, with squared-off fingers that had wrapped around her own hand. Jone's hand had seemed to hold it all together, but then they had objected to Jone's staying in the delivery room so her hand had been replaced with another, softer one. She couldn't remember the face that went with the second hand. The only memory she had of the delivery room was of the new hand, muffled voices, and finally a blurred picture of an upside-down baby doused in a cocoon of blood. She had wanted to look into its eyes, but hands had held her down till the placenta had been expelled and by then—she had heard them say—the anemic baby had been taken off somewhere to see if it could be saved.

Now Jone put her hand on Angelica's shoulder but Angelica gave no sign of noticing. For all of Angelica's bluntness, Jone had never known her to be rude or abusive. She was one of those people who seemed able to say anything, honestly, without being mean or hurtful. Until today Jone had never felt her sting.

"What are you thinking?" Jone asked huskily.

"That grief is tedious, that I should go back to being a schoolteacher, that I ought to marry a dentist and live somewhere with a green lawn and my own washer and drier."

"And that's all you're thinking?" Jone was afraid to leave her alone.

"That's all," Angelica replied without looking up.

Jone felt ridiculous arriving at the Palm Court and being led to a table with Whit and his parents gawking at her while a tuxedoed violinist played a squeaky rendition of "Fascination." Dumb, she told herself. This is dumb.

Whit stood up as she approached and his father, seeing that this was *the girl,* leaped to his feet, leaving Mrs. Russell momentarily stunned, caught in the middle of a sentence. Jone smiled, the way she had been taught by Elizabeth, and said all the right things. From Westchester to Texas, she thought, it was all the same. Her family was interchangeable with Whit's.

The meeting went well, as Whit had known it would, and two hours later they were back in their loft. Jone felt like a dog who had been groomed for a big show and who now wanted to go out and roll in the dirt.

"Yeah, but you look fan-*tas*-tic!" Whit circled her, licking his chops and loosening his necktie. "You got to wear this to the Whitney opening . . . maybe even the *celebration*."

"I can't wear a black dress to my wedding!"

"You're so conventional." Whit pulled up her dress and peeked at the lacy teddy he had bought for her. "Jeezus!"

"Freak!" Jone darted out of his grasp and pulled down her dress, pretending to be outraged by his boldness.

"Couldn't you tell I was thinkin' of doin' that all the time my mother was tellin' you how cute I was when I was four and how I wanted to wear nail polish so I could be like her? She cites that as my first artistic inclination."

"You were always a freak." Jone stumbled as he grabbed for her but managed to escape his clutches.

"A Texas freak meets a Westchester freak." Whit lunged for her again and missed. "Let me have another look, ma'am. I promise all's I'll do is look."

"How often have I heard that?" Jone said prudishly. "All right then . . . one." Whit crawled over and wriggled his head up between her legs until she moaned with pleasure.

"I beg your pardon, ma'am"; he withdrew quickly, smiling and bowing in his imitation of an Oriental imbecile. "Did I do something wrong, ma'am?"

Flushed with excitement, Jone shook her head and began stripping off her clothes, until she stood naked before him.

He started to prolong the joke by slobbering at her feet with the same idiotic expression but suddenly he broke off with a look of wonderment.

"Jeee-zus shit," he said, shaking his head incredulously, "man, did I ever strike the jackpot!"

"Angelica, I'm begging you, let me show Aron your work. I've been raving about it. He keeps asking me." Ferris walked across the studio to where Angelica was putting the finishing touches on a compelling if disquieting portrait. The new painting was of herself with the image, the only one she had, of her bloodied child reflected in her eyes.

"I can't risk it," she said automatically.

"You have to risk it!" Ferris exclaimed. "Angelica!" he turned her toward him and took the brush out of her hand and put it firmly aside. He kissed her mouth gently, for a full minute, as if to capture her attention, then he studied her closely.

This was the first time they had kissed since the conception of their child, thought Angelica. He knew it had been their child though he had said nothing. She thought she was grateful to him for that, although sometimes lately she wasn't sure if she was grateful for anything.

"Do you think we'll ever . . ." He hesitated, then forced himself to go on, ". . . ever make love again?"

She shook her head. "I don't think so."

"Well, I don't want to push," he said quickly.

"It's the furthest thing from my mind." She glanced back at the painting.

"I understand."

Angelica sighed. "I have to go to work, Ferris. It was nice of you to stop by."

"I'll drop you off." He followed her out of Cathy's studio.

"If you want to," she said and disappeared into the bedroom to change her clothes.

❀

"I just can't reach her," Ferris told Jone when he met her at the Spring Street Bar. "She doesn't see me."

"I know." Jone put out her cigarette and took a sip of her martini, thinking it wasn't as good as the ones Whit fixed.

"I guess she probably told you . . . about us, about what happened in France that made her pull out."

Jone nodded.

"Do you hate me?" Ferris clenched his fists together. His face was grayer than usual.

"No," Jone shook her head. "I was prepared to, but I don't. You've been there for her."

Ferris nodded. "I suppose that should be a comfort to me, but I want more. I want to have her back." Ferris signaled for the waitress to bring him another beer.

"Let me ask you something," Jone began as she flipped the ashes off the end of her cigarette. "Why do you want to show her paintings to your gallery now when you didn't before? Has her work grown that much?"

Ferris ruminated painfully. "Well, it's matured."

"But it was always exceptional, wasn't it?"

"She's her own worst enemy." Ferris looked away from Jone.

"Why is *she* her enemy?" Jone was amazed at the steady line of her thinking.

"Well, we both know she did everything she could to lose the baby."

"You don't believe that?" Jone controlled her reaction.

"It was obvious," Ferris affirmed brusquely.

"How was it obvious?"

"Come on, Jone, she never pulled back, she was busting her ass right up to the wire."

"What *should* she have done?"

Ferris looked at her hard as if he suspected a trap. "She should have told me the truth."

"What truth?"

"Look, it was my child, too. I feel a loss, too, for Christ's sake!"

For an instant Jone thought she was going to upend the table and shake him. If he had been that positive the child was his, why hadn't he done *more*? Now that she thought of it, what had he done for Angelica other than take her out to dinner and offer to loan her some money after the baby was born, and pester her about resuming their old affair!

"Admit it, Jone. You know the truth."

"I don't know," Jone denied it willingly. "You know how secretive Angelica can be."

"You know," he said accusingly.

"I don't understand you," Jone said. "If you wanted to help her, why wait till now? Why didn't you offer to show Aron Loden *The Woman with the Pink Powder Puff* when you first saw it? You were the first one to see it. You thought it was good. Loden's as good as gallery as Porter."

"Because she had already met Porter."

"Come off it, Ferris. People court two galleries at a time, it puts a person in a stronger position. She wouldn't have been putting all her eggs in one basket. Why didn't you even mention it? Or when she was worried about the outcome with Porter, why didn't you take the onus off her by saying if it didn't work out with him you'd have Aron there the next goddamned day to see her work!!"

"I thought we were friends." Ferris shifted defensively in his chair. "I thought you liked me."

"I did," Jone said sullenly, "until a few minutes ago. Until I started thinking and it finally dawned on me how much you could have done for her with all of your power."

"I've never believed in mixing my professional life with my personal life."

"Bullshit! Then why are you being so gallant now? Now that the child you *think* was yours is dead?"

"Know," Ferris said defiantly. "*Know* the child was . . ."

"So now you feel guilty . . . or maybe you don't. Maybe you just see how, now that she has sunk so low, you can raise her up."

"That's not fair!"

"What is?" Jone said rigidly as she stood up.

"You don't understand," Ferris said pathetically.

"Maybe not," said Jone, "but neither do you."

Jone half expected that he might come after her but he didn't; she was relieved because she was bigger than he was and would have been tempted to heave his skimpy body in front of one of Angelica's lumbering mail trucks. She was angry with herself, too. It was true that she had not thought of it until now—had not seen that Ferris Brown, being the important artist he was, could have quite simply pulled any number of strings for Angelica—had he chosen to do so. There were other galleries besides Porter, besides his own Loden Gallery. The city was full of galleries and with Ferris's clout he could have placed Angelica's work in one of them even if her work had been inadequate. But her work was far from inadequate. Any of her earlier paintings, the pastels, the gouaches, even the drawings might have been placed in a gallery and even if they hadn't sold she would have felt the connection, she would have known there was at least a chance. Anyway, Jone was convinced, there would have been some sales—enough to have boosted her morale at a very crucial time. As early as October, when he had first seen what Angelica had been working on since her return to New York, he might have done something.

Instead he had offered to loan Angelica some money and like idiots both she and Angelica had lauded his tact and generosity. It had not occurred to either of them that his response to Angelica was not only miserly but depraved and utterly selfish. Cathy had done more. Cathy, who was not even a terribly close friend, had arranged for Porter to come down, had taken Angelica into her home, had gone to Porter to try to convince him to take the pressure off Angelica, and had eventually pulled out of a long-term, very profitable relationship with him because of his callous behavior.

Jone let herself in to the Obil Garage. The place had never smelled good, not even after Angelica had splashed Joy on the floor the night of her arrival. Now it stank of the usual stale gas, turpentine, and, so it seemed to Jone, all that blood. She understood how impossible it was for Angelica to set foot in the place again.

She was risking their friendship and she knew it. Angelica's present condition was so erratic and unfamiliar there was no guessing how she would react. Jone gathered up the four paintings which Zed Porter was supposed to have picked up and went back outside.

Well, Georgia O'Keeffe's friend Anita Pollitzer had been the one responsible for bringing O'Keeffe's work to Stieglitz. What would have happened if she hadn't? Life and fortune, Jone thought, often hung on a very slim thread, and action mattered more than anything.

❁

"You have to," Jone said bluntly to her agent, David Epstein.

"You don't understand, Jone. It's not ethical. You're not behaving professionally."

"I don't know what that means," said Jone, doggedly gesturing toward Angelica's paintings. "These are good; you're a good agent. You can place them in a gallery."

"You're very talented at what you do. But you have to allow me to do my job. You can't give orders." Epstein pushed his glasses back onto his nose with a confident smile.

"I'm sorry." Jone tried to think how she might be tactful, of the words someone like her mother would use to charm and amuse someone polite and intellectual like David.

"You said you liked them." She rejected delicacy and forged ahead.

"I don't want any new clients now."

"You mean any that you don't choose yourself."

"Yes, that's my prerogative, isn't it?"

"Sure. But if you don't find a gallery that will handle Stein's paintings by Friday I am going to find another agent."

"Jone!"

". . . and I'm going to find another gallery. After they see *Peloria* at the Whitney, I'll have my pick. That's *my* prerogative," she stated firmly.

"Your ego is all out of kilter, Jone. You're not in any position to . . ."

"Do you want to keep the paintings and think about it or should I take them with me?"

"I think you should take them with you," David said quietly, "because nobody is going to tell me what to do."

"Fair enough," said Jone, hoisting the four paintings onto her shoulder. "Call Laurent and tell them the deal for April is off. That means London too."

"You can't break a contract."

"I can and I will," Jone said calmly. "I'm the one with the talent. And I didn't ask you to do me a favor, David, I did you one by bringing these in."

By the time Jone got home with the four paintings Whit was beside himself.

"I can't believe you did it!" he stormed. "What are you? An egomaniac? David called and asked if you were having a breakdown, flying on drugs, pregnant, or just hysterical!"

"No to all four." Jone put Angelica's paintings in the large closet where she kept her supplies.

"David's upset. You should call him."

"Let him call me."

"Joneeeeeeee . . ." Whit was aghast. "You're blowin' it!"

"I don't think so. They love *Peloria* at the Whitney. After the show opens David will be eating his heart out for being so power-hungry."

"It seems like you're the power-hungry one here. Jone, people don't do what you did."

"I do it."

"Professional people don't promote their friends."

"Oh, shit, what a laugh. What do you mean, it's done all the time. Don't tell me it isn't done . . . I may not have done it the way it's usually done, but don't tell me it's not done."

"David said you demanded . . ."

"The shortest distance between two points," Jone interjected and went into the kitchen for a beer.

Whit gaped at her. She was standing in the middle of the kitchen, a beer in one hand, one hand on her hip, one leg thrust formidably to the side like Lachaise's *Standing Woman*. He knew he would never be able to change her mind on the matter and the knowledge made him feel insubstantial. He could not reconcile the image of her now with the lazy, warm-bodied woman he loved to lose himself in. He wondered for a moment is she might not have severe mental problems; perhaps she was a split personality?

The phone rang and she gulped the beer as she ran to answer it. When she returned she was beaming.

"A compromise is in the offing . . . he can't relinquish all that power so easily, after all. David's going to place one painting—*The Woman with the Pink Powder Puff*. He's put a price on it of five thousand dollars!"

Cathy had the *New York Times* delivered to her front door every morning and every morning with her tea and toast Angelica pored over the Jean Harris trial which was being held at the Westchester County Court in White Plains. It was the first time in Angelica's memory that the *Times* had ever continuously run a murder trial story on its front page. It was, thought Angelica, a sign of progress that a paper like the *Times* interpreted this trial not as mere sensationalism, but as an important documentation of the hard and complex realities existing between men and women in the eighties. The story of the death of the sixty-nine-year-old Scarsdale Diet Doctor at the hands of his fifty-seven-year-old mistress of fourteen years had struck a responsive chord in women everywhere, and, when on January 30, the *Times* quoted Jean Harris as saying, "I was a person sitting in an empty chair . . . ," there was no ambiguity in her meaning.

That Friday Angelica phoned Far Out Inc. to say she required a day off and by nine o'clock she was on the train to White Plains to stand outside the courthouse waiting for a glimpse of the accused murderess. It was the first time she had been out of the city since her arrival in early June and it was the first time since the baby's death that she had not been merely sucked into a visual spectacle, usually against her own will.

The trial junkies, mostly female, were lined up outside the municipal building. There was no chance of getting inside the courthouse, but simply being there had solidified her commitment. She waited for two hours in case Mrs. Harris could be glimpsed on her way to lunch, and when that did not happen she found a coffee shop near the train depot, ate a tuna fish sandwich, and downed a glass of milk. She felt oddly hungry again. She boarded the two o'clock for New York City and on the train she took out her sketch pad and made a few drawings and notes of ideas for a new painting: *The Person Sitting in the Empty Chair.*

PART FIVE

"... my life was a solo.... And that is what gave me a strength and gave me my independence. And it gave me truly a great deal of sorrow. It's a total price."

Louise Nevelson, sculptor

FEBRUARY 1981

New York City

On her first night home Cathy slept fitfully, alone in the guest room (which she had come to think of as Tony's room) instead of in her and Lester's bedroom (which she now thought of as Angelica's room). Actually, Angelica, much to Vinnie's disappointment, was moving into Whit's old loft at the end of the week and then, until Tony returned from a week's visit with his mother in Pasadena, there would be just Cathy and Vinnie. Lester had gone on to London for a week but even when he returned he wouldn't return here. It was a huge game of musical chairs, she decided.

And she wondered why, after a marvelous six weeks in Europe where she had been satiated in every possible way—intellectually with Lester, sexually with Tony, maternally with Vinnie, metabolically with all of the epicurean feasts provided by the chef Lester had hired for their two weeks in the chalet outside of Grenoble—did she again feel herself on shaky ground? Maybe because Jone's wedding was the day after tomorrow? Could that be it? Was she irritated because Angelica's paints were strewn all over her studio and the canvases there were Angelica's, not hers?

Cathy shook her head, burrowing deeper into the pillow. No, she wasn't bothered by the plenitude of Angelica's work. She was relieved, in fact, that Angelica was painting. She did wish that she knew what had happened between Zed and Angelica but apparently Jone did not even know the full story.

"Don't hurt your back, dummy," Cathy cautioned herself as she sat up and swung her legs carefully over the side of the bed. "Be very conscious—no bending over from the waist, easy . . . relaxed."

She broke off talking to herself. Maybe it was the painting Angelica was working on, *The Person Sitting in the Empty Chair,* that had triggered off her uneasiness; that and probably the usual dislocation of returning home to the realities of life after an idyllic vacation. Yes, but mostly it had been Angelica's painting plus Tony's absence and the realization that she could not go back to living as she had lived before the trip. She wished he hadn't felt the need to fly off to California the moment they got back. She couldn't help feeling he was trying to escape something! But what, she fretted. They had had such a stupendous time in France!

Cathy sank back down on the bed with a transfixed expression. She crossed her left arm in front of her breast and massaged her right shoulder rhythmically.

Last night's dream began to take shape in her memory as magically as the faint image of a Polaroid turns into a sharply focused picture. How was it possible that she had had an erotic dream about her first husband? But of course that was what had happened! She had dreamed of Rosen in a schoolroom with wooden desks like the kind she had grown up with in Wayne, desks with round inkwells and a place underneath to slide your books. At the front of the classroom there had been the blackboard, all chalky and indistinct—in the dream nothing had been clearly written.

Rosen had entered soundlessly, stalking like a giant to the teacher's desk, singling her out—Cathy Harder—with his needful eyes. Although there was no one else in the room, they shared the sense that they might be interrupted at any moment, might be caught. Rosen had walked down the aisle toward her desk, she had pressed her legs together, touching the tops of her knees to the underside of the desk, scarcely able to breathe because of her desire for him. At first he had seemed formidable and toweringly godlike approaching her. It was only as he came closer that she had seen more than ardor in his eyes, more than passion. In the dream she had a complete understanding of Eros, the spiritual and lustful blend of the creative force.

She had risen from her desk, feeling the frustration of her desire for him, knowing that he felt the same. He had run his hand along her bare arm and she had agreed, in the unspoken language of dreams, to meet him later in the cloak room where it would be dark and the smell of wet wool and rubber boots would fill the air. Instantly, the dream-Cathy had projected them onto the floor, still half-clothed, writhing and groaning, but they were still in the classroom, unfulfilled, and there were other unspoken plans for clandestine meetings. The dream had made it clear that they would have to meet, that their desire would have to be consummated or they would be doomed.

Remembering the dream made Cathy feel frustrated all over again. It was too real and it was poor timing. There was no way to release this pent-up energy. And why have such a sexually frustrating dream when Tony had only left yesterday? Besides, why hadn't the dream been about Tony? That she might have understood. Why Rosen? Why did she desire a man who had never treated her with anything but disdain?

Angelica would tell her it was karma, that her connection to Rosen had not been broken by his death. But she didn't believe in karma. Yet the way the dream still lived in her body made her feel that Rosen was once again haunting her.

Cathy felt disgusted with herself as she slumped out to her kitchen to put on the coffee. Funny, how you went along thinking your life was falling nicely into place and then some dream comes along and zap, if you knew how to interpret it, you saw that you had been fooling yourself. She guessed that was one of the benefits of being in therapy for almost twenty years. It was a good thing she had an appointment with Dr. Metcalf today. Still, the thought of going to see him depressed her. Hell, she had done without him when she was in Ohio and for six weeks in Europe. And the life arrangement the three of them had worked out in Paris had seemed right at the time. Maybe the dream about Rosen wasn't ominous, wasn't a bad dream. Maybe it was a good dream. What about that?

Angelica staggered out into the kitchen rubbing her eyes sleepily.

"I wish you wouldn't move to Whit's loft," Cathy said. "You should stay here with Vin and me. He loves you. I've never seen anything like it. You could take an outside studio for less than what you'd pay for the loft."

"That's nice of you." Angelica tossed a grapefruit in the air before slicing it.

"But you won't," Cathy said.

"Right."

"So . . ." Cathy poured them each a cup of coffee. "Catch me up. I was surprised to hear Jone and Whit were getting married . . . it was so rocky when I left."

"Yes." Angelica held her coffee cup in two hands and stared into the black liquid trying to see a hint of her face. "Rivalry. I think Jone can handle it though. If anyone can."

"And he's no slouch either," Cathy observed, then jumping down off the stool she ran to the kitchen door and yelled, "Vinnie, are you up?"

"Of course." Vinnie materialized under Cathy's nose and Angelica laughed. "Anyway, it's Sunday and I have jet lag." He sat down next to Angelica.

"Am I invited to the wedding?" he wanted to know.

"Of course," said Angelica. "Only you mustn't call it a wedding in front of Jone and Whit. It's a celebration."

"What are you wearing?" asked Cathy as she handed Vinnie some orange juice.

"Who me?" Vinnie asked with a knowing look at Angelica.

"No, not you!" Cathy said, reaching for the cereal.

"We're both wearing roller skates, aren't we, Vinnie?" Angelica winked at him.

"Hey, great! Do you have skates?"

"I'd like some," Angelica said. "Maybe I'll buy some and we'll wear them to the wedding. Jone said everyone was supposed to come the way they felt best."

"How strange." Cathy turned quizzically and stared at her son and Angelica.

"What, Mom?"

"I was just thinking," Cathy said pensively, "the idea appeals to me. Funny. I was thinking I'd wear that gray Ted Lapidus silk I picked up in Paris and then I thought, no, Whit will obviously wear cowboy clothes and God knows what other people will wear and I don't want to feel like an old square. Forty-six isn't old. You know, in a way I'm glad Les and Tony aren't here. And I hate designer jeans. Even I am not that phony. But . . . I thought, it should be special . . . they're a special couple and they're calling it a celebration . . ."

"We could all three wear skates!" Vinnie nearly toppled off his stool in excitement. "And I could bring my transistor and plug out if I didn't understand what was going on."

"I don't think there's any chance of that," Angelica laughed.

"But first we'll have to make sure Jone and Whit haven't sanded the floors." Cathy's eyes sparkled. "We won't say why we're asking but . . . we wouldn't want to damage the floor if they've . . ."

"Oh, I hope, I hope, I hope they haven't!" chanted Vinnie.

"Oh God," said Cathy with a little jump, "me, too!"

Angelica sat on a bench just across from the Beresford inside Central Park, relieved to be by herself, away from Cathy's constant bubbling and Vinnie's elfin smiles. At breakfast she had heard herself laughing, heard herself contemplating the purchase of roller skates. Now she could only think of the baby, and the snatches of her old self which had somehow slipped out earlier made her feel even more unreal.

It was a mild day, the park was crowded as it usually was with Sunday walkers, joggers, earphoned disco skaters, dogs, baby carriages, baby strollers, smiling pregnant women. It was one thing to live in Cathy's life-teeming apartment when Cathy was absent and quite another when Cathy returned to enliven it further with her own effervescent energy and the rollicking energy of her child. Although she had laughed, the contrast Angelica felt in the presence of Vinnie and Cathy made her feel closer to death than before.

When Jone had called to say she wanted to talk to her it had given Angelica an excuse to leave. She glanced at her watch, then looked around expecting to see Jone's blue hooded parka bobbing down the path toward her.

Skates? She had actually been talking about buying skates when sometimes she felt unable even to walk, felt all wobbly like a newborn colt. God, she dreaded facing Zed Porter again and she was certain to see him at the Whitney's black tie affair celebrating the Ten American Sculptors show. She knew her fear of seeing him was irrational, that she had no reason to feel embarrassed or humiliated by the outcome of their brief acquaintance. But she was embarrassed and, yes, she was humiliated and she could not imagine what she would say to him or what she might do. It had occurred to her that the sight of his charming smile (no question that he would smile) might trigger some violent reaction in her, that all the things she thought she had forgotten—the blood, the smell, hope, frustration, *everything*—might flood in on her and cause her to go finally and perhaps irretrievably mad. Yes, she was afraid the sight of him would make her lose the last shred of her sanity, for it was all, she thought, still very tenuous and she was not sure who she was or what she was capable of.

She closed her eyes and turned her face to catch the few rays of winter sun. She was moving to Whit's old loft because there wasn't anything else to do, because the logistics of buying a plane or a train ticket to Savannah seemed monumental, like climbing Mount Everest without a pickax.

She felt like a winter-sun-baked corpse. Ferris had offered to take her away to St. Barts, to have her lay her body on the warm sand, to glide her wasted body with its loose skin and sagging muscles into the water, then to cover her body with his body—to fill her with life. He thought he could fill her with life. The idea of anyone touching her, least of all a man, repelled her. She still could not look at her body because it had betrayed her. Vaguely she recalled the special tenderness she had felt for Vinnie the last time she had stayed with Cathy. She had loved squeezing his thin little frame, loved the feel of his delicate child's rib cage, the narrow, undeveloped shoulders, his jumping, twisting vitality. Now when he came near her something in her turned cold. She had canceled two postpartum doctor's appointments because the idea of lying on the examining table with her feet in those cold stirrups was now abhorrent to her. She would not, could not, do it—she did not care to have the stitches removed where they had sliced her body to allow the child an easier entry into the world.

She could always move back to Chicago, live with her parents, teach school, and walk along the lake. But there were too many things to explain and she grew weary even thinking of going back to a place which had been foreign to her from the start. It all required too much thought. Even the move to Whit's loft loomed as a logistical impossibility.

"Hey!" Jone nudged her. "Let's go to the Museum Café. I called from the subway . . . they're saving us a table. The new loft is still in shambles," she confessed as they crossed the street. "I don't know how it'll be ready for the wedding in two days but Whit says it will. He's got a gang of guys down there working and drinking beer. What a production! I hadda get out. So how is everything now that Cathy's home?"

"Fine," Angelica smiled.

"But not really," said Jone.

"No, it's okay. I'll be glad to leave though. I feel funny painting now that she's . . ."

Jone nodded. "So what's new in the Aimsley domestic drama? Who's ahead this week?"

"Holding pattern," said Angelica. "They're both away. Tony's at his mother's in California for a couple of weeks."

"Well," Jone smiled critically, "she would have let you know if anything had changed. You know, I'm curious . . . did they all sleep in the same bed . . . all four! Poor Vinnie, he seems like a nice kid, too."

That, thought Angelica, was an uncommonly bitchy remark coming from Jone. She looked closely at the blond as they entered the Museum Café and after they were seated at a table in the glassed-in area next to the sidewalk she felt the need to clarify the situation for Jone.

"Vinnie *is* nice, and no, they did *not* all sleep in the same bed. They each had a room . . . with a lock. I really don't think you need to worry about Vinnie, if that's really what you're worried about. He's not going to be tainted by Cathy's sexual proclivities. He's a lot saner and certainly more sensitive than most kids his age. For that matter, I think Lester and Tony and Cathy are a lot saner than the folks down home who pass for normal."

Jone gave a negative shrug. "I mean, but what kind of game is she playing?"

"What kind of game is any of us playing?" Angelica responded. "You play with what you're dealt."

"No!" Jone insisted. "If you want to be symbolic, and I can see you do, you wait for the right card . . . before you play. You reject the cards until you get a full house."

"You're talking to the wrong person," Angelica said tonelessly. She was perturbed at how lightly Jone could dismiss Cathy, speaking about her as if she were simply a fool.

"Oh, I know she's not *just* a fool." Jone waved her hand impatiently. "Listen, I'm sorry—prenuptial nerves."

"And what about the show? It opens Tuesday before the celebration, right? Or did you forget?"

"It's weird," Jone mused. "I'm not nervous about the show but I am about the other. I wonder why?"

"I can think of a few hundred reasons," Angelica observed dryly. "Did you ever talk to Whit about the little surgical procedure you had last summer?"

"Tonight," Jone confessed, trying to sound casual.

"You waited a long time." Angelica felt a new wave of hopelessness.

"Well, I guess that's why I'm so strung out, if you want to know. Not that I'm worried . . . I mean, can you imagine Whit as a father? I can't imagine that for at least fifty years and by then I'll be too old so . . ." She laughed, then gave up the pretense and lit a cigarette almost angrily.

"What do you think he'll say?" she asked Angelica after she had taken several deep drags.

Angelica looked up, confused. "I'm sorry, I didn't hear what you asked me."

"I asked if you thought Whit would understand."

"I don't know," Angelica lied.

"You do know . . . you're not telling me."

Angelica felt drained. She had nothing to give Jone and she was irritated that so much was being expected of her. "Jone, what good is my opinion in all this? It's between you two. But you have to tell him."

"Of course I do," Jone affirmed quickly. "I really forgot to bring it up till now. I swear. It's been one thing after another, I mean, I *really* forgot."

Angelica softened. "Why don't I believe you? You're afraid to tell him."

Jone nodded slowly. "I'm afraid I screwed up. I think I should wait till after we've settled into the marriage."

Angelica's mouth flew open but Jone rushed on.

"Whit and I have come a long way in our relationship in a very short time. The competition thing is solved. I mean he's handling the Whitney show fabulously and we just have this very open, direct way of communicating. If one of us is jealous and feels the other is encroaching on their space, we come right out with it. We've written it all down, too, like a contract, so we're clear about everything. We're really going to be equals in this union."

"Then you've got to come out with this, too," Angelica counseled.

"You're the only one who knows," Jone whispered .

"Well, I'm not going to say anything." Angelica was upset. "Jone, you can't . . ."

"I know," Jone went on urgently, "I can convince him that what I did was a necessity . . . for me. I know I can do that. By the time the idea of having children even occurs to him, our marriage will be so secure that he'll understand. I know it!"

Angelica lowered her eyes, unable to comment.

"I don't feel like eating . . . if you don't mind."

"I'm sorry." Angelica reached across the table for her hand. "You knew what I would say, didn't you?"

"My God!" Jone fought back the tears, "I feel like praying only I don't know who to pray to."

They left the Museum Café without having lunch, Jone to go back downtown to Whit, Angelica to wander through the park to the Metropolitan Museum where she spent the rest of the afternoon looking at the collection of French photography from the Bibliothèque Nationale. The day seemed interminably long. She was glad tomorrow was Monday and she could safely pass the time at Far Out Inc. working on a new record album cover.

"Jone says call her," Cathy hollered when Angelica came home from work the following day. "And also they haven't sanded the floors so it's 'Go' for the roller skates if you're still game. We can go shopping for them before dinner."

May as well, thought Angelica, unless the wedding is off. She went into her room and dialed Jone's number. Jone answered on the first ring. "Have I got good news!"

"Thank God," said Angelica, relieved.

"Listen, I wanted to see your face when I told you but if you could see what we have to do before this time tomorrow . . . and I couldn't wait. Angelica," she paused and Angelica heard her take an excited breath, "David, you know, my agent, David Epstein, placed *The Woman with the Pink Powder Puff* at the Circle Gallery in Soho and it sold this afternoon at three to a collector for three Texas universities! . . . Are you there?"

"I'm here," Angelica said calmly, wondering why she couldn't think of anything else to say.

"Don't you want to know how it happened?"

"Yes."

"And how much?"

"Yes."

She listened as Jone explained what had happened, how Jone had put it all on the line and how David had finally given in. Angelica forced an enthusiastic response and Jone rushed on.

". . . and they'll take more on consignment. David is sending the Atlanta missing children trio down and he wants to see what you're working on now. I told him about the Jean Harris painting and he's really excited about it, so show him that," Jone advised. "It's already sensational. You know, I meant to tell you, there's something about it that puts me in mind of David's *Marat* . . . I guess the way you've understated the violence. You always said you wanted to paint something political and . . ."

Angelica tried to concentrate on Jone's heartiness but her thoughts keep slipping back to the night she had stood, belly staunchly protruding, painting *The Woman with the Pink Powder Puff*. That night she had been so full, so certain. It might have been the happiest night of her life.

". . . and my grandmother's coming to the Whitney!" Jone continued. "My mother wasn't sure Grandmother could last for the wedding, but I said I'd rather have her see the show."

"Of course," said Angelica.

"I thought you and Ferris could plan on getting to the Whitney around six so you wouldn't miss her."

"I want to meet her." Angelica stretched out on Cathy's bed where she had first had the visions of the reflections.

After she hung up the phone she lay with her eyes open, staring at the blue ceiling, praying that the dullness would soon wear off and she would feel something other than despair.

She knew her friends considered it a good sign that she had continued to paint, if only as a form of therapy. Only nobody understood that her painting was in a vacuum, disconnected from anything she saw for herself, in a space, in a time which most people referred to as the Future. She painted as she ate: as a matter of routine, because she had to, without really wanting to, without tasting or enjoying.

❀

The Whitney show of Ten American Sculptors was a glittering black tie affair and had there been any way to get out of it without hurting Jone, Angelica would not have gone. Ferris had phoned earlier to say he had a flu bug and would be unable to make either the Whitney or the Beele-Russell nuptials later the same evening. Angelica knew he was malingering, but it hadn't mattered much to her one way or the other. He had hinted strongly that he was not amused by the three of them wearing roller skates.

"Just look straight through Zed," Cathy advised as Lester's limousine pulled up in front of the museum to let the two women and Vinnie out.

Angelica felt a dizzying tension sweep over her as Cathy referred to Zed Porter, whose presence at such an important art function was all but guaranteed.

"Stick with me," said Vinnie, their appointed escort, squeezing Angelica's hand as he helped her out of the car.

Angelica allowed the small hand to lead her into the museum, feeling very much as though she were being led to her execution.

"Just think," he said, holding open the door for her, "as soon as we put in an appearance here we'll be able to put on our skates!"

"Yes." Angelica managed a smile.

"That's gonna be really weird," he rhapsodized. "We could get in the *Guinness Book of Records*, huh, Mom?"

"How did you know about the *Guinness Book of Records*?" Cathy looked quizzically at her son as she often did, stunned by his eclectic nine-year-old's mind.

"The guy who sets up the dominoes . . . three hundred trillion of them or something. He's always on TV."

Thank God for Vinnie, thought Angelica, and Cathy. Both of them were touchstones of reality.

"Hey, Margot!" Cathy screamed at a fat woman with flaming red hair and rushed off.

"She always does that," observed Vinnie. "My mom is one of the friendliest people I ever knew." Vinnie made it sound like he was ninety-one years old and knew the entire world.

Angelica laughed unexpectedly. "She's nice."

"Yeah," Vinnie nodded, and they moved through the crowd into the first gallery. In her black harem pants and black sweater Angelica was like a shadow slipping through the sparkling colorful throng.

Vinnie felt Angelica tense up as a deep male laugh rose above the hum of voices. "Don't worry, I got my eye open and when I see him coming I'll squeeze your hand three times like this. Mom's right, if you don't want to see him you should just go out and wait in the car."

"Aye, aye, sir," saluted Angelica. "I hope we'll always be friends, Vin . . . even when you're as tall as I am."

"Or taller," said Vinnie.

From the gallery on the main floor they moved downstairs where a crowd of admirers surrounded Jone's *Peloria*. For several moments Angelica forgot her terror about seeing Zed and allowed the magnificence of Jone's piece to overpower her. She had watched the sculpture grow from a small strip of bronze and was deeply moved to see it standing proudly in one of the most respected and innovative museums in the world. She craned her neck, hoping to spot Jone to congratulate her.

"Let me know," she leaned over and whispered to Vinnie, "if you see a very, very old lady in a wheel chair who appears to be having a miserable time."

"Jone's grandmother." Vinnie nodded professionally and scanned the crowd.

"Angelica?"

She felt Vinnie squeeze her hand three times and was amazed that she did not stop breathing. She had dreaded ever seeing Zed Porter again, as if she had done something drastic to him and had reason to feel humiliated and embarrassed. To her surprise she did not bolt, as Zed rushed forward to greet her, kissing her on the cheek.

"You're looking wonderful," he exclaimed, "and it's Vincent," he chucked Vinnie on the chin, "which means Mama and Papa can't be far. Please, if I miss them in all this craziness, give them my best."

"Okay," said Vinnie somberly.

"You know," Zed gave a functionally self-deprecating smile, "I felt awful about that misunderstanding."

"I'm sure you did." Angelica lowered her chin involuntarily as if to ward off a blow.

"The moment my secretary got through to me in London I tried phoning you directly to straighten it out. There's been no answer at your home for weeks. Listen, if there's anything I hate it's a misunderstanding with one of my clients . . . or prospective clients, I should say. It seems I've had my share lately."

"I'm not a prospective client," Angelica said faintly, her chin still lowered, her hand perspiring in Vinnie's.

"You see," Zed looked confused, "we have really had a breach in communications."

"Excuse me, Mr. Porter," Vinnie stepped forward, "we're supposed to meet my mother now."

"That's right." Angelica and Vinnie were squeezing each

other's hands rapidly. The movement enabled her to smile at Zed and extend her other hand.

"Please do call me when we can talk . . . or I'll call you."

Angelica nodded.

"Oh, by the way." Zed touched her shoulder. "How is the baby?"

"Just fine," said Angelica. "Everything is just fine. It was a pleasure seeing you again."

❀

"Jesus!" Cathy swigged from a bottle of Tanqueray gin as the limousine drove toward King Street. "You carried on a conversation with the sonuvabitch? Shit, I wish I'd been there. How'd you do it?"

"I did it," Angelica started to feel teary, "with Vinnie's help. Because he's a good friend."

Vinnie smiled in embarrassment.

"I didn't think I could ever . . ." Angelica broke off. She did not want to cry in front of anyone, least of all in front of Vinnie, but there wasn't any choice now.

"She was really cool," Vinnie said, taking Angelica's tears in stride and peering out his window.

"It's okay." Cathy put her arms around Angelica and cradled her with the gin bottle still in one hand. "You're going to be okay, kiddo. You really are."

"Yes, you are," echoed Vinnie.

❀

The wedding celebration which was held in Jone and Whit's sixty-by-one-hundred-foot loft with eighteen-foot ceilings and three north-facing Gothic arched windows was as wild and wooly as Whit had intended it to be. The loquacious Beeles of Westchester and the somewhat subdued Russell contingent from Texas were beyond being shocked.

Jone's father said not once but a dozen times that it was the first wedding he'd ever gone to where no one had cried and as far as he was concerned that made it the best. Even Elizabeth, who cried at birthdays and anniversaries as well as at weddings and funerals, had been too awed and confounded to squeeze out a single tear.

"Leave it to that Whit," said Mr. Beele, while Mr. Russell, who had never approved of his son's occupation, and knew little about art, raved on and on about his daughter-in-law's sculptures and how happy he was that someone was finally going to make the Russell name legitimately famous. When, as part of the ceremony which Jone and Whit had written themselves, Jone declared that she would retain the name of Beele, Mr. Russell thought it was just another joke and laughed loudly until the bearded young priest who was officiating gave him a warning glance.

Above the lily-covered altar which had been rigged up at one end of the rectangular room there were two blown-up, grainy, black and white photographs; one of Jone and one of Whit, each a posterior nude shot. Rising above the lilies the nude photographs were simultaneously shocking and inspirational.

Strands of white sheets hung like banners from the ceiling and the only light during the rites came from large Gothic candelabras strategically placed throughout the room to cast eerie shadows. Music was the low wail of an oboe playing an original Oriental-sounding piece written by a friend of Whit's especially for the occasion. There were several dogs at the ceremony and one thin horse stationed at the door as a silent butler. Vinnie was momentarily disappointed to find there were four other guests on roller skates, one of whom was wearing a fake arrow which appeared to have pierced his head, and another of whom was a flamboyant transvestite with a painted purple body and only a few crucial sequins and ribbons for clothing. Toddlers crawled between the legs of unlikely young parents with matching Mohawk burr haircuts, decked out in gaudy "carnie" outfits held together with glittering "punk" safety pins. Young women in saris rubbed elbows with sophisticates in Halston and Chloe. There were men in black ties and an older woman in a tulle prom dress from the fifties, plus a plethora, quite naturally, of cowboys and cowgirls.

Nobody had been prepared for the primeval, ritualistic nature of the "celebration." The reason no one cried, Cathy commented later, was because everyone was spellbound, waiting for the next unpredictable moment. There was an air of suspense and the guests were hushed, like children at a Halloween party; there was the sense that anything could happen. Elizabeth Beele nearly fainted when, shortly after the appearance of the bearded priest, there was a loud noise like a bomb hissing, then a sudden cloud of dense fog in front of the lilied altar. But it was only the theatrical explosion of the dry ice pellets which Whit had deployed to cover the entrance of the bride and groom. When the fog lifted, the coughing guests ooohed their approval, for there, standing arm in arm beneath their nude photographs, were Whit, in black and silver western attire, and Jone, all in crimson with her blond hair swept up on top of her head the way Whit liked it. There was a smattering of applause before the priest began the ceremony.

"Of course I do!" cried Whit when the priest asked the crucial marriage question; and Jone had answered softly, "Without a doubt."

Then in instantaneous contrast to the ritualistic sobriety of the ceremony, the loft was flooded with flashing strobe lights and a rollicking country band picked their way into the midst of the startled guests. From that point on there was utter madness with people roller skating and square dancing, dogs yapping, champagne corks popping, a magician in one corner, a juggler in another, a miniature chuck wagon offering everything from caviar to Whit's chili with onions and sour cream. It was a carnival, a celebration, a wedding that no one would ever forget.

For Jone the only detail to mar an otherwise perfect occasion was her Grandmother Mary's last-minute refusal to attend the Whitney show.

"I just don't understand," Elizabeth said earlier in the day when she was helping Jone with final preparations. "I know how much it meant to you, honey, to have her see your show but maybe we can get her to come another time." For once Elizabeth had not covered over Mary's actions by declaring that the old woman was sick.

"She won't." Jone had tried to shake the sense of foreboding she felt at Mary's absence from the Whitney show.

"Now Jone, honey . . ." Elizabeth had comforted her daughter, "don't take this personally. You know how she is."

"How is she, Mother?" Jone had faced Elizabeth, expecting more rationalizations, more lies.

"You were right, Jone," Elizabeth had said tremulously. "Mother tried to kill herself . . . yes. She tried twice before last summer—once when I was a girl and that time at Christmas." Elizabeth shut her eyes but managed not to cry. "But Jone, I never believed it was simply us children who kept Mother from painting. I know that's what you think. We were rich . . . Mother could have afforded help, Papa was a pushover, he would have given her anything she wanted."

"What stopped her?" asked Jone.

"I don't know," Elizabeth replied sadly, as if she were referring to herself.

"Don't worry." Jone put her arm around her mother's narrow shoulder and hugged her. "Thanks for telling me the truth. It's better to know."

MARCH 1981

New York City

"It was incredible!" Cathy wound herself into Tony's arms as she finished an animated description of Whit and Jone's wedding. "If Whit doesn't make it big as a sculptor, I tell you, Tony, he could direct huge spectacles, movies like Cecil B. De Mille. The whole evening was perfectly planned to be as spontaneous as the . . . creation of the world. I mean, when that dry ice exploded . . ."

Tony laughed. "Would you like that, babe?"

"What . . . would I like what?" Cathy nudged her nose into his armpit and nipped him.

"A lunatic wedding like that? I always thought you preferred the classic touch—a brut champagne, string quartets, Beluga caviar, and smoked Scotch salmon."

"That's what *you* prefer." Cathy giggled and rolled on top of him, feeling his lean young body beneath her. She propped herself up on one elbow and studied his face, which seemed to have become younger during the month they had been apart. Sometimes, like now, with his cheeks still flushed from their love-making, his youth shocked her into silence.

"Do you like what you see?" he asked with a cocky smile.

"I do." Cathy lowered herself and kissed him softly. "I missed you terribly. Why did you stay away so long? Why didn't I cancel the whole trip when I learned we'd have to be separated for so long?"

"Because you are a power-mad woman," Tony teased, stroking her back. "And there was no reason to cancel your trip."

"Switzerland's so expensive." She felt herself sinking lazily into him as he massaged her.

"What do you care? You're rich."

Cathy sat up suddenly. "What did you mean by that?"

Tony laughed and hugged her back to his chest. "Absolutely nothing."

"No, you meant something," Cathy persisted. "Does it bother you that I make so much more money than you?"

Tony folded his hands behind his head and smiled. "No, Cath, it does not."

"It bothers Whit apparently. Jone is always protecting his ego."

"So . . .?"

"Why doesn't it bother you?" Cathy wanted to know.

"Do you want it to?" Tony asked, still smiling.

"Of course I don't want it to but I know last year was a lean year for you. You weren't teaching full time and . . ." Cathy squirmed out of his arms. "I feel weird talking about this. We never talked about anything like this before."

"Domestic conversations have never intrigued me that much," Tony said. "I always figured you'd had enough of them in your life."

Cathy winced. "It really doesn't bother you that I pay . . . or even that Lester pays your way much of the time?"

"I pay my own rent," Tony said defensively. "What's this about? Are you starting to think of me as a gigolo?"

"Of course not," Cathy protested vehemently, but she was not sure he wasn't right.

"Yes, you are." Tony interpreted her tone accurately. "I flew to France because I was asked. I did my work while I was there, played football with Vinnie, chess with Lester. I couldn't have afforded to pay my own way."

"Don't be mad!" Cathy followed him into the bathroom.

"I'm not mad," he turned on her. "I'm hurt."

"It was the way you said 'rich,'" she explained. "It made me feel tawdry, old . . . like I was buying you."

"Guilt. What's really bothering you?" Tony stepped into the shower and turned on the water.

Cathy hopped in next to him and flung her arms around him. They stood holding each other a moment as the steaming water coursed over them.

"You stayed away so long. You said you'd be back in a week and it ended up a month. If I'd known you weren't coming back till the first of March I'd have canceled the trip to Bern. Now I'm leaving and . . . and I don't understand why you stayed away so long visiting your mother."

She had sworn to herself not to say what she had just said. Her voice had a petulant jealous ring to it, and she was ashamed. She stepped out of the shower, toweled off, and threw on her bathrobe. She didn't look at him as she left the bathroom and trudged irritably down the corridor to the kitchen.

She had no right to be suspicious. No one did, for that matter, but she least of all, considering the ongoing ambiguity of their arrangement. Of course he wasn't a gigolo, but what was he to her and what was he likely to be? Why had life been so easy and simple in France and why was it again so confusing?

She would make his favorite Sunday sweet—an oven omelette with fresh strawberries. Maybe she could even talk him into canceling the class he was going to teach and convince him to come to Switzerland. She dashed frantically around the kitchen separating the yolks from the whites, whipping them, melting the butter, slopping them into the skillet.

He was going to leave her. Cathy stopped speeding and sat on one of the stools with her head in her hands. How did she know?

She knew.

"I fixed your favorite . . . the oven omelette with *fraises*," she smiled at him as he came into the kitchen. His hair was wet, slicked back straight, and shiny black.

"Cathy." He reached for her but she darted over to the oven to see if the omelette was puffed up. What if she were to finally bring up Lester's crazy idea that Tony move in with them? Would that solve the matter once and for all? She shook her head anxiously as she stood up and turned to him. She knew it wouldn't solve anything.

"Did you fall in love with someone else?" she asked stonily as she poured his coffee.

"No." Tony accepted the cup solemnly.

"But you had . . . an affair. That's why . . . never mind. Forget I said that."

"We're both free to do whatever we want."

"You're right," snapped Cathy. "And of course what *we're* having is just an affair."

"Words don't really do justice," he said sadly. "I don't want to play games, Cathy."

"Someone younger?" She could have slapped herself for asking.

"It's irrelevant," said Tony. "I don't want to make you feel bad."

"Thanks." Cathy jerked the sash on her peach satin robe.

"Look, I had no intention of getting into this just before you hop a plane to Europe."

"You were saving it for my birthday? Well, it's coming up . . . maybe you could give me another nice present."

"Knock off the cynicism," Tony shouted. "It's a totally wasted effort because you do it so poorly."

"Shit!" screamed Cathy, "the omelette burned. Damn you!" She collapsed onto the kitchen stool in tears.

"You're amazing." Tony looked down on her confounded. "See, you think I'm going to leave you but it's the other way around and it always has been. You and I are never going to have a life together and don't harp on your age because that has nothing to do with it. *You* don't want anything permanent with me. You don't want to live with me and that's the truth."

"You never asked me," Cathy accused.

Tony leaned forward on the stool until he was gazing directly into her watery eyes. "Do you want to move to Paris with me in April?"

This is where I came in, Jone thought acerbically as she listened to Cathy's melodramatic lament. Nothing ever changes, nothing ever changes.

As part of their egalitarian arrangement Whit and Jone had agreed to have two nights a week when, even if they wanted to, they were not allowed to see each other. Tonight Whit was off somewhere (he liked to keep his whereabouts mysterious) and Jone was having Angelica and Cathy to dinner at the new loft. But Angelica, who continued to be remote and unreliable, had phoned at the last minute to say that her boss at Far Out Inc. had given her a special assignment and since it involved a substantial amount of money she was going to work late. Jone wondered if that wasn't a lie, if Angelica wasn't just avoiding her.

"Did you hear what I said?" asked Cathy. "Jone, are you okay?"

"I'm fine." Jone poured them each another glass of white wine.

"I said I still want to paint you and Angelica . . . *The Girls Downtown*. I know you're busy but . . . if I could just nab you guys for a few hours sometime."

"Sure," Jone nodded congenially, glad that Cathy had finally abandoned her domestic tragedy in favor of some other subject.

"Lester and I have been legally separated for a year and a half," Cathy lapsed back onto familiar ground.

"He's a nice man," said Jone.

"Oh, shit, don't I know it. Lordy lord!" Cathy crossed her legs and stared at the shiny pointed toe of her tan leather boot. "So . . . Angelica sold another painting."

Jone nodded. "But it doesn't seem to matter."

"It can take a long time to heal, Jone," Cathy said thoughtfully.

"Maybe." Jone lit a cigarette and gazed at the shrouded marble statue in Whit's work space. Whit's work had grown in its proportions and he had managed to convince her that because of the racket and the fumes created by her welding, she should work downstairs in the storage room. To demonstrate his good intentions he had even installed a fan and rigged up a new lighting system. Only there was something denigrating about the place, though he had a point about the fumes. Retreating into the basement everyday had become a descent into negativity and resentment.

"Are you angry?" asked Cathy after a moment.

Jone laughed. "Why would I be . . ."

"With Angelica . . . or me?"

"I think I'm disappointed in Angelica. You know how ridiculous she thought Far Out Inc. was. Remember the scandalous things she used to say and draw? Now when I talk to her she goes on about this album cover or that one and how so-and-so loved something she did and somebody asked expressly for her to do a job. It's like she's really involved in that stupid job."

"*Oi*," said Cathy. "*Oi vey*."

"What a waste!"

"Well, I understand," reflected Cathy. "It's a helluva lot easier operating inside the structure with regular money coming at you, regular old praise, pats on the head . . ."

"But Angelica is a genius!" Jone exploded. "I wouldn't be surprised if she went back with that creep Brown."

"Ferris?" Cathy looked askance. "No, she wouldn't. Nah!"

"Stranger things have happened."

"You seem depressed," Cathy said after a moment. "How's the work coming?"

Jone wrinkled her nose the way Whit was always doing. "I don't know."

"I don't mean to pry," Cathy said quickly, sensing Jone's impatience. "You know, maybe you need to be alone. I'd understand . . . I can rustle up something . . ."

"I wouldn't hear of it," Jone protested, aware that she sounded just like Elizabeth. "Damn!"

"What?" Cathy looked concerned. Lately she had come to look on Jone as a daughter, whereas she recalled that her first impression of Jone, nearly a year ago, had been of someone older than herself. It was as if in the course of the year she had grown older and Jone had grown younger.

"I just . . ." Jone stopped as soon as she began. "I don't know what's expected of me anymore."

Cathy waited and when nothing was forthcoming she asked, "Can you elaborate?"

". . . since we got married," Jone's voice trailed off. "It's like I feel I should be doing something."

"You are," Cathy pointed out. "You're working on a new show."

Jone poured herself some more wine. "I remember once

Grandmother Mary getting very upset because my mother, who she considered not only a radical, for God's sake, but an unfit wife, did not get up and cook breakfast for my father before he went to work. I remember Grandmother on the verge of tears almost because of my mother's negligence. And I thought, she's right, Mother is a horrible person. My poor father clumsily poking around the kitchen . . . Jeee-zus!"

"Funny," said Cathy. "I wouldn't have thought you could have had these thoughts."

"Me neither," said Jone, gulping down the rest of her wine and pouring some more.

"But Whit doesn't want you bopping around the kitchen in a little ruffled apron."

"I know," Jone said glumly. "But I feel sorry for him every time I see him putting on the coffee or scrubbing the bathroom floor. And he's neater than me so he's always scouring something."

"But you lived together before," Cathy began.

"That was different," Jone interjected. "When we were lovers I adored him bringing me breakfast in bed, thought it was sexy the way he tossed the salad with walnut oil. Now I feel I'm not doing my job."

"Shit," said Cathy, helping herself to more wine, "the old waitressing syndrome. Funny, you either have it or you don't, and you and me got it. Angelica I don't believe has it. I betcha anything she never . . ."

"Yeah!" Jone gestured drunkenly. "Yeah, you're right. She said once. She always felt great about Ferris being a gourmet cook, figured that was one of the few breaks Providence had bestowed on her. So big deal . . . all that stuffed quail and what did it get her?"

"You know," Cathy narrowed her eyes portentously, "I think I still love my husband Lester Aimsley."

Jone was too soused to be annoyed. "What a relief," she said dryly.

"Yeah, I think I do 'cause when I think who I would most not want to live without, other than Vinnie of course, I think of goddamn Lester Aimsley."

"Maybe you can hire Whit to write you guys a remarriage celebration," Jone giggled.

"Outside," dreamed Cathy, "on the beach at Saltaire in the spring before the crowds come, at sunrise with the Goodyear blimp passing overhead and skywriting declaring: 'The brush is mightier than the sword.' "

"We're drunk," said Jone.

"I'm glad," said Cathy, stretching out on the floor with her back against the sofa. "Listen to me, kid . . . are you listening?"

"I am." Jone slid down next to her.

"I am going to extemporaneously extemporize on the subject of guilt with which I am well acquainted. It is a suh-lippery subject and it is the most difficult skin to shed in the erstwhile metamorphosis of sexual equality.

"If I were not absolutely certain of what I am saying," Cathy continued ceremoniously overenunciating each word, "I would shut up. But I am sure! Of one thing! That there exists what I call *female guilt* . . . a gift from the gods, no doubt, which is a nagging, self-imposed form of continued slavery allowing us to suffer by placing everyone else's real or *imagined* needs before our own. Beware the Ides of March, Jone."

Jone nodded her head attentively. "That's from *Julius Caesar*."

"It is indeed," said Cathy sagely as she reached for the nearly empty gallon jug of wine.

❀

The agreement between Jone and Whit was that they were not to ask each other what they were doing on the assigned nights out; not because, as Whit explained, he wanted to prowl like a tomcat, but in order to maintain the "mystery of their union." He read Jone passages from Carlos Castaneda's *The Teachings of Don Juan,* in which the crafty old Indian sorcerer advised Carlos to periodically disappear from friends and colleagues in order to gain personal power. Whit was a firm believer in personal power and peyote and although Jone had never given metaphysics much thought, she tended to agree, in principle. In theory it sounded exciting; but invariably Jone found herself at loose ends on those nights while Whit seemed invigorated and fortified by them. She wondered what on earth she had done with her time before Whit and why, when he absented himself at night, she felt more inclined to wait for him to come back than to strike out on her own. The idea of working on these assigned nights made her feel inadequate, because if she always resorted to her work, didn't that imply she was not as resourceful at Whit in other areas? She had already exhausted Cathy as a dinner guest and Angelica seemed always to be working late at Far Out Inc.

The fact that Whit was gregarious and she was and had always been a loner was no comfort. She began to measure herself against him and found herself wanting. She missed Angelica deeply and was confused and hurt that Angelica's life seemed to have veered off in another direction.

In an attempt to feel better about herself, Jone took the train to Connecticut to visit her grandmother whom she had not seen since Thanksgiving. She had determined in advance to be direct in her attempts to discover why Mary had abandoned her art so completely. It had been a foolhardy determination, however, and the old woman, wily and cunning as ever, had sidestepped all of Jone's questions with the sort of trivialities which Elizabeth usually found so comforting.

"Do you remember the Irish setter your grandfather had? The one that always went nuts whenever I made those little Swedish pancakes with the lingonberry syrup?"

"Yes," Jone had replied politely to the hollow-cheeked old woman.

"It was always amazing to me, Jonie, how he could tell when I was making those pancakes. Now how do you suppose he knew? Never bothered when it was Aunt Jemima mix but just let me reach for the sour cream . . ." The old woman had shaken her head in remembered disbelief. "Were you too young?" she had asked. "Do you remember?"

Jone had hidden her disappointment with a smile. "Of course I remember."

"I always liked setters." Mary had seemed comforted by the exchange. Obviously she did not want to hear about Jone's success, for she had neither apologized for missing the Whitney opening nor inquired how it had gone. Briefly Jone entertained the idea that Mary had simply forgotten, that senility had finally set in. But she did not believe that. She had come for a blessing and was leaving, as she had after her visit last summer, in a panic.

She went directly back to the loft praying that Whit had returned early, knowing full well he would not. Tonight she did not want to be there waiting for him. Something in her wanted him to worry about her the way he had done the time she had lost track of time mulling over her future at the Temple of Dendur. But there was no place to go unless she hung out at McSorley's Bar. She called Angelica but there was no answer. There was, she thought at times, considerable liability in being a loner.

She went down to the basement and worked on her latest piece, a circular structure with radiating spirals reminiscent of mystical symbols. *Beware the Ides of March,* she thought, and was suddenly and for the first time in her life consumed with jealousy and suspicion. How had she been stupid enough to believe that Whit was out gaining personal power? Usually when he came home on these nights she was already asleep; once she had glanced at the clock and seen that it was four in the morning . . . and stupidly she had thought nothing of it. She continued working furiously, firing up her rage and indignation as she dominated her metals, forcing them into submission. She channeled her rancor into the metal and it grew along with her fury. She despised him for arousing such mean emotions in her and mostly she despised herself for allowing herself to be victimized.

Three hours later, her hands and face smudged and grimy, she let herself into their loft. Whit was sleeping peacefully in the new four-poster bed, a sweetly satisfied smile on his face. Jone gaped at him and then at the alarm clock. It was only midnight.

APRIL 1981

New York City

Jone stood purposefully in the rain outside the old Obil Garage wearing a bright yellow slicker over her rolled-up baggy pants and sweat shirt. Her tennis shoes were soaked; they squeaked when she shifted her weight. If she stood for a long time without moving she could feel the water accumulating and turning slightly tepid from her body heat; then she would move, squoosh out the old water and new fresh cold water would ooze in. An acquaintance of Angelica's had taken over the Obil, she didn't know his name, only he was a former scientist who worked with the synchromatic movement of light and called himself a "light painter."

February had been like May and now April was a disappointment, even though today was mild. April Fool. She had expected more. What had she expected? She frowned. Angelica was making jokes again, growing cherry tomatoes in her loft and still talking about moving to Savannah. She had let her hair grow, shed the black wardrobe for a violet one, and was working ten, sometimes eleven hours a day at Far Out Inc. Jone found it difficult not to be critical on the afternoons she met Angelica for lunch at one of those trendy midtown restaurants . . . the type of place Jone's mother might have frequented. What had she expected after all?

Everyone kept telling her how extraordinary she was, how

she had accomplished so much in one year, yet when she looked back, reflecting on the days which had led her to this one, she saw only that this time last year, as lonely and uncertain as she had been, she had been happier. She searched her soul to find the reasons why and came up empty-handed. Her acceptance into the art world had been practically effortless; she called it luck. In one week she was supposed to fly to London for her first European exposure. Next year when the Whitney opened its new ground-floor sculpture garden at the Philip Morris corporate headquarters on Park Avenue and Forty-second Street, there would be a new large-scale piece by Jone Beele included in the glass-enclosed space. On top of all this she was married to a man so incredible she had never even entertained the notion of finding someone like him. When she thought of life without Whit she thought of death.

But they could not get along. Despite Carlos Castaneda and Simone de Beauvoir, their egalitarian relationship was tumultuous to say the least. They loved and fought, loved and fought, swore peace and found new avenues of resentment. Whit might have handled Jone's first acceptance by the Whitney chivalrously, but additional commissions from the Philip Morris Gallery and the Los Angeles County Museum had triggered off all of his old insecurities. Now he was refusing to come to London with her, proving his independence by staying behind when all along they had planned the trip as a honeymoon. The opportunity he had thought was going to materialize for a Paris showing of his work had been postponed, perhaps indefinitely, and in the past two weeks he had all but stopped even trying to make a pretense of working on his marble pieces.

It was her fault. Jone sloshed past the Obil Garage and leaned against a grimy mail truck. Usually a walk in the rain cleared her mind, but not today. Whit never actually said his slump was her fault, but she felt it. There should have been something she could do or say to pull him out of his lethargy but even her genuine praise for his work seemed to drive him further into a feeling of worthlessness. She could not love him enough. The only times she felt adequate to soothe and comfort him were when they made love, but lately she felt such a compulsion to please him that she was unsatisfied. It didn't matter.

"Was it good?" she would ask him and when he would tell her yes and smile, for the moment freed from the terrible competition, she would feel almost like her old self again.

A month after he had instigated the two nights a week "free time" he decided he had accumulated enough personal power on his own and that it was important for the two of them to share in more social activities. For the remainder of March they had scarcely spent an evening home, unless it was entertaining Whit's friends. Jone didn't mind that they were his friends; as she had done with Angelica, she allowed herself to be stimulated by his buoyancy. But not only had Whit become compulsively sociable, his expectations of her were different than Angelica's had been. With Angelica she had been able to say no, leave early, or remain silent for an entire meal without feeling she had failed.

Jone kicked the dented bumper on the mail truck and began jogging down Charlton Street. Damn if she wasn't turning into a proper phony like her mother.

"Everything's terrific!" she had told Angelica yesterday at lunch, not knowing why it seemed impossible to confess her difficulties with Whit now that they were married. It was as if the marriage had sealed her off. She felt obliged to smile and confirm how wonderful married life was. "He wants to move." Jone had humorously hinted that she had a few very minor reservations about leaving New York City.

"Well, I understand why he would," Angelica had replied dreamily. "I can't lose my fascination for Savannah and I don't know why."

"You're just saying that about moving to Savannah," Jone had teased with some of the candor they had once shared, and Angelica had smiled briefly as if she had been caught. There had been no way for her to tell Angelica how she had longed for the Obil, for of course Angelica did not feel the same way. Angelica had been unable even to step inside and claim her few belongings and had relied on Cathy and Tony and Vinnie to move her into the new loft.

Jone was drenched by the time she walked from the Obil to the loft on King Street. The yodeling record was blaring and above that she could hear male laughter—no doubt another beer-drinking confab between Whit and his friends. Jone started to press the elevator button for the top floor, changed her mind, and went down into her basement studio to work, ignorant of how soaked she was from standing for hours in the rain.

She kept one eye on the clock so that Whit would not feel hurt if she stayed too long with her work. She felt pressured at least to make a start on the Los Angeles piece before leaving for London. The prospect of leaving for London depressed her. She had been so excited about their first trip together and now, in exactly seven days, she would be flying off alone.

When she entered the loft punctually at six that evening Whit was stuffing clothes into a backpack.

"Vermont," he announced with a tipsy smile. "Larry and Sanders know of a hundred acres cheap . . . on a lake. Doesn't that sound great? Jeeee-zus, am I fed up with this shit-filled city. If I get into one more train that smells like a urinal and stalls for ten minutes in a dark tunnel I could turn into a . . . what'sa matter?"

Feeling the clamminess of her wet feet, Jone kicked off her tennis shoes and crossed angrily to the kitchen to get a beer. "I'm not sure I want to move to Vermont."

"Of course you do!" Whit bounded up behind her and kissed her neck.

"Maybe I don't," she glared at him. "Were you just going to leave? No, you'd leave me a note, wouldn't you? Why are you looking at the land with Larry and Sanders?"

"Because," he said sullenly, "I need to get away."

"Your answer is always to get away."

"It's a waste of time arguing." He walked out of the kitchen and Jone followed him.

"Whit, don't go. Please. If you have to go wait till I'm in London. It's going to be hard enough being separated from you for two weeks . . . I don't see why you want to go now!"

"I'm supposed to plan my life around yours?" he shouted fiercely.

"I never asked you to!" Jone was already crying. "We talked for so long about driving from London into Scotland . . . of being on the moors . . . the heaths like Cathy and Laurence Olivier . . . shit, I mean Heathcliff!"

"Stop crying!" he demanded and Jone sobbed harder. "I said

stop, damn it! If you want to have a conversation, talk, but don't whimper and make me feel like a rotten shit."

"Oh shit!" Jone leaped up, screaming at the top of her lungs. "Make me feel, make me feel, make me feel!"

"I don't want to go to London," he said viciously. "I have had it with cities. I have to get out!"

"But what about me?" whimpered Jone.

"I'm going up to Vermont tonight," Whit explained, "for *us*. Jeee-zus, we gotta get outta the city before we kill each other, Jone. Can't you see? It's no good bein' cooped up. You're always complainin' about bein' in the basement but how in the hell can you expect me to work with those fumes, huh? In Vermont we'll have space. Space, damn it! Space is what people need. Once we have space, I guarantee you, we'll be fine."

"But I like the city." Jone stopped crying.

"You've never lived in the country."

"I lived in Westchester," she replied.

"Hardly the country," Whit said snidely, throwing his backpack over his shoulder. "I'll be back day after tomorrow."

Jone stopped herself from running after him. She was shivering and seething all at one time. She took a hot shower, four aspirins and two stiff belts of brandy, and went to bed.

The next morning she was awakened by her anger, flying out of the four-poster like a crazy person, cursing and shouting so loud her voice reverberated in the high-ceilinged loft. For the next two days she worked at that high pitch of fury, waking every morning more hostile than when she had gone to bed the night before. He did not call. She was so afraid she would miss his call that she left the answering machine on even when she was upstairs and not in the basement working. He had removed himself but it was not personal power, she thought, that he was gaining. His withdrawal, she saw, had been about power but not his personal power.

He arrived home three days later than he had said, walking in on her with an innocent, boyish smile, telling tales of deer and crystal mountain lakes, saying how the five days had clarified everything for him. He gave no indication of remembering that she was due to leave for London in two days.

"I put five hundred dollars down on an old farmhouse," he

said after he had fixed himself a cup of tea. He was also no longer drinking, he said—only herb teas and fertilized eggs and vegetables. He was going to put in an organic garden as soon as the ground thawed enough to work it.

Jone had counted on her anger but it deserted her in the face of the finality of his plans. Once again she began to cry.

"Please, Jone." This time he was loving and gentle. "Honey, I shoulda called. C'mon now. It's gonna be just fine now."

He unbuttoned her shirt and buried his head in her breasts, taking the nipple of one gently in his mouth as his hand massaged the other.

His hair, thought Jone, as she nuzzled him, did smell of crystal mountain lakes. It mightn't be so bad after all.

He unfastened her jeans, sliding his hands down her hips and back and under her buttocks, then around to the mound of her stomach and slowly down.

Jone squirmed away from him, suddenly caught in the terrible grip of her anger. She crawled on her knees across the Navajo rug, but he caught her by the heel and thinking it was a game tugged at her jeans. He was aware of nothing different in her attitude as he stripped off his clothes and stood above her, straddling her body as she looked up at him.

Jone struggled, undecided, praying that the irrational anger would dissolve in his arms. There was a new glint in his eye; he stood for what seemed to Jone a long time looking down at her. Their eyes seemed locked together, the sound of their breathing matched perfectly though they were not touching. They seemed, thought Jone dizzily, to belong this way.

Suddenly then she grabbed his arm roughly and pulled him on top of her.

"God, I missed you," she groaned, digging her fingers into his back. Too hard, she thought, too hard. He was overcome, unable to sustain himself as she moved furiously beneath him, and then she was aware that the marks she was making on his smooth back were drawing blood and she could not help but dig deeper. He seemed aroused by her violence and he thrashed harder and more determinedly inside of her and memories of all their days and nights rushed by her—the way he had first touched her in the phone booth, the hours he had spent photographing her, his hand turned to one side, limp, with the long fingers curled slightly against the pillow, as he slept next to her in the bordello bed.

Jone fought him with the power of her body as if without words she might finally obliterate his fears. When he was depleted she moved against him until he wanted her again and then again until she was weak and the frustration and the anger were once again diminished.

"It has seven bedrooms." Later they sat at the kitchen table drinking beer (Whit was making an exception to his new healthful regime) while he drew a diagram of their new Depression farmhouse.

"Who needs seven bedrooms?" Jone laughed. "Whit, please change your mind and come to England with me. Then when we come back we can . . ."

"We do," Whit grinned and continued with no acknowledgment of her suggestion. "You and me. We can knock a coupla walls out of two of 'em—make a big studio. That leaves five. One for you 'n me, one for Angelica . . . I don't see why she shouldn't move in . . ."

"Maybe she doesn't want to move to Vermont," Jone suggested tentatively. "Unless we tell her it's Savannah."

"So we'll tell her it's Savannah. Anyway when she sees it . . . when *you* see it . . . whatta buy! That leaves one other guest room and two rooms for kidlets."

"What?" Jone felt a new surge of anger.

"Babies, Jonie. You've heard of them . . . little human creatures that go goo."

"Why are you talking about babies? My God!" She sprang to her feet. "You're planning everything! This is not another Cecil B. Russell extravaganza like our wedding, this is my life."

"Mine, too. Listen, I didn't mean . . ."

"The shit you didn't!" Jone stormed off and retreated back to the refrigerator for another beer.

"Look, I am doing my damndest," Whit said, "to save our very brief marriage."

"And the answer is a houseful of kids in Vermont? That is your answer to what's going on between us? I can't believe you," Jone raged on. Some of the words she was saying she recognized from her early morning tirades to the empty walls; the words had been lying in wait, they tumbled out more naturally than they had ever in her life done.

"You're talking like somebody out of the fifties," she yelled. "You . . . you, you actually think that children are going to solve . . . that's retrogressive thinking . . . unworthy of you. Please now . . . just think about it."

"I've thought about it," Whit said cooly. "Living here is unnatural. The city is no place to bring up . . ."

"Who wants them?"

"What?"

"I said who wants children?"

"Jeeee-zus!" Whit stood up and heaved the oak table over on its side.

"Listen." Jone went to him, trying to remain calm. She put her hand on his arm and jerked it back because she could not stop it from shaking. "It's naive of you to think that we're in any position to be talking about having children . . . even about moving to the country. These things take time. We have to be able to talk about them and decide together."

"What did you mean by *Who wants them*?" Whit raised his voice.

"I just meant what I said," Jone said belligerently, her anger rekindled by his hostile attitude. "I don't want them. You know how I feel about . . ."

"I don't know how you feel about anything," Whit said in a digusted tone, "because you are like a fuckin' zombie, you keep everything to yourself."

"Not true," snapped Jone. "I've tried to get you to talk about . . ."

"What good is talk. I'm trying to *do* something."

"Like hell," said Jone. "You avoid everything . . . like pain and how you feel about my . . ."

"My life doesn't revolve around you, baby."

"Don't call me 'baby.' " Jone faced him, too blind to see that his frustration and anger were as agonizing as hers. All she felt were his attacks and she had to fight back, to let him know she could not be beaten.

"If you want babies you'll have to go find someone else to

have them because . . ." She stopped abruptly, stunned at how easily the truth had tumbled out.

"What?" Whit demanded. "What did you mean I'll have to . . ."

"Because I can't have them!" Jone replied in a low, disdainful voice. "I can't have them, by choice."

"What do you mean by choice?" He took a menacing step toward her and Jone felt her fury reignited.

"I went to a doctor, that's what," she shouted. "I had my tubes cut, tied, blocked, burned apart, fixed forever and thank God I did!" She knew she was saying too much but she rushed on, glad to see the suffering look on his face. If he could make her suffer by going off to Vermont and not even phoning, then wasn't it fair play to twist the knife in him? The words were easy. She had more words now than she knew what to do with and each one of them, she saw, stung him and that was what she wanted.

When she finally finished he simply stared at her with no expression on his face. Then she felt the panic; she knew she had gone too far.

"It was before I met you, Whit." She was shaking. "I did it as the ultimate protection. I told you what happened to my grandmother, how I was afraid of being sucked into . . . of not having the time and the . . . spiritual space to do my work. I told you. And I never expected to meet anyone like you."

Whit averted his eyes but held the same rigid stance.

"Say something," Jone pleaded, then after a moment continued in what she thought was a controlled, logical voice. "I'm still glad I did it. You see, you proved me right."

"I didn't prove anything," Whit said softly.

"Yes, you did!" Jone ducked down and tried to meet his eyes but he looked away again. "You proved me right because . . ."

Whit began walking slowly into the other room and Jone followed with a new urgency in her voice. "See, I loved you . . . *love*, I mean, I love you so that . . ."

"I don't believe that," Whit said sarcastically without looking at her.

"I do. You can't doubt that. If you had asked me to have children I know I would have. I wouldn't have resisted you for long. You could have talked me into it, like you talk me into . . ." Jone floundered, then made a feeble stab at a joke, ". . . into Japanese food when I want Italian."

"Hardly." Whit gave her a disgusted smile.

"But I should have told you. I never meant it to come out like this . . . I'm sorry I . . . I was wrong not to tell you. But you have to understand how afraid I was. Now," Jone tugged at his arm, "I have to make you understand that with it all in the open we can really make our lives together into the . . ." Jone stopped, she could not think of the word. ". . . the union," she finally said, "you want it to be . . . and me too."

Whit's eyes moved around their bedroom as if he were searching for something valuable, then he looked back at Jone with an indifferent expression.

"Please say something!" she moaned.

"Not right now," he said impassively as if there were more important matters on his mind.

"I meant it to come out when we were close, when I could explain it to you and you would hold me and . . . and understand that . . . that I did it because it seemed like the only way I could survive and . . ."

"I'm going out," he interrupted her nonchalantly and Jone watched him walk through the loft and disappear out the front door.

Jone did not go to London. On April 8, the day she was scheduled to leave, she simply did not go to the airport. When her agent, David Epstein, phoned to find out what had happened she said only, without rhetoric or mumbled excuses, that she could not go.

"Are you all right?" David had been alarmed.

Of course, she had said. Yes, she was fine, only the Los Angeles piece was coming along so nicely she hated to interrupt her momentum now.

Jone waited for Whit for nearly two weeks, during which she spoke to parents and friends as if nothing out of the ordinary was taking place. She made nonchalant references to Whit as if he were still chipping away at his block of limestone, yodeling contentedly to himself. Every morning at seven she left a note on the kitchen table in case he returned while she was in the basement working. Every evening when she emerged all grimy and tired the note was still there. She would throw the note away, preferring to write a fresh one every morning although the brief message was always the same: *Darling . . . am downstairs working. Love, Me.*

As long as she was working with her metal the world did not exist, but when she wasn't working her breathing was shallow and controlled, as if she was consciously conserving both her own energy and the oxygen in her immediate environment. Casually she phoned his friends, all of them men, who might have known where he had gone, but there was no information and there was nothing in anyone's attitude to suggest that they were lying. No one had seen Whit, no one knew anything.

At night after she had showered and dressed Jone wandered over to the fashionably bustling section of Soho, moving silently from bar to bar, convinced that she would eventually run into him. She phoned his agent, his gallery owner, and finally, inventing a pathetic excuse, she phoned his parents in Texas saying that Whit had a yen for some ruby red grapefruit and she wanted to surprise him by having some sent up north. Everything was fine, she told Mrs. Russell as she strained to detect any duplicity in her mother-in-law's responses.

There was no sign of panic in her behavior, even to those few people who knew her well. She lunched with Cathy once and twice she met Angelica midtown for dinner. When Angelica noted the shortness of breath, Jone attributed it to heavy smoking and nerves about finishing the Los Angeles piece by the deadline.

Finally, at the end of the second week, she thought of calling the Vermont real estate agent and for purposes of simplicity she for the first time identified herself as Mrs. Whittemore Russell. The real estate agent's Yankee punctiliousness almost shattered her shell but once she was able to convince him that she was indeed Mrs. Russell and that she had to reach her husband because of an emergency, he grudgingly allowed that Mr. Russell had phoned a week ago to say he was forfeiting the five hundred dollar deposit on the house and ten acres.

Jone was scarcely breathing when she hung up. She had not cried since the night Whit had left; she had gone about her business with her usual unwavering discipline and alacrity, refusing even to speculate on what was going on in his mind. Now she understood that he was not simply off somewhere on a binge or shacked up with another woman in an effort to gain revenge. He was methodically taking care of business, living his new life, and he had no intention of coming back to her, not ever.

She phoned his agent for the second time and this time, no doubt according to Whit's master plan, the agent admitted that he of course knew where his client was, but he had been given instructions not to give out the information to anyone.

Although she did not feel like moving after she hung up the receiver, Jone forced herself to her feet, put on her jacket, and took the elevator to the main floor. She checked the mailbox, feeling ridiculous for harboring a remaining shred of hope. There was the usual assortment of junk mail plus a white bond envelope decidedly un-Whit-like and addressed to her. She threw out the junk mail, stuffed the envelope in her pocket, and went out onto the street. It was drizzling slightly and she shivered. She felt the futility in the face of the predictable cycle of the seasons as she walked to the corner and pulled the envelope out of her pocket. The return address in austere black lettering read: "Materson and Materson Attorneys-at-Law."

How expediently he had dealt with all of the ambiguities, thought Jone, as she ripped open the envelope. She scanned the letter which notified her that Mr. Whittemore Russell had made the necessary applications, both legal and ecclesiastical, for having his marriage to Jone Beele annulled on the grounds that Jone Beele had *misrepresented herself.*

Jone did not bother reading the remainder of the letter which spelled out the situation in unfathomable legal jargon. She wadded up the letter and threw it in the gutter. Like a robot she walked three times around the same block, feeling her body winding down until she had hardly enough stamina to push the button for the elevator which would take her back upstairs. In a daze she phoned Angelica at Far Out Inc. She had difficulty forming the words because of the lack of breath.

"I'll be right over," Angelica promised and did not ask any questions.

Jone sat next to the phone staring dumbly at the composite Whit had made of her nude photograph superimposed over several perspectives of Lachaise's *Standing Woman*. Now she knew what was happening and where it would all lead. There was only one remedy, only one way to pay for her own stupidity, and that was simply to kill herself.

There was no telling where Whit had gone. He was clever, she had always relished that about him. He was a master of theatrical entrances and exits and Jone knew that his disappearance would be another in a line of masterful feats. Like the wedding celebration so unexpected and bizarre . . . there was just no telling what else he might have in store. One thing she felt certain of, however, and that was that *when* he appeared it would be too late for any reconciliation, for Whit was smart in addition to being clever. He would know when time had made him inviolable and he would not reappear until then.

But even so, Jone reflected as she stuffed the chisel into the pocket of her denim jacket, he would not anticipate her move, for he, along with everyone else, had underestimated her. Yes, and she too had underestimated herself. There was also that. She smiled vaguely, remembering how once she had believed she lacked passion; she had believed herself so different from her nervous tearful mother. She had so wanted to be immune from histrionics and self-destructive, energy-sapping relationships and now look how it had ended.

Jone walked out of the apartment leaving the door wide open behind her. He was not the only master of the great gesture, she thought, as she exited from the building onto the rain-soaked April streets.

❁

Cathy chewed off the nail on her little finger as she mulled over the five outfits which she had spread across her bed: the gray silk dress, the mauve suit, the skin-tight brown corduroy pants, the plaid skirt with the black velvet jacket, and the jeans which were his favorite. She couldn't very well wear the jeans later at Le Cygne even if they were French. And anyway, it didn't matter. She was prolonging the agony by spending so much time deciding what to wear . . . as if the last image he had of her would be more powerful and indelible than the past year and a half of their affair.

Cathy sniffed, dabbed her eyes, and reminded herself to remain calm and not to pick up anything off the floor except with a straight back. She'd be damned if she was going to have her back go into spasm this time. The new rule was no more self-inflicted torture.

She chose the gray dress because it was her favorite and she could wear the new pearls Lester had given her with it. Her hand shook as she touched up her makeup. Her mascara was sure to run. She was tempted to take it off so that his last glimpse of her would not be that of a sobbing woman with black streaks on her face.

"Hello." Cathy jumped when Tony's face appeared next to hers in the bathroom mirror.

"My God, you scared me!"

"Sorry." He kissed the nape of her neck as if this were any other day.

"Why aren't you nervous?" Cathy winced at the ugly sound in her voice. "Never mind," she rushed on. "Just let me leave a note for Vinnie in the kitchen so he'll know where he can reach me if he needs to."

"Catherine." Tony put his hands on her shoulders and kissed her gently. "You are doing the right thing."

"Oh, Jesus." Cathy slipped out of his arms and hurried toward the kitchen. "Don't tell me that. Do I need to hear that from you when I'm falling apart?"

Tony laughed uneasily. "You're not falling apart. Anyway, you can always change your mind."

"Ah, yes. I know, it'd be great for Vinnie to go to school in Paris and I could have a studio overlooking the Seine on Quai St. Michel and we would live happily ever after—for how long?

Never mind. I've been wavering all day. But you don't know when or even if you're coming back to the States . . . it'll be a year at least. Oh, I've been through all this a zillion times."

"But you haven't changed your mind?" Tony eyed her warmly.

"No." Cathy ground her teeth until her jaw ached as she scribbled the note to Vinnie.

Angelica found it easy to walk right into Whit and Jone's empty apartment, since, oddly, neither door was locked, but waiting there with a gathering sense of disaster was torturous. Finally, after an hour, she phoned Cathy, because she didn't know what else to do.

"Another fight with Whit." Cathy sounded distracted. "Poor baby. Don't worry, Angelica, you know Jone . . . the kid's solid as a rock. You and I should be so solid. She'll be fine."

Angelica glanced around for any clues she might have overlooked. "It's too still here and the door was wide open. There's no sign of a struggle, no ashtrays brimming with cigarette butts, no beer cans . . . no sign of marathon conversations."

"I'm afraid you've caught me at a rotten time," Cathy replied apologetically. "I can't talk. I'm sorry . . . I know you're worried, Angelica, but . . . look, I'll try and phone later. Okay, hon? Oh . . . and don't forget this Saturday you two are posing for me. Okay, hon? Don't worry now."

Angelica hung up the phone and made another tour of the apartment. She opened Whit's closet and saw his clothes hanging neatly inside, his several pairs of cowboy boots lined up in an even row on the floor. She counted the toothbrushes in the bathroom and noted that Whit's shaving cream was on the sink and that there was a full box of tampons next to the toilet. She wondered if she should call the police. She couldn't imagine that they would listen to her fears.

She glanced briefly at her worried face in the bathroom mirror. Her dark hair, now longer and very shaggy, was fastened behind her ears with two lavender barrettes. She tossed some cold water on her face and tried to think of a reasonable course of action. She could try the Spring Street Bar or walk over toward the river, but those were both long shots. No, she was better off staying here in case Jone telephoned.

Angelica returned to the couch and tried to concentrate on a battered copy of *Arts* magazine, but that was impossible so she stretched out on her back and tried to connect her positive thoughts to Jone. It had been hard for her, losing touch with Jone over the past few months, but it had been necessary to remove herself from almost everything and everyone with whom she had been connected during her pregnancy. The one exception had been her job at Far Out Inc. Over the past two months the layouts which she had once found tedious and inane had become her *raison d'être*. She did not question why this was so. She was content to accept the mitigation of her pain in whatever form it came to her.

Just over a week ago she had made what she considered to be her definitive break with Ferris. She had finally realized that her bitterness precluded friendship and that the energy she had spent trying to overcome her resentment against him could better be channeled into other areas of her life. Although she had shed her black attire for violets and lavenders, the life she led was solitary, an almost cloistered existence which included almost no time in front of her easel. The gallery which had sold *The Woman with the Pink Powder Puff* had accepted five more paintings on consignment. One of the paintings had sold immediately, but in the past two months there had been no further sales. Lately she had given little thought to any income she might or might not receive from her paintings. *The Person Sitting in the Empty Chair* remained half finished. She had had little inclination to work on it since the jury had returned a guilty verdict on Jean Harris.

But she was making money and for the first time in her life there was enough not only to support herself but to indulge in luxuries not connected with her art. The hours formerly spent painting were now devoted to overtime and independent freelance projects which she could work on at home or on weekends. To her own wry amusement Angelica fancied that she had become something of a consumer, spending lunch hours at Bloomingdale's, reading shopping ads instead of editorials. Her loft, entirely transformed since Whit's western residency, was nearly a greenhouse environment, stocked with a collection of rare plants, herbs, and several vegetables, including a thriving cherry tomato plant. One corner was taken over by a large (and expensive) ficus tree, its roots tenderly tucked into a terra-cotta pot imported from Italy. She thought of the pot as the green-growing equivalent of a pair of Gucci shoes. She was still paying for the rose-hued Oriental rug which was the focal point in the large and still sparsely furnished space, and recently (Jone would die when she learned this) she had purchased a deluxe Cuisinart and a complete set of china, for which she was paying in monthly installments. She had become obsessed with creating an environment for herself, a comfortable home to insulate her, she thought, from the world. She had sensed Jone's disappointment in her choices but had been both unwilling and unable to defend them. Now, however, she felt a twinge of guilt for the self-absorption which had put her so out of touch with her friend.

Jone walked with her chin tucked down and one hand inside her pocket resting lightly on the chisel. She was not aware of having any destination until she saw the gentle Gothic arches of the Brooklyn Bridge rising out of the late afternoon mist. She heard herself squeak with surprise as she wondered if this, then, was her choice. She saw her body hurtling over the bridge and then she saw her mother's pinched, grief-stricken face.

Jone sprinted across the street, dodging traffic and unaware that several cars had screeched to a halt and someone was yelling at her. It had stopped drizzling but there was no one else, she thought, stupid enough to be walking across the vast stretch of the Brooklyn Bridge with heavy black storm clouds still threatening. It occurred to her briefly that Whit would approve of her bold approach. She wished he had been around so she could see his reactions. Yes, he would be impressed if she jumped.

She increased her pace. Anyone seeing her would have taken her for an overzealous jogger, a big, healthy, strong woman panting and perspiring as she mounted the span. She ran across doggedly, unseeingly. As she approached the other side she felt a stab of pain in her side and leaned against a post, gulping for air. Her hands clutching the post were white. Peering over the edge into the swirling, muddy waters, she knew that she could not jump. As her knees started to buckle, her mother's face swam before her eyes again. She could not do it, not even for Whit.

Still gasping for breath, Jone found herself in the snarling Brooklyn Heights traffic and heading for Joralemon Street, where the old Gregory mansion had been—where Grandmother Mary had lived "when I was a girl." Jone thought of one of Grandmother Mary's pictures which her mother had hung in their living room until Mary had demanded it be taken down. The painting of bright pink peonies had been no more than four by six inches, a delicate oil, meticulously realistic except for its size. It had always struck Jone as odd that her grandmother, with her tyrannical personality, loud voice, and acerbic wit, had made such delicate paintings. Of course that had been the style for young ladies at the turn of the century but Jone had always wondered if there hadn't been other paintings, paintings which had reflected something of Mary's true nature.

Just down from Joralemon, on Sidney Place, stood St. Charles Borromeo, the same church her grandmother had attended seventy-five years ago. Jone tried the door but it was locked. She sat down on the steps panting. When the renovated brownstones for which the Heights was now famous began to blur, she got up and walked bleary-eyed down to Columbia Heights and watched the gray western light fade to black.

If she had had a gun, she thought, she would have been dead by now. It would have been so easy simply to pull the trigger on some silver pistol hidden in her lingerie drawer. But she didn't have a lingerie drawer, she had never even had lingerie before Whit. Before Whit she had had pants. An abrupt laugh escaped. Now she had a drawer full of lacy lingerie and that suddenly struck her as outrageously funny. Still laughing, she removed the chisel and regarded it. There were tears streaming down her face and the few people who were walking along the Promenade were staring at her. Had she really thought she was going to stab herself to death with his goddamned chisel? Her large body shook with the absurdity of her thinking. To have been so wrong and there was nothing to do about it, nothing! Jone heaved the chisel over the railing and watched it fly through the darkness against the spectacle of the vaporous Dream City with its twinkling lights and its concrete and steel shafts which seemed to leap upwards into the night.

Cathy huddled against Tony in the back seat of the cab as it inched its way through rush hour traffic on the Van Wyck en route to Kennedy International Airport. Leaving her apartment they had laughed together over the symbolism of the stormy weather, but the laughter had stopped suddenly and though Cathy continued to wrack her brain desperately for something to say, neither had spoken a word since the Triboro Bridge. She felt oddly awkward with her chin resting on his familiar trench coat, as if she were taking liberties with a stranger. They held hands too tightly, in a suddenly pointless gesture of union.

She had dreaded this moment practically from the first night they had spent together, only it had not happened the way she had imagined it. She recalled the delicious anticipation of their first afternoons together, how she had relished the warm tingling which preceded his arrival in his tiny Village apartment, how the languid, long hours of their lovemaking had made everything else in her life seem insignificant and trivial. By her own choice her work had virtually stopped during those first months with Tony. Nothing else had mattered and she had struggled to lose herself in him just as she had lost herself in her Wayne boyfriends who preceded Rosen and the long line of international lovers who followed him. The difference, and what a difference, she thought affectionately, was that Tony, far from demanding her obedience, had teased her ceaselessly about her use of their affair as a cop-out. And he had accused her of trying to trap him into a domesticity which neither of them wanted. He had not wanted her every waking thought to be of him and for the longest time that attitude had threatened her.

As recently as six months ago she would have had no choice but to follow him. She would have fallen into a panic, stopped painting, jerked poor Vinnie out of school, rationalizing that it was best for him—and she would have followed her lover. Six months ago Tony's decision to move to France for an indefinite period would have been enough to shatter her ambivalence and prompt her to divorce Lester. She would have given up everything as proof of her passion, her love for him. Women, she thought; we always leave, following, reorienting ourselves in the name of love, assuming that the agony of separation from the beloved is worse than anything else we might lose in the process.

It's for the best, Catherine, she thought. What a worn-out, simplistic phrase that was and how she hated its puritanical connotations. There was nothing brave in her attitude, for now that he was actually leaving she was typically frightened and insecure about the decision. But that ambivalence, she had recently decided, was something she was stuck with for the time . . . or maybe even for always. Maybe she would always be poised in the middle, feeling herself pulled in two opposing directions. She would have preferred to have been endowed with the decisiveness of a Jone Beele, but as Angelica so often said, "You play with what you're dealt."

Of course she dreaded the nearly inevitable letter telling her that he had fallen in love with someone else, probably a woman his own age, one with whom he might have a family and share a long life. He was perhaps that sort of man, after all. She glanced up at his strong Gallic profile. It was only a question of time, she knew, until that letter came. The incredible thing was that with all of her ambivalence and yes, even fear, she knew that that letter would not destroy her. Still, she thought, snuggling in more closely on his shoulder, it would have been a hell of a lot easier to let go of a man of lesser quality. Forget lover, she would miss him as a friend!

"This is so strange," she said after he had checked through his baggage at the TWA counter and they were having a drink in the bar which overlooked the boarding gate.

"For me, too." Tony took her hand and studied it forlornly.

"I know for you, too." Cathy felt tears in her eyes for the first time that day.

"And Lester's moving back in?" he asked reluctantly.

"How did you know?" Cathy stiffened.

Tony smiled ambiguously and sipped his drink.

"How?" Cathy repeated. "Am I that obvious? Oh, I know

what you're thinking . . . that I'm doing it because I can't stand the idea of being without a man? Is that it? Really, Tony, is that what you think of me?" She blinked back her tears. "I can't believe we're having a goddamned fight!"

"I'm not having a fight." Tony looked at her steadily.

"Now I'm going to cry." Cathy choked and fumbled in her purse for the bundle of Kleenex she always carried. She blew her nose too hard, then felt her face flush. "Anyway, I haven't decided. I'm considering."

Tony drained his drink and ordered two more. Cathy glanced at him surreptitiously, trying to gauge what he was thinking. He was freshly shaven and his skin glowed. He was wearing a brown tie sprinkled with a few delicate pink flowers and he looked, she thought, like a student going off to college. He only wore a tie on special occasions and this, she guessed, was one. He seemed so desolate, so unabashedly sad, yet his strong, magnificent body which seemed to rise out of the chair gave off a contradictory message. He was resilient, energetic, solid.

A painting began to form in her mind as the waiter came with their two drinks and Tony raised his glass in a small toast for good times.

As soon as she finished *The Girls Downtown* which he had posed for yesterday and for which Jone and Angelica were posing this week, she would paint him as he was now. She could call it *The Departure*. But what was she going to do for a model . . . who would be her inspiration?

"To your departure." Cathy touched her glass to his. "This is so strange," she said again. "All I'm thinking right now is that I want to be lying next to you, that maybe I never will . . ."

"You'll come to Paris," he said, "you said you would."

Cathy nodded. "I will, too." She smiled quickly, thinking that it wouldn't be the same, not even in Paris, no matter how often she saw him there. "You were right," she went on, "I have decided that Lester should move back in . . . that we should try to work things out."

Tony nodded with a tentative smile playing around his mouth.

"It's funny," Cathy continued, "I didn't want you to know and that was a sort of game, wasn't it? It was my kind of game . . . an old-fashioned game. We don't need those games, do we?"

"No." Tony met her eyes evenly.

"I never thought I'd ask Lester to . . . well, I don't know if it'll work but I want to try and not just for appearances' sake. God knows I've let go of appearances, a lot thanks to you. Why is everything such a contradiction!"

Tony pulled out a handkerchief and wiped his eyes, then he laughed. "I guess I didn't think it'd be *this* hard."

"So it's another soppy farewell scene in an airport bar," Cathy laughed as she blew her nose again. "What did you expect from me, Tony?"

"Just this," Tony smiled.

Twenty minutes later Cathy, wearing a wary expression as though she were being followed, hailed a cab outside the TWA terminal.

"Fifty-three east Fifty-fourth Street," she told the driver as she stuffed two pieces of Trident Blue into her mouth. She chewed the gum vigorously, looking out the window with the same alert intensity. "That's Le Cygne." She leaned forward to the driver. "It's a restaurant."

"I know what it is, lady." The driver swerved to avoid a collision with a Carey bus that was spewing clouds of noxious fumes into the air.

I'm not crying, she thought. I'm not crying. She put her hand over her heart to see how rapidly it was beating or if it was beating at all. It was beating forcefully and regularly. She swallowed, removed the wad of gum from her mouth, wrapped it in paper before putting it in the ashtray. As she leaned back into the seat with her eyes closed her hand went automatically to her throat: she had not even broken her pearls!

There was, she thought, something almost religious about bidding farewell to a lover one has really honestly liked. Well, she was probably exaggerating as she did with most things but in any case it was an extraordinary feeling and one she had never had before. Bless Tony!

She sat up and rummaged in her purse to make sure she had brought along her address book with Jone Beele's phone number in it. No doubt everything was fine but she would call from Le Cygne to be sure. Jesus, what a Jewish mother she was but she did love those two dames . . . the girls downtown and dear Tony. For an instant she wondered if her excitement wasn't hysteria. Maybe she was *too* excited and just fooling herself again. She leaned back against the seat again. No, the threesome Lester had so seriously suggested as an alternative lifestyle had only worked as a diversion, in France. Her rejection of his plan as an ultimate solution had nothing whatever to do with morality. From her standpoint a threesome was simply too time-consuming. Even for Tony, she guessed it was both too limiting and too unstable an arrangement. And for Lester, now that things were more or less resolved, it had been a weightier and weightier compromise. Oddly enough, the person it had worked out best for was Vinnie. Now who would have thought that?

Wasn't it odd that she still wasn't crying? Well, it wasn't, she realized, as if his leaving hadn't made her sad at all. She was sad, but not *that* sad. It was just amazing! The possibilities for her new life seemed limitless. She was going to spend a few more weeks in Ohio completing the unfinished paintings she had left there and after that, when Vinnie was out of school for the summer, the three of them (Vinnie and Lester and she, that is) were taking a trip to Egypt. They would take a house outside of Cairo and she would paint. Maybe nothing would come of it, but it was an old dream of hers to explore the pyramids and absorb the atmosphere of the pharaohs. Then in July she had been invited to participate in an art teaching symposium in Bar Harbor. She would go unencumbered, while Vinnie and Lester stayed in New York, and after that she and Lester, just the two of them, were going to Finland, then ferrying to Leningrad (though it was still St. Petersburg to her) to view the art collection at the Hermitage. So many new sights would feed her, she knew, and this time next year there was no telling what new tangent she would be off on.

The thought of Lester waiting for her at Le Cygne brought a curious wave of excitement as if she were meeting him for the first time. Perhaps he was not merely an erudite old friend after all. Now wouldn't that be something! Perhaps there was a new way of making love she had not yet discovered—not merely a compromise but something between the earthshaking, blinding passion of first encounters and the stultifying, mechanical ritual of a long-standing relationship.

Cathy's eyes opened again and she caught herself smiling broadly. From where she sat at this moment it seemed she had finagled herself into a pretty damned good life. Finagled, hell, she thought, she had *worked* herself into a hell of a good life and she was bloody well going to enjoy it.

❁

"Where the hell have you been?" Angelica screamed at Jone when she staggered into the apartment, flushed and bleary-eyed, at ten o'clock that night.

"Oh, shit!" Jone held her side and fell into a chair gasping for breath. "Running."

"Running!" Angelica clasped Jone to her, both hugging her and shaking her. "What happened? I didn't know what to . . ."

Jone's face distorted and a great hoarse cry came out as she slipped down to the floor sobbing.

"Jone?" Angelica knelt next to her, tentatively patting the strong shoulders of her friend, but the mixture of sobs and groans did not stop. Angelica sat cross-legged, waiting.

"I almost killed myself," Jone said between sobs, finally pulling herself to a sitting position and facing Angelica on the floor. "I did. I can't believe it . . . I went crazy. I just went . . . like I was someone I didn't know. I mean, it didn't seem like that then. Then it seemed like I was me but now . . ." She looked around wildly. "I went crazy. What time is it?"

"Ten," Angelica answered.

"Oh, God, I'm sorry!" Jone reached out for Angelica. "You must have been . . ."

"It's all right," Angelica soothed.

Jone blinked several times, then she started to shiver and Angelica put some water on to make coffee.

"He's gone," Jone said when Angelica came back to sit next to her on the floor.

"What do you mean he's gone?" Angelica asked.

"Whit." Jone gulped for air and continued. "I threw it out . . .

someplace, can't remember. I got a notice. He's having the marriage annulled. He's gone."

"When?"

"Two weeks ago."

"Two!" Angelica shrieked. "I've seen you twice. You didn't say a thing!"

"I thought he'd be back. I mean, it seemed like he had to come back . . . after the shock of my news wore off."

"You didn't tell him about having your tubes blocked before the wedding, did you?"

Jone shook her head. "I screamed it at him . . . in the middle of a bloody battle about his scheme to move to Vermont and raise kids. Why did I do it? Why did I do it like that?"

Jone fell back onto the floor pounding her fists angrily.

"And then he left?" Angelica asked. "Just like that, he left?"

"Of course!" Jone pressed her lips together.

Angelica looked perplexed.

"Of course he left!" Jone screamed at her as if the whole thing were Angelica's fault. "I betrayed him, Angelica! *I* did it!"

"He left because all of a sudden he wanted to move to the country and have children and you wouldn't."

"Because I *couldn't* have them!" Jone jumped to her feet irritated. "Angelica, why are you acting so dense?"

"And he never called, just sent you a . . ."

"That's what I said," Jone cried impatiently. "I got a letter from his lawyer stating . . ."

Angelica went into the kitchen and took the singing kettle off the stove. Jone followed her and watched her make coffee in Whit's big scorched campfire coffee pot.

"But the two of you had a marriage," Angelica said softly as she handed Jone her coffee. "You don't just walk out without a word and send a letter to . . ."

Jone shut her eyes against another onslaught of tears.

"You should have told him before, of course," Angelica went on, "but how could he just leave? I could see why he'd be pissed at you for keeping it from him but . . . It's not unforgivable, Jone. You mean he didn't even try to find out *why*?"

"I kept it from him because I knew he wouldn't understand. Why am I so stupid?" she asked after a moment.

"You're not stupid," Angelica said.

"Everything I've done has been stupid," said Jone. "Probably not jumping off the Brooklyn Bridge was the most stupid."

Angelica smiled softly and Jone caught her eye with a rueful smile of her own.

"I ran across the bridge and I actually thought what such a grand gesture would mean to Whit, I actually thought . . . he'd approve."

"And why didn't you?"

"Would you believe it?" Jone began crying again. "Because of my *mother*. My poor, sad, hysterical, nervous mother!"

Angelica wiped the tears out of her eyes as Jone continued.

"She was always so afraid I was like Mean Mary. You know? I mean, my own mother, Lady Elizabeth herself, has lived her life knowing that her mother tried three times to kill herself. No wonder she's so friggin' nervous! Jeee-zus! I just couldn't do it to her, Angelica! I just couldn't!"

"Thank God!" Angelica found herself crying along with her friend.

"Goddamnit!" Jone slammed her fist on the table and sprang to her feet. "I'm not going to kill myself! But I'll tell you what I *am* going to do. I'm going to move out of this place tomorrow even if I have to camp on the street. I'm getting my metal out of that cruddy dark basement; I'm calling Cathy's goddamned shrink to talk things over a bit and then I'm going to buy myself not one, but two golden retrievers! Maybe you'll come with me and help pick them out."

Angelica opened her eyes and considered her reflection in the mirror above the loft bed. The smooth, prepubic bunnies had been taken down along with the bordello red drapes so that the reflection was only of Angelica framed by two leafy corn plants and covered by a North Carolina Rose quilt. Pressing the small of her back into the hard mattress, she flexed her stomach muscles until it hurt. She repeated the exercise ten times, then throwing back the quilt she bent her knees, did twenty fast sit-ups, and without glancing at her naked body sprang to her feet, climbed down the ladder, and ran into the bathroom to take her shower.

Her body was coming back. Every morning she felt tighter, more resilient and ready. Five minutes later she emerged, barefooted, wearing jeans and the violet silk shirt. She stood in the center of the room admiring the way the soft early morning light fell on her rose-hued Bokhara rug. The room had a spare, clean look and it smelled of the mixture of cinnamon and cloves with which she had filled the Oriental ginger jar Cathy had given her as a housewarming gift.

She had stayed with Jone for nearly a week and though she had stopped by her loft after work everyday to water her plants, coming home alone last night had been something of a celebration. For the first time in her life she felt she was actually coming home.

She switched on the radio and her rapture was reinforced by the strains of the Brahms horn trio. She danced into the kitchen area, flinging her arms out in a wide sweeping movement. After putting her copper kettle on to boil she ground fresh coffee, putting the grinder to her nose to enjoy the warm, rich aroma of her new custom-blend beans. While the coffee was filtering into the pot she filled a white ironstone pitcher (another recent acquisition) and padded happily around the loft watering and talking to her plants. Out her window the Hudson River was choppy and the cumulus clouds were mounded deep one layer upon the other in a sky that was fading from pale blue to gray. No doubt there would be more rain. She smiled and popped a cherry tomato into her mouth as she turned off the grow-light above the tiny vegetable garden. She had not been to a museum since Jone's February show at the Whitney. She glanced at the stack of free-lance design work which she had figured would take care of the final payment on the rug, then abruptly she put down the pitcher and called Jone to see if she wanted to spend Sunday afternoon at the Frick Museum.

Jone answered drowsily. "Jee-zus, what time is it?"

Angelica craned to see the clock. It was not yet seven-thirty. "I'm sorry. Go back to sleep." She heard Jone giggle. "What is it? Are you alone?"

"I'm never alone," Jone mumbled, then let out a little squeal. "Why did I think two dogs were necessary? I swear they're in league against me. Lipshitz!" she shouted and Angelica heard the high yipping of one of Jone's new golden retrievers which was joined momentarily by the equally persistent yipping of the second puppy, Louise.

"I think they're more trouble than kids," Jone came back on the line.

"Only thing is," Angelica interjected, "you won't have to worry about them taking drugs or wrecking your new car when you get it."

Jone laughed. "Anyway, you didn't really wake me up. Lipshitz has been vocalizing since six. I think he misses you. I'm already getting *so* anthropomorphic. Stop it, Louise! Angelica, I'm sorry."

"I remember the morning mayhem well," Angelica said.

"I've decided to rent a car today and take them to see my parents," Jone went on. "I mean, if they could make me laugh in my state I'd think they'd be able to elicit a smile out of my folks. After you left last night I got all awful again and . . ."

"I told you to call if that happened," Angelica scolded.

"I called Dr. Ramiriz. She said I should call anytime if . . . you know. Anyhow, we had a good talk and after we hung up I decided it was time I broke the big news to everyone. I'm terrified . . . I feel like I'm telling them I murdered someone or I'm on heroin or . . . my mother will probably take to her bed for a week and I know Dad will never forgive me for allowing Whit to slip through my calloused hands."

"Why don't you present your father with all the cowboy boots Whit left behind," Angelica suggested.

Jone chuckled. "Maybe I will. It's going to be a hell of a day. I'd much rather be at the Frick. You're sure you don't think I'm being vindictive by leaving all of Whit's stuff here when I move on Monday?"

"So what if you are." Angelica stretched the extension cord to the phone so that she could pour herself a cup of coffee. "Good God, Jone, how much could he care about his limestone piece if he didn't even think to have his agent pick it up?"

"I guess," Jone replied faintly. "But he's . . . upset. I don't know . . . I think I should have the movers drop his work off at his gallery."

"I think that's nice of you," Angelica said.

Jone sniffed at the other end of the line and Angelica could hear her muffled tears. After a moment she came back on. "Wanna come to my new place for dinner after you finish work tomorrow? I can throw together one of my casseroles with thyme. God knows I got plenty of *time* now."

"I'll be there by six." After Angelica hung up she wandered ambivalently back into the living room and stood in front of the window which looked out onto the river. She felt the familiar hollow sadness growing inside of her and began to waver about going to the Frick. If Jone had been coming it might have been different but she still dreaded the silence that formed around her when she was not actively engaged either in work or in shopping. When she imagined herself standing alone in front of Rembrandt's *Polish Rider,* or any of the other masterpieces in the Frick collection, she felt frightened. Anyway it was probably going to rain.

Every day it was the same: she would open her eyes and feel a heady rush of excitement, convinced that during the night hope had been finally restored. Lately, as had happened this morning, she had felt positively giddy, bursting with life and enthusiasm, loving her loft, her new things, the aroma of the coffee. Only it all dissipated so fast, unless of course she had to rush off to work or could immerse herself in the free-lance work stacked up at home. She was unable to sustain her zest for life for more than an hour after waking up and invariably the plans which had seemed so alluring became too complicated, too fraught with possible emotional consequences. The week spent ministering to Jone's needs had given her a sense of purpose and optimism which had been misleading, for here she was, less than twelve hours home after leaving Jone, and she was already feeling the same old angst and inertia. The contrast to her earlier feelings left her even more hopeless. She felt that there was some emotional hump which she would never again have the energy to surmount.

By eleven o'clock she had nearly completed the free-lance work which, according to her earlier calculations, should have required all day. She thought anxiously about the long tedious hours of the increasingly dreary Sunday afternoon and wondered if there were any movies left that she hadn't seen. She was irritated with herself on all counts—for being nervous and weak and for not bringing more work home as a protection against the loneliness. Cathy and Lester had gone to Montreal for the weekend and there was no one else she wanted to call. The idea of painting did not cross her mind.

At one, just after she had completed the layout for the last movie ad, the phone rang. It was Ferris and he wondered if she wouldn't like to join him and some mutual friends for a late brunch . . . not for his sake, he insisted, but because their friends were anxious to see Angelica. Angelica snapped at him that she was busy. When she hung up she was shaking, amazed that her animosity seemed to increase rather than subside as time went by.

Her anger seemed to propel her out into the blustery April day. She found herself heading east across town to take the Lexington Avenue subway north to Sixty-eighth Street and from there to walk the remaining blocks to the Frick Museum which was just off Fifth Avenue.

Because of its abundance of portraits, the Frick had always been one of Angelica's favorite museums. That the collection was housed in such a magnificent old mansion lavishly furnished with antiques only enhanced the aesthetics of the art. She loved it that the Frick was small and though she had not visited it in well over a year she recalled precisely where everything was located and plotted her tour as one plans a gourmet meal, saving some but not all of her favorites until last. She was still anxious, but once inside the Frick she felt the heady rush that generally only occurred the first thing in the morning.

As always on Sunday the museum was crowded with an assortment of faces. Angelica realized that she had missed the ritual of observing people almost as much as she had missed her old favorites, the Rembrandts and the Vermeers. As she walked through the flower-filled interior courtyard on her way to the largest gallery she felt a new urgency ticking away.

She stood in front of David's *Comtesse Daru* for some time before moving to Goya's *Doña Maria*, and then on to Whistler's elegant portraits of three women. Except for the portrait of Rosa Corder, so haughty in her black bustled dress, holding her brown feathered hat in one hand, the Whistlers did not touch her. They were pretty, to be sure, and Whistler's technique in painting misty Oriental-like tonalities could not be denied, but for all of their prettiness Angelica found them lacking in power, in the real thrust of artistic commitment. Her pulse quickened as she left the small room where the Whistlers were located and entered the next gallery. She walked through the room without looking, for this was the gallery with the Rembrandts and her favorite Vermeer. This was the real feast and she was saving it; after this there remained only the two Vermeers in the anteroom.

She thought of Françoise as she studied Fragonard's playful, opulent *The Pursuit*. Then there were the Holbeins and the Van Dycks and finally it was time to cut back through the courtyard and regard the earthen colors of Rembrandt's *Portrait of an Artist*. She always enjoyed comparing this painting with the later *Portrait of Himself* on the opposite wall. Perhaps the titles had been assigned by someone other than the artist, but Angelica had always been fascinated by the difference. As an artist Rembrandt had given himself a penetrating, dark countenance, while the *Portrait of Himself*, painted when he was much older, exuded an almost divine gentleness, a wisdom, so it seemed to Angelica, that was in no way egotistical. The eyes of the older Rembrandt, who held a walking cane in one hand, were compelling in their expansiveness, they followed her as she shifted her position to view the portrait from different angles. She felt she knew much of the man by looking into the eyes of his portrait.

To the right of the Rembrandt was a painting that never failed to inspire her: Jan Vermeer's *Mistress and Maid*. She liked to think of it as two portraits really, a significant moment, frozen in time, a complete narrative told with utter simplicity.

In the painting the lady's maid, dressed in muddy gray, was reluctantly handing her mistress a missive. There is trepidation on the part of both the women. The mistress, elegantly attired in yellow cut velvet trimmed with ermine and seated at her writing desk, had obviously been penning something of great concern to her. As the maid approaches the mistress's hand has just gone to her chin as if to ward off a blow—and that is the moment Vermeer has captured: the maid with her outstretched hesitant hand holding the note and the mistress with her hand tentatively touching her chin. There was nothing, to Angelica's thinking, that could surpass the Vermeer. In every aspect, from the luminous lemony yellow of the mistress's gown to the detail of the tiny iridescent seed pearls which encompassed her blond bun, the painting shone with intelligence, sensitivity, and technical virtuosity.

The longer she stared at the Vermeer the more intoxicated she felt. Finally she retreated to the courtyard and sat on one of the marble benches along the colonnade which overlooked the pool in the center of the courtyard. Hundreds of paperwhite narcissi had been planted around the perimeter of the pool and their heavy scent permeated the air. Several times she had caught a trace of it while looking at paintings. She rested a moment, drinking in the peaceful beauty of the rectangular area with its Ionic columns and the paned glass ceiling which allowed the soft artificial light to fall on the plants. She wondered why she had deprived herself of so much nourishment at a time when she had most need for what existed in this place—the tranquility, the inspiration, and the beauty were the very essence of what she valued most in life.

Good God, she had been all wrong in her approach to *The Person Sitting in the Empty Chair*. She had taken Jean Harris's poetic remark—"I was a person sitting in an empty chair"—too literally. The painting might well turn out to be of the two of them—Harris and Tarnower—a portrait-narrative that might capture the essence of Harris's remark as simply and eloquently as Vermeer had rendered the moment between the two women. Yes, it was important to free herself from all preconceptions, to address herself to the *implications* of the moment and not the historical fact of the moment. The moment could always be changed. Tonight when she went to work on some more preliminary sketches she would pare down the details in her work so that those nuances she chose to accentuate became more significant. It was always a question of choice, wasn't it?

Angelica felt like an antenna, sensitized to everything around her, a sieve for all the passing faces. She considered the other Sunday patrons who were enjoying the tranquility of the courtyard: three earnest, unsmiling adolescent girls whispering intensely on the marble bench nearest the pool; two tanned, middle-aged men in tennis shoes who weren't sure that sitting and listening to the flow of the waters was what they ought to be doing; an attractive interracial couple in their twenties: the man blond and Ivy League, the woman exotic and sophisticated except that she was wearing white bobbysox.

A tense, fortyish woman appeared and jerked her head to the right, then to the left while at the same time trying not to seem anxious or irritated at not finding whomever she was looking for. She too was deeply tanned but Angelica decided it was a Caribbean, not a California tan. Probably the woman only wore 18-karat gold jewelry, had married just out of college (Smith or Vassar) and had two adolescent children who were a constant irritation to her even on a Sunday at the Frick. The woman jerked her head to the right again, then rushed along the colonnade past Angelica, pounding her square, sensible heels into the pale green carpet.

Angelica stretched lazily, then retraced her steps to have a second look at the Vermeer and the Rembrandts. As she entered the gallery she caught sight of a woman, probably in her late seventies, with a blue and white feathered pillbox hat perched jauntily on her white head. She was chatting quite intimately with one of the black guards. Her red, white, and green plaid skirt hung well below her shabby black coat and on her stockinged feet she wore a pair of old brown suede men's shoes.

"But isn't it just remarkable?" Angelica moved closer to listen to the woman's velvety, cultured voice. "It really is so magnificent," she enthused to the attentive guard. "Just look at this." She handed him a small print and he nodded as he studied it. He said something to the old woman and she smiled and nodded at him before toddling off.

Her squeaking men's shoes cut through the silence of the

gallery, and Angelica wondered that everyone else didn't turn and stare. She watched mesmerized as the woman limped across the glossy wood floor, moving from side to side like a sailor walking on a slippery deck. She halted in front of one of the Goyas and put on the glasses which she was wearing around her neck along with a necklace of red and green curled Christmas ribbons. She moved very close to the painting, shielding her eyes with one hand as though she were looking directly into the sun. Had the guards not known her, thought Angelica, they would have asked her to move back, for her nose was almost touching the canvas. After a moment she moved back from the painting and nodded amicably as if she were having a conversation, then she sidled across the room to another of her favorites, again shielding her eyes.

Another detail! Angelica noted the woman's wispy white hair was escaping from a braided bun which she had covered with a crocheted snood. As the woman left the room, Angelica waited, not wanting to alarm her or to invade her privacy. There was something so dynamic and joyous about her. By the time Angelica walked into the next room the woman was already deep in conversation with another black guard who was clearly delighted that she had broken the monotony of his all too silent workday. The woman's face was strong and serene. In her youth she had probably been a ravishing beauty with thick, cascading locks, perhaps red, judging from the tint of her now white hair.

There was a magnetic purposefulness in the way she swayed down the room to study the Vermeer. If her walk reflected the pain she was in, her face did not. She was no idler. Again she smiled, shaking her head incredulously at the Dutch masterpiece, then off she hurried. Like Angelica she was only concentrating on those paintings which had some special meaning for her. Perhaps she was an artist—an unsuccessful one, judging by her attire.

That should have been a murderously grim thought on a rainy Sunday in April, but oddly it held no power over Angelica. She trailed the woman at a respectable distance, wishing she had brought a pad and pencil. Her absorption was complete and she was without any past. She was free and in hot pursuit.

She felt almost that this woman was a vision, a creation of her own resurrected hope, yet the woman was so real, just short of being a comic figure, but for her great dignity.

"How are you, Sally?" the woman greeted the only female guard Angelica had noticed at the Frick. The two chatted briefly and then the old woman labored toward the exit in her squeaky shoes.

Angelica thought about going after her and introducing herself. She might ask her to pose. She stopped herself with a smile. No, the event had been complete, she would just have to trust that she would be able to impart to her canvas the magical power that the feather-hatted, squeaky-shoed woman had instilled in her. She glanced at the clock in the foyer as she wandered back into the courtyard. She had been here for nearly three hours and the museum was about to close. She leaned over the pebble-filled pool trying to see her reflection, but the narcissi planted along the pool made it impossible for her to gaze directly into the water. Because of the rough texture of the small brown and white pebbles and the softness of the diffused light there were no reflections. To make sure, Angelica leaned forward, straining to extend one arm out over the water: there was only a dim wavy line.

Interesting, she thought, directing her attention to the bronze frog spouting water out of his mouth. The sound of the overflowing water from the tiered center of the fountain was lulling her into a deeply relaxed state, the heavy perfume of the flowers aroused a long-dormant desire and she was reluctant to leave. She turned away from the pool, looking at the colorful array of flowers planted around the opposite side of the walk—the fuschia azaleas, purple and white primroses, and the blatantly erotic red amaryllis with its seductive stamens protruding out of its immense bell-shaped blossoms.

"I grow them," said a man's voice with a thick, almost guttural working-class English accent. "One I grew had eight blooms on it at one time. I had to cut my broom in half to make a stake for it."

Angelica was on the verge of laughing as she turned toward the owner of the deep, resonant voice—a tall, disheveled man of around forty whose face was partially obscured by large, very dark glasses. His shaggy hair was long and graying and he wore a star-shaped earring in one ear.

"Here now, look at this one." He pointed to the long tubular stalk of an amaryllis which had not yet burst into bloom. The orange bud had just forced a slit in the protective green which enclosed it. "I give it another day or two," he declared in what Angelica identified as a North Country accent. "They say it's quite unusual to get them to give more than two flowers the second year but I've had four bulbs for more than three years now and each year it seems I get more flowers than the year before."

"I've never grown them." Angelica clasped her hands in front of her, smiling and trying to figure out what there was about him that seemed so familiar to her. They stood silently for a moment studying the orange bud which peaked out of the green like an Egyptian eye.

After a while he said, "I saw you watching the lady with the peculiar blue and white feathered hat."

"Oh, no!" Angelica flushed.

"Oh, yes," he nodded with an amused smile. "It's all right though. You were awfully subtle. I observed your subtlety. You were very careful. Believe me, she didn't notice. I did. I was watching you."

Angelica laughed. There was something of the clown in him, yet his appearance was almost depraved, shoddy, burned-out. Yes, he was like a wasted ex-hippie, a disillusioned British ex-flower-child.

"Aside from looking at you, I also looked at some paintings. I agree about the Vermeer. You liked that. However, I prefer *Officer and Girl* to *Mistress and Maid*. It's happier."

"Yes, it is," Angelica said, wishing he would remove the dark glasses so she could see his face. There was something very likable about him in spite of his looking as if he could use fifty cents for a cup of coffee.

"Come here often?" he inquired briskly, then laughed at himself. "I should be able to do better than that now, shouldn't I?"

"Why do I think I know you?" Angelica wrinkled her nose looking up at him.

"I give up." He smiled. "Why?"

"Are you famous?" she asked.

"I'm a gardener."

Angelica gave him a dubious look. "I'd better go have a look at the other two Vermeers before the museum closes. Good luck with your amaryllis."

As she was studying the other two Vermeers in the foyer below the elegant stairway that rose to the second floor of the mansion, Angelica could feel his presence behind her. He intrigued her. She found it hard to buy his story that he was a gardener because despite the working-class accent there was an ease about him, a sophistication almost.

When she turned away from the Vermeers he had removed the dark glasses. Even though he was smiling his gray eyes were sad as if he had used up their sparkle in another life. She would have to paint him, just as he was, in his still youthfully tight jeans with a black turtle neck and a worn leather jacket, standing at the base of the gleaming, aristocratic staircase.

"Angelica Stein," she extended her hand. He shook it, then let it go, still gazing at her with his tired eyes.

"Harry Riley," he said with a resigned smile.

"I knew it!" exclaimed Angelica. "You're Harry Riley!"

"I know," said Harry. "That's what I said."

"The Harry Riley who's the lead singer with . . ." Angelica paused impatiently, ". . . with . . ."

"Ah, how soon they forget." Harry closed his eyes briefly, then stared expectantly at Angelica.

"I didn't forget . . . Soldiers of Fortune! Right? You're the lead . . ."

"Wrong," said Harry. "*Was* the lead singer. Haven't made an album in ten years."

"Technicalities." Angelica smiled. "I thought I recognized your voice. I swear."

"Good ear." Harry looked off quickly as if someone had called him, then he looked back at Angelica uncertainly as if he had no idea what to do next.

Angelica felt sorry for him and struggled with herself about suggesting that they go somewhere for coffee. She had been eager to get home and haul out her sketch pads but there was something so needy about him.

"I have to go," she caught herself. The last thing she needed was to feel responsible for a washed-up rock singer turned gardener. "Nice meeting you, Harry."

"I was sure from observing you," Harry said, walking along beside her as she moved toward the exit, "that you were into plants. Anyway, I hope you're not a vegetarian."

Angelica looked sideways at him and laughed. "No. Why?"

"My ex-wife was a veggie. The experience left me with a degree of skepticism about people who only exist on veggies and nuts and berries."

"I'm an artist," she said, "a painter." Harry smiled as if he'd known that all along.

They stepped outside the Frick Museum into a soft shower and Harry took her arm and guided her out of the rain under a nearby awning. The touch of his hand sent a shiver of desire through her body that startled her. They looked at each other for a moment and then Angelica looked away, watching the raindrops bounce off the hood of a sleek, silver limousine. It had been a long time. She could almost feel his naked body next to hers. She could tell it would be very easy with Harry; she would hate to miss the opportunity.

"Do you come here often?" he repeated with a slow smile which made her pulse quicken.

Why him, she wondered as she fished in her purse for her address book. "I could call you sometime, Harry."

"You could," he smiled, "but I don't have a phone."

Angelica nodded. Great, she thought, an ex-rocker turned gardener who doesn't have a phone. She sure could pick 'em, but what the hell! At least he had a sense of humor, which poor old Ferris certainly did not have.

"It's not in yet." Harry laughed at her. "I mean I'm broke, but not *that* broke. I put all my bread into a little plant shop that specializes in succulents, The Bloomin' Desert."

"You're kidding me!" Angelica hooted, wanting very much to throw herself into his arms right there under the awning.

"No." Harry smirked. "I'm outa the music business and into succulents."

"Harry." Angelica turned to him excitedly. "What would you think if I told you I wanted *everything?*"

Harry looked skeptical for a moment, then his eyes softened and he nodded. "I'd say go ahead. I guess you're old enough."

"Would you know what I meant, though?"

He pondered this a moment while his eyes followed the people who were leaving the Frick and darting through the shower for cover. "You want to be fulfilled in your work and in your life. You would hope that your life and your work would merge . . . at least sometimes . . . same as me. It never did for me with the music and I made a bloody fortune . . . all gone now. But you're not an ordinary person, whatever that means. I imagine you've had a rough time of it but my guess is . . ."

He paused and looked hard at Angelica. ". . . my guess is you're a woman who knows what she wants and is going to get it."

"Yes." She touched his arm emphatically and allowed her hand to linger as she continued. "I do want . . . a lot." Angelica backed away from him waving. "I'll call you, Harry. I'll get your number from information."

"The Bloomin' Desert," he called after her, looking almost happy.

"How could I forget?" Angelica turned and ran toward Fifth Avenue where a Number Three bus was just approaching the bus stop. She sprinted and squeezed in the door just as it was shutting and dug for some change in the pocket of her ancient trench coat. She was going someplace—going home—and she was going to eat her dinner and meditate lying on her back on her lovely rose-hued rug and then she was going to sketch, going to set up her new work area in a place that was home.

The bus was nearly full. No doubt with Sunday art lovers, she thought. She searched for a seat. The faces all seemed to be looking at her and they all seemed to be smiling.

At the next stop Angelica threw herself eagerly into the only empty seat. Mondrian had painted a beautiful picture of an orange amaryllis against a pale blue background—an early painting, very realistic, before he veered off into the geometric works using only primary colors. She would have to tell Harry Riley about it. Last winter a New York gallery had put a price on it of one hundred and forty thousand dollars. Now how many people knew anything about that obscure Mondrian amaryllis, and how many people had spent a day like she had, culminating in making the acquaintance of an ex–rock star who grew amaryllises? It was a sign! It had to be. The day was an omen and it was telling her that it *was all* going to happen.